I slide a little, going downhill fast. Almost immediately, a flashlight beam shines weakly through the trees. But the dense trees screen the beam, reflecting the light backward.

In the darkness, a dog barks. I try to time my moves with his sound: bark bark bark. . . .

My eyes have adapted, somewhat. I see more now, not that there's a lot to see. Trees. No lights. My breathing slows. I try to compensate for my high-altitude disorientation.

Then I hear a very slight sound close by. At the same time, I smell him. He must have a shop rag in his pocket. . . .

I hear him breathing. He's moving quietly for a big guy but still making noise. Other than the pounding of my heart, I'm not.

Very slowly, I try to hide. I crouch down. It's no use running. He's got the whole forest here, and he's coming straight for me. . . .

Also by Suzanne Proulx:

BAD BLOOD

Books published by The Ballantine Publishing Group are available at quantity discounts on bulk purchases for premium, educational, fund-raising, and special sales use. For details, please call 1-800-733-3000.

BAD LUCK

Suzanne Proulx

THE BALLANTINE PUBLISHING GROUP • NEW YORK

Sale of this book without a front cover may be unauthorized. If this book is coverless, it may have been reported to the publisher as "unsold or destroyed" and neither the author nor the publisher may have received payment for it.

A Fawcett Book
Published by The Ballantine Publishing Group
Copyright © 2000 by Suzanne Proulx

All rights reserved under International and Pan-American Copyright Conventions. Published in the United States by The Ballantine Publishing Group, a division of Random House, Inc., New York, and simultaneously in Canada by Random House of Canada Limited, Toronto.

Fawcett is a registered trademark and Fawcett Crest and the Fawcett colophon are trademarks of Random House, Inc.

www.randomhouse.com

A Library of Congress card number is available from the publisher upon request.

Manufactured in the United States of America

First Edition: August 2000

10 9 8 7 6 5 4 3 2 1

Acknowledgments

The following people have helped, in ways great and small, from lending moral support to providing facts and anecdotes which I have cheerfully distorted and twisted into fiction.

The usual suspects: Vic, Marcel, Dylan and Sam; Olivia de Castanos, Dan Thomas, David Thomas, Jim Rase, Judy France, Sue and Wayne Meis, Sarah Schoentgen, Meredith Russell. Accomplices: Nancy Yost and Shauna Summers. The usual unnamed but highly reliable sources: you know who you are. Rocky Mountain Fiction Writers, particularly Janice Ford, Chris Goff, Dave Jones, Janene McCrillis, Mary McPhee, Gwen Schuster-Haynes, Bob Strange, Dianne West, Louise Woodward, Lisa Bleyley, and Dolores Johnson. The CompuServe Boot Camp group, especially Michelle Powell (for advice on astrological matters), Alex Keegan, Paulette Rommel, Diana Forrester, and Vida Evelyn.

1

Lucky Is My Middle Name

Don't talk to me about luck.

I nearly collide with Harley Sloane while stomping into my office. I'm in a vile mood after going all over creation on the stupid bus. I am temporarily without a car but got a ride to the meeting of the Colorado Hospital Association of Risk Managers, otherwise known as CHARM. Then my ride had to deal with a sudden crisis and couldn't drive me back. "Be glad this isn't happening at *your* hospital," she said. "You're lucky. I'd a lot rather ride a bus back downtown than deal with this."

Oh, and the CHARM meeting was really a bore.

Whenever somebody tells you how lucky you are, what they mean is things could have been worse. For instance, three weeks ago when my car caught fire, I was lucky—I had just completed a round of errands, ending with dropping off my dry cleaning. I was on a major street, not on the highway. Found an empty place to pull over on Grant Street, at rush hour. Lucky! It didn't blow up. Fortunate, indeed! A man working in an office building came right out with a fire extinguisher. And hey, my car could have been totaled, but it wasn't. What a godsend!

Would a lucky person's car catch fire in the first place? It's not a very old car, nothing like the wrecks I drove throughout nursing school and law school, and *they* never caught fire.

"Hey! Lucky I caught you," Harley says. I think he means

he's lucky, but he could be saying my name. Actually, my last name—spelled Lucci, pronounced Lucky. It would sound so much neater if it were my middle name.

"Whatcha need, Harley?" I try not to sound too surly. He is, after all, the chief operating officer, a decent human being, and my boss's boss.

"We have a problem. Nobody's seen Jette all day." Jette Wakefield, my boss, is our vice president of legal affairs. Geri, her assistant, nods and tries to assume a worried look.

I shrug out of my coat and reach around my door to hang it up. "So? That's a problem?"

"She's missed a *meeting*. And she's got some other things on her schedule that are important." Harley puts his jacket on, armoring himself for wherever he's going. "A deposition in some personal injury case."

I lean on the ledge that we still call the secretarial corral, even though we now call the people behind it assistants. I believe the ledge is there to keep us away from their office supplies.

"Jette probably took the day off," I say. "She's probably on the golf course. It was a pretty nice day, off and on." It was a nice day when I was on the bus and lousy whenever I got off to walk or to wait. Our bus system has been known for years as The Ride; its clientele ignore the Madison Avenue moniker and call it "The Walk and the Wait."

Harley paces around the coffee table in the reception area. "She's so meticulous about calling in. She doesn't miss meetings. I'm worried."

"All right." I assume this falls under my job description. I'm the risk manager for Montmorency Medical Center. I guess that means I'm supposed to find her. "What do you want me to do?"

"I don't know. Her job, I guess." Harley spreads his hands, giving me the serious look that makes him resemble Alfred E. Neuman. "Check with Geri, check Jette's calendar, make sure things she needs to do are covered. See if you can find anybody who's seen her."

"You're the boss."

When I first started here, I reported to the CEO. So did Harley, and so did Jette. Then the old CEO left, a new one, Dr. Langstrom, appeared, and almost instantly things were changed so that Jette reported to Harley and I reported to Jette. In other words, in one pen stroke I slipped two rungs on the corporate ladder, through no fault of my own.

Doing her job is not going to be a problem. She already gives me all the dreary stuff, while she keeps the exciting stuff—like policy meetings and deciding what sort of corporate entity our new sports clinic should be—to herself. Yeah, I know—choice of entities, exciting?

Still following the line of the secretarial corral, I move to Geri's desk and address her. "Guess I'm covering for Jette," I say. As if she hadn't been sitting right there during the entire discussion.

Geri nods. She doesn't like Jette. In fact, nobody does. Not that Geri looks thrilled to be working for me, either.

"She missed a lunch meeting," Vanessa says significantly.

Vanessa is the assistant to Dr. Ben Langstrom, the CEO, who is not a doctor, at least not a medical one.

"Well, she's dieting," I say. We all know this because Jette's been quite vocal about it. "Hey! Maybe it worked, maybe her diet suddenly took. Maybe she's in there, in her office, only she's so skinny none of us has noticed her."

Behind me, Harley chuckles.

Geri sniffs. "Very funny. She missed the meeting with the board representatives and the physician recruitment meeting— that was the lunch meeting. She's supposed to cover a depo with a doctor today at five."

"Okay," I say, visualizing a nice, posh, downtown lawyer's office. "I'll go hold his hand."

"*Her* hand, okay?" Geri says. "The doctor, that is. It's at . . . Let me get the file. I hope Jette doesn't have the file with her, wherever she is."

"She won't, I'll bet," I mutter. I am a veritable pack mule, taking my briefcase and lots of heavy documents with me wherever I go, but Jette often breezes into a meeting carrying only a notepad.

"No, it's right here." Geri drags a legal-size file folder out. "Okay. It's a personal injury case and the doctor was the on-call in the ER when the patient came in."

Simple enough.

"But she hates lawyers," Geri adds.

"Who doesn't?" Vanessa puts in.

"The depo's at—wow, 6312 South Fiddler's Green. Is that in the Tech Center? It just says Arapahoe County."

"Arapahoe County!" And me without a car. "*Shit*. I just got *back* from fucking Arapahoe County, on the bus, and it took me two hours!"

"Really, Vicky?" Harley's anxious look changes to feigned innocence. "The whole county? And it only took you two hours?"

"I thought you were leaving."

He grins.

"Hostile work environment," I say. "Somebody write me up a complaint." I throw my pen at him. He dodges.

"Harley, I can't do this. I don't have a car," I moan. "The bus schedule is not that regular." And if you think the schedule's irregular, you should see the passengers.

"Take mine," he suggests.

"I don't know. The depo starts at five," I say. Probably in deference to the doctor's clinical schedule. "It could go on, it could be late . . ." This is overreacting. It will last one hour, as scheduled.

"That's okay," Harley says. "Bring it in tomorrow. I'm meeting Bebe downtown. She's got some kind of awards banquet. I can go home with her. It's the big one." He means the car, not the awards banquet.

"I guess you'll drive the little one in tomorrow," I say. "And then put it in the backseat of the big one to take it home."

"We'll work something out," Harley says. "I'm not meeting Bebe until seven or so. Give me a call when you get back, but if I'm not here, don't worry."

He tosses me the keys, much in the same spirit with which

I threw my pen at him. "The access card's in the pocket on the driver's side. The windows are automatic. Try not to set it on fire."

2

Black Cats

How ironic it is that I'm going to be driving a stupid sports utility vehicle instead of needling Harley about driving one. Lots of people are against SUVs, practically everybody, you'd think, judging from the letters in the newspapers. Except: Everybody *has* one. I'm not kidding. You can't drive anywhere in Denver without being surrounded by these gas-guzzling, road-hogging behemoths. If they're not blocking your vision in front, their headlights are blinding you in the rearview mirror. I've cursed them from all possible angles.

Perversely enough, once I'm in the driver's seat of Harley's fortress on wheels, a Mercedes ML320, *I love it*. I love the clear, unobstructed vision. I love the powerful bursts of speed. (Of course, it probably gets about nine miles per gallon. But gas is cheap.)

When I signal for a lane change, the drivers of lesser vehicles *drop back* to let me have the lane. They are probably struck dumb by the idea that anyone driving an SUV would bother to signal a lane change or anything else.

As I cruise along, readjusting the dials on Harley's radio so as to hear jazz, not country-western, I tell myself I would really, really hate to take this thing into, say, the Tattered Cover's parking garage, where turns are sharp, space is limited, and the cement pillars have plenty of gouges to attest to the fact that people don't always make the turn.

Parking's not a problem at the law offices of Rivers and Wright. These are attorneys for the defendant, an insurance company. Even though I'm wearing my feel-good Anna Sui suit, I'm a little underdressed; this office calls for the herringbone Les Copains. Oh, well.

At least I'm better dressed than the doctor. She's wearing a long flowered skirt, a shapeless jacket (which, if I was wearing it, I would call "unstructured"), kneesocks, and Birkenstocks. She eyes me suspiciously as I give her the standard depo prep (Don't make things up, Don't speculate, and Try to avoid using the phrases "to tell the truth" and "honestly"). She manages to follow these simple instructions while I sit there, giving her no further reason to hate lawyers. When it's over, she shakes my hand without noticeable revulsion.

One of the great things—maybe the *only* good thing—about the Tech Center is its view of the mountains. One of the worst things is the traffic. Even now, well after rush hour, I crawl along in first gear, on my way to Interstate 25. I find it quite boring, moving along at 2.4 miles an hour. I get out my phone. I hate being bored.

I call Harley and tell him I'm heading back. He wants to know how the depo went. Well, he doesn't *really*, he just can't think of anything else to say.

"I don't know how people can drive and talk at the same time," he says nervously.

On the phone, I assume he means. I assure him that, for those of us who can chew gum and walk at the same time, it's a no-brainer. "Hey, don't worry. I'm only going one point nine miles per hour."

I dial my home phone number. In one part of my mind is the hope that my neighbor, Glenn, will already be stretched out at my place, having a beer. He likes my place, I think, because there are more places to sit. I envision him there, waiting for me. Ready to rub my neck, which is stiff. Ready for a happy hour.

BAD LUCK

Both of us used to spend a great deal of time after work in bars. Separately. Now, at least when we get home at reasonable hours, we spend that time in bed. It's perfect, a great way to unwind. Since hooking up with Glenn, my alcohol consumption has gone way down.

He doesn't answer at my place or his. Still bored, I call my office phone to leave myself a message of things I need to do. This is much less hazardous than writing notes on paper while driving. On the final approach to the highway, I hang up and toss the phone into my purse.

The cycle of the light on the ramp is slow, causing traffic to back up on the ramp, which in turn causes jams on the street. This is why it's taken me fifteen minutes to go two blocks.

It's maddening to sit here, waiting to make a left turn onto the ramp (so that I can wait some more), and to have to watch traffic from the other direction turning onto the ramp and *filling it up*. By the time the green arrow signals my turn, the ramp is full. And by the time there *is* room, the arrow is off and traffic from the other direction is filling up the ramp again.

Damn it, I don't want to sit here and wait fifteen minutes to get on the fucking highway; I want to go home and have my neck massaged. It's after six, you'd think these people would have had time for chrissake to *get off the highway*. Where are they all going? What's their problem?

Finally it's my turn for real. Munificently, I allow a woman in a lesser vehicle, a white Pontiac, to pull out of the HOV lane in front of me. This noble gesture not only saves her from the humiliation of blocking two lanes, it will contribute to the general well-being of traffic.

Wait a minute; she's an idiot! With a car full of people, she blocked traffic in two lanes so that she could get *out* of the high-occupancy-vehicle lane!

"You idiot," I tell her. "Lady, you're stupid. Stupid!"

Cars in the HOV lane don't have to wait for the light. Had I been in the HOV lane when she got there, I would be on the highway *now*. If I got into it now, I would be on the highway in two seconds.

"Jesus Christ, what a moron!" I pound on the steering wheel.

To get into this lane, people put their groceries into the baby seat and throw a blanket over it. They put a dummy in their front seat. But this lady—

"You sorry boneheaded broad!" I screech.

We inch forward. She may be stupid, but she's ahead of me.

"God, you're dumb." Of course she can't hear me.

"You fucking *blocked* traffic to get out of the HOV lane. You could be *on the highway right now*, you pea-brained bitch!" If I had her car phone number, I'd call her up and say this in person. Too bad phone numbers aren't part of the license-plate number.

See, I have this ability to express my hostility verbally; it's a safety valve that keeps me from committing road rage. "Someone ought to *hit* you," I hiss. "You *deserve* it."

Typically, she misses the green light. If I knew where the horn was on this vehicle, I'd honk, but there's no need; the person behind me honks. "Hey," I growl to the rearview mirror, "stupid doodyhead, who do you think *you're* honking at? I am blameless here, you queer." (In real life I have nothing against queers. I have already used up all my mature road-rage language and have to revert to junior-high epithets.) I glare into my rearview mirror. Then I pull onto the highway and forget the whole thing. Well, almost.

The first thing I do is pass the lady in the white Pontiac. Which is to say I get in the lane going five miles per hour, while she's in the lane that's stopped.

"Ta ta, y'old bat," I say. "Hey, learn to drive!" She remains oblivious.

And now, frustration defused, I cruise along the highway with no further problems until I exit at Logan.

Denver is a city that does not have enough highway to go around, which is too bad. Logan Street was narrowed to discourage through traffic. It didn't work, although I'm sure if I habitually drove a vehicle like this one, *I'd* learn to avoid it.

I don't see the cat in the street until a beat too late. I hit the brakes just in time to skid right into it, and, Goddess, what a bump.

They say it's bad luck to have a black cat cross your path. If you're driving an SUV, it's worse luck for the cat.

"Oh, shit." I dawdle down the block, cursing owners who don't keep their cats restrained. I feel kind of sick, even though I don't particularly like cats and I know it wasn't my fault. I mean, I was going *slow*. I was *not* speeding down the street. The cat was suicidal.

By the corner, I've convinced myself that there was no cat. I have a small battle with myself. I told Harley I was on the way back with his vehicle. But I don't want to leave an innocent animal, even a cat, lying in the road to be squashed further.

I stop at the corner and peer into the rearview mirror. It's just that time of day when streetlights don't help, and there are no headlights behind me.

I tell myself it won't take that long to circle the block, just to make sure.

3

Bumps in the Night

On my second pass around the block, I still don't see a body, but I do see two women who are calling, "Here, kitty, kitty, here, kitty."

I pull the Mercedes into the only parking space on the entire block, for which maneuver I could use the help of a tugboat, and walk down to the scene of the crime.

The women are trying to coax a cat out from under a parked car. (Another SUV. They're everywhere.) It has to be the same cat. And yet, it seems to me, it can't be. This cat's not only alive but spitting. And very small.

I go over the *thump* in my memory. Obviously, my memory is exaggerating.

The cat, understandably, is reluctant to move. The only reason I know it's the cat I hit is, the smaller of the two women keeps cussing out the asshole driver who hit it. The cat also sounds like it's cussing, in cat.

"Assholes. I can't believe it. Fucking pervert assholes just drove right on like a bat out of hell. They hit a defenseless animal and then just drive right on by."

"Yeah," the other one—the one with curlers in her hair—says. "Here, kitty, kitty . . . come on, baby."

"Come on, Tarbaby," the first one says. "It's gonna be okay, sweetie pie. They were speeding. I wish I'd have got their fucking license plate."

She named her cat Tarbaby?

I stand there for a minute, thinking maybe I should get back into my chariot from hell and drive on.

"You," the first woman says. "Get over there and grab her if she comes out that way." She indicates the street side.

Great. I get to test my karma by standing here in the street, to see if anybody will hit me. In my black leather coat. Like some kind of automaton, I move into the street.

"Some asshole hit her and just breezed on by," the woman says. Not a woman, now that I can see her. A girl. Fourteen? Sixteen? I would think the woman in curlers was her mother except who talks like that around their mother? She's as small as me, very slight. Her dark hair is plastered flatly to her head, making her look like she just surfaced from a swimming pool. Or just got out of the shower. Her teeth gleam in the dark.

"Uh, that was me," I say. I don't *have* to say this, but I think I should set the record straight: I am not an asshole. "I couldn't find a place to park, so I came around the block. Anyway, your cat shouldn't have been at large."

The girl sniffs. "Oh, at large, pooh. She just got out for a minute. Come on, Tarbaby, come on, sweetie."

I crouch down to look under the car. The cat, which must have had a death wish, heads straight for me and leaps into my arms, sinking its claws into my coat.

It looks awful. Scraped down to the bone on one side of its head, its ear torn, its eye bloody and bulging. I hold it gingerly, prying its claws out of my coat, until the girl takes it. Sorry about the repulsion, but this is a good coat.

"Come on, sweetie," she says. "Oh, what a mess, what a mess. Let's get you home." She cradles her pet, ignoring the blood. And why should she care, anyway? She's wearing about a triple-extra-large T-shirt, black, and possibly nothing else—not even shoes. Real street-urchin. She gives me a serious look. "Thanks for fucking over my cat, but at least you came back to help me find her," she says. Ah. I've been dismissed.

"It could have internal injuries," I say, from my wealth of medical knowledge, none of which is about cats. Note to Vicky: Shut up and get the fuck out of there. Dumb Vicky disregards good advice, keeps talking. "I think you should take it to a vet and get it checked out."

"Prolly," the urchin says. "No car, though."

"Oh." Well, damn and double damn. "Okay. I can drive you." *Who said that!?* Harley is going to love this. I've moved the seat, shifted the mirrors, changed the radio station, and now I'm going to put a dying, bleeding cat in his car. I point to the vehicle. See? I'm no asshole.

She hangs back. "I gotta tell my boyfriend," she says.

I pull my phone out. "What's the number?" I should just hand it to her, but she looks the sort who would run off with it. Like the people at the bus stop, who lined up and started offering me quarters to make calls. *Right.*

She shakes her head. "We don't have a phone. I live right over there." She indicates a large, shabby white house. I'm relieved to hear she lives someplace.

"Okay," I say, still holding the phone, thinking I'll call

Harley back and tell him the plans have changed. Or I could do the sensible thing and just split. As the other woman, the one with the curlers, has done.

"Maybe you could grab a towel or something." Harley's Mercedes has leather seats.

"You have to come with me," she says. "So he'll believe me."

Wait a minute. No, I don't. No way. But I follow her.

Why do I have a bad feeling about this? Sure it's an awful neighborhood, but probably no worse than mine. If a fourteen-year-old waif isn't afraid of it, why should I be?

"Also I've got a cat carrier at home," she says. "That might be a good idea. She doesn't much like riding in cars."

I shrug and follow her across the street. We go down a driveway of sorts, to the back of the white house. We climb two flights of rickety fire-escape stairs. The top story is small enough, you'd think, that there would be only one apartment up here, but there are two doors off a dingy hall. She opens one of them.

"Hey, it's me!" she yells. "Tara got hit, I'm taking her to the vet. This lady is driving us." We go through a hallway, off which is a tiny kitchen. The main room—and I assume it's the only other room—is larger. A waterbed mattress takes up most of the floor space, with an authentic (i.e., tattered) tufted quilt on it. On top of the quilt is a large guy, a bleached-blond surfer type, watching *The Simpsons* on a large color TV while listening to a baseball game on the radio. He looks a little old for this girl, although not quite old enough to be her father.

"This lady hit her," the girl says brightly, "but she's taking me to the all-night vet. You hear me? So that's where I'm gonna be at, for a while. With her."

The guy turns to her. "How long you gonna be?" he asks in a thick surly voice.

She shrugs. "Dunno." Everything in her body language says she's afraid of him, as if I couldn't have guessed from the desperate way she had to let him know where she was going.

I get the idea he doesn't care about the cat at all, and not much about the girl. As if she picks up on my sudden wave of sympathy, Catgirl glares at me. "She's a lawyer," she says. Then she disappears into the bathroom.

He looks at me with more interest. "Oh, yeah? What kinda law you do?" His eyebrows are so dark, they look like they've been charcoaled onto his face.

"Ah, corporate," I say. "Medical. I work for a hospital." I'm trying to remember when I told her I was a lawyer, and I'm pretty sure I didn't. In fact, I'm goddamn certain of it. So how did she know that?

"Huh," he says. "A lawyer, working for a hospital?"

Oh, come on. Even he should be able to figure that one out. "Montmorency Medical Center," I say helpfully. If he reads the newspapers at all, he should know why hospitals have lawyers; they get sued constantly. "But all hospitals have them. Us. Lawyers, that is."

He's already turned back to the TV and made a switch. Now he's watching basketball and listening to some annoying death-metal group. The girl comes out of the bathroom. She has put on leggings and sandals and done something to her hair—sprayed it with superspray, it looks like, then run her fingers through it so it stands straight up. No bad-hair days for this girl. I like the idea of a hairstyle like this; she did it quick, and while holding an injured cat in one hand. She hands me the carrier. Nothing fancy: a cardboard box with airholes. I open it, and she stuffs the cat in. When closed, the flaps turn into handles. Very convenient.

Without saying another word to the surly guy, the girl tears down the rickety stairs. I proceed a little more cautiously, feeling old and out of it.

The feeling persists as I unlock the car and we climb in (*climb* being the operative word, for both of us). She starts babbling as soon as we get in, talking alternately to me and the cat.

"S'lucky you came back," she says. Here we go again. If I'm so lucky, why didn't I drive down a different street?

She elaborates. " 'Cause, you know, it would have come back on you if you didn't, three times. I mean, it would anyway, but more so because I'm a witch."

Like maybe Harley's SUV will catch fire? This makes me wonder what I did that caused *my* car to catch fire.

"A witch, huh" is what I say.

"Yeah, and my mother is one, too, even though she's married to a Mormon priest. I mean, my mother's a good Mormon, too, and all that. I know Jewish witches, Christian witches ... People think we worship Satan, but we don't."

Right. "I guess you're psychic, too."

"Only a little bit, sometimes, yeah. I mean, like, I can't tell you what the Lotto numbers are gonna be."

More's the pity. "So that's how you knew I was a lawyer?" I glance at her as I say this. She looks puzzled.

"Well, no, you know, like, I thought you told me that."

"I don't think so."

"One way or another," she says, "you told me. So, like, yeah, I'm psychic, I know I am, some other things have happened. Like—"

"Excuse me," I say. "I have to make a phone call." I dial Harley's number to tell him I was wrong, I'm going to be late. I'm already late. He doesn't answer. I picture him standing in the parking lot, waiting for me to dock, and growing increasingly apprehensive about his expensive vehicle.

What must I look like to this girl? I try to see myself through her eyes: a middle-aged woman, wearing nice clothes, driving a big Mercedes, talking on a cell phone. I'll bet I look like money. And my actions indicate I'm a soft touch. For some reason—not because I'm psychic—I start feeling a little nervous.

"Like now," she says, "I see your aura and I see there's a club in your future. Some kind of club."

"You mean like a card? A club, a spade—"

"I don't know what kind of club. I see a club, is all. These things are, like, not explained, but it'll all be clear later."

And thanks so much for the free fortune-telling session. I feel like the club is hanging over my head, ready to bop me.

"I hate these fuckin' SUVs," she says violently.

"Yeah, me, too," I agree. "I'm only driving it because my car caught fire."

She looks at me with interest. "Wow."

Shut up, I tell myself, and drive.

Shutting up is no problem. Arinda—that's her name, she tells me—talks pretty much nonstop. She's a singer. She's Irish. She's eighteen, which I don't believe. She ran away from home because the Mormon priest, who's really her stepfather, was too hard on her and didn't like her singing. She's studying the Celtic harp. She has an old one, but antique harps are basically no good because they warp and won't stay in tune. She stayed with her real father for a while, but things didn't work out. He drinks too much. When he was married to her mother he stopped drinking, but when he started again her mom kicked him out. She works at a Kentucky Fried Chicken place and sings at a nightclub called Charley's, but only for tips. She's gonna be awesome; she's already got a following.

She does have a pretty nice voice.

She *knows* she's gonna be awesome, because witchcraft helps you get what you want. Helps you focus. I assume she's a recent convert, because, in the way of recent converts, she's very enthusiastic.

My own flirtation with goddess worship isn't much, just a bit of feminism. Not witchcraft. I always figured sure, they *tell* you it's a harmonious, nature-based religion, then once you're initiated you get the real truth.

But she keeps going on with plugs for witchcraft, like how witches aren't so bad really, they only work for good. How witchcraft helps you get what you want but comes back on you if you use it to hurt somebody. Right. Like when she was cussing me out for driving away.

All in all, it seems like a pretty long drive. At the vet, Arinda fills out the information sheet while the cat is examined. The vet thinks the cat may lose that eye and might also have internal damage. We leave the cat, then it's another long drive back and more personal history.

At one point Arinda leans forward and her pendant catches my eye. A silver circle, with a fairy recumbent on a slice of moon, it gleams up at me in the streetlight, advertising its presence. "Your pendant," I say.

"Yeah," she says, "it's my totem, like. Like Tara's my familiar. My moon goddess. I got it in a magical way, at my first Sabbat, which was Imbolg. You know, Groundhog Day? It's funny, the newspapers all write up Samhain, that's Halloween, and Beltane, that's May Day, but they never say a word about where Groundhog Day came from, and it's my favorite Sabbat. . . ."

She goes on and on and doesn't let me tell her that once, long ago, I had a moon-goddess pendant exactly like hers, one that I thought was unique in the world.

Probably, I tell myself, it wasn't exactly like hers. And anyway, I lost it.

"You're a Leo, aren't you," she says. "Hey, can I have a cigarette?"

Harley didn't have to tell me not to smoke in his car; asking me not to set it on fire was sufficient. I figure the smell of frangipani—Arinda's—will cover up everything else. So, even though I'm contributing to the delinquency of a minor (probably), I give her one. And roll down all the windows.

She lights up and tells me she's working on astral projection, which is harder than you'd think. At least, controlling it is. The first step is lucid dreaming, and it's taken her almost two years to get good at that. When she gets good, she says, she'll be able to go anywhere. Inside people's offices, for instance, or into their apartments. Or to other continents, maybe even other galaxies. She'll be able to meet up with the astral projections of other people who can do this. She'll be able to attend closed city council meetings—although, of course, she won't be able to say anything. Or vote.

When we get to her place, she sits in the car, finishing her cigarette, while I fan smoke out my window. I hope she doesn't ask me to go back with her and attest that yes, we have taken the cat, and we didn't go anywhere else. She doesn't. She mutters something about a fucking materialist SUV, but she's in no hurry to leave its confines.

I'm sending psychic messages: Get out, please. *Now.*

Psychic no more, she tells me a little more about astral projection. "You've done it," she assures me, "everybody has.

Ever been asleep and then you suddenly wake up and it's like you were dropped into your bed? Like, *yanked*? That's your astral self, coming back. It's attached with, like, a long cord of light and it pulls you back. Or when you dream you're flying? *You're really flying,* or at least your soul is."

"Yeah?" I glance at my watch.

"Or when you get a déjà vu?" she says. "That's when you're somewhere your body's never been but your astral spirit's been there."

She hasn't mentioned the cat since we left the all-night vet. Finally I do.

If the cat makes it through the night, it needs to be picked up before nine tomorrow morning. I agree to come by at, Goddess help me, six in the morning to go fetch Tara (the cat's real name; Tarbaby was a diminutive). Arinda gets out, slams the door, and heads to her pad. The proper thing would be to wait until I'm sure she's safe inside, but from where I'm parked, I can't even see the fire escape.

What's happened to me here? I just spent over an hour driving around with a wounded cat and a crazy teenager, probably a runaway, and I don't even like cats, and all I wanted to do in this world was get home. I must have been bewitched.

4

Astral Projections

I duck my head as I pull into the parking garage because the ceiling's so low and the SUV's roof is so high. I dock the thing in Harley's space so he can find it if he's still around.

Then I call Glenn to see if he would like to drive seven blocks to pick me up.

We've known each other to nod at for several months but we've only been lovers for a few weeks, so he says of course he will come and get me. Then he gives me a bad time all the way home for not walking seven blocks.

"What a day," I moan, hoping it sounds in the nature of a lament rather than in the nature of a whine. "I am dead."

"You're not dead," he assures me. "I'll bet you're hungry."

He's right; and he's what I'm hungry for. He gives me a back rub, which leads to a full body-to-body rub. Happy hour delayed is not happy hour denied. And then we raid our refrigerators while I tell him about my day. Or most of it. I hit the high spots. He is properly concerned about the cat I hit. He's not so sure about the girl.

"One of those street people you're so fond of living around," he says. "Who gives color to the neighborhood."

"She had a place, therefore she wasn't a street person. She seemed like a tough little thing, anyway," I say. "I guess the cat is, too. If I ever get hit by an SUV, I hope I come out as well as that cat did."

When my phone rings, some hours later, my astral body is far, far away from the physical one. For all I know, it's still out there as I try to process what a person named Agnes is telling me.

Agnes seems to be an aide on the Psych Unit, and as such is a person who should *not* have my home number. She says her boss told her to call. I tell her to put him on; she says he's busy. "He just wanted me to let you know we lost a patient."

Honey, we lose patients *all* the time. And speaking of losing patience . . .

"I mean, she disappeared. She went out onto the third-floor fire escape for a cigarette and she got away."

About the time my astral body makes it back into my physical one with a *whump*, another person comes on, the real Agnes, a supervisor.

"The switchboard has you down as the officer on call,"

Agnes explains. I'm glad somebody let me know; I wouldn't have thought of that.

I guess I'm on the rotation because I'm filling in for Jette. This is distressing news, or it would be if I stopped to think about it. I don't. I tell Agnes to alert Security and call the police if the patient is considered dangerous. Then I hang up and send my astral body off in a quest for more sleep.

I am running through the woods, in the snow, with holes in my socks, when the phone rings again. Eventually I answer it. It's now 3:30 A.M. I don't know how many times it rang. Many. It was just so strange to hear a ringing phone in the woods. I assumed someone else would get it.

"Uhnn," I say.

"Just wanted to let you know we have a situation," says a crisp voice.

"Uhmmm?"

"An emergency patient. Apparently he's been assaulted by someone and he wants to leave."

I wake up a little more, enough to figure out who I'm talking to. Larry, a third-year trauma resident in Emergency. He tells me a cabdriver involved in an accident was brought in by ambulance. He was unconscious, but his vitals were good. However, he was pretty much squashed in his cab and had to be removed with the jaws of life. The paramedics immobilized him and the Emergency staff put him under observation; they wanted to wait until he came around to perform tests to rule out spinal-cord trauma.

Next thing they knew, the cabbie was screaming his head off in an unknown tongue, and while most of the people rushed around trying to figure out what kind of translator should be called, and to call such a translator, Larry ran into his room, where he was still immobilized but . . . And here Larry breaks down.

"But what, Larry?"

"He was . . . there was a woman in there with him. Naked."

"Oh, good, a naked woman. Please go on." Glenn changes his body posture somewhat. I think he's asleep, but he could be eavesdropping.

"She was, ah, performing a sexual act on him."

"And this made him scream?"

"Well, we didn't have a translator at that point."

"Come on, Larry. Surely you don't need a translator to tell you if someone is screaming."

"Right," he says, "but we didn't know, we couldn't tell if it was pain or what."

"Or what" is my guess. Hell, maybe pain, too.

"Where did this woman come from?"

"Ah, it turned out . . . when we got a translator, it turned out he thought she was staff, but she wasn't."

"She wasn't wearing an ID?"

"She wasn't wearing . . . anything."

"That's good." I make a semiconscious astral leap. "Was she our escaped mental patient? From Three?"

"Oh, man," Larry says. "I didn't know about that. Well . . ."

"I guess you ruled out a spinal injury? Obviously he has feeling below the waist."

"Well, yes, that was a good sign. But he's, well, he's a Muslim—or is that an Islam?"

"Christ, I don't know, what difference does it make?"

"The act she was performing is against his religion, apparently," Larry says delicately.

"Muslims don't do blow jobs?" I say, indelicately and taking a wild guess.

"Apparently not."

At least they didn't have to surgically remove her. She ran away.

"So now he's unclean and disgraced," Larry says, "and of course he wants out of the hospital, but he won't sign an AMA, even though the translator read it to him. He won't sign anything."

Ah. We arrive at the gist of the problem. Patient wants to leave Against Medical Advice. Yeah, this is my area, all right.

"Do a rape kit exam on him," I say.

"What! On a guy?"

"Yeah. It's been done, don't worry. If he's claiming sexual assault, he'll need it."

"What if he won't consent?"

"He probably won't. Then you *document* that he refused an examination for evidence of sexual assault."

"I get it," Larry says. "Document."

"And try to get him to sign the AMA," I say. "Naturally he's free to leave without signing it. Document that, too. Try to get him to wait for someone to pick him up, if he insists on leaving. Document everything."

"Right," Larry says.

"Check your Policies & Procedures manual to make sure I've covered everything," I add, mostly to remind him what I just told him is also in the P&P manual, if only he'd looked.

"Right."

5

Possessed

Quite understandably, I'm in sort of a stupor in the morning. I guess Arinda put me under some kind of a spell because I get up at some ungodly hour.

I don't know what I was thinking when I said I'd come pick her up to go get that cat. Why didn't I just tell her I had no car? I'd already mentioned that it had caught fire.

Grumbling, I borrow Glenn's Alfa and proceed to Arinda's apartment with the top down even though it's very chilly. Okay, I said six, but I'm no more than half an hour late when I ascend the rickety fire escape. It looks even scarier in the light. This has got to be some kind of building-code violation. It's like walking a tightrope. The thing sways in the breeze.

I try to recall why I have a bad association with fire escapes. Something that happened in the night? A dream?

Probably the memory of this particular fire escape.

The outer door is open. I pound on the inner door—hard, because loud rock music is on inside. Really loud, considering how early it is. This happens in my neighborhood all the time. What's the matter with people? You don't play loud, intense rock 'n' roll at this hour. Late at night, okay, but at six o'fucking clock in the morning people should be asleep.

My pounding fails to rouse anyone. If they can sleep through the death-metal racket, what are a few raps on the door? I can't knock hard enough to compete.

Now, the logical thing would be to assume, since I was late, that Arinda had found another ride, freeing me to go home and get ready for work—or go home and go back to bed. But I'm bewitched, so I drive to the all-night vet. Arinda has not been there. I get a full report on the cat's condition, *write a check for $105* (and yes, I signed my own name), and then take the cat over to its regular vet, as suggested by the after-hours vet.

Both the all-night vet and the regular vet bore me with the details of this feline's health. Like: It's lucky to be alive. (See what I mean? Your truly lucky cat would have stayed out of my way.) Its chief problem is, it was recovering from being spayed a week ago, so they are concerned about internal damage.

In my own view, its chief problem other than being a cat in the first place is it looks like FrankenCat, with one ear kind of chewed and lopped off, raw skin on one-half of its head, some stitches in heavy black thread to hold its eye in and its scalp on, not to mention a nasty-looking hematoma in its eye.

"Look," I tell the vet, "I hit this cat. *Not on purpose.* Its owner was supposed to come with me to pick it up, but she didn't show. I'm not paying another cent for this cat! I don't care if it lives or dies."

And the vet thanks me. She tells me she'll take good care

of the cat. "The owner still owes us for the spay, but don't worry. You've done more than enough."

Yes. I have.

Back home, I work a spell of my own and get Glenn to drive me to Hertz, where I plop down my plastic and drive off in a Ford Taurus.

Now it seems a little wasteful to rent a car, since I've arranged my life so virtually everything (except my dry cleaner) is in walking distance. You would think I could get along without a vehicle for a couple more days, particularly since I have to pay for it. (Don't worry. I will write this off on my expense account. I may even write the cat off on my expense account.) But for some reason, as soon as my car caught fire, I kept having meetings in the damnedest places—the Tech Center, Broomfield, places not easy to get to by bus. And my best friend, Melinda, who lives in a bungalow near Washington Park, is out of town on an extended project, so I've been watering her plants. Too bad she drove her snazzy red Porsche. I could have borrowed that.

Harley's Mercedes is not in its space. Good, he picked it up last night. Jette's car isn't here, either. Nobody's is.

In my office, the message light on my phone is flashing like mad.

"Vicky, I'm not able to get Jette, so I need to talk to you, please call me back."

"Vicky, I was working on this thing with Jette, but she's not calling me back . . ."

"Hey, I'm calling you because Jette's voice mail is full . . ."

"Note to me, check Jette's schedule if she hasn't come back . . ."

"Lady, you're stupid! Stupid!"

"Jesus Christ, what a moron!"

I sit up straight and swallow. Time to call Security, I think. I've had threatening messages before. They know how to deal with it.

"You sorry boneheaded broad. God, you're dumb. You fucking *blocked* traffic to get out of the HOV lane . . ."

Uh, forget Security. This is me. This is my own voice (and I hate the sound of my voice, particularly now), cussing out the pea-brained driver on I-25. I sound much better when I'm giving myself notes. I must not have hit the END button on my phone hard enough. Or I hit the SEND button by mistake. Well, obviously, I hit the SEND button, otherwise this would not be a separate message.

Damn it, that kind of thing wastes batteries. And cellphone budget, which I would like to spend getting a newer, sleeker model. With an easier keypad lock so these things wouldn't happen.

I erase the lady-you're-stupid message. Sheesh. Five minutes. You'd think there'd be a time limit.

I take a large breath. I'm *lucky*. The phone redialed the last number I called; it could have been Harley. Or somebody else important. Wouldn't that have sounded nice?

The next message is Larry in Emergency, saying please call quickly. This message came in at 3:34 last night and I've already dealt with it. What was *he* thinking? Risk managers don't work at 3:30 in the morning.

At least not at their desks.

That reminds me that I should check Jette's voice mail. Then I decide I shouldn't. If she shows up, she might think I was snooping.

Instead, I start dealing with the stuff on my desk and reflect on how I don't feel like I'm doing lawyerly stuff. Except for the depo, I'm doing things a trained monkey could do. Okay, I have already reviewed our whole stack of policies and procedures to make sure they conform to changes in state law. This was a big project, and I suppose it required a lawyer to oversee it, but you have to admit, it's not like being Melvin Belli.

I think I would have made a hell of a good trial lawyer, even though during my first and only mock trial, I impeached my own witness. Oh, it was a perfect opportunity. I did it with style and élan. And in a friendly way so that it did not seem like I was attacking the witness. I did it because it was a chance to show off my incisive legal mind, and my skill at thinking on my feet, and because I couldn't resist. But yes, my own witness. This may have been the misstep that took my career in a whole different direction.

The memory spurs me outside to the Smoker's Showcase—a patio, visible from many windows of the hospital buildings but hidden from the public—for my morning nicotine fix.

It's a great way to keep in touch with the hospital grapevine. The big items today are: the escaped mental patient. The assaulted cabdriver, who turns out to be Tanzanian. And the continued unexplained absence of Jette.

The cabbie, I fear, is destined to become an urban legend. It's almost frightening how many of these urban legends are started by nurses—the one about the gerbil, for instance. I believe I know the person who started that one.

The folks in Admin, the ones who supposedly run the place, haven't heard about the cabbie and the escaped mental patient, but concern about Jette has escalated. Today it's full-scale panic with a seasoning of character assassination.

"Vicky," Harley says, "I want you to go around and find out from everybody when they last saw Jette."

"I don't see the point. She's not here now. What good's it going to do to locate the last person who saw her?" This is not my kind of investigation.

"The last place she went was on Wednesday night, that Disease of the Year dinner," Geri says. "I mean, the last place she went where she was supposed to go."

The Disease of the Year is something the Montmorency Foundation puts on, to focus on through the year. Just like it says, it picks out a disease, preferably an obscure, media-starved disease. No breast cancer, no AIDS. Then it does the usual charitable things—luncheons, balls, auctions, Las Vegas nights, Mardi Gras carnivals—to provide money to support research, or the patients, or public acceptance, or whatever. This year the disease is hardly obscure, nor is it in my own opinion a disease. It's eating disorders. I call it the too rich supporting the too thin.

Every year the foundation selects a hospital official as honorary chairman, for credibility. This year's chairman is Jette.

She's a peculiar choice for honorary chair of this so-called disease, because she's always on some kind of diet and she always tells *everybody* about it. Slips it into every conversation. Announces there are doughnuts in the break room but of course she can't have one 'cause she's on this diet.

She does this even though she isn't fat. Big, yes, and she does have these piggy cheeks. But let's face it, she's about six-two, large boned, broad shouldered. She's *not fat* in the way professional football players are not fat. I mean, she could roll me up into a ball and slam-dunk me. What good's a diet going to do?

But hey, what do I know, maybe it's helped. Because Jette has the lowest body-fat percentage of any woman in our office. I know this from when our Executive Wellness team came in to evaluate us. They drew blood to check our cholesterol levels, took our blood pressure, pinched our body fat, and gave us a questionnaire to fill out about our family history and overall health practices. The Executive Wellness computer analyzed all this data and returned individualized profiles, after which the Executive Wellness director gave our office a presentation on the importance of keeping fit.

I happened to be alone in the office the day the evaluations came back, and, well, I peeked. I couldn't help myself.

I was shocked to learn I have a body-fat measurement of twenty-four percent. Yes, that's right, folks, twenty-four percent, or roughly one-fourth, of my body is fat. Yuck. And I consider myself a skinny person.

Vanessa, who is two inches taller than me and very slinky, was twenty-four percent fat, too, which made me feel a little better, even though she is twenty years older.

Geri, who's thick in the middle but has skinny legs, topped out on the fat percentage with thirty-one percent.

Anita, Harley's assistant, rated twenty percent on the body-fat scale and thinks she needs to lose ten to twenty pounds. Get real.

And, bringing up the rear, giant Jette. Fourteen percent body fat. *Fourteen.* She was lower than some of the men. It must be her Viking heritage. Or maybe, like I said, the diets are working.

The men, disgustingly enough, were all way under twenty percent body fat. Life isn't fair.

But back to the current problem, which is: Where *is* Jette?

She didn't leave any clues. Geri keeps a copy of her appointment book. Luckily for me—since I'm picking up all these appointments—Jette doesn't schedule anything for Friday afternoon, ever. The last thing on her calendar for this week is lunch.

"Should I keep this lunch date of hers?" I ask Geri. "Or is it personal?"

"Personal," Geri says distractedly.

Jette already passed along three of the four things on her official to-do list: insurance for the new sports clinic, physician contracts for the new sports clinic, and corporate structure for the new sports clinic.

For the last few months we've been adding new entities at a dangerous pace. What we say is, we want to serve the needs of the community, but of course we are just trying to make ourselves look attractive to the large for-profit hospital chains who want to move into this market. And in fact are moving in.

Either we join them or we compete against them. Bummer. For this reason we recently established the Executive Wellness Program and bought a home health service and a sports clinic. All very risky ventures, in my opinion, but I'm only the risk manager. Who asks me?

The fourth thing on Jette's list is a response to interrogatories from someone who's suing the hospital, and of course it's due today. The person who's suing is one Andrew Dorrey, who was the risk manager before me, and it was thought I might not be totally objective.

Or maybe it was thought that this suit might give me ideas.

I feel a leap of excitement at getting to do actual legal work. The excitement dies when I ask Geri if Jette's gotten started on this.

"Oh, yeah. She put one of our law firms on it. They've sent

a draft over. All you'll have to do is read the response and then sign it."

That takes some of the fun out of things. But I still get to sign it. Hey, I'll get to see my attorney registration number on something.

"But, Vicky, we've got to find her."

"Right," I say. *Why?* "I assume we've called her house."

"Duh!" Geri says.

"And we've called her family?"

"I didn't want to alarm them."

I point out the obvious: It may not alarm them. If Jette had a family emergency, she may have just taken off. Geri gives me the numbers: Jette's mother in Minnesota, her sister in Michigan, and her brother in Deer Trail, Colorado.

"Yeah, he has a ranch or something out there," Geri says. In Deer Trail? Like, what else is out there?

Since he's closest, I call Derek first. He hasn't talked to Jette since a week ago Monday. She had just gotten back from spending the weekend in Wyoming, where she goes a lot, since that's where her boyfriend lives. There's no family crisis. He's sorry he can't help me.

"Should I come into the city?" he asks. "It isn't like Jette to take off like this without telling somebody."

As lax as she is about her job, and as little work as she does, Jette is good about letting people know where she'll be. Or if not exactly where she'll be, that she won't be in.

"I'll let you know," I say. "Meanwhile, is there anybody else we should call?"

"I'll call Mom," he says. "Do you think somebody ought to file a missing persons report with the police?"

Yeah, I do. I think somebody ought to check out her apartment, too. Call her friends. Surely she has some friends.

"Her ex-husband," Derek suggests. "It's not like you think. They were on pretty friendly terms."

I didn't even know Jette had an ex-husband. I don't know why; they're like SUVs, everybody's got one but me. And my friend Melinda. Melinda and I do catch-and-release.

"So who should call the police?" Derek asks.

"Everybody," I say. "I'll call them, you call them. I have no idea what kind of questions they'll ask, but you'll probably have more answers than I will."

He doesn't have phone numbers for current boyfriend and ex-husband, but he gives me their names. Randy Cryer of Laramie and Steve Hutton of St. Louis, Missouri.

All the police ask me is her age (thirty-three), physical description (large, blond, low body fat), how long she's been missing, and when she was last seen (Wednesday night, at the eating disorders dinner). Irreverently, I wonder what the menu is at an eating disorders dinner. A cracker and a slice of apple per person, or do they go the other way and serve a seven-course meal that nobody eats?

"What about checking out her apartment?" I ask.

"Yeah, we'll do that," the cop says. "Are you a friend of hers?"

"Yes," I lie, and agree to meet him at her place in half an hour.

I get a listing for Randall Cryer in Laramie and call it. No answer, no voice mail. I strike out on Steve Hutton. There are only about twenty S, Stephen, or Steven Huttons in the greater St. Louis area and the operator will give me only two numbers at a time.

I also try to get into Jette's voice mail. I know it's full. About twelve people have told me that, as they were filling up my voice mail. But Jette has hers password-protected, which is annoying.

Geri doesn't have Jette's password. "She's secretive about some things," Geri says. "Also, a lot of her stuff is confidential." She gives me Jette's log-in code, on the off chance that they're the same.

Damn near all of my stuff is confidential, and my voice mail isn't password-protected. The four-digit code is the same as the extension.

I try Jette's log-in code. I try her extension. I try her birth date. I go into her office and look under her desk. People have been known to tape their passwords under their desk or put them on little pieces of paper next to the phone. Jette hadn't.

I try the last four digits of her social security number. *Nada*.

I ask Geri to call the phone people and get them to change the password so that I can get into Jette's voice mail. She nods and reaches for the phone as I head off to Jette's apartment.

6

Deductions from the Closet

On the way to Jette's, I'm still bewitched enough to go by Arinda's place and give it one more try. Still the loud rock music. Still no answer. This time I scribble a note on one of my cards and wedge it in the door. "Your cat is at your regular vet's and it's fine."

This is it. I am not coming back here again. I give the place a last look as I creep down the creaky fire escape. In general the neighborhood seems to be improving, but this place is a dump. The brighter the light, the more obvious that it's a dump. But in the back, an old woman is setting out flowers. "You know Arinda?" I ask. She glares at me suspiciously. "I took her cat to the vet. Just let her know the cat's okay." The old woman narrows her eyes as if this is some sort of cryptic message. It's possible she doesn't speak English. What the hell. I gave it my best shot.

Jette's place, by contrast, is sparkling and lush, as befits the vice president of legal affairs. It's a town house in Cherry

Creek, three stories, with a backyard deck on the first level, a covered front veranda on the second level, and a balcony overlooking the creek on the third level, off the bedroom. The cops procure a key from the condo association.

My bad feeling about Jette gets worse when we enter and are met by a desperate cat. Oh, Goddess, another cat. This cat, white with orange spots, leads us daintily into the kitchen, where it meows piteously over an empty bowl. I go as if by magic to the cabinet that contains a box of dry cat food, pour a bowl, and give the cat some water. See, I'm not heartless.

Then I run up to the second level, to Jette's study. She has the whole setup, just as if she were going to work here. Computer, fax, file cabinet, bookcase full of the usual law-school flotsam (but most of it's in her office at work). *Prosser on Torts,* Colorado Collection Law, hornbooks. I open the office drawer, which is full of files, neatly and colorfully tabbed. Old research files, old cases—lawyers never throw anything away. The study looks like it was arranged by a set designer, even down to the Smith College alumni newsletter, set at an artistic angle on the desk, with a distinguished-looking fountain pen lying next to it.

This reminds me of my first indication of Jette's tyranny. When I started working at Montmorency, Jette had a great secretary. (Back then, three years ago, it was still okay to call them secretaries.) One day she overheard somebody mention that her secretary had a B.A. from Harvard. Jette immediately insisted on hiring a new secretary—somebody who hadn't done her undergraduate work at a better school than Jette's. So the Harvard grad was duly reassigned—to another building, in fact, where she was probably much happier—and Jette brought in Geri, who has no undergraduate degree whatsoever but who was qualified by virtue of having worked for Jette before.

"Don't look like she's been here," says the superobservant policewoman who accompanied me. "Her bed hasn't been slept in."

It's the first time I've heard anybody say this line in real life. It's a line that always bothered me, in movies and in books. The cops come in, look at a bed, and say it hasn't been slept in. From what sophisticated analysis do they get *that*? From the fact that it isn't warm? Maybe it was slept in and then whoever slept in it made the bed. Maybe they even put on fresh sheets. Maybe they even made it up so that a quarter would bounce off the coverlet. I mean, please.

And how long since it's been slept in? One night ago, two nights? The whole place is permeated with the odor of Red perfume. Judging by the smell of it, Jette could have just left. After making her bed.

I feel a small stab of guilt. Anyone walking into my bedroom would know the bed had been slept in, for an absolute fact.

Plowing through her bedroom, Supercop and I discover a set of luggage, empty, from which Supercop observes that she *seems not to have packed anything*. From the condition of the cat's litter box in the otherwise immaculate house, Supercop concludes that *she hasn't been around for a couple of days*. However, based on the fact that her car isn't there, Supercop feels that *she probably took her car, wherever she went*.

I guess this is helpful information. There's no sign of forced entry, no indication of any kind of a struggle.

"We'll check with the ex-husband," Supercop says.

"Her brother says they were on good terms. Anyway, he's in St. Louis."

"Yeah," Supercop says. "Did you know that, like, ninety percent of violence toward women is committed by their spouses?"

Everybody knows that. No one's talking violence here, Jette just disappeared.

Supercop leafs through the clothing in the closet. "Do you happen to remember what she was wearing last time you saw her?"

As a matter of fact, yes. "A teal Carole Little jacket, a black silk shell, and a swirly African-patterned Carole Little skirt—rayon, I think, but maybe silk—with kind of a flair at the hem.

Lots of colors—teal, orange, red. Bright. Black stockings and black Nine West wedgies. But she might have changed since then. She went to a fancy dinner."

Supercop looks at me in amazement. After a moment she recovers. "Well, do you see anything like that . . . that outfit in here? Like maybe she came home and changed?"

Well, yes, everything in Jette's closet is like that; it's like a Carole Little trunk-show-in-a-closet, with a nice smattering of Liz Claiborne and some Ann Taylor for more subdued occasions. However, I don't see the specific outfit.

"So that's what she could still be wearing," Supercop mutters.

Yeah, or it could be at the dry cleaner's.

As we're walking out, my phone rings. I feel kind of dumb, asking the caller if he can hold, please. It's Hawkeye.

"Don't give me that," he says. "Call me back." And hangs up before I even have a chance to say okay.

Hawkeye, otherwise known as Dr. Endymion Lassiter, the chief of staff of medicine, is one of the people I always call back. But reaching him by phone is damned hard, so I say a quick good-bye to the police officer, give her my card, and try to call back while Hawkeye is still in the same place. In a stroke of what may be either good luck or bad, I get him.

I identify myself breathlessly.

"You should quit smoking," Hawkeye says.

"Thanks. You called to tell me I should quit smoking?" How did *he* know I was smoking?

"Ha. You should be so lucky. No, I called to tell you that Harley said to brief you on an incident that happened last night. One of those incidents that's gonna turn sour on us in the press, three or four different ways, if the press gets hold of it."

"That's very good, Hawkeye," I say. At the moment I am driving past the offices of Channel 9. They are probably picking up this very conversation on one of the multitude of dishes and stuff on top of their building.

"I don't know if you should come in on this or not," he

says. "I can't get hold of Nolan." Nolan is our media relations director.

"Okay," I puff. "Let me have it then, since you called."

"It's sensitive I said."

"I'll be back there in five minutes," I promise, a trifle optimistically.

"Find me. I'll brief you." He hangs up, leaving me to wonder.

I locate Hawkeye in the fourth-floor doctors' lounge, a place with food. He's almost always in a place where food is available. In here it's free.

"So," I say. "Is this a secure area? Do you think we can talk here?"

"Best place in the world," Hawkeye says. He's eating a burrito. Normally, watching Hawkeye eat is enough to take my appetite away. But I missed breakfast. Hawkeye tells me to help myself. I grab a lukewarm cup of coffee and a cold banana.

"So brief me," I say. "This has to be about the cabbie and the mental patient, right?"

"Hell," Hawkeye says. I ruined his surprise, aw, gee. "You're up on things. Well, anyway, he wasn't hurt. Not by our patient, not by our staff. That's what counts, right? She was performing fellatio. Not hurting him."

I shut my eyes. Instead of counting to ten, I think liability. Do we have exposure on this? What's our insurance company going to say? What are the damages?

Doesn't sound to me like there are any damages. If the cabbie wants to file a criminal charge against the patient, that's not our problem.

Well, let's see. We let a crazy person escape. Psych patient on the loose, that's bad. If the Muslim guy was upset enough, maybe it resulted in a spinal injury he wouldn't already have, so he could sue for damages. Pain and suffering?

"How's our patient, and I don't mean the lady. She was a lady, right?"

Hawkeye snorts. "Wait, it gets better," he says.

"I mean an adult. Not one of our adolescents?"

"Free, white, and over twenty-one."

"Not exactly free," I mutter. "But go on. How's the patient?"

"Contusions," Hawkeye says. "Possible concussion. Bruising of cervical spine but no insult. Coccyx bruised but intact. Fractured ulna, fractured femur. And once we got a translator he calmed down a little bit, although not too much. He's very, very upset."

He's probably meeting with his lawyer now.

"But I said it gets better. Okay, when our staff member goes in and finds this scene, the girl—'scuse me, I mean the woman, the female patient—kind of laughs and runs off. Naked. And at this point they are concerned about this cabdriver, who is after all screaming his fucking head off."

"Screaming his head off, huh."

"Bad choice of words. Anyway, they get him calmed down—somewhat—and make sure he's stable, and the woman has disappeared. She's a redhead."

I feel a thin smile form on my lips. I'm a redhead. We should become a protected minority if you ask me. "Other than being a redhead, did anybody notice what she looked like?"

"You'll love this," Hawkeye says. "She was Miss Wisconsin, or some state like that, a few years ago."

"Aw, shit. You're kidding, right?"

"So she tells people. So everybody's combing the joint for her. And they find her, too. In the parking garage. Blowing *another* joint."

"You mean—"

"More fellatio, right. Not a patient this time."

"Good, Hawkeye," I say, almost a whisper.

"I loved watching you eat that banana as I was telling you about the fellatio, by the way," Hawkeye says. "You should see yourself, biting off those little pieces—"

"If you'd like a sexual harassment lawsuit, just keep going with this, Hawkeye. I could write you up and send you to diversity training."

Hawkeye rolls his eyes. "Okay, sorry, forget I said anything. Anyway, she's in a car. In the parking garage. With another victim." He waits expectantly for me to ask who. I don't.

"What's she in for, treatment of nymphomania?" He shakes his head. "Okay, I give up. Who?"

His eyes alight. He's gotten me back, for already knowing the assault on the Tanzanian cabbie was performed by an escaped mental patient. "One of our Environmental Services people," Hawkeye says. "One of the contract ones."

"You mean—"

"Yeah, one of the retards."

"Diversity training, Hawkeye," I warn.

"Well, what do you call them?"

I call them the people from the sheltered workshop, although I believe "developmentally disabled" is the appropriate term. Another one is "trainable." Environmental Services contracted with the workshop to hire them. They are good workers. They don't mind doing boring things like mopping floors endlessly. They don't mind working all night. They are usually cheerful and amiable. They are cheap.

There are times when mopping floors is a job that sounds pretty good to me. Not so many headaches. You can see instantaneous results.

"I guess this guy's been fired," I say thoughtfully.

"Yeah. Well, no, I think he was just sent home. I'd hate to be the one who had to explain to him what he did wrong. It was kind of a touchy issue. We didn't want to turn him over to the police because the lady in question, her husband—"

"Oh, shit!" I howl. "She has a husband?"

"Yep. And he works for the police." Hawkeye is pleased; he knew something I didn't.

"Wait . . . back up . . ."

"Okay. The staff had called the husband to alert him that she'd escaped."

"They shouldn't have done that," I mutter.

"What else should they do? That was before they knew she was still on the premises and looking for love. So the husband came over, all outraged, to help find her."

"He brought his cop buddies?"

"No. Security had called the police, also to help find her."

"So they considered her dangerous."

"Doesn't she sound dangerous? I don't know if the husband heard about the Tanzanian guy, but he was right there when they found her in the car with the janitor."

"I guess we're lucky nobody got shot," I say.

"Right. Well, not exactly. The husband is a shrink for the cops. Not a real cop."

A shrink. For the cops. Of course; that makes perfect sense. I rub around my eyes carefully, so I won't get mascara under my contact lenses.

"So, that's bad," Hawkeye says. "Of course the husband is a little upset we let her escape. Wants AIDS testing and a full refund for her stay."

"No, that's good," I tell him. "I'll bet it won't get written up on the police report, which means no reporters can find it, which means they can't spread it all over the papers tomorrow." My mind is ticking off what I need to do. I'll need to find out if the patient was a voluntary admission or was committed, possibly by her husband. I'll need to talk to the cabdriver and assess his level of rage—just as a formality. Check out any precedent for this kind of thing, patient assaults patient. Does Montmorency have exposure? And see what's being done with the guy from the sheltered workshop. All that ought to eat up the rest of the day.

"Great," I say. "Thank you so much for briefing me on this."

"You have a plan, right?"

I have a plan. I'm going to go home. I'm going to go to bed. I'm going to pull the covers over my head—no, wait, first I'm going to drink a glass of wine or maybe two. *Then* I'm going to pull the covers over my head . . .

"I thought you'd want to know," Hawkeye says. "By the way, if we ever get another Tanzanian, call Ed Waffen. He translated. Swahili."

"Thanks, Hawkeye. I'll make a note of it."

"Wanna know how to say 'blow job' in Swahili?"

I roll my eyes. He tells me anyway.

By the time I get back to my office, I've forgotten—not that I believed Hawkeye anyway. I grab a couple of notebooks out of the closet next to Anita's desk.

"Jeez Louise, Vicky," Anita says. "You sure go through those things fast. Are you taking them home or what?"

"Lawyers do that," Geri says helpfully. "I don't know why."

"They teach it to us in law school." Then I think maybe that's wrong and I developed this habit at my first job, but anyway. "I like to have a separate notebook for each separate incident. That way I don't have to paw through one notebook looking for everything related to one specific incident or case."

Anita turns to Geri. "That explains why Jette's files are always half filled with legal pads, perfectly good legal pads that have one or two pages written on."

"I guess," Geri says.

I go into my office, log on to the system as Jette, and in between phone calls peruse her directories.

Lots of us have our Rolodexes on our computers, usually called ROLO with our initials. If Jette does, maybe I can get the phone numbers of her ex and possibly other people to call. She does have a file called ROLO.JW, but it's locked. She has a lot of locked files. Some of their names are intriguing as hell. Literally.

Three of the most interesting, DEVO.MEM, TOGO.GAY, and SATAN.DOC, were last saved on Wednesday at 21:43, 18:30, and 21:45, respectively. Just before and just after the eating disorders dinner. Because of this, they'd be worth looking at even if they didn't have interesting names. But I can't view them because they are password-protected and I don't have the password. I go out to check with Geri. She doesn't have it either. It could be different for each file.

"Jette's become a lesbian devil-worshiper," I suggest. "That could explain her disappearance."

"Ha-ha," Geri says without mirth.

"Well, what was she working on that was sensitive?"

"She thinks everything is," Geri says. "If I knew her voice-mail password I'd try that, but . . . well, you know, I don't know that."

"Yeah. Did you call HR?"

"Left a message."

"If it's locked, it's locked," I say. "What can you do?"

I go back to my office and change the sort mode to look at the files by date. Jette didn't have a lot going on on Wednesday, but at 14:43 she saved a file called TIME.SHT, which is also locked. I try a few more common passwords, such as various combinations of her initials. They don't work. A call to Information Systems removes any hope that I could get into these files.

"We don't have those passwords. We can't get those passwords. We can't get into those files. If you forgot your password, you're sunk. Try to remember it." Words to live by.

I go to Jette's office to seek more clues. A quick flip through her in-basket indicates that she's been keeping up with her workload, except for the reading. I knew that—she's been passing her workload to me! A couple of supplements have cases flagged. The ones I check pertain to medical records. Something about why they should not be E-mailed.

If she'd told me she was working on a medical-records issue, I could have given her lots of stuff, piles of it, from the risk management perspective. Now, of course, I can't, because then she'd know I was snooping through her files.

As long as I'm in here snooping through Jette's stuff, I open one of her file drawers and scan the tops of the files, looking for complete legal pads. As Geri said, the files are stuffed with them. I pull out the first one I come to—a pretty old file. As noted, the first couple of pages are written on, the rest of the pad is blank. The notes themselves are cryptic, as notes tend to be, but it looks like this particular file predates Jette's reign as VP of legal affairs. It's notes on collections procedure. Maybe it's even personal. I'm not above reading personal stuff, but some other day. I cram the file back into the drawer and go back to my office.

I call a couple of people I know who are on the Disease of the Year Committee, who confirm they saw Jette at the dinner but not afterward.

One of the people I call is my friend Kate, who comes from old Denver money and flirts with heading into the society spin. She also flirts with extreme political activist groups and rock stars. I never know what I'm going to run into when I talk to Kate.

She did not attend the eating disorders dinner, but she is on the committee. And she would love to spend a few minutes yakking with me. For some reason I get on to how I'm fed up with not really practicing law, but I can't bitch about it because everybody I know who *is* practicing law claims to just hate it.

Kate, who briefly considered a career in law, thinks I'm an idiot. We met when I was running an independent legal clinic, of the sort that recruits lawyers to volunteer their time—or at least take a lower rate—for people who are not quite destitute enough to qualify for the bar's official indigent-client program. She wanted to volunteer, to see how she liked it. Not being a lawyer, she was given a great deal of stuff to copy and file, so she decided she'd like nothing better.

She thought it might be fun to run a newspaper, so she started one: a real estate weekly. After a year she was bought out to the tune of about three times her original investment. Typical.

"So what would you like to do instead of law?" she asks.

I don't even think about this for a minute. "Train polo ponies," I say.

"Hah," she says. "Remember when I asked you about your ideal day? I hate to tell you, but shopping all day and training polo ponies are two incompatible choices."

Okay, so I'd alternate days.

After hanging up, I alternate roles. I switch from being the risk manager to being the VP of legal affairs, and as such I need to review and sign those responses to interrogatories.

I take the stack of papers outside, to the Smoker's Showcase. I spend about six minutes (one cigarette) with the thing and then I'm ready to vent. It's a mess—typos, errors of fact, names misspelled—sloppily done by some dude Jette went to law school with. Why would we pay an outside firm to do this? We could have made a hash of it ourselves.

Meanwhile, six people come up to me and ask me what's the deal with Jette. Three people ask me what's the deal with the cabdriver, and one person, one very informed person, asks me what's the deal with the police shrink's wife. Our grapevine is very, very good. Everybody has some theory about Jette. Like, maybe she eloped.

Jette has, of late, been softening her image. For instance, she's let her short, spiky blond style grow out a little bit and gotten some kind of perm so it's wavy. A few more months and it might be chin length. Just the sort of thing that could indicate sustained romantic interest.

Naw, she didn't elope. She would have bragged about it.

Nolan Horowitz, Mr. Media Relations, sits down beside me and waves his cigar. "So, is it true that Jette's picture's going to be on a milk carton next week?" he asks.

"Sad but true," I say. "Think what that will do to the Got Milk? campaign. Are you in charge of procuring the photograph and contacting the dairy?"

Sitting in the spring sunshine, I find it necessary to light up yet another cigarette, to aid in my edit.

"Penny for your thoughts," Nolan says.

"Not worth selling," I say. The truth is, I don't want to share this thought: If Jette doesn't come back, I can fire this incompetent law firm and hire somebody *I* went to law school with.

7

Games of Chance

Debriefing (my term) the victims (or worse, the victims' survivors) is touchy. I have to be two people at once: the sympathetic hospital representative who is sorry sorry sorry it happened at all, and particularly to them; and the risk manager protecting the hospital's assets, reputation, and money, trying to convince the victims (or worse, their survivors) not to sue, then assessing the likelihood that they will sue anyway. (And figuring out how much they could get, should they prevail, but that's more of the fun part. It's not my money.)

At these moments, it's a great relief to remember that everybody fucks up.

I try to put myself in the patient's position. How would I like it if I had an awful accident, was ambulanced to a hospital, immobilized, and then sexually assaulted?

I must be a terrible person. What I think is, it would depend on the assailant.

It's not that I'm cavalier about sexual assault. It's just that, considering all the indignities one is subject to following an admission to a hospital, not to mention the trauma of being in an accident in the first place, the severity of a sexual assault, particularly the kind this guy suffered, recedes somewhat. Me, I'd be a hell of a lot more pissed about being immobilized, and on this point I speak with assurance.

The patient's right arm and left leg are in casts. He's in a much better mood today and, as he says, has the English. For everybody's peace of mind, Ed, the translator, remains, acting as a chaperon.

The cabbie doesn't mention the sexual assault, and neither do I. Instead I offer him two weeks' worth of home-health services, up to three hours a day, since he's going to have trouble with daily life. I did, when all I had was a broken finger. I offer to pay his transportation costs for getting back to the hospital for follow-up. These are known as proactive maneuvers, in the hope that should he be inclined to sue, he'll remember how nice it was of me to volunteer this assistance.

Harley and Geri are the only ones in the office when I get back. Geri's sitting morosely at her computer.

"Go home," I tell her.

She turns a sad face to me. "The police are coming to talk to us about Jette," she says. "I'm really, really worried about her."

"We all are." And some of us are pretty fucking tired of hearing about it, too. I sit down on the couch and stare at today's *Wall Street Journal*. Usually, someone has taken it home by now. The circumstantial evidence points to that person being Jette.

Harley and Geri don't tell me to hang around and join them in their conference with the cops, but they don't tell me to leave either. Two uniformed officers stroll in, equipment clanking on their belts. They are both portly and middle-aged, which is reassuring. I tend to distrust the new breed of cops, the ones who are smaller than me and about fifteen years younger.

They tell us what they are doing, which is, basically, keeping their eyes open. We assure them that we do not know of anyone who might have kidnapped Jette.

"Sometimes people just split," one of them says. "Come back of their own accord, when they're good and ready." Geri shakes her head. She thinks Jette was too responsible to pull that kind of stunt.

Then they get into some nitty-gritty. Do we know who might benefit, if Jette was done away with?

Well, me. I might get her job. Officially, that is. I don't mention this. Let them figure that one out.

Did she have any enemies? Come on, guys, *think*. She's a lawyer.

"Whatever you do, don't try to pursue this yourselves," the cop admonishes. "We've got her on a list. We've got her car plates and vehicle description out in all fifty states." This seems like overkill. We're in the west, after all. These are big states. "If you hear of anything that might pertain to this matter, call us." Business cards all around. Okay.

When they leave, Harley corners me. "You heard them, Vicky."

"Harley, I wouldn't dream of going in search of Jette," I say. "All I've done is what you asked, finding out where and when she was last seen. But surely you don't mind my keeping my ear to the ground."

He grudgingly admits he doesn't, as long as all information I might obtain goes straight to the police and I don't act upon it myself.

"Well, sure, Harley, that's a given."

"If someone abducted her, there could be danger," Harley says.

Well, duh!

8

Skating on No Ice

"Guess what?" I say to Glenn, who's laid out on my couch, drinking a beer. "I talked my boss out of being on the pager this weekend—that is, I'm not on it until midnight." I feel like Cinderella.

Glenn sits up. "Great!" he says. "And I don't have the kids this weekend."

I knew that. He had the kids last weekend.

I have never met the kids, because he always goes to them and then takes them somewhere. I believe he thinks he doesn't have room for them in his apartment, but maybe he just doesn't want them to run into me.

"We could go for a ride on the motorcycle," he says. "Maybe go up to the Central City casinos and try our luck."

"Uh . . ." How do I say this? I am in no mood to try my luck. Just yesterday I ran over a black cat. "I don't think so."

"You're afraid to ride on the back of my motorcycle," he says.

I scratch my head. "I'm not a riding-on-the-back type of person. I want to drive."

"I've only got one motorcycle."

"Glenn, riding on the back of a motorcycle is boring. You can't talk. You can't listen to music. You can't even see very well. And half the fun of being on a motorcycle—hell, *all* the fun—is driving it."

"Oy vey," he says. And he looks pissed. "How come we always have to do what you want to do?"

Instead of happy hour, we're having our first fight.

I suppose this is a good sign. I have always considered that people who don't fight have wimpy relationships.

Or maybe I just like to fight. I don't think so, but look at my job; is this the kind of job a nonfighter would have? It's a stupid fight anyway.

"We don't always have to do what I want to do," I say. "But I don't see why we should *ever* do what I don't want to do. Is this reasonable or what? If you want to ride up to Central City and gamble, go right ahead."

"Okay, I give up. What do you want to do?"

"Go someplace with loud music and dance. Second choice, go someplace with loud music and drink. Or both. Or go for a walk. I never get enough exercise to work the kinks out."

"And with your particular set of kinks, you never will," Glenn says. "I didn't mean now, though. I meant tomorrow."

"Rollerblading," I say. "Hey, the weather's gotten good, the snow will have melted off the bike path. . . ." He shakes his head.

"Okay," I say. "I'm a mature adult and I can go Rollerblading by myself." I got these skates, see, and I haven't used them all winter.

"Good," he says. "I'll cycle up to Central City." Okay. It's settled.

When we get up, he's changed his mind. We outfit ourselves with pads, elbow protectors, and wrist guards, so we look like people from the science-fiction future. Glenn wears a helmet. But then Glenn has never done in-line skating before. I have, and I draw the line at wearing a helmet.

"Some *risk manager* you turned out to be," he says.

"I do this all the time," I retort. "Skinned knees I get. Concussions I don't get."

"At least you've got a padded butt." He pats it.

Every time we pass someone wearing a helmet, he points it out. "Hey, look, an expert. And *she*'s wearing a helmet."

We are both tired and sore when we get home. We are soaking in the hot tub downstairs when my phone rings. The cell phone, which, true to Harley's prediction, has been with me all day.

"Aha," Harley says. "I knew you'd answer this phone. I just tried your apartment."

Damn it, he takes the pager, then as soon as it goes off he calls me. "Hey, this is supposed to be my day off. I don't do the pager thing until midnight."

"Want me to call back after midnight?"

"*No.* Since you've already disturbed me, go ahead and tell me now."

"It was the police."

Numerous possibilities flash through my mind. I pick the most felicitous. "They located Jette?"

"No. Now don't get riled up," Harley says. "I don't know

what it was about. They wouldn't say. They asked all these questions about an apartment at Eleventh and Logan, what was I doing there, how long was I there, I kept saying I wasn't there, I was never there. Finally it dawned on me that maybe that was when you had the car."

"*Maybe* it was when I had the car? You know damn well when I had the car."

"Right, I know when you had the car, but they wouldn't tell me the time frame. I gave them your number."

Could I have been speeding in Harley's SUV? No; they'd either have nailed me on the spot or taken my picture with the new photographic speed enforcers. And then they mail you the ticket.

Shit, did I park illegally or something? It couldn't be hitting the cat. The cat lived. Or maybe the cat died, but still. It was just a cat.

I turn to Glenn. "Boy. I borrow a car and the cops track me down."

"Hey, they called me, too," Glenn says. "I forgot to tell you. They left a message asking me to call them. At my convenience. It hasn't been convenient yet."

"I drove your car there, too," I say.

"What? When?"

"They got Harley's license, apparently, from when I drove his car to Eleventh and Logan, where I hit the cat." I use the cellular to call my voice mail. Sure enough, the cops have already left a nice polite message. Call at your convenience.

They must be having a very slow Saturday in District 3 if they're calling people up about hitting cats two days ago.

We're dry, relaxed, and two glasses into a nice Merlot when the phone rings again. I pick it up, expecting the cops and ready to face the music. It's not the cops. It's Harley again.

"I don't come on till midnight, remember?"

"I'm on my way to the hospital," he says. "I think you'd better head there, too. As the risk manager, not as the corporate counsel." He won't tell me why, just that it's not about Jette.

Something in his voice inspires me to make a lightning change from my hot-pink sweatsuit to a more sedate gray knit outfit from Lands' End. It's still a sweatsuit, make no mistake, but it's a more respectable sweatsuit. I say a quick good-bye to Glenn, who's standing by the couch holding his wineglass. "Go ahead, finish the bottle," I say. "I'll be home as soon as—"

I stop. One bad thing about this job: I never know when I'm going to be home.

9

Weekend Special

Being many, many miles closer, I get to the hospital way before Harley does. Adrenaline has won out over the wine, and I'm completely sober. As I walk in, I hear Hawkeye being paged to the Intensive Care Unit, so I also head there, figuring that Hawkeye can tell me what's going on.

A patient came out of surgery with no apparent complications and went into the recovery room, where patients go to gradually regain consciousness.

She didn't. Not gradually or any other way.

The staff has no idea what's wrong with her. It isn't anything cut-and-dried; her heart hasn't stopped, she hasn't stopped breathing.

This pisses me off. Why can't Harley deal with it, at least until midnight? It's not clear to me why this situation would throw Harley into a tailspin. The surgery was over at 10:30 this morning, and it's only a little after one. Too early to panic, I would say. I'm an inveterate panicker, so I should know.

For one crazy moment I picture myself gowning, gloving, and going in to stand over the patient and pronounce the diagnosis, something simple and obvious that nobody else has noticed. Like, "Oh, she's not plugged in, see?" I don't know where I get these crazy heroic fantasies. Instead I listen to one of the nurses tell me the patient's hypotensive and her pupils are equal and reactive to light, but she is not responding to pinpricks.

Some patients are just slower to recover than others. As a nurse, I would let a doctor know about this, but I wouldn't panic. Yet.

I'm steaming up inside my sweatsuit. Too warm for this kind of thing. "What kind of surgery?"

"A brow-lift," the nurse says. "Endoscopic."

In other words, not a full-scale face-lift but a sort of touch-up.

"Good God, when did we start doing elective outpatient plastic surgery on Saturday morning?"

Hawkeye sneaks up behind me—for a large guy, he's light on his feet—and answers. "When the wife of the chief of staff of surgery requests it, that's when."

Oh. That's why it's a major incident. The nonresponsive patient is Bootsie Devoss, wife of Dr. Dennis Devoss.

Hawkeye is the highest-ranking physician at the hospital, the chief of staff of medicine. Dennis is right behind him, and he has a lot more class. Dennis looks like a chief of staff. Hawkeye looks like a fat slob.

For instance, Hawkeye hangs around in scrubs, often scrubs stained with splotches of food, even though his duties don't often call for him to wear scrubs.

Dennis, however, wears respectable, expensive, well-cut suits. Monogrammed French cuffs. Gold cuff links. I don't think I've ever seen him in scrubs, even though he spends half his life in surgery. He showers, scrubs, operates, then changes back into business attire.

In a way, Dennis is Dr. Montmorency. When we need a top-ranking presence to appear at, say, a news conference, that doctor is Dennis. Never Hawkeye. Dennis also makes news every year or so when he assembles a team and travels to some third world country to perform surgery, *gratis,* on children who otherwise would grow up stunted, if they grew up at all.

I turn to Hawkeye. "So, how bad is this?"

"Real bad. Potentially awful. She should be awake enough to answer simple questions," Hawkeye says. "The anesthetic should have worn off to the point where she's barely groggy. She should be feeling discomfort. She should react to stimuli, but she's unresponsive."

"Who was the surgeon?" Almost unconsciously, I have pulled a notebook out of my bag.

"Elliott Stillwell, assisted by Keith Cowan."

"She had general anesthesia?"

"Sodium pentothal and nitrous oxide–oxygen anesthesia," Hawkeye says.

When we have an incident like this, I am charged with investigating, submitting a report, and seeing that the guilty are disciplined and the innocent exonerated, whether the victim is an old homeless person on Medicare or Bootsie Devoss, but the fact that it *is* Bootsie will make it harder.

"I like the way you just dive right in," Hawkeye says.

The next person to join our glum little group is Harley.

"How could this happen?" he moans. "This is like *Air Force One* crashing. You know planes *do* crash from time to time, but you know it's not going to happen to *Air Force One*."

Then Dennis Devoss comes in. He's a tall man, a bit wide around the middle (but nothing like Hawkeye); his well-cut suits disguise this. Even in casual clothes he looks elegant. He would be imposing except that his body language radiates friendliness. He hugs me.

Unlike a lot of surgeons, Dennis is a warmhearted and physical guy, and I find his hug pillowy and comforting, even though he needs the comfort more than I do.

Usually, when I talk to the next of kin, I can be very, very professional, because these are people I don't know. They are not people I have just hugged.

I don't know Dennis all that well—not like Harley, for instance—but I do like him, and I like Bootsie. In fact, Bootsie is someone I admire.

Bootsie has class. She's one of those golden people, a natural beauty, like my friend Melinda. Great bone structure, a cute figure, good hair. Like Melinda, she is nice. Unlike Melinda, she's short, but still very classy.

Bootsie—even before the face-lift—looks a good ten years younger than Dennis, but she's not. She's his original wife, married to him since medical school. Most doctors shed their medical-school wives shortly after they graduate, and by the time they're Dennis's age, at Dennis's high level of income and achievement, they're on their second trophy wife. I give Dennis some points for not doing that, although it's possible the credit should go to Bootsie.

She and Dennis together have a sheen of perfection and success. They could be poster children for the American dream.

When Harley stands up to shake hands with Dennis—at least I assume that's what he was doing—Dennis embraces him, too.

"Don't worry," Dennis says, comforting *us*. "I'm sure everything's going to be all right."

My usual questions, calculated to put the patient's family at ease in the strange environs of the hospital, just won't work. I'll have to come up with something else.

I decide it's time for me to get out of here and chase down the operating team.

I head back to my office in Admin to get a fresh notebook. Harley follows me, like a lost puppy dog.

The Admin reception area smells musty, of old flowers. We get fresh flowers every week from the hospital gift shop, for appearances. We also get lots of arrangements that are on the verge of collapse. I don't know where those come from.

I open the supply cabinet next to Anita's desk and pull out a new notebook for my investigation. Then, for the benefit of Anita, I make a check mark on the supply list and initial it.

"Comas are pretty bad, right?" Harley says.

This is the COO of the hospital talking here. Hasn't got a clue. Sometimes, I kid you not, I have to wonder how Harley insinuated himself into top management. He's a nice guy, but really. Not that our CEO knows any more about comas than Harley, and Langstrom is not a nice guy.

I probably have the most medical knowledge of anyone in Admin and look where it's gotten me. Am I in line to become CEO? Not a chance. But Harley is.

"Sometimes they're bad news," I say. We've had several recently that have made headlines and a lot more that didn't.

One of them was a hang glider who augured in, as they say. She was wearing a helmet, which probably saved her life. Six days in a coma, then complete recovery.

Another was a young mother, who died. Lots of press on that one, and an investigation into her care, which was deemed adequate. And then we had an alcoholic, about seventy years old, who had the added problem of having a separated shoulder. He presented, as we say in medical terms, in Emergency, holding his shoulder, which he said he hurt when he got off a train; it was obvious to the medical staff that he had *jumped* off the train and that he was a little too old for that sort of shenanigans. During treatment for the shoulder, he passed out and went into a coma for a period of weeks. I don't remember what happened to him. Maybe he's still in one.

"The thing to remember is, comas aren't great medical mysteries, or they aren't supposed to be," I say. "What you have to do is find the underlying pathological condition. That's usually the problem. Not the coma."

"I thought that young mother was a curious case," Harley says, so I know he was thinking of her, too.

"The *coma* wasn't a mystery. The mystery was why an apparently healthy thirty-year-old woman had a massive heart attack. It was the heart attack that caused the coma."

You have to wonder where the health-care system broke

down in a case like this. The last act of this young mother had been to nurse her seven-week-old daughter. Then, still holding the baby, she called out to her husband and told him she felt awful. They called 911 and got her to the hospital, where she was diagnosed as having had a massive infarction and where she had another before going into the three-week-long coma that preceded her death.

She had passed her six-week postnatal checkup only a couple of days before. Her husband said her maternity leave was up and she was planning to return to work the next week. His theory was that the thought of leaving her baby in day care literally broke her heart.

It's a tearjerker all right, and I, ever susceptible to tearjerkers, went through a tissue or two before reverting to my usual cynical stance. *It literally broke her heart?* Come on, folks. Hundreds of women, probably millions, would rather not go back to work, but they don't just up and die from broken hearts. Of course, I didn't say this to the survivors. Somewhere along the line this woman's health-care team struck out, but I couldn't say where. Nobody could.

"They don't seem to know what caused Bootsie's coma," Harley says. "They were rushing around, drawing blood like mad and performing various tests."

"Well, sure." I flip open my notebook and jot down questions in shorthand. "They'll need the usual lab work. They'll also check the blood for drugs, although they'll have presurgical samples of that, I'm sure. The usual things—urinalysis, blood pressure, respirations. They'll run an EEG, and maybe a CT scan. By that time she may have woken up; some people are just slow to rouse."

Harley rubs his hands together. "Dennis called in Brian Marrote," he says.

I nod. "The Brain" Marrote is a big guy in Neurosurgery, but it makes perfect sense. Being a big name himself, Dennis could get any neurosurgeon in town off the golf course to supervise treatment of his wife. Marrote is not who I'd pick to get me out of a coma, but he knows his stuff. You have to assume all neurosurgeons know their stuff.

"What did Hawkeye tell you?" I don't add, *to get you in here on a Saturday*.

"Don't put me in your notes," Harley says dourly. "Ask him."

Okay, fine.

I write down things I need to ask. Saturday morning is an odd time to schedule surgery. As a doctor's wife, Bootsie must have known that. Perhaps she was being secretive about the surgery, it being cosmetic in nature. But those things are hard to keep secret, given the fact that there's kind of a long recovery time. I add another question to my notebook: Why was this done in the hospital? A brow-lift is commonly done in the plastic surgeon's office. Did her surgeon expect trouble, or was it one of those insurance things—covered if done in the hospital, not covered if done in the office?

Not that I've ever heard of cosmetic surgery being covered by insurance at all, unless it's reconstructive.

It's possible that Bootsie had some condition that made a hospital procedure more prudent. That would be in her record. I flick on my computer. My jinxed computer.

Ever since I moved back over here to Admin, my computer has given me problems. It refuses to follow my instructions. It goes on slowdown strikes. Most perplexing of all, it often saves my files with the date of January 12, 1980. While the rest of the office worries about the Y2K affliction, I'm twenty years behind. The Y80 affliction. Someone in Information Systems told me they'd have to revise the master-slave conditions, or something like that, but I think it's just a plain old ordinary gremlin. Anyway I turn it on and instruct it to head for EMRAM, Electronic Medical Records At Montmorency.

Since it takes quite a while for my gremlin-possessed computer to boot up and get to EMRAM, I head back to the clinical area to get the operative report, which is dictated right after the surgery and includes everything that happened during surgery: the room, the duration, the procedures, the personnel.

I also pick up the patient's charge log, which is a record of everything used in Bootsie's surgery: drugs, implements, medical equipment.

On it is listed every item that goes into the room and every item removed from the room. One reason for the charge log is so that every scalpel and sponge is accounted for. This serves a number of purposes, the main two being: so the patient can be charged for them, and so the operating staff can be assured that nothing was left in the patient. Sure, this sounds crazy. It sounds like there must be a better way—like, check the patient before you sew her up. But if you count eleven retractors going into surgery and only ten coming out, chances are that the missing retractor could end up somewhere it shouldn't. In at least one case I know of, the uncounted retractor, which was fairly large, ended up in the patient, where it remained for approximately six weeks, causing pain, damage, and a big settlement.

Since the OR has already been wiped down and disinfected, the OR narrative and the charge record are important in reconstructing what went on. Other pieces are the printouts from various monitoring devices, which are reliable but not infallible, and the memories of those who took part in the operation, also reliable but not infallible.

And the best time to probe those memories is when they are fresh. The OR records and the printouts will not change with time; memories might. In other words, it's time to track down and interview the players.

The first one I catch is the anesthesiologist, Pham Nguyen.

Okay, call me a racist. Call me ethnocentric. Call me nationalistic. I have a problem with people whose English I can't understand. I am, so help me Goddess, a sympathetic person, and not only that, I am a person with a good ear, and not only that, I can speak French. Okay, I can understand spoken French. I can read written French. I probably should not attempt to speak it myself, despite all those years of study, because my spoken French would probably come out even worse than Dr. Nguyen's English.

And it's pretty bad.

To illustrate the nature of the problem, his name is pronounced "Winn," or a close approximation. I am mangling his name as badly as he's mangling the English language. For which I accept full responsibility and apologize. After all, he's bilingual. Even counting my college French, I'm not.

This guy speaks English less well than our Tanzanian cabdriver, who needed a translator.

I remind myself that Bootsie was a far more sophisticated and cosmopolitan person than I, and probably she could communicate with Nguyen. I'm giving Nguyen the benefit of the doubt, because in my mind this could be a factor in why Bootsie's still out.

"She wife of doctor, she know all that." This is Nguyen's response to the standard question of whether he discussed with the patient any known or potential allergies or reactions. He has to repeat it six times before I get it.

"And she didn't have any? She knew what you were asking?"

"She know it all, thees vhooman." Nguyen keeps making his answers simpler and simpler, until I can understand him.

"Did you check out her chart?"

Another big whoosh of Vietnamese-accented English. I'm getting a headache. *"Parlez-vous français?"* I ask hopefully.

Nguyen smiles largely. *"Oui,"* he says, delighted, and then goes into a cascade of lovely French, spoken with the same accent that threw me when he used it on my own native tongue. But—maybe because French is not my native tongue—I pick something out that I had not heard before. *"Je pense qu'elle a menti au sujet de son âge."*

He thinks she lied about her age.

"Pourquoi?"

He starts explaining in French that it is not unheard of for a woman of a certain age to become coy, et cetera, so I have to go back, pluck the French words out of my sparse vocabulary to ask again, "No, I mean why do you think . . . I mean, *pourquoi pensez-vous qu'elle a,* uh, lied about her age?"

He speaks some urgent French about how the EMR accesses records for previous hospitalizations (assuming they were recent enough to be in the computer). The EMR flagged inconsistencies in Bootsie's birth date, as given on previous hospitalizations, and of course the birth date is part of the patient identifier.

"But is this material?" I wonder out loud and in English. "I mean, whether she was born in 1950 or 1948, would that matter?"

"Also 1946," Nguyen says. "A thing of definite wonder, this." I think he means this is something he'd like to know.

"But in surgery, fine," he adds. *"Aucun mauvais signe."*

This discrepancy could mean nothing. Someone hit a wrong key or two, or heard it wrong, or else Bootsie lied. I note it. But people don't go into comas because they lied about their age.

While I wait for the plastic surgeon to meet me, I read the charge log, where I find something curious. Phenol is listed on the charge log but not mentioned in the operative report. Phenol is a tissue-destroying chemical, used in chemical peels, but it jumps at me for another reason. It was the culprit in a recent, highly visible malpractice suit that occurred (luckily for me) at another hospital.

Dr. Elliott Stillwell, Bootsie's surgeon, is a distinguished older man, with wavy silver hair—quite a lot of it. You would think he would try to look younger.

On the other hand, he's a guy. Guys look better than gals when they're older. Sometimes, unfair but true, they look better than they did when they were younger. That hardly ever happens to women, which is why Stillwell owns a big house in the country, a little condo in the city, a ranch, and half of a movie production company.

"You're on my side, right?" His first question.

"Yeah," I say, none too heartily. I'm on the side of truth and justice. I'm on the side of the angels.

"I just wondered if my attorney should be present. I've put my professional liability company on notice, of course. I assume you have likewise alerted the hospital's insurance company."

"First thing I did," I lie. I should send them a fax. "This is for my internal report. The questions I'm going to ask have nothing to do with liability or fault. It's an inquiry into how this happened."

"I've dictated the narrative report," he says.

"And it's been typed up and I've got it," I assure him.

Stillwell exhales—and ages. "Dennis and I have been friends for years," he says. "Bootsie and my wife are friends. This has been really hard. And I guess it's not going to get any easier."

"Probably not," I say.

"My wife—Barbara—the first thing she asked was if it had something to do with Bootsie's being diabetic," Stillwell says.

I take note: We're four hours postsurgery and not only has he put his carrier on notice, he's discussed the situation with his wife.

"Well, Christ," he goes on, "I didn't even know she was diabetic. It's not in her record. It should have been flagged."

I draw in my breath and start thinking more clearly. Maybe this is *not* just routine. "Did you notice any other discrepancies in the record?"

He frowns. "I don't remember any."

I make a note about her age. "Would diabetes have affected the outcome?" I ask.

"Hell, yes," he says. "It's something we need to know. In Bootsie's case I understand she was controlling it with diet, which can be done in certain cases."

"Wouldn't that have come through in her blood work?"

He sighs heavily and rubs his temples again. "Well," he says, "we would have had a baseline preop, but we wouldn't have known we needed to watch her glucose during surgery. We just did the standard chemistries."

I think Stillwell is the sort who likes to wield the knife and lets his assistants deal with the underlying medical realities. Like: Is this patient fit for surgery?

"So Bootsie could be in a coma because of her diabetes," I say.

Stillwell, frowning, nods. "We can't rule it out," he says. "You know, I wouldn't call it a coma at this point. I would say she's unresponsive."

Okay, let's call it that. "How about her age? Would the fact that she lied about her age be of any significance?"

Stillwell massages his chin. "Oh, that's what you were asking about before . . . on the record. Yes, I saw that. I do like to know how old my patients are. But, honestly, it's not a big concern. The type of woman who's going to lie about her age is the same type, naturally, who's apt to consider this type of surgery."

Naturally. "Okay. Among Bootsie's medical concerns then, how about her hypotension?"

He lifts his head and juts his chin out. "That problem occurred after surgery," he says. "Her blood pressure was monitored, as always, during surgery, as you no doubt know. And she exercises a lot, so her BP is normally low. For her, in fact, I don't even consider this hypotension."

A pressure cuff checks the patient's blood pressure constantly and beeps quite alarmingly for any number of reasons: blood pressure drops below a certain point, rises above a certain point, or if its power supply is interrupted. However, the one used in Bootsie's surgery did not leave a paper record.

"What do you use phenol for in plastic surgery?"

Stillwell frowns. "I wouldn't. It's not one of my drugs."

Doctors are like that. They have their own stable of preferred drugs, often influenced by visits from friendly sales reps from pharmaceutical companies, price breaks, kickbacks, and other great stuff.

"It's used in chemical peels," he explains.

"I know that; I meant what was its use in this particular case?"

"I don't even do the chemical peel anymore. I use the laser method. But when I did, I used TCA, not phenol. And this was not a peel. I certainly wouldn't have used it in this case. I'm sure it's not mentioned in my report."

"It's not. So you didn't order it?"

"Absolutely not. Didn't I say that? Dr. Cowan assisted—maybe he ordered it."

Interesting.

"Why did you do surgery here and not in your office?"

He grimaces. "Bootsie had to be done on her own timetable," he says. "Normally, yes, I would do this in my office."

I make another note to the effect that he might not *know* what's routine in the hospital. He answers my next question, which would have been "Why the hospital?," even before I ask it.

"My office is not staffed on Saturday, and Bootsie felt more comfortable doing it here, given her time constraints."

He means that Bootsie wanted to be all fixed and presentable for some occasion two or three weeks down the road. She didn't want to have to cover her bruises with pancake makeup.

He shuts his eyes. I can tell a big dramatic moment is coming. "But she trusted us here, as she wouldn't have trusted anyone else. And we let her down."

10

Message from the Tooth Fairy

Dennis Devoss is sitting outside Bootsie's room on the usual plastic hospital chair, his head lolling to one side. He perks up when I pad down the hall. He looks like he'd rather be anywhere else—but, perversely, he doesn't look bad. He looks vital and alive. In the gray-green corridor he looks colorful. He hugs me again and updates me on Bootsie's condition. No change, but she appears stable. There's still hope, and he's upbeat.

I mumble something like "Just need to ask you a couple questions," and he sets me at ease: of course I need to ask him questions. He can't wait to answer them.

"Was Bootsie diabetic?"

"Christ, no," he says.

I sit there with my little pen poised above my little pad.

"She wasn't?"

"She was not."

"Some of her best friends thought—"

"Here's what happens," he says. "I've seen it a hundred times. We go someplace for a nice dinner and someone offers her something scrumptious for dessert. Or we're in the buffet line with some of her friends. Now, she and all her friends are on diets half the time. She could just say that. But instead, instead of saying three simple words, *no, thank you,* she goes into this spiel about how it looks simply divine but of course she can't eat it because she's diabetic, and they ought to know that, and it's such a burden, blah blah blah." He shuts his eyes as if he has a killer headache. "Who cares? Just don't take the goodie, right? She just couldn't seem to do the simple thing."

I wonder idly if Bootsie is on the eating disorders committee. She must be. It's a given. Rich doctors' wives make up the essence of the foundation, and Bootsie, a few years ago, was the director of the foundation.

Dennis runs his hands through his hair and then reaches out and touches my arm. "Look, I'm sorry. I didn't mean to get hysterical there."

"Oh . . . you didn't."

He gives my arm a faint squeeze and removes his hand. "I'm a little wound up," he says.

"Well, sure."

"I know you have to ask these questions," he says. "In fact, I appreciate it."

"Okay. Would she have lied about her age? To her doctor?"

"Yes," Dennis says. "Or to anyone. Would she have disregarded her doctor's advice? Yes. Would she have . . . Well, never mind. There I go again."

This time I reach out and pat him on the shoulder. He covers my hand briefly with his.

"You've heard this before, doctors make the worst patients," he says. "Let me tell you, their wives aren't a hell of a lot better."

I nod sympathetically.

"I have total trust in this team," he says. "I'll tell you, I'm not going to be one of those doctors who has to lay blame somewhere, when something goes wrong in my own family medically."

I continue my sympathetic nodding.

"She had the full-scale face-lift a few years ago—the chin, the cheeks, the neck—even though she already looked damn good. And, frankly, I wouldn't mind if she put on a few pounds, you know? Or if she looked her age. She kept saying she was doing all this for me, but I didn't care."

He runs his fingers through his hair yet again. Dark, curly hair, with a few silver threads dispersed throughout. A little on the long side, and lots of it, despite his age. He's not bad, even if he is old enough to be my father. Attractive, nice, warm . . . I don't blame Bootsie for trying to maintain her looks.

Dennis assures me that he will be delighted to answer any more questions I come up with. Since he's the medical expert, I ask him if there's anything I missed.

"Neurological stuff isn't my strong point," he says. "We're specialists, you know. What I knew about it, I've forgotten. It's like me asking you what you know about admiralty law." He's got me there. What a thing to think of. Admiralty law.

He could have hit a lot of other legal specialties while he was at it. But this helps me focus. My function here is not to figure out what's wrong with Bootsie and fix it. I am looking for evidence of medical malpractice and/or hospital negligence.

"You might talk to her internist," Dennis suggests. "Patricia Duty. I don't know whether Trish knew she was having this surgery, but at least she can confirm that Bootsie didn't have diabetes."

"Hey, I believe you." I take the name down, but now that I'm focused, I don't think I'll need it.

I go in search of Dr. Stillwell's assistant. Now, there would have been a good question: Why did Stillwell have an assistant? A brow-lift is usually done in the doctor's office, so why would such a procedure necessitate *two* specialists, along with two OR nurses? So there's one more person to bill?

Of course, when I had my broken finger reset, two doctors were also present, along with *three* nurses, a medical technologist, and the anesthesiologist. The room was so crammed, it was a wonder anyone could get to my finger. And with all those experts in the room, you'd better believe I stayed awake for the procedure.

When I see Dr. Cowan, I realize he probably assisted as a learning exercise. He is the youngest doctor of the bunch, and the most loutish. This makes me think he's the most likely to have screwed up, even though such an assumption is false. Just because someone's an asshole doesn't mean he doesn't do good work.

Everything was routine, he assures me. There were no complications of any kind; things went very smoothly. He has never lost anyone on the table, never. He operates *only* on healthy people. He even insists that they quit smoking twenty-one days before the surgery. Not that most of them smoke.

This guy's probably twenty-six years old and he has a lot of gall saying he's never lost anyone on the table; how many people has he even *had* on the table?

"Did Bootsie smoke?"

"I've never known Mrs. Devoss to smoke," Cowan says coldly. "But if she did, she would have had to quit twenty-one days before she was scheduled for surgery. *Or I would not have done it.* What's the point of having this kind of surgery if you're going to smoke?"

This kind of talk makes me long for the Showcase. Just for a minute.

I get him to describe the surgery in detail. Everything went smoothly, he says again. It was a quick surgery. Routine. (Right; he's done it hundreds of times, in the three years he's been an M.D.) It took approximately one hour and forty-five minutes. He was changed and on the golf course by eleven, which meant, of course, that he was still on the golf course when he got the call from the recovery room that his patient did not seem to be recovering. And he came straight back— for all the good that did.

As he talks, I figure things out. Board-certified plastic surgeons have to go through three years of surgical residency and then some further time in constructive and cosmetic procedures before they're certified. Even though he acts like it—insisting that *all his patients* quit smoking or he won't do the surgery—he's not the main guy, although he may have wielded the knife.

But is that material? The problem as defined does not seem to have happened during the surgical procedure.

Because he's a rookie I quiz him on this a little harder than I put the questions to Stillwell. I pull out the operative report and, while reading it, ask him to go through it step-by-step. As he does, his arrogance slips away.

"Did you or the nurses inject anything—like lidocaine— during the surgery?"

"No. Is that in the report? Shouldn't be. Sometimes we would do that, but not this time."

"So she couldn't have gotten any of the phenol?"

"Phenol? No, we wouldn't use that."

"So why was it in the OR?" He shakes his head. He didn't see it. He doesn't think it would be routine to have it. He didn't order it.

He looks over the operative report. "There was one thing," he says. "I didn't dictate it, and neither did Stillwell. Just for a brief, very brief, moment, the nurse put a drape back and thought the patient seemed uncommonly cold. Of course you know the OR is always fairly cold."

Yeah. Around fifty degrees.

"So we checked and the anesthesiologist said everything was okay. That was toward the end of the surgery, and, in fact, everything had gone well. But it wouldn't be uncommon for the patient to be cold. It wasn't a feeling like we were losing her. Well, I suppose it wasn't my feeling at all; it was what's-her-name, the nurse. Have you talked to her?"

I haven't. However, neither the anesthesiologist nor Stillwell mentioned this incident. Why should they? It was a nothing incident. A fleeting moment. Still, it bothers me that neither of them mentioned it. Now I'll have to ask them again.

As I leave, the nurse on duty gives Dennis and me a rundown on Bootsie's condition. Intact pupillary response, intermittent abnormal extension of extremities, sustained hypotension, but no indication of cardiac arrhythmia. What all this means is that Bootsie's still in a coma but her brain is working.

I head out to the Showcase with my cellular phone. The nurses who assisted during the surgery are harder to track down than the physicians. That's because neither of them was scheduled; they came in as a favor to Stillwell. I catch one of them on her cellular at a soccer match. She hadn't even heard about the bad outcome.

"I just have one question," I say, "then I'll let you go. Do you remember any particular incident during surgery?"

She thinks for about four seconds and says no.

"Okay, do you remember asking, or hearing anyone ask, about the patient's temperature? Specifically, that she seemed cold?"

"That's two questions," she points out. "Yeah, I remember that. I redraped her and noticed her skin seemed kind of chilly. The drape had come away from her shoulder, so I checked to make sure the tube was still there—the breathing tube, on facial surgery we check those very carefully, because of the drape—and her shoulder seemed cold. It's usually their hands that are cold. But Nguyen checked and all the levels were okay. It wasn't a big thing and not unusual."

"Okay. Thanks." I let her go back to her soccer match, and I check over my notes.

A damp wind is blowing and riffling my notebook. The other OR nurse is unreachable. I need to talk to the staff nurses who were on duty when Bootsie was taken to Recovery before their shifts are over. I leave messages on their machines. I get Nguyen on the phone, and he *does* remember checking a couple of times when the operating team asked him about things. At least, I think that's what he says.

I trudge back to my office, where my computer has finally loaded everything it needs to get me into EMRAM. I key in my password and EMRAM boots me out.

Grrr.

I remember that Jette was working on something about the security of medical records. I hope she hasn't been in here horsing around. She thinks she's a real technical person computerwise. It would be just great if she changed the administrative password. I consult some sticky notes on my desk, to make sure I have the right one.

Pooh92 (case-sensitive). I type it in again. This time EMRAM lets me in.

Most people can look only at what's pertinent to their area. A radiology clerk can access the radiology portion of a patient's record; the staff on a nursing unit can access records of patients on their unit; physicians can access only their patients.

My EMRAM privileges pretty much describe my whole job here: I can look at *everything* but can't change anything.

In the old days of paper records, people could go in with some bleach on a Q-tip, wipe out the bad thing on the chart—the wrong dose, the wrong patient, the wrong drug—and put in the right thing. Then, months later, when the medical record became an exhibit in a trial, it looked like things were done correctly. Sometimes forensic document examiners could prove the record had been tampered with and sometimes they couldn't.

But with a paperless medical record, to which lots of people have access, this became something of a problem. So now each entry is date-stamped and somehow linked to the authorized user. I don't even know if the program shows that I looked at a certain record. Probably.

If it shows I got into Bootsie's record, it will be lying. Her EMR appears to consist of one page, and that can't be right. I grind my teeth and go to the next record to see if it's a one-page record also, and my computer hangs up.

Back in the good old days—like, six months ago—I would simply run over to Medical Records and sign out the paper record. However, at this point in the implementation of the EMR at Montmorency, neither the paper version nor the electronic version contains the whole record. It's a transitional thing. The EMR is supposed to either contain everything or have notes saying what's missing and where it can be found. Maybe it did, only the gremlin shut my computer down before I saw it.

I mutter a few curses at the computer screen and try to go back to Bootsie's record. The computer unlocks. There's more of the record here now, but it still isn't the whole thing. It's supposed to contain the patient's history, family history, risk factors, findings from physical examinations, vital signs, test results, known allergies, immunizations, health problems, therapeutic procedures and medications, and responses to therapy. The only things I see on Bootsie's record are vitals and test results from earlier today.

The EMR is also supposed to link in any previous hospitalizations. Some of them also link to the medical record from the patient's primary-care provider (not necessarily the admitting physician, although it can be). That isn't here. A typical record will also include the physician's assessment and plans, along with the patient's advance directives, consent to treat, insurance information and consent to disclose the record to insurance companies, and sometimes even images of, for instance, X rays or EEG scans. All of which I'd like to print out, take home and study. None of which is in here.

Nor is there a winking electronic note saying these records

are not available in electronic form and try the Medical Records Department.

This could mean that someone is putting new test information or something into Bootsie's EMR right now, which is what's making it slow. Either that or my computer is fucked. Or both.

So. If it's not on-line, it had better be in Medical Records. I won't be able to sign the record out because it's "live," as they say, rather than "dead." I picture myself standing in MedRec over a hot copy machine and decide to wait.

Harley sticks his head in my door.

"Find anything out?"

"Not really," I say. "I could use a new computer."

"I meant with regard to fault," Harley says. Once again, as when I asked him what Hawkeye told him about this incident, I get a weird beat.

"It looks good, with regard to fault," I say. "For us, that is. Looks like just one of those things." I don't need to tell Harley that we are at a point at which Dennis's interests and those of the hospital may diverge. Or at which Dennis's interests as a hospital official and his interests as a spouse may diverge. "There are a couple of things, though." I tell him about the phenol, my difficulties with the EMR, and how Stillwell's wife thought Bootsie had diabetes.

"No diabetes, huh," Harley says. "That's funny, because Bootsie and my wife are friends, too, and Bebe specifically remembers a time when Bootsie was taking insulin."

"She just says that," I mutter. "So people won't force her to eat brownies."

"No, I think Bebe saw her shoot herself up with something."

I feel a shock of excitement. "You mean drugs? You mean she could have OD'd?"

Harley rolls his eyes. "I didn't mean drugs. I'll have to ask Bebe."

"Insulin is a drug."

"Not a *drug* drug. You know the difference."

I certainly do.

I back off. "Do you mean Bebe *saw* her shoot up, or did she just say something like 'I have to go get my fix now, g'bye'?"

"I'd have to ask her," Harley says. "I think she saw her. In the ladies' room."

"This could change things," I say, speaking as the hospital's risk manager and not as a friend of a friend of Bootsie's. "If she was known to do drugs, that kind of drugs, that's always the first thing we check for when someone's brought in comatose. Or maybe she was in withdrawal."

"Vicky, I don't think so. I'm sure they checked that. And either it was insulin or it was nothing and I remembered it wrong. Bootsie was not a druggie."

"Is there anything you know that I should know about this?"

He hesitates. "Naw. Not a thing. I don't really know anything. I don't know Bootsie that well."

I hate it when people don't tell me everything. But since Harley's my boss (in the absence of Jette) and he's skittish about this, I glide over it.

"The phenol bothers me," I say. "You know why? Because of the case that was just settled, where the guy was mistakenly injected with phenol instead of something else and he ended up a vegetable."

"Yeah," Harley says. "That one."

We love this one because it happened at somebody else's hospital, making it less likely that such a thing would happen in ours. It was one of those situations where Murphy was in full charge. As I remember it—and being that it was someone else's hospital, I am not privy to the details—a man went in for a routine nerve block to decrease the ghost sensation in an amputated limb. Somehow, no one is sure how (or they aren't telling), he got phenol instead of the nerve block. The injection of phenol threatened to shut down the vascular system in what was left of his arm. So they put him into surgery the next day, in the hopes of saving his arm, or what was left of it. During the surgery, his breathing tube came out, resulting in severe brain damage, and he was left a vegetable. This incident, not surprisingly, generated multiple lawsuits, the last of which was settled a few weeks ago; it made headlines because it went to a jury, which awarded something like four million dollars for his continued care. (Of course, this means it was *not* the last lawsuit. The hospital, or its insurance company, or whoever's supposed to fork over the four mil will surely appeal.)

Harley rubs his face. "So what's the verdict, counselor?"

I pull on my hair. People who know me see this as just Vicky, pulling out her hair again, but I have heard it relieves tension and prevents headaches. "Maybe somebody fucked up or maybe Bootsie's number just came up. It would help if the folks in ICU could say what caused the coma. A diagnosis here could tell us everything."

"I guess they're working on it," Harley says. "And she could wake up at any moment."

Normally, we would lighten this "ain't it awful" discussion by throwing in some irrelevant, disrespectful humor, something in very bad taste. But since it's Bootsie, the wife of the chief of staff of surgery, we don't. The strain is telling on us both.

"Sleeping Beauty," I say. "Has anyone thought to give her a kiss?"

"I think Dennis did."

Hell, that should have done it; a kiss from the magnificent Dr. Devoss would certainly jump-start *me*. In fact, the arm squeeze almost did.

"So," Harley says. "When will your investigation be wrapped up?"

"Jesus, Harley. Give me a break. It only just happened. She could still come out of it."

He gives his head the faintest of negative head shakes.

"What, you know this already? Did Marrote say something to you?"

"Ah, no," Harley says. "You're right. She may come out of it just fine. What do I know?"

What, indeed? I stare at him for a minute. He looks away first.

"Could Dennis somehow get blamed for this?" he asks.

"Would the president get blamed if *Air Force One* crashed?" I counter.

Harley shakes his head.

"Why would you ask that, Harley?"

"I didn't ask that, you did. You said, 'Would the president get blamed—' "

"Har*leee*. I meant about Dennis. Why would anyone blame Dennis?"

"Because she's his wife," Harley says uncomfortably. "A person's wife ought to be safe in a hospital where he's the head surgeon. I mean, if she's not, nobody is."

"Nobody is. Which is why we have them sign that little consent sheet."

"Is it possible something went badly wrong during the surgery and all those people are lying to cover it up?"

"Harley, that is so farfetched. . . . This is a hospital, not the Oval Office!"

This gets a grin. There. We feel a little better now. But not much.

Even though it's almost dark and has turned very chilly, I have another smoke before going back to my office. What the hell, it's Saturday. And damned hard to believe that only this morning I was out Rollerblading.

As I smoke, I mull over the very bad luck that brought this upon the Devosses. I'd also like to know what Harley's not telling me. Harley's not great at giving people direct answers.

A nurse I know, Candace Bothman, joins me. She's a big toothy blonde who's doing what I once did—working double shifts on the weekends, going to law school during the week. She's kind of on my shit list because she told a mutual friend I had discouraged her from going to law school. Not true: She asked me what was involved and I told her the kinds of things she might expect. If she found that discouraging, it wasn't my fault.

She sits down and assures me that Bootsie is a real bitch, as a patient.

"Are you taking care of her? How could someone in a coma be a bitch?"

"Not this time. When she had her face-lift, or maybe it was her tits. She was really a drag."

I take a puff. I don't have to ask why Bootsie was a drag. Candace is ready to vent.

"Doctors' wives, I swear to God. She wanted a pain pill. I looked on her chart, and she wasn't due for another one for ten minutes, so I told her that. She called in my supervisor, complained about my bad attitude, and then she sent letters of complaint to everybody in the universe about why she had to wait ten fucking minutes for relief from her pain. Jesus."

"Um." I'm kind of with Bootsie here. Ten minutes seems a lot longer to someone in pain than it does to the nurse. If a patient is complaining about pain, then take care of the pain.

"It wasn't that I got in trouble or anything. I mean, I followed procedures. But I had to go in, have meetings with my supervisor. It's in my record and all that. You know. It was that she was shitty about it, being a doctor's wife and all. Plus it's extremely unpleasant to have a patient ripping you apart. She wasn't nice about it, not at all."

She drops her butt on the ground and grinds it viciously under her toe. "When I heard she was in a coma, I was glad."

Thanks, Candace, for cluing me in that the nursing staff might have a grudge against Bootsie.

"You know of anybody else on the nursing staff who felt that way?"

Candace's face shuts down. "Is there a problem?" she asks. "Wait, of course there's a problem, she's in a coma. But then I don't have a clue who's taking care of her this go-round."

I follow Candace back inside the hospital, thinking she will make a hell of a better lawyer than she does a nurse.

I make one more foray up to the ICU. Dennis is still there, holding his vigil. I sit down beside him. "No change?"

He shakes his head. "I had a coma case once," he muses.

"A skier. Practically a kid. I think she was twenty or twenty-one. Airlifted down from Vail. I did an open reduction. It took a long time, because she was an athlete and preferred not to have screws, and then she didn't come out of it. She was in a coma for—I don't know—a couple of weeks. Brian would remember. He pulled her out."

So that's why he picked Dr. Brain to be Bootsie's expert.

"But as I recall, she returned to full function," he says.

"Well . . . good." What can you say? This is a good sign? There's good karma here; your patient pulled through, so maybe your wife will, too?

"That was years ago," he adds, as if it matters.

"If you think of anything that might help my investigation, let me know," I say.

He shakes his head, but more as if he's trying to clear it than as a negative gesture. "It's funny, I've been on the other side of this so many times."

As chief of staff of surgery, he's the chairman of the peer review panel that scrutinizes all bad outcomes, which is probably what he means.

I would dearly love to know what goes on behind the closed doors of the peer review committee. I think of it as a very exclusive club, composed of extremely brilliant, well-educated, egomaniacal murderers. Because when you get a bunch of surgeons together, who among them has not made some error or omission, at some point in their career, that resulted in the death of a patient? Not many.

"Wait, there is one thing," Dennis says. "I should have mentioned this before. I did tell Brian. A few weeks ago Bootsie passed out after she had her teeth cleaned, and it was kind of scary."

"She passed out after having her teeth cleaned?" It's *during* the cleaning that I would like to pass out but never do.

"Right, well, it was that full-scale thing, where they go down into your gums, and she was totally out. She was a little woozy when she came home and then she sort of passed out."

"She sort of passed out?" This is a highly developed technique, repeating the last phrase the interviewee said.

"She was sitting on the couch and then she just fell over. For a bad couple of minutes I thought I wasn't going to be able to wake her up, but I finally got her to open her eyes. She was talking gibberish. I started getting her dressed to take her to the emergency room, because I feel that doctors shouldn't treat members of their own family and anyway I'm a bone man, and while we were struggling to get her into her clothes, she said she was fine, just very sleepy. She said I would be the laughingstock of the hospital if I took her to the emergency room when she just needed a nap. We called Trish, her regular doctor, and Trish asked her a few questions and told me it sounded like I should let her sleep it off, so I did."

"An odd reaction. Yeah," I say, pulling my notebook out again. "When was this?"

Dennis gazes over my right shoulder as if the answer is to be found there. Apparently, it *is* found there. "The ides of March," he says. "We went up skiing the next weekend and she was fine. So, three and a half weeks ago."

I'm sure it's beastly of me to think this, but I wonder if Bootsie was having an affair. Big-deal teeth cleaning followed by face-lift. I push it out of my mind. It has no relevance. Instead I note the dates and the reaction, along with my notes about Dennis's case that resulted in coma, because you never know.

Finally, I get out of there.

At my place, Glenn is standing almost where I left him, holding a bottle of wine and a corkscrew, as if he's just been waiting for me to get home to open another bottle of wine.

Shit. Even though I've been working for hours, I'm still on the pager, starting at midnight. Cinderella, I believe I called myself.

I move over to him. Before he can say a word, I give him a kiss.

Here's what happens when I kiss Glenn. There's a moment of anticipation, during which I look at his face and admire it and my heart pumps faster, the better to speed the blood through my system. I gaze into his eyes and watch his pupils dilate. Then

BAD LUCK

our lips connect, softly at first, then more firmly. By now the extra blood is sparkling through my veins, first from the chest up, sending messages to my arms to hug, to my hands to caress. Which actions they duly perform. Then the messages shoot downward, the increased blood flow increasing sensation from my hips down to my toes. Yes, even my toes are ecstatic! It's amazing. I get warmer. My warmth connects with his warmth. Skin seeks skin. Gradually every inch of skin on my body lights up and glows.

I'm a clinical person, and I have studied this. Really. This is what happens.

My mood improves. (My mood becomes irrelevant; moods disappear.) Colors become brighter, noises louder, smells more intense—the wine, the oranges on the counter, Glenn's breath, the faint odor of chlorine in his hair from the hot tub, the perfume I put on earlier. I get lighter, in much the same way you get lighter on an elevator going down fast, and with a similar rush of adrenaline. Some other hormones kick in and contrive to weaken my legs, but this is not unpleasant. At the same time I get lighter, I feel a warm heaviness in my abdomen, kind of like leaning against a hot clothes dryer. Or maybe I just think this because Glenn and I originally connected downstairs in the laundry room. But that's a psychological explanation, not a clinical one.

Glenn's hand touches my face, sending showers of sensation down my cheek, my neck, and directly to my crotch, with a side trip that wakes up my nipples. His other hand touches the other side of my face, sending a similar cascade down the other side, which ends up in the same places, intensifying the sensations. These are the same kind of prickles you get when your feet fall asleep, but perhaps because of the presence of heightened endorphins, nature's pleasure drug, these reactions feel simply wonderful.

All the blood in my body, it seems, and all the nerve endings, too, have concentrated in my pudenda, which responds by seeking his crotch, groping in its way for corresponding engorgement. Which, most gratifyingly, it finds.

So: Electrified lips, throbbing labia, ultrasensitive fingertips, a squirt of some lubricating hormone, tingling nipples, and a willing partner who's forgotten to pour the wine he just opened. At this point, the clinical part of my brain that records all this is pretty much turned off. Nullified. Gone. There's time for just one more rational thought, which turns out not to be so rational: If the phone rings, now or in the next few minutes, I will *kill* the caller. I will send powerful brain waves *through the phone* and the unfortunate person on the other end, receiving them, will *drop dead*.

Fortunately for all of us, the phone doesn't ring.

11

Cooking with Glenn

I went through law school living on instant junk food. I never learned the culinary arts. Cooking bags—some kind of meat, sealed in plastic, that you plunk into a pot of boiling water for a few minutes—were my salvation.

They've gotten a hell of a lot better since then. If Glenn objects to eating this stuff, he can take me out to dinner. He doesn't offer.

"You didn't tell me your boss had turned up missing," he says as we stand in the kitchen, hugging and waiting for the water to boil.

"I didn't?"

"I had to read about it in the paper."

I plop the three cooking bags—*three* bags, see, I told you it was deluxe—into the boiling water. "It's in the paper? Let me see."

While he pages through to find the article, I set my watch for seven minutes. This is too hard; next time I'm getting something microwavable.

" 'Montmorency VP Missing,' " Glenn reads.

I look over his shoulder. There's a fuzzy picture of Jette, probably from her driver's license.

" 'Police have no leads in the disappearance of a high-ranking official of a local hospital,' " he continues. " 'Jette Wakefield, the vice president of Montmorency Medical Center, disappeared from her home late Wednesday night.' "

"*The* vice president?" I mutter. "Give me a break."

"Right," Glenn says. "I thought *you* were the vice president of Montmorency." He keeps reading. " 'Wakefield, thirty-one, was last seen Wednesday evening at her office, where she headed legal affairs. Police have questioned coworkers and neighbors in connection with her disappearance.' "

They got her age wrong! Now, how could they do that? They had her driver's license. Maybe she, too, has been lying about her age.

" 'Wakefield, a graduate of Smith College, was a partner at Morrison & Foerster before joining Montmorency as head counsel. She is blond, six feet two inches tall, and weighs about 145 pounds.' "

"And has a body fat rating of fourteen percent," I carp. "In the interests of full disclosure, they should have said she's one of about twenty-seven vice presidents. And that she was an *associate* at Mo-Fo. For about four months."

"Now, now," Glenn says. "Come on. The poor woman's missing."

"She could be somewhere having a hell of a good time," I grouse, although that doesn't sound like Jette.

"Anyway, it's not about her? What you were doing today?"

"Has nothing to do with her," I snap. The timer on my watch beeps. Good. Maybe food will distract him.

"Hey, is there a problem? You don't have to tell me anything if you don't want to."

"There's nothing to tell. It was just my usual job. Finding

out if something went wrong—I mean, something did go wrong—but mainly finding out if it's our fault."

"Why would you think it was your fault?"

Good question. Mostly because of the suspicious bottle of phenol.

"Well, there were some questions," I say. "And I couldn't get into her medical record. Some people thought she—the person this happened to—was diabetic, only her husband, who's a doctor, says she wasn't. And there's a suspicious bottle of phenol that was logged out of the OR but wasn't logged in. . . ."

Just as there was a good explanation for Bootsie's age discrepancy—she lied—there's probably a good explanation for that bottle of phenol. I just haven't found it yet.

"And phenol wouldn't have been used in that procedure, which was a face-lift. Or rather, cosmetic surgery. Not an actual face-lift . . ."

Glenn's eyes are glazing over in a way I cannot possibly misinterpret as rapt attention, although it might be hunger. While I pour stuff from the bags onto plates, where it looks like something that a real cook could have concocted, Glenn pours us wine and lights a candle.

I sure wish I could have collected that particular bottle of phenol. Don't ask me why. It wouldn't have any incriminating fingerprints, because if the person who introduced it into the OR had malicious intent, that person might have worn gloves. Even if the person *hadn't* had malicious intent, the person had probably worn gloves. There are latex and nonlatex gloves in dispensers all over the hospital.

We sit down to our home-heated meal.

"I've got the kids next weekend," Glenn says. "You know I'd love for you to meet them."

Oh. This scares me.

"Um . . . if things calm down a little."

"No. Come on, Vicky, they have to let you take a weekend off every once in a while."

"That's true."

"We could all go up to Keystone."

"There's still snow up there!"

"Right, that's the point. Snow," he says. "The boys love to ski. Stephanie, well, she's a little young for that."

Stephanie is three.

"I don't ski. Remember?"

"Right. You Rollerblade. You ride horses. Okay, how's this: We go to one of those dude ranch places. I'll bet they have openings this time of year."

"Oh . . . okay." What scares me about this is that I'm afraid I will fall in love with his kids and they will hate me. The boys are eight and eleven. Prime ages for hating their father's new lady.

I pour myself a second glass of wine.

"How come you always do things with your kids?" I say. "Um, that didn't come out right. I mean, why don't you just bring them up here and let them hang around?"

"In this neighborhood?"

"There's nothing wrong with this neighborhood. I've lived here for years."

"The kids though . . . no yard. They have a lot of excess energy. They'd bounce off the walls. Or they'd go out and join a gang."

I choke on my wine. "We could take them to Melinda's house. She wouldn't mind." Is this true? Melinda has nice things, but they are not irreplaceable. Still, she's just a block away from Washington Park.

I'd rather just hang around and do something with his kids in Denver. We could take them Rollerblading and introduce them to my friend Maurice, the homeless guy, who lives under the bridge at Downing and Speer. He doesn't consider himself homeless. He tells people he lives at the Denver Country Club and his cats use their sand traps as litter boxes. I'm sure Glenn would love introducing his nice suburban children to a colorful city dude like Maurice.

"Skiing's good, because you drop them off at the ski school and you don't have to pick them up for three hours. We wouldn't have to ski. We could go sit in the hot tub or something."

"Or something" has a certain appeal. "All right," I say.

"Good," he says. "I know they'll love you."

Oddly enough, I'm afraid of that, too. Afraid they'll hate me and afraid they'll love me. I know, it doesn't make sense.

Probably that's why I haven't met his kids yet.

I should mention that this neighborhood is *improving*. When I first moved here, the police had a special number for residents to call when they suspected gang or drug activity and it was always busy. Now it's disconnected.

"Oh, I forgot to tell you," Glenn says. "The cops called you again while you were at the hospital. I meant to tell you as soon as you got in."

Can't imagine why he forgot. "They still didn't say what they wanted?"

"Same thing they wanted before. You to call them, at your convenience. They were very polite."

How nice of them.

Maybe it will be convenient tomorrow.

12

The Club in My Future

Glenn invites me to come along and watch him play golf. What an idea.

"It may be fun when you're playing, but it's a sorry-assed excuse for a sport," I tell him. "You're too young to be playing golf."

"Hey, I've been playing since I was nine. It's good exercise. You keep saying you need exercise."

"Watching golf is not exercise. I'm not even sure about playing it." My mother has been known to sing its virtues. Ditto gardening. I suppose they are better exercise than playing bridge, which she also does. The trim figure she maintains despite these nonactivities is genetic. Thank goodness.

"There are two kinds of people in the world," Glenn says. Before he can go on to say what they are, I tell him my mother's favorite Saturday-morning saying. " 'Oh, Vicky, look what I found behind my golf clubs in the closet! The *vacuum cleaner*! Why don't you use it while I use the clubs?' " Now does he see why I have bad associations with golf?

"Anyway, I have to call and confess to the cops," I say. "If they arrest me, see that I get a good lawyer."

"Your pager would have been a problem anyway," he says. "I don't think they allow them on the course."

"Good for them." Nice of him to think of the pager. I'd forgotten about the damn thing. Hey, it didn't go off in the middle of the night!

"You could think of it as a nice brisk walk in beautiful surroundings. But since you're playing golf, you have a purpose."

It's Sunday. I don't need a purpose. I think I might go back to bed. This *has* to be the club in my future Arinda mentioned. The Golf Widows Club, because I am *not* learning that dumb game.

Glenn has a Golf Outfit: the old-fashioned knicker thingies, argyle knee socks, a baggy sweater. Thankfully, he isn't wearing it. Instead he's dressed in a somewhat frayed, poisonous green shirt, which he was wearing when he got his last hole in one. My understanding is that it was a fairly old shirt even then.

Once he leaves, I decide to let the cops call me. Better they should get my voice mail than I should get theirs.

I dig into the mammoth Sunday paper, read the funnies, read the lifestyle section, scan the front section for any bad news. Luckily enough, there is none, at least none that relates directly to Montmorency. The one that gets me is the story about thirty-seven-year-old Lindy Fogg, who collapsed at mile 24 of the Boston marathon. She insisted she'd just hit the wall and she needed to run through it. However, despite her protests, she was taken to the nearest hospital, where she suffered a massive heart attack and died.

The story goes on to say that this was the fourteenth marathon for Dr. Fogg, a local OB-GYN. I guess this does relate peripherally to Montmorency: she had privileges there. She is survived by her husband and two children, a seven-year-old and a two-year-old.

This story makes me sizzle with that strange displaced sorrow you get for people you didn't know. In my empathy I include the bereaved spouse, the motherless children, and the staff at the hospital in Boston, who now have to do some kind of investigation about why they allowed a young woman in great physical shape to have a heart attack at their facility.

This leads me on a quick trip down memory lane. I'm probably empathetic because my first nursing job was at Boston City Hospital. It was one of those experiences, like a bad vacation, that you think you're just barely going to live through (if you do live through it), but ever afterward you're glad you had it. There was a head nurse who must have been the model for Nurse Ratched in *One Flew Over the Cuckoo's Nest*. There was a nasty old cardiologist who thought it was fun to call the nurses by insulting names. ("Nurse Fucky? Oh, sorry, it's Nurse Lucky. My mistake.") There was a lascivious OB-GYN, whose desk, in his garden-level office, was situated so that he could look up the skirts of women walking by on the sidewalk outside. You'd think he'd get enough of that in his profession. There was a chief resident with a habit of fondling women's breasts under the pretext of checking out their hospital IDs.

And there was the usual charity-hospital horror show of patients, people who, because they had no health insurance and no money, let things go until they were convinced they were about to die, and in many cases, they *were* about to die. Of course, a lot of this was just getting used to the horrible things you run into in a hospital, all the weird diseases, bizarre mishaps, and messy bodily functions, and toughening up to the reality of what you were doing. It was my boot camp, my apprenticeship, my initiation—and I'd probably feel the same way whether it happened in a charity hospital or at the Mayo Clinic.

Finally, I concentrate on what needs to be done about the Bootsie incident. I call the ICU to see if Sleeping Beauty is still sleeping.

The ICU nurse delivers what she says is bad news: an EEG performed at 6 A.M. recorded background activity of 4 Hz, interspersed with frequent bursts of 1 to 3 Hz activity, and her cerebral oxygen uptake was 1.1 cc per 100 gm. per minute, which means her brain is not getting enough oxygen.

"So what's normal?"

"A normal EEG would be 7 Hz activity. A normal cerebral oxygen uptake would be 3.3 cc per 100 gm. per minute," the nurse tells me. "And still no one has determined what the initial insult to her system was."

I need to get Bootsie's medical record together and send it for review to two or three members of my panel of experts. I don't think my experts will find any wrongdoing on the part of the medical or hospital staff. If the medical staff suspected wrongdoing by the hospital staff, or vice versa, they would have let me know about it.

The easiest way to get the record is to have EMRAM print it. I shower, futz around with my bangs, which are hanging down into my eyes, and put on leggings and a tunic, since nobody seems to have washed my jeans. I walk to the hospital for a change, just to see what it's like.

It probably beats watching golf.

The ICU is quiet. Dennis spent the night at Bootsie's side. He's wearing the same clothes he had on yesterday along with the look of a man who hasn't slept. Puffy eyes and a version of the thousand-yard stare, as if he is in some sort of stupor himself. When I touch his shoulder, he runs his hands through his thick, curly hair, shaking loose a good quantity of dandruff.

"No change?" I ask. Meaning since this morning's EEG.

He shakes his head.

I pat him on the shoulder, which he seems to appreciate. He doesn't ask me about my report.

I wander around the hospital until I find Hawkeye in the doctors' lounge, eating celery sticks of all things.

"Turning into a bunny?" I ask. Usually you see Hawkeye eating things like greasy double cheeseburgers with bacon, a diet that is reflected in his girth.

"I'm hitting forty-five next week," Hawkeye says. "Got to start worrying about the old ticker."

For some reason this strikes me as hilarious. Next thing you know, you'll see Hawkeye on an exercise bike in the hospital gym. I manage to contain my mirth and grab a carrot stick.

My own diet is not that great either, I'll admit it. But at least my excesses haven't yet led me into danger. And while we're at it, when would *I* ever see Hawkeye in the gym? I was there once, on my orientation tour.

"You see that thing in the paper about—"

"About Lindy? I sure did." He shakes his head. "You know, she almost made the Olympic team, only she thought it was a better idea to go to medical school. A person like that, just keeling over."

I'll bet that was what prompted the celery stick—not the impending birthday.

"If you've got some time, I'd like to talk about Bootsie's case," I say.

"So that's why you're in here on a Sunday. I should have known." I give him a certain amount of credit for knowing it's Sunday. Hawkeye is here all the time, day and night, weekends and holidays. It's rumored that he does have an apartment somewhere, but why would he?

"Yeah. Here's who I'm thinking of sending her record to," I say, and throw out the names.

Hawkeye nods. "Those sound good."

"Good. Also, I had trouble pulling up Bootsie's medical record yesterday."

"Try my login," Hawkeye says. "The computer geniuses

have been messing around again. *Improving* stuff." He pulls a card out of his pocket and scribbles his password, MD1—how original—and his EMRAM access code, HawkI.

"Oh-kayee." I'm torn between telling him he shouldn't give out his passwords to just anybody and feeling pleased that I am not just anybody. But when I go back to my office, his codes don't work any better than mine did.

I call Medical Records. "I need a complete copy of Bootsie Devoss's medical record," I tell the clerk. I need three or four complete copies, but the hard part is fixing up the original record. After that, I can take it to Kinko's.

The clerk emits a loud sigh and asks when I need it. This afternoon? Sure (another loud sigh), no problem.

I could emit a loud sigh of my own. Using EMRAM, you tell the computer that you want patient identifiers purged, and it prints the record with patient identifiers purged. On the paper record, this stuff will have to be manually blanked out. On most of the pages it's only at the top of the page, but it is on *every* page. I use white Post-it tape.

I love the idea of spending Sunday afternoon sticking white tape over Bootsie's name, which will be pointless because every doctor in Denver will recognize this case but which I need to do because that's the procedure.

I ask the records clerk who I should talk to in Information Systems about the EMR and get two names: Barney and Regina. No last names.

Barney's not in, but Regina answers the phone cheerily.

"Hi, this is Vicky, the risk manager, and I'm having trouble accessing somebody's medical record. And yes, I have authorization."

Regina asks for various things, like my access code and Bootsie's patient number, and says she'll get back to me.

Then, ever hopeful, I log back into EMRAM and try Bootsie's record again. I still don't see the history, but there are some more tests—this morning's EEG—and some notes. This seems like progress.

I start calling my experts, to alert them and to convey the basic information—I have this case to review involving a patient who is still in a coma—and get their opinions. But these doctors won't offer any guesses as to what's happened, even though they know that's what I want.

"Surgery is a risk you take," one of them says. "I feel like I'm going to die whenever anybody puts me under. I get my affairs in order. I'm not kidding."

I believe him. I do that whenever I get on a plane.

"Bootsie had to know the risks," he says. "God, I feel sorry for Dennis."

Whoa, did I mention Bootsie? I think not. I may have to reconsider spending the afternoon with white Post-it tape.

I *know* these people have their own ideas on what occurred just before, or just during, or just after Bootsie's surgery, but they aren't telling me. Here's what I mean:

"If she was diabetic and that information didn't get into her chart, could that have been a contributing factor in her coma?"

"It's certainly possible."

"How about if she had eaten something, unbeknownst to anyone, in the six hours before her surgery?"

"Ah, well, there's no indication that she aspirated during the surgery, is there? But sure, it's something to look at."

"Could the low temperature of the operating room have contributed?"

"That hasn't been my experience, but I wouldn't necessarily rule it out."

"If a man had a sex change, could he then get pregnant and deliver healthy twins?"

"Vicky, don't be silly!"

Okay. Well, they will *almost* never give you a straight answer.

In Bootsie's case, everybody seems to be leaning toward the just-bad-luck theory, and so would I, except for the mystery of the phenol. There is something about this phenol that just gets me, I don't know why.

I head to the Medical Records office to see if they've finished copying Bootsie's record. On the sign-out sheet I see that I'm getting a whole eight pages.

"Hey, what is this, eight pages? She should have accumulated eight pages this morning!"

The records clerk taps her finger on the top sheet. "Explained in here," she says, and then, apparently doubting my ability to read it, she tells me. "The whole record was sent directly to Information Systems for scanning. After they're scanned, they don't come back here right away. They go into a vault."

"Damn it," I say, "nobody told me they'd changed the procedure." As the risk manager I should have known about this.

The records clerk shrugs. "It's this electronic system," she says. "Although it seems like a bad idea to me. God help us when the system goes down. We took good care of these things."

Jette's office clutter indicated a current interest in medical records. It would be so like her to change the procedure, particularly to something that didn't work. And then not to tell me.

All I've got in the paper record are the tests performed since 6 P.M. yesterday and a further note that this record will be moved to IS for scanning within twenty-four hours.

I call IS back, get Regina again, and ask her what the hell is going on with EMRAM. She's either modest or dodging responsibility; she tells me that the person who really knows this stuff is Barney, her boss, who didn't pull Sunday duty. Barney deals with SATAN.

Then she has to explain—and fast!—that SATAN stands for System Administrator Tool for Analyzing Networks. It's something IS installed, temporarily, to check for weaknesses in our electronic security.

Whew. For a minute there I was wondering about the gremlin in my computer.

SATAN's the name on one of Jette's files, which takes some of the intrigue out of those files—but not all of the intrigue.

"So what did SATAN do with Bootsie's EMR?" I ask.

"Funny," Regina says. "There should be more of it, that's

all. I know that record was scanned in. Not to worry. I'll get the paper record out of the vault."

"Whose brilliant idea was it to put them in the vault instead of back to MedRecs?"

"I think it was something Barney cooked up, in case we crashed the system during testing, so we'd have them here to rescan. It's just temporary."

"Until you get the kinks out?" Sounds to me like they *had* crashed the system. Or at least part of it.

"Are you kidding? These are computers. By the time we get all the kinks out, there will be a whole new software system."

"Oh."

"When do you need that record?"

"Two hours ago."

"Come on over," Regina says.

IS is probably half a block away—not that far in distance, but farther when you have to wind through corridors. As soon as I get there, Regina dumps Bootsie's official medical record in front of me. A great big fat stack of paper, just what I was looking for. I have to sign for it again, in order to lug it back to Admin to copy it.

I consider taking it back over to MedRec and letting someone there copy it. MedRec has a superfast machine for just that purpose. But they always charge the copying to somebody—like my budget, for instance. If I take it to Admin I can save my budget for better things.

As I'm (uselessly) sticking white tape over Bootsie's name and social security number, I see, as Dennis said, a "no" in response to whether she'd ever had diabetes. In response to a question on whether she'd ever had a bad reaction to a drug, she said she hadn't. But there is a note in someone else's handwriting on the page, "During teeth cleaning?" No date. Probably she filled this out before she fainted after having her teeth cleaned, but somebody obviously knew about it.

A couple of pages later, on a sheet asking the patient to list all drugs ever ingested, Bootsie has listed a veritable pharmacopoeia: Valium, Librium, marijuana, cocaine, heroin(!),

Xanax, Fiorinal, Halcion, quaaludes, Fen-Phen, and mescaline. If I didn't know her I would read this as: former hippie marries doctor and becomes hypochondriac. Since I *do* know her, and she's somewhat hyper, I wonder how she managed to miss crystal methedrine; she seems like that kind of person. And diet pills. Did she forget those? If she would mention heroin, why wouldn't she mention that?

All these drugs and she never had even *one* bad reaction? Give me a break.

I don't *know* this about Bootsie. I'm extrapolating based on the fact that she's something of a live wire and from my own drug experience, sadly far in the past. Which is, I'm sure, the case with Bootsie—except for the Fen-Phen. I can't believe Dennis let her take that. But here it is, in her own hand.

I drop the redacted record off at the Kinko's across the street, tell them to call me when it's done, and sit at the Showcase for a few minutes making notes about things to ask.

I call Regina back to ask if there's a durable medical power of attorney in the record, and she cheerfully checks for me and says that, in fact, there is, with Dennis as Bootsie's attorney-in-fact. She also has some more interesting information. EMRAM has an audit log that can check when the record was accessed and by whom, and for some reason this audit trail is missing on Bootsie's EMR.

Not only that but the incremental time-stamped automatic backup recorded that Bootsie's EMR was 465,664 kilobytes last Tuesday, the same number on Wednesday, but only 16,565 on Thursday. It was constant on Thursday and increased slightly on Friday and quite a bit yesterday.

"Of course, we're scanning it in again, so it's going to increase again," Regina says. "But this is weird. Sometimes there's a blip, but EMRAM is supposed to note those. I have no explanation for why the audit trail is missing. I've never seen this before. It must be something to do with SATAN."

"What *is* this program?" I ask, almost rhetorically. "How bad was the original problem, anyway? Jette never tells me anything."

"Any word on Jette?" Regina asks delicately, ducking my question.

"Not as far as I know," I say.

Boy. Harley told me not to try to find her, and I didn't. She's been the last thing on my mind. It's almost a shock to realize that she's still missing. Along with sizable portions of Bootsie's EMR and the audit trail.

I pick up the copies at Kinko's and dump them on my desk. Then I go back up to ICU, where Dennis is still sitting around. He's more animated than last time, possibly because he's now speaking with Bootsie's neurosurgeon, Dr. Brain Marrote.

But they are not talking about Sleeping Beauty. Instead they are rehashing Dennis's old case, the skier. In fact, they are arguing about it, Dennis insisting that the young woman returned to full function and Dr. Brain saying nope, she had to drop out of college because she couldn't concentrate.

"But that could have been because of the closed-head injury sustained in the skiing accident, not the coma," Dennis says.

"I take the position that the closed-head injury contributed to the coma," Dr. Brain says. "Most people recover completely from closed-head injuries, or at least about eighty-five percent do. Of course, a person in a coma at that age, you'd expect her to recover, too."

Well, gee, I hate to break in on this interesting postmortem, but I was wondering if I could get a medical record release signed by Bootsie's designated representative, so I can see even more of her fascinating personal history.

Dennis whips out an expensive pen and scrawls what looks like a butterfly on the bottom of the page. Hell, I could have done that myself.

Dr. Brain walks out with me and tells me Dennis wants him to do some kind of surgery. "These orthopods think surgery can fix anything," he says. "Now, I could go in there and I'd probably know more about the source of the insult. But it wouldn't help her recovery. And putting her under anesthesia again, until we know what caused the problem, is not a great idea."

I walk home, arriving at the same time Glenn does, but in a somewhat worse mood. Not that his mood is great. I gather the golf did not go well. I don't know why people get so upset over a silly game.

13

Monday the Thirteenth

I always try to wear a serious suit on Mondays, because you never know what can happen, even on a good Monday, if there is such a thing. Today probably won't be. For one, as we say in the office, "Friday the thirteenth falls on a Monday this week."

The pale aqua Carolina Herrera seems serious enough. It's a suit I've hardly ever worn. Mainly because I don't have the right shoes to go with it, but I fudge that, stepping straight into last year's Maude Frizon chunky-heeled oxfords. The shoes give me a big lift, and I don't mean psychologically. It looks like I'll need it.

By the time I get to work, "Top Doc's Wife in Coma at Montmorency" has screamed at me from various newspaper vending machines, when I wasn't even looking, in case I might have forgotten what was going on at the hospital.

I sit down with Harley and Hawkeye to tell them how my investigation is going. Turns out we're not calling it the Bootsie thing. Both Harley and Hawkeye ask me how the Sleeping Beauty investigation is coming.

"I don't think we're going to find any liability here," I say. "I've only just gotten the medical record out to my experts." This is a little white lie; the copies of the medical record are stacked on my desk, where I'm hoping Harley won't see them. I'll messenger them over as soon as I get out of this meeting.

I turn to Harley. "Did you check with your wife about whether she saw Bootsie shooting up something?"

Harley's ears redden. They're the kind of ears that are quite noticeable anyway, particularly the day after he gets his hair cut. "I forgot," he says. "I'll ask her tonight."

"Say what?" Hawkeye says.

"Nothing, really," Harley says. "Anything else?"

"Somebody seems to have horsed around with Bootsie's medical record. That is, I couldn't pull it up, so I went over to IS and got the paper record, so everything's complete now. But if her physicians were relying on the EMR, there might have been things missing."

"They would know that, Vicky," Hawkeye reminds me gently. "You aren't the only person who knows what's supposed to be in a medical record. She didn't go into a coma because her EMR was missing."

Good point. Still, it bothers me. And it's not the only thing that bothers me. "Okay, then there's that bottle of phenol. Nobody will admit to having ordered it or even seen it."

"So what?" Hawkeye says. "You checked the narrative, right, and nobody mentioned it? It was unopened?"

"I don't know that it was unopened," I say. "I didn't see the bottle, and now it's gone."

"So how do you know it was even there?" Harley asks.

"The nurse peeled the label off and stuck it right on the patient's charge log, that's how I know it was there. Both Stillwell and Cowan deny they ordered it and say there was no reason to order it—"

"But there's no reason to think it was used," Hawkeye says. "Probably just a mistake."

"*Just* a mistake," I say. "The same exact mistake that cost another hospital four million dollars, when phenol was mistakenly placed in the operating room and then mistakenly used. Turned a guy into a vegetable."

"No, he was gorked during surgery to repair the damage done by the phenol," Hawkeye says. "A cautionary tale for all of us, though. You're right."

"Vicky, will you drop it with the stupid phenol?" Harley says. "Okay. We don't know how it got there, but it was sealed, unopened, not used. So drop it!"

So. I drop it.

With the elimination of these two irregularities, I have no basis of substandard care on the part of hospital personnel or medical staff. Pending review of the file by expert physicians. This makes everybody happy.

Back in my office, I dispatch the copies of the medical record to my experts. It may not have been a factor, but I'd still like to know how Bootsie's medical record disappeared. I call Regina, who tells me that Barney is in today and I should probably talk to him, but right now he's on the phone. I head for the cabinet next to Anita's desk, to replenish my supply of notebooks, and find Anita haranguing Nolan about using the word Xerox as a verb.

"I believe in the importance of words," Nolan says. "But give me a break. I just asked if anyone had Xeroxed the article in the paper about Sleeping Beauty."

Anita shoots me a look. "You're a lawyer," she says. "Is this or is this not copyright infringement?"

"It's not copyright infringement," I say. "*Trademark* infringement maybe. I don't think Xerox is going to come in and slap Nolan in handcuffs." It's possible that the reason she gets so upset about this is that her husband's a Minolta salesman. But I think it's just Anita's control-freak nature. It's too bad; it's people like her who have deprived the world of a verb beginning with *X*, which apparently the English language needed desperately.

The weird thing is, our copier *is* a Xerox.

As long as Nolan's being chewed out, I figure I'll add my two cents worth. "Do not, repeat, *do not* let the press get ahold of the fact that we're calling Bootsie Sleeping Beauty. Got it?"

"Aw, they wouldn't print that."

"The hell they wouldn't. Try this on: 'Hospital officials have no comment on what is being known, unofficially, as the Sleeping Beauty incident.' Take that phrase and plug in the headline of your choice."

"I'm the media expert here," Nolan whines.

When I walk past Jette's office, I do a double take. Someone is sitting at her computer.

"Oh," Anita says, "I forgot to mention, this is my son, Tristan." She twists her mouth slightly. "I cleared this with Harley last week. It's his spring break."

I nod and try to head back to my office. I don't make it.

"I hope it's okay that he's in Jette's office," she says.

"Fine with me," I say.

"He's too old for the spring-break day-care programs," she says.

Hey, no problem.

"He'll be here all week," she adds. "Maybe he could stuff envelopes or something."

I nod. What envelopes?

"His older brother got in a lot of trouble one spring break when I was working," she says. "That's why I felt I had to bring him in. Boys! You just can't trust them."

"Or men either," I mutter.

"Tristan!" she calls. "Come here. This is Vicky Lucci, the risk manager."

Tristan hasn't started his growth spurt yet, so he's still at my eye level. He's a cute kid, with unruly hair and a slight hint of mischief in his gray eyes.

"Pleased to meet you," he says formally, holding out his hand. He has a nice firm handshake, although the hand feels a little sweaty.

"He's not to bother anyone here. It's only for a week." Anita looks hard at Tristan when she says this. She might as well be saying, "Tristan, go to your room!"

He heads back to the computer.

"His brother is twenty-one now, and he turned out okay, but it's been hard," Anita says. "With Bill being on the road so much, I'm practically a single parent, and I live so far away, after all."

In the suburbs. So who asked her to come work downtown? There are places to work in the suburbs.

Behind Anita, Vanessa feigns unconsciousness. She's probably heard this sad tale a lot more than I have and she's sick of it.

"I guess I let that situation get out of hand," Anita says. "It's not going to happen again. I couldn't go through it."

(Vanessa shakes her head as if to indicate that *she's* not going through it again, either.)

"You just can't trust a kid that age alone," Anita says.

(Vanessa purses her lips: naughty, naughty.)

Frankly, I can't fathom Anita ever letting a situation get out of hand. Jared, the older son, must have quite a lot of willpower to have ended up in trouble—whatever it was—under his mother's watchful eye.

I try to break up her monologue by asking Tristan questions. Not that I have a clue as to what kind of questions would engage a thirteen-year-old. Doesn't matter anyway; as soon as I ask, Anita jumps in.

"So you're in middle school?"

"Eighth grade," Anita says.

"Yeah? What are you taking?"

"He's doing algebra II already . . ."

"Harley said it was okay to use her computer," he says. "I asked him."

"You like computers?"

"Tristan, *we* have work to do."

Dumb question. A thirteen-year-old, of course he likes computers.

I tell him to help himself to the pop in the refrigerator. I tell him he can microwave some popcorn if he wants. We also have things like V8 and Cup-A-Soup, not that he'd be interested in that.

"Is it hard to make the popcorn?" he asks.

"I'll show you when I get a minute," Anita says.

"I'll show him." I lead the way back to the kitchen, with Tristan behind me and Anita behind him. We'd be a parade except Anita hears her phone ring and, ever the watchdog, steps back to answer it.

"How's life?" It's a trite question and I don't expect him to answer it, but he does.

"Many ancient civilizations had a tough ritual, a hazing process, through which adolescent males had to pass in order to achieve adult status within the tribe," he says, pushing his glasses up his nose. "In order to attain manhood, they had to battle pain, the elements, fatigue, and possibly even ridicule. In America, we get middle school."

He's got it down perfectly—the language, the delivery. It takes me by surprise and I snort. He snorts back. He doesn't seem like a particularly troubled kid.

"I'll bet you're pretty good with the computer," I say.

"Yeah," he says. "That's a pretty cool one in Jette's office. I mean for an office."

I show him how to run the microwave—not that he couldn't have figured it out in about twenty seconds. I walk him back to Jette's office. The popcorn bags we have are huge, when popped. He doesn't offer me any.

Anita pokes her head in. "Stay out of trouble, Tristan."

Out of her view but in mine, he grimaces. "Right, Mom."

"He can't mess anything up in here?" Anita says. "Jette's files and stuff? I know she had a bunch of confidential stuff."

"All locked up," I say. "Don't worry. He's just going to play Solitaire or those other ones . . ."

"Pinball," Tristan says helpfully. "Or JezzBall. And I brought some on a disk, only she doesn't have a joystick or a sound card."

Anita pulls back to pick up her phone again.

I lower my voice. "I have a list of some files that Jette's put a password on. Nobody has her password, and we need to get into them."

He instantly grasps my implicit plea.

"Mmm," he says, also lowering his voice. "Well, I *probably* couldn't get into those anyway, so not much chance I'll screw them up."

"Do you do any hacking? I mean, we can't figure out how to get these files open."

Oh, my. Contributing to the delinquency of a minor.

His face lights up. Then he blushes.

"Um . . . probably not," he says. "I'm not much of a hacker."

"No problem," I say. "If you do, if you have time and you think you could do it. I have no idea what's in those files, but it might be something I need. Of course, you could never tell anybody what was in them. Or even that you got into them." I write down the names on a sticky note: SATAN.DOC, TOGO.GAY, DEVO.MEM, TIME.SHT.

"Mmm." He pulls something up on the screen. I leave him to it, shutting the door on my way out.

The ethics of this troubles me only slightly. I don't think these are personal files. What worries me is, will he tell his mother I told him to do it? Somehow, I think not.

I finally make it back to my office. But, apparently, not for long. I have a message from Father Gifford, saying that he needs to talk to me fairly urgently. I call him back and ask him what's so urgent.

"I'd rather not get into it on the phone." I remember this about Gifford; he always thinks the phones are tapped or something.

"I'll be right over," I promise. I'm wrong about that.

The phone rings again. It's the Capitol Hill Animal Clinic. If I'd known that, I wouldn't have answered. Assuming they're after some kind of donation, I try to brush them off and then I get what they're calling about. The goddamned black cat that I hit. They are giving me a report. The cat spent a nice easy weekend, and, in fact, is ready to go home.

"Fine with me. I'm not her owner," I say. And I don't want a report. This is what I get for promiscuously handing out my business cards.

The girl on the phone mumbles, fumbles. Does she have the right person?

"I brought her in. But . . . it's a long story. I'm not involved. Her owner doesn't have a phone."

As soon as I get that cleared up—mainly clarifying the fact that I left a note on its owner's door stating quite clearly where I'd left the cat—Anita buzzes me.

This is peculiar, as her desk is virtually outside my office. You can judge your rank by how close you are to the secretarial corral and my rank is pretty low. Anita tells me someone is here to see me. A cop. Yikes.

I put on my talking-to-cops face, or try to. This face is just like theirs, a face that reveals nothing. In my case, I've been told it's a lost cause, but I try it anyway. I escort the guy in uniform into my office.

It occurs to me to be very serious. I'm thinking this is about Jette. I even mention that. He knows nothing about Jette. Or at least that's what he says.

No, he's here to inquire what I was doing, parked at a certain address on Logan Street, on more than one occasion and in at least two different vehicles, none of which are registered to me.

"My car's in the shop," I say. "It caught fire. Oh, right. I was supposed to call you guys back."

"Yeah. The rental company gave us your phone number. So did someone else, a Harley Sloane."

"Also Glenn Rossmore," I say. "I mean, you called him, too. I drove his car over there, too."

He smiles at me. "So what were you doing there?"

God. "I hit this girl's cat," I say. "I'm sorry and all. I did everything I could, but the cat just ran in front of me. And then she didn't have a car, the girl, I mean, so I took it, the cat, to the vet, the all-night vet—that was the night I hit it—and then I went over to get her, the girl, the next morning to go pick the cat up, only she didn't answer the door. So then I went back . . ." I rack my brain. Was it only three times? It seemed like I was swinging by there at every opportunity. Because I was bewitched. "Yeah, I went back one other time. Left her a note. And the vet just called me. The cat's fine."

"Yeah. We found the note."

On another one of my stupid business cards, which is how they knew where to find me.

"You took the cat where?"

I tell him, adding helpfully that if he's going over to talk to Arinda, then could he please convey to her that the cat is ready to go home.

"I don't think so. This girl—you call her Arinda? You only met her the once?"

"Right." I'm getting a bad feeling.

"You never saw her again?"

"Uh, no. I went up to her place and knocked, but nobody answered."

He stares at me for a minute. "So you never went inside."

Now, this is the way to conduct an interrogation. If I were a doctor, I'd say it's possible I went inside. I couldn't rule it out. He's got me nervous, and it's more than the feeling I'm going to be booked on cat slaughter. Has the cat decided to press charges?

"I went inside that night, the night I hit the cat. Just for a minute. To get the cat carrier."

"Anybody else there?" he asks, too casually.

"Oh, my God," I say. "He did something to her, didn't he, that guy. She seemed almost afraid of him, afraid to go back in. Oh, my God. I should have left the cat in the street and taken *her* someplace."

In retrospect, this all makes perfect sense. I knew Catgirl didn't want to go back in there. "She had to, she made me go inside to tell him where she was going," I say. "What, I mean, what happened?"

"Do you think you could identify this guy from a photo?" The cops never tell you *anything*.

"Um, yeah, sure. I mean I think so." I try to get a mental image of the guy. All I can think of is Sean Penn in *Dead Man Walking*, and the guy didn't look like him at all. Big. Kind of blond. Seemed dumb. "Well, I only saw him that one time."

"Maybe you could give a statement," he suggests.

"I can't imagine what I could say in a statement that would be helpful," I say. "There was another woman around there, helping us look for the cat after I hit it. She seemed to know Arinda. She had curlers in her hair."

Good show, Vicky. She had curlers in her hair last Thursday. What are the odds they're still in her hair?

"Her name wasn't Arinda," he says. "Her name was Phyllis Atteboro."

Was. I thought of her as Catgirl. Phyllis doesn't work at all.

I arrange to go to the station sometime today, *at my convenience,* to speak to the lead investigator. Never mind that this is a day when it's never going to be convenient. I promise him I will get there. And then he reassures me that it's no crime to hit a cat, and not even a crime, in this municipality, to hit a cat and then drive off. Which, of course, is what I should have done.

After he leaves, I take a deep breath and head down to Gifford's abode. He's sitting behind his desk, dwarfing it, but he leaps to his feet to press the flesh with me and then doesn't sit down.

"Sorry to make you come all this way," he says.

It's two flights.

"It's okay," I say. I'm distracted, thinking of Catgirl. Was there anything I could have done?

"The problem is, I got this information last week and called Jette with it, but she never got back to me, and it's the kind of thing that might need some follow-up. I've been kicking myself that I didn't call you last week."

"Okay. I'm ready."

Gifford shakes his head and paces around his desk. "It's hard to figure. You know I run kind of a day camp for these kids in the neighborhood, keep them out of gangs, and it's pretty successful. We meet at the gym most afternoons."

"Right." In the three years I've been here, Montmorency has gobbled up various bits and pieces of the neighborhood including an abandoned grade school. We demolished most of the school for a parking lot; however, the gym survived.

"So these kids trust me, and they give me information in confidence. Only in this case I think somebody ought to know what went down."

I can't stand it. "What went down?" I ask.

"Some guy came to them, to a bunch of them in the park, asked them to start a riot."

"Now, there's a new one." Then I remember it's not, exactly. "So did they?"

"Not these guys."

The incident that prompted Gifford to intensify his community outreach, and prompted Montmorency to back him up, happened just after I started here. An employee drove out of our parking garage and into a turf war, took a bullet in the shoulder. Of course we fixed her up gratis, but then she quit, not surprisingly.

"So what happened with the riot, and why didn't I hear about it?"

"You didn't hear about it because it didn't happen. But it troubled me. So today the boys came by—they're on spring break—and I talked to them a little more. I got to thinking we oughta try to find this guy."

"Good idea. Did they have a description?"

Gifford ignores my question. "These guys are very reliable. I thought it was possible they were just making it up, you know, wanting to sound big and like they knew something. But I think it happened just like they said."

"A description?"

"Yeah, I'm getting there. They've got one, but . . . You have to remember, they're just kids. And I figure if I push them on this, they'll just book. So I've been taking it pretty easy."

Oh, boy, something *else* to tell the cops. Maybe. Our policy is to call them as soon as we know a crime has been committed. In this case a crime was planned but not committed.

"I forget—when did they come to you?"

Gifford shuts his eyes. "Thursday. Yeah. I talked to them in the afternoon, then I called Jette to let her know I had a potential situation."

"Why'd you call her?" I ask. "Why not me? I'm the risk manager. Or Mary Lou." Mary Lou is the director of safety.

"Babe, I know that. I wish I had called you. What happened,

I called Mary Lou and she's on vacation and she's got her voice mail routed to various places, depending on the situation, and for this situation, threats to the hospital, she routed it to Jette."

"Mary Lou is an idiot," I say roughly. "I wonder how many other potentially threatening situations I don't know about." I need to get into Jette's voice mail!

"Aw, come on. I called you as soon as I realized Jette wasn't calling back. Anybody heard anything about her?"

"If they have, they're not telling me. But I have to go down to the police station, like right now, so maybe I'll find something out."

I plod back to my office, wondering if I should mention this new incident. I've thought it before and I think it again: Why does everything happen at once?

Then I think: Does this have anything to do with Jette's disappearance? What if she drove out of the parking garage just as the riot was starting and was kidnapped by the rioters or by the guy who instigated the riot?

I order myself to calm down. There was no riot. If there *was* a riot, Jette would not drive into it. Anyway, we'd have heard about it.

I ask Geri to please follow up on changing Jette's password so that I can get the rest of her messages. Then I head for my office, Harley following close behind me to ask how Sleeping Beauty's coming.

"Frankly, Harley, I haven't had a minute to check on her."

"Don't pretend you don't know what I'm talking about. I mean how's the investigation?"

I get up, stroll past Harley, and shut my door.

"What's the deal?" I demand. "What is so important about *this case* that I have to finalize the investigation right now? I've just sent the record out to be reviewed!"

"I just want to know if we have a problem," Harley mumbles. "You know, headlines, top doctor's wife, all that."

"Yes! We have a problem! Our corporate counsel has disappeared, Bootsie's gorked, and we don't know why! But so far, to me, it just looks like one of those things, like the runner who collapsed and died in that race."

Harley makes a sorrowful face, the expression that always makes me think of Alfred E. Neuman. When he's being silly, oddly enough, he resembles Harrison Ford.

"I knew Lindy, too," he says. "This has been an awful weekend."

"Back to the point," I snap. "My gut feeling is we have no liability here. Just bad luck, just one of those things. I know it's hard because Dennis is our friend, but this is what it looks like."

"But you're not a doctor."

"True. I do get a feel for these things, though."

"What contributes to your feeling?" Harley asks.

"Lots of things. Consistency in the stories. Believability of the accounts. Seems to me, if anyone involved suspected anything about anyone else involved, they'd mention it. Well, I know they would. And nobody has."

Harley clears his throat. "Which experts did you send the record out to?"

I tell him, adding that I cleared it with Hawkeye before I sent it and Hawkeye concurred.

"I worry about Dennis," Harley says.

"Sure. We all like Dennis and we all like Bootsie—wait a minute, what do you mean?"

"Just that," he says, too quickly. Harley is a terrible liar. "That we're all friends. I'm worried about him."

"But not about her?"

"Sure, yeah, I'm worried about her. But Dennis could be . . . well, he might have trouble about this. About the circumstances."

"Harley, you mean you think Dennis had something to do with the coma?"

"Not at all," Harley says stiffly. "But somebody could think that. It would be easy to think."

"Why on earth would he do it?"

"He wouldn't," Harley insists. "It never crossed my mind."

"You liar. Why would he do it?"

"These things can be misinterpreted. In your report. The phenol, the record . . . It could look like someone was trying to cause something."

"Why would they think the person screwing up the case was the patient's husband?" I ask. Harley stares at the floor.

"You think this? You seriously believe this about Dennis of all people?"

"It's just how it looks," Harley says.

"All right. Supposing Dennis *did* have something to do with it. He put the phenol in there or whatever. *She didn't get any phenol.* Supposing he did screw around with her medical record. It disappeared, in fact. But it didn't disappear until last week, and I'm assuming the surgery was set up long before then. The staff knows where to find the medical record if they need it."

Harley bites his lip.

"Anyway, my investigation isn't going to change anything. What, did you want to get him out of town if things look bad for him after I finish investigating? In that case, the longer it takes, the better, don't you think?"

Harley frowns, like he can't quite figure this one out.

"Honest to God, Harley, this guy is one of your best friends and you suspect him of trying to do in his wife?"

"I don't," Harley says, shaking his head. "It was a devil's advocate sort of thing."

"Ah," I say, feeling very dim. "I get it. You thought—no, you *know*—he wanted to get Bootsie out of the way. Maybe he was tired of her? Had somebody else?"

Harley's ears flap. Okay, they don't really, but obviously I have hit the nail on the head here.

"No, he didn't. He wouldn't."

"That's it, isn't it? Wow. Who is she?"

"There's no one—that's not it," he says unconvincingly.

I blow air up through my bangs. "Not one particular woman? He is known to be a bit of a flirt."

"That's not what I meant and you know it!"

I don't know it, and I sense the opposite. I started off kidding, but this has the ring of truth. What's baffling is, usually when someone has action on the side, everybody knows about it. Even if everybody doesn't know about it, *I* know about it. I didn't even get a glimmer. At least not from gossip.

I have to admit I've gotten glimmers of some sort—from Dennis. Mostly, though, he just seemed like such a nice person. What the hell, nice people have affairs. At least he was nice enough to keep it very quiet. Which is to his credit. As is still being with his original wife.

I don't believe he tried to get Bootsie out of the way. Still, I play along. "Here's what I'll do. I'll drag this out as long as possible while you get his escape route planned."

Harley's now red in the face, probably red all over, although all I can see is his face. "You're not taking this seriously," he says. "And the main thing here . . . I'm thinking, what with it hitting the papers and all, it would be real nice to have a document from the risk manager saying it was nobody's fault."

"I see your point, Harley, and I'm with you. But the document will carry a lot more weight if the investigation is thorough, if you see *my* point."

Harley nods, but he looks as if he has no idea why he's nodding.

"Anyway, remember, my investigation is confidential. Not discoverable. Whatever's in the written report, and the written findings of the expert doctors, I'm not going to hand it over to the cops. Or the media. I might summarize it."

He nods some more, even more blankly.

"Now, if you'll excuse me, I have to go talk to the cops."

The look on his face is priceless. His mouth falls open, his blue eyes widen. Alfred E. Neuman in *The Scream*.

"About the incident with your car on Logan Street," I add.

This great exit line is unfortunately marred by my ringing phone. As Harley staggers out of my office, I field two calls: one from Jette's brother, Derek, who is now camped out at Jette's place and feeding her cat, and one from our insurance guy, who wants to know what the hell is going on over here and what's the deal on Bootsie. "Coma, natural causes suspected at this point," I say. "I haven't heard anything new since I faxed you the incident report."

"You want me to reserve a million? Christ. This sounds like the kind of thing that could get ugly," Andy says. "They're saying the doc had something to do with it."

"That's preposterous." I narrow my eyes in the direction of Harley's office. Did he mouth off to somebody, or is this just something everybody knew but me? "Who's saying that?"

"People in the office," Andy says. *Right*. People whose bonuses might be affected if they have a big payout. "On the radio, I guess. I don't know. I prefer to hear these things from you."

"I haven't heard anything like that," I assure him. "Not a word." Unlike Harley, I am a good liar, particularly over the phone. "There's no evidence. I've been going over and over the records, I've interviewed everybody. Even my experts say there's no indication of anything but bad luck, in which case you're off the hook. Don't worry."

"Easy for you to say," he grumbles. "It's not your money."

We already paid the insurance company our money, quite a lot of it.

I don't know why he's so jumpy. It's not his money either.

14

Silver Charm

After spending much of the last twenty-four hours interviewing people, it's interesting to be on the other side of the desk.

Lucy Montoya looks too young and too glamorous to be a detective, but she's very professional. I have to admire the way she takes me through my actions at Catgirl's door. She does this in the same way I took everybody step-by-step through Bootsie's operation, helping them remember without prompting them.

I go through it just the way I want people I'm interviewing to tell it to me. It's harder than I thought. Montoya's questions don't interrupt, they expand. Like "When she opened her door, did she use a key?"

I think back, concentrate. It was just dark. There was still light over the mountains, a blue light. But there were no lights on the stair and no lights on the landing. Did she have a key? It's not that it's any harder on this side of the desk. Just different.

Detective Montoya and I spend about twenty minutes discussing what the boyfriend looked like. Big—my impression, although I have to admit I'm guessing. He didn't stand up.

Heavy eyebrows? Dark eyebrows? Yeah. Mustache?

Damn, I'm an awful witness. I can't remember if he had a mustache. Why would I notice? Maybe a mustache. Yeah, I think a mustache because he was drinking a beer, sloppily, and there were drops of beer on it.

Or is my mind telling me that if he had a mustache there would be drops of beer on it?

I remember all sorts of weird little details. From not being able to remember if he had a mustache, I end up remembering that his mustache was a different color than his hair. Darker. Could I be making this up? My blond brother has a red mustache. I, a redhead, have blond eyelashes, damn it. So this guy's hair was blond, though almost certainly bleached.

"Like lifeguard, out-in-the-sun bleached, like he worked outside? Or chemical?"

Chemical. He didn't strike me as outdoorsy in the least.

"Why don't you ask the landlady?" I ask. "Wasn't she the one who took down my license-plate number every time I went there?"

Montoya gives me a look. "That wasn't the landlady, just the lady downstairs," she says.

After a thrilling few minutes in which I explain why I went there three times driving three different vehicles, and I neglect to mention that I was bewitched, Detective Montoya asks if I want a break before looking at some pictures. I guess I look like I need one.

I go out to the smoking section, which is the porch of the detectives' trailer. It overlooks a park, the football stadium where many of the city's high schools play, and a track where a number of young athletes are running wind sprints.

"Healthy young things," I mutter as I light up.

"Yeah," says another detective who's out here with me— the same one who was out here smoking when I arrived. An old grizzled guy. "Inspirational, isn't it?"

We smoke for a moment in silence, then he asks how I'm getting along with Detective Montoya. I myself detect something in his attitude, possibly a resentment that women are allowed to be detectives.

"Oh, fine," I say. "I'm sure glad I'm not a suspect, though, the way I'm being grilled."

He laughs. "What makes you think you're not a suspect?"

"Please," I say. "For one thing, I have not the least clue *how* she was killed. For another, I'm pretty sure I was somewhere else at the time, whenever it was. I mean, I'm *damn* sure. I don't think she was being killed at the exact moment I knocked on her door. Maybe tortured by Metallica at a loud volume, but—"

"Wasn't Metallica. Marilyn Manson."

"Whatever." And they aren't gonna tell me when or how. Okay by me. The less I know, the better. "And nobody gave me a Miranda," I add.

He chuckles. "Well, obviously we screwed up there. I'll have to mention that to Ms. Montoya. It's her first murder case."

"Ha-ha."

"Really." He flicks his cigarette into the parking lot even though there's an ashtray of sorts—a coffee can filled with sand—on the porch. "Nine times out of ten it's the spouse or the boyfriend, and we don't even look at anyone else. We don't even have to. Doesn't mean we shouldn't. You came up pretty suspicious, the way you kept going back there, but we'll see what Ms. Montoya makes of it. Like I said, it's her first. She's being thorough."

After the first couple of pages all the mug shots start to look alike, whether they have mustaches or not. I keep shaking my head. Finally we close the book.

"Can you think of anything else?" the detective asks.

In much the same way that people I interview come up with the salient point as I'm walking out the door, I remember the pendant. Not that it's a salient point.

"This is weird, it's crazy," I say. "But a few years ago my place was broken into and one of the things I lost was a necklace. Or I wasn't sure I lost it then, but at any rate I lost it. It wasn't expensive, but it was unique. It had a circle with a sliver of moon with, like, a fairy asleep on it. Little, about the size of a quarter. Anyway, she—Phyllis—was wearing a necklace exactly like that. I noticed it. I mentioned it and she said it was her lucky charm, but . . . I mean, it had been a long time since I saw my necklace, but I thought it was unique, you know?"

Detective Montoya nods, looking slightly pained. *This* is my great revelation? But she writes it down. As the guy outside said, she's thorough. She even asks, "So you think she might have been the one who broke into your place? All those years ago?"

I shake my head. "I mean, I lost the thing like five years ago. It couldn't have been the same charm." Shut up, Vicky.

Am I giving myself a motive for murder? Sure. I killed her to get my lucky silver charm back. Right.

As I walk into Admin Geri tells me HR has authorized the phone people to change Jette's voice-mail code and it has been changed to our all-purpose security code, which is . . .

1-2-3-4-5. Anybody could figure that out, right?

Finally, I listen to Jette's messages. All of them came in

before Friday. Many of them are not important. Some of them are.

The first message is the big surprise. Of all people, Dennis Devoss: "Hey, Jette, got your message, called back as soon as I could. For . . . well, I've missed you or you're on the other line. For what it's worth, I think you should hold off on this, I don't think you should risk a confrontation, and at the very least take somebody from Security with you. But I . . . we, well, we hadn't considered that, had we? That somebody might break into the system on somebody else's terminal? Sure, we should have thought of that. Well, listen, if you get this tonight, feel free to call me back. I'll be in surgery tomorrow, probably all day; I'll be down there on Saturday on various matters. Take care."

This message gives me a chill. Received at 2131 last Wednesday, about the time Jette was saving those password-protected documents. Take along somebody from Security? Don't risk a confrontation? Boy, the timing is sure lousy, but I'm going to have to ask Dennis about this.

At least it didn't sound like the message of a lover. I don't know why that should cheer me up, but for some reason it does.

Then I listen again and this time I'm not so sure. "I've missed you." That could mean Oops, phone tag, you're it, or it could mean he's been longing for her.

For Jette? I tell myself not to be ridiculous. Dennis might have been having all sorts of intrigues with all sorts of people, but if he'd been having one with Jette, I'd know.

He talks about somebody breaking into the system. Medical records? This does look bad, considering that IS has a problem with his own wife's medical record. I listen again.

Spooky. He leaves Jette this message, then she disappears. Except it's a new message. She didn't get it.

There are more. An extremely long message that's personal in nature, although not revealing. A message from Jette's dentist. A message from someone in Radiology inquiring about the steps necessary to fire someone and what grounds are needed, if any. A long message from a clinical administrator detailing a Medicare patient who comes in every twenty-one days for administration of an orphan drug, and it costs us $1,500 to procure and administer this drug but Medicare only pays $900, so we lose $600 every time this guy walks through the door, and is there any way we can send him to another hospital? I make a note to call this administrator back and get more specifics. Like, what's the drug? And no, we probably can't send the patient to another hospital.

At last here's Father Gifford: "Yo, Legal Eagle. Got some brothers here who have some interesting information. Important but not urgent, but I'd like to run it past you before the weekend. Your call."

That's Gifford, revealing nothing over the phone. Given how hard it was for me to get this message, it's not likely it could have fallen onto the wrong ears.

Well. Saturday night has come and gone and, as Gifford said, there was no gang war, real or faked. So I guess I was right not to mention it to the cops. I still don't like it, though. The message was delivered at 4:15 Thursday afternoon, giving this weirdo, whoever he was, plenty of time to find some other group of kids. Okay, I tell myself, but *he didn't*. So move on.

The rest of the messages are either inconsequential or hopelessly out-of-date. Many of them are also extraordinarily long.

I have pretty much trained people to leave me short messages. I do that by ignoring long messages.

I make several calls. To the garage, to see if my car is fixed. It's not, but hey, would I like a new super-duper security system? It has seven different warnings for various situations, none of which is "I'm about to catch fire."

Um, no thanks, just fix the fucking car, okay? Like, *today*. *Right*. They'll call me.

Almost out of habit, I dial the Laramie number of Jette's boyfriend, which I've been calling for three days—well, once a day, anyway—and somebody answers.

"Randall Cryer?"

"The same," he says. "Be fast. I'm beat."

"I work with Jette Wakefield," I start, but he interrupts me.

"Yes, I know she's missing. I've received a personal visit. The last three days I've been flying all over the place, looking for her."

"Flying?"

"You know, in an airplane. I've already answered every possible question about our relationship and I'm in no mood for more. Particularly from an amateur."

"We're all very concerned," I say.

"So am I," he says. "And that's the only reason I'm even picking up the goddamned phone." Whereupon he slams it down.

If Jette ever surfaces, I'm sure those two will be very happy together.

I call a couple of nurses to ask if phenol routinely goes on the tray for plastic surgery and then Patricia Duty, Bootsie's GP, to ask if she has any pertinent information on Bootsie's preop condition.

Then I check my incoming messages. Capitol Hill Animal Clinic.

An OR nurse calls back with the less-than-edifying news that sometimes phenol is put on the tray, sometimes not, depending on the habits of whoever is loading the surgical tray for whatever surgery.

I'm pulling on my hair when the Capitol Hill Animal Clinic calls me. Again. That cat. This time I speak to a veterinarian and not the receptionist.

"I tell you I am not responsible for this cat." Then I remember; they don't know her owner is dead. Shit.

"The cat is fine," the vet says. "She's a very healthy young kitten, and she is just the sweetest thing. But we can't keep her. We didn't even need to keep her for the weekend. We're going to have to take her to be destroyed if someone doesn't take responsibility here."

Hey, it's not gonna be me. I already paid out a hundred bucks for that cat.

"We're not asking you to pay the bill," he says as if reading my mind. How do people do that over the phone? "If you could just pick her up and take her back home. We haven't been able to reach the owner."

"I think her owner's . . . dead," I say. "That is, the police called me. I mean, I didn't even know the person—"

"That's awful," he says. He doesn't say it with awe. *He thinks I'm lying.* "I guess we could give it one more day before we have this kitty destroyed. It seems a shame, to bring her back from the brink only to have her put to sleep."

It only seems like a shame if you like cats. Or if you've spent a hundred bucks to keep one alive.

Uh-oh. I'm softening.

"Yeah, give it one more day," I say. "I'll work on it."

"Were you kidding about her owner being . . . dead?"

"I'm afraid not." Give that kitty a sympathy card.

"Oh, dear."

Yeah. Now the spay bill will probably never be paid.

Before the phone can ring again, I take off for the ICU, hoping to find Dennis and ask him about that message to Jette. He's not there, and Sleeping Beauty has not awakened.

"I think he went to get some food," the charge nurse says. "He's been here around the clock for two days, poor man."

In search of Dennis, I encounter Hawkeye, who's standing in the hall waving a bunch of papers at somebody. He turns to me and seamlessly starts talking. I seamlessly interrupt him.

"Have you seen Dennis?"

"He headed down to his office to shower and grab a bite," Hawkeye says. "I think he's beginning to get the idea Sleeping Beauty is never gonna wake up."

"This is bad," I say.

"You bet it's bad. Haven't you said it a million times: It's better to just kill them outright than to turn them into vegetables. From a liability viewpoint."

"I never said that."

"Yeah, you did."

Hell, I probably *did*. It's true, too. Wrongful death has a statutory cap of $250,000, but restitution for someone you've disabled can get into the millions. Which is why we have insurance companies.

I walk down to Dennis's office and ask his secretary if she's seen him. "He's inside," she says. "Go on in."

He doesn't look distraught. He hasn't fallen apart. He's wearing fresh clothing—his usual sharply creased outfit.

"Hiya," I say. "I have a couple of questions, and I know the timing is terrible, but . . ."

He waves it off and invites me to have a seat. For some reason, I'd rather stand. He sits, tying his shoelaces.

"You and Jette were working on something together, about medical records?"

He looks blank, but at least he doesn't look guilty.

"Christ. Jette. I'd forgotten all about that," he says. "Any word on her yet?"

I shake my head. "What exactly were you working on?"

"We had a couple of things in peer review where it sort of looked like practitioners were entering unauthorized information in the medical record. You know, we give the doctors twenty days after discharge to complete the record, they don't make it, they lose their privileges. So it looked like some of them had figured out how to fudge the date. I mentioned this to Jette, and she was concerned that if they fudged the date, they could fudge other things. You know, go back in and clean up the record. You know how that works."

It's a no-no.

"So she kept me posted, since I introduced the subject. Really, that's about the size of it."

"You left her a voice mail last Wednesday night," I say.

He squeezes the bridge of his nose. "Um, yeah, that's right. See, she was working with IS on this problem, and they had some software that checks your system for holes. A hole being—"

"Please don't get too technical."

"Right. Anyway, I ran into her at . . . oh, that dinner, and we talked about some of the security holes the program had located. She said something, I can't recall exactly . . . Oh. Okay. She wondered if the system would flag users by terminal *and* by password or just by password, so I said I'd go back to my office and log into EMRAM so that she could check. So I did, and she did, and then she called me back, very excited, to say she'd located an unauthorized user and the program did flag that terminal, but the password was strange, so she was going to go right over and find out who was on that terminal. I mean, she left the message on my voice mail, because by then I had gotten out of the program and gone to check on a couple of my patients, so I didn't get her message until I got back, but she sounded very hyped. And I was a little worried about her confronting someone. You know she can be abrasive."

"She sure can."

"But this thing with Bootsie just wiped it out of my mind. I'm sorry."

He looks up at me, very concerned, very warm. "I didn't make the connection. And then nobody ever saw Jette again?"

"Not that we know of. You logged on with your password?"

Dennis crinkles his eyes. "First mine, then Hawkeye's."

"How come you know everybody's password?"

Dennis leans back. "I don't, but lots of us use a system," he says. "In fact, that was one of the things that drove Jette crazy. Like my password's DDVMD, my initials and title; Phil's is PSDO since he's a D.O. and not an M.D. Of course, Hawkeye's is—"

"MD1," I say. "I can see why Jette was concerned. Do you realize the havoc someone could wreak if this got into the wrong hands?"

"You're not going to use it," he points out. "We all have a few other things on our minds other than what password we're going to use. We pretty much keep it among ourselves."

And, believe me, I'm quite honored to be among this select little group.

"Did you by any chance log into Bootsie's record as part of your experiment?"

"No. In fact, what I did was I pulled the charts of a couple of my patients and then I changed to Hawkeye's login so that I could more or less ramble around the system. Then I saw something I needed to check on, so after a couple of minutes I went up to the floor. On the floor, I logged in as myself and updated the record. I'm not even sure I can get into Bootsie's record. She's not my patient, after all." Suddenly he looks very sad.

"Okay. Sorry, but I had to ask." Of course, he could always log in as Brian Marrote, since they all know one another's password.

He massages his face.

"And I do understand why it slipped your mind," I add. "Did you by any chance save Jette's message?"

"I don't think so. They automatically delete after, what, three days? Here." He swivels around and punches up the number with the phone on speaker. And there it is: Jette's voice. "Hey, Dennis, this program's great, works like a charm. I got a live one here, along with you. Don't know what password he's using, but I've identified the terminal. You're identified by password, but he's just a string of zeros. Something's not kosher here, but I can see where he is, and I'm going to nail him. Oh, I'm working on a memo, I'll send it over tomorrow. G'night!"

This adds a lot of credibility to his story. "Can you forward that to my phone?"

He grimaces. "I'm pretty good with computers, but phones? Well, let's give it a try—or do you want to do it?" Even as he says it, he's forwarding the message.

On my way back to the office to see if it worked, I run into Nolan.

"Nolan! Need a cat?"

Nolan does a double take. "Whatever might have made you think that?"

"Just wondering. Idle curiosity. I happen to know of a nice cat that needs a home. Spayed, even."

"No, thank you," Nolan says politely. "If you recall, curiosity *killed* the cat."

Not this one, unfortunately.

Dennis correctly forwarded Jette's message. I listen to it again, wondering what those two were *really* up to, and then

BAD LUCK

decide it's what it seems like. Unlike Hawkeye, Dennis does not try to micromanage, but neither is it uncharacteristic of him to get involved in something like Medical Records.

Then I call Bob's Bump Shop again. Just to bug them.

"Oh, sure, it's ready," a guy says, in a voice that implies it's *been* ready and sitting there for hours and where have I been? Oh, and they close in thirty minutes.

Now here's a challenge: How do I get to the Hertz rental place, check in my rental, and still get to South Broadway in time to pick up my car? The answer is, I can't. If I skip the part about taking the rental in, I have an outside chance. I head toward Broadway and call Glenn, trying both my place and his. He doesn't answer at either.

I leave the rental on the street.

A guy with the name Rick stitched on his collar gives me an enthusiastic rundown on everything they replaced and how the work was much more extensive than they originally thought, blah blah blah, and how lucky I am that I had an estimate because they can't charge more than ten percent over the estimate no matter how much it costs. . . .

What kind of idiot would even consider taking a car in without an estimate? Frankly, I think it's a state law.

You never know. We do have a state law saying it's okay for a car salesperson to tell you lies. Okay, maybe it doesn't specifically state that it's okay to lie. The statute in question* specifies that the contract for sale of a motor vehicle must include, in 12-point type, or three point sizes larger than the smallest type appearing in the contract, the statement that only those terms *in written form* embody the contract and any *conflicting oral representations* made to the purchase are void. (Emphasis mine.) Now, what does that suggest?

I have never been wild about this car, and now, frankly, I don't trust it. It smells different. Like it's catching fire. But it

---

*Colorado Revised Statutes 12-6-104(k)(I)(C). C.R.S. 12-6-102(2)(5)(b)(II)(3) defines "coerce" as "the failure to act in good faith . . . except that recommendation, exposition, persuasion, urging or argument shall not be deemed to constitute a lack of good faith."

manages to get me home. Glenn opens his door as I'm unlocking mine. Good; he hasn't moved to the suburbs yet.

"Hey, handsome," I say. He grins and embraces me. His skin is cold. Bracing. He probably drove home with the top down.

Our hello kiss sweeps us into my place, and we are making nice progress toward a happy hour when the phone rings.

One ring. Probably some idiot telling me something they could tell me tomorrow—or it could be something big. Good news or bad. It could be Father Gifford, with his band of non-gang members for me to meet with. I did leave the office a bit early.

Two rings. They can leave a message. I'll call them back—or not, as the case may be. If they are desperate, they can have me paged. If they *dare*.

Three rings. Well, hell. The call has just gone to the answering machine, but the mood has been broken and, furthermore, I am curious. Haunted by ringing phones.

Glenn sighs. "Wouldn't it be nice to be somewhere where there were no phones?" he says. "I don't mean that. I've spent the last two days in an office without a phone on the desk. It's been strange."

"But someone could reach you if they had to?"

"Nobody has to, these days."

I pick up and dial in for my message. The Capitol Hill Animal Clinic. They have made an unfortunate mistake. The shelter will not take Tara, the cat, because her stitches are not healed. The clinic cannot keep her another day. They thought I would like to know.

Thanks so much for calling to relay that death sentence. And what do I care? I say as much to Glenn.

He takes me in his arms and nuzzles my hair. So I guess we are starting over.

"They're driving me crazy, that clinic!" I screech. He pulls away.

"I don't need this! I wish that cat was out of my life." I calm down a little. If I just let things take their course, it will be.

"That cat bothers you, doesn't it?"

He doesn't know the half of it.

"We could go take her to her owner's. But if her owner doesn't care enough—"

"Uh, Glenn? Her owner is dead."

"Oh. Shit. That's awful."

"Yeah. The police called. I had to go down there and look at mug shots—a total loss—and the vet is gonna put the cat to sleep."

"For God's sake, let's go get the cat then. We can keep it a couple of days," he says. "I know it's against the lease, but cats are pretty nonintrusive."

Right. My place or yours?

Uh, about that lease? The building is managed by 1911 Properties, a limited partnership whose general partner is FLS Interests, a corporation. A corporation started by me, Joe Feeney, and Ken Sharpe so that we could invest in real estate back when we were first-year associates and needed a good shelter for our seemingly enormous new salaries, not to mention flexing our corporate-structure skills. So I'm not particularly worried that cats are against my lease.

I call the clinic back. They're open till nine. They are very, very nice. They explain that Tara is such a sweet cat, they would love to be able to keep her, and they are sure I will find her a home.

So. Instead of a nice, comforting happy hour, we get into my car, drive down South Broadway, pick up the rental car, which I left parked on the street. Glenn follows me to drop it off, then we go to the clinic.

Tara still looks like FrankenCat. Her eye isn't as red or as swollen, but she has these god-awful stitches and her ear is never going to be the same. The vet puts her into her cardboard carrier, telling me he thinks Tara has vision in that eye, they aren't sure yet. He is so happy not to have to kill the cat that he doesn't charge me. In fact, he gives me a disposable litter box and a whole sackful of cat-food samples.

No litter, though.

With FrankenCat yowling in the carrier, we head to Safeway

to pick some up. In the pet aisle, two young girls are giggling about something. No, they would not like a nice kitty.

When I step outside, I can hear the cat screaming as if it's being killed. I rush to the car. How do you calm a freaked-out cat? "It's okay," I say as I scramble into the seat with my five-pound bag of Jonny Cat. Glenn looks far from okay.

"I should have killed this cat," I mutter. "Less overall liability." I set the carrier on my lap. The noise stops.

"Aw, Vicky," Glenn says. "You know you don't mean that."

"I do, too. I've spent a hundred dollars on this cat. The only reason I'm taking it is to protect my investment."

"Right." Glenn smiles his fabulous smile. "Look how nice she calmed down once you got back to the car." He starts the engine.

The cat, being a terrible judge of character, purrs.

15

Nine Lives

One of the questions asked to rule out heart attack (or confirm one) is whether you have a heavy feeling, like an elephant sitting on your chest. Waking up, I have that feeling. I even have the brief thought that maybe it's time to quit smoking.

Then I realize the elephant on my chest is purring. And drooling. It's FrankenCat. Er, Tara.

Gah, *cat* drool. My first instinct is to fling her off in panic. I control myself, remove her gently, and get into the shower. When I come out, she's disappeared.

Who can I give that cat to?

I open my closet. A box containing sandals lands on my head, scaring me half to death. The cat is on the overhead shelf, knocking things off. A black cowboy hat I never wear. Another shoe box. It looks as though I'll have to remember to close the closet door while this animal is in residence.

I put on a cherry-red coatdress. I am rolling up one of the legs of my tweed-patterned Donna Karan tights when FrankenCat leaps out of the closet, attacks the other leg, gets her claw hung up in it, and takes off. Mind you, these are $12 tights and now they're ruined. The damage mounts: $105 for the vet, plus $3.69 for the cat litter, and now she's ruined my outfit. Cursing, I unwrap a package of Hanes and take them into the bathroom, where I get them on without snagging them. When I look in the full-length mirror I realize that sheer black was a better choice for this outfit than patterned anyway. Now I can wear my red shoes.

Grrr. A cat with better fashion sense than I have.

I whip out the colorful Fendi scarf Melinda gave me for Christmas, and FrankenCat leaps to the top of the bookcase beside my bed. "Yeah, you'd like to get your sharp little claws into this, wouldn't you," I sneer at her. "It's a two-hundred-dollar scarf. That would make your day."

Goddess help me. Talking to a cat.

I step into the red snakeskin pumps while the cat stares fixedly at my scarf, now safely knotted around my neck, her green eyes glittering.

"Who can I give you to?" I ask her.

That's what's foremost on my mind as I drive to work, but I forget all about it once I get there. Harley has set up an emergency meeting of the major incident response team.

Sleeping Beauty, by virtue of headline intrigue, has become a major incident.

The team consists of the risk manager, a legal representative, the PR director, and the COO or another ranking hospital official. I guess I'm doing dual duty as risk manager and legal, since Jette is not available. Her continued absence is part of the story.

"Last night," Nolan intones, "I informed the media that as far as we knew, there was no police investigation into Sleeping Beauty, nor is there any reason for one. Somehow a rumor got started that we were investigating Dennis in conjunction with this incident. I've denied this rumor. My contacts at the police department say they have likewise denied it. So now that I've denied that there's an investigation, the press is clamoring for one."

"Just a minute," Harley breaks in. "Why do they need to know anything at all?"

"They have a duty to their readers," Nolan says. "And, frankly, there's not a lot else going on. Super Bowl's over, Rockies' opening day isn't till next week, the Nuggets are in the cellar as usual. It's not an election year, everyone's tired of political scandals, and unemployment's at an all-time low."

"We could announce massive layoffs," Harley mutters.

"Also," Nolan says, "Dr. Devoss is big news. The *Post* did a whole series right before Christmas on his outreach team, when they flew to Rwanda to do all the reconstructive surgery on victims of land mines. And it's also big news by virtue of his being a hospital bigwig."

"I think we should be real low-key here," I say.

"True," Nolan says. "But that's not our call. I'm thinking our strategy should be open, up-front. Get Dennis out there in front of the cameras saying he has faith in our team."

"No, no," Harley almost shouts.

"Why not?"

"I just think it's the wrong thing to do. To put Dennis through something like that at a time like this," Harley says.

I chime in. "And I think it gives too much importance to something that's not that big a deal in the grand scheme of things." In case anyone cares what I think.

"I see your point," Nolan says. "Okay. We'll continue to be low-key. If anyone sees any camera crews, give me a call."

We are just winding up the meeting when our CEO, Langstrom (make that *Dr.* Langstrom, since he's a Ph.D.), enters the conference room. He rubs his hands together. "Well, what have we decided?" He addresses this question to the room at large.

"We're issuing a press release and keeping things low-key." I never learn; the first person to open his or her mouth gets the heat.

"I thought your advice was to face these things heads-up." Langstrom looks directly at me when he says this.

"I can think of times in the past when facing things *head-on* has been the best plan, but this is internal," I say. "Besides, we *are* facing it head-on: talking to the media, issuing press releases."

"What's your thinking on this, Ben?" Harley asks. That's why Harley's in upper management; he's a diplomat. I use Langstrom's first name so infrequently, I'd almost forgotten it.

Langstrom, who probably has not done *any* thinking on this, intones that he's sure we have the situation well in hand; it's just that he's heard these rumors that people are saying it's Dennis's fault.

"That's just gossip, Ben. Our best plan is to be straight and reveal no weakness." This is not how Harley talks to me, but it mollifies Langstrom.

"Vicky's working up a sort of preliminary analysis of the situation," Harley says, handing it back to me.

"Just the usual incident investigation," I say. "Sending out the file to experts and so on. They should be getting back to me soon, possibly even today, but as of now it looks like everything has been handled properly."

"I'd like to be in the loop on this in the future," Langstrom says.

"Right, Ben," Harley the yes-man agrees.

"Absolutely," Vicky the yes-woman repeats. And we all head back to our offices, hopefully to get some work done.

I go into Jette's office to look up a couple of statutes. Tristan is in there, typing away.

"I'm working on it," he whispers. "I have a plan. Even if I can't open the files I think I can print them."

"Excellent," I whisper back. "Jette has her own printer."

"I know that," he says in a normal tone. Of course he does; it's sitting right there next to the computer.

I get back to my office just in time to pick up my phone. It's Patricia Duty. She gets right to the point.

"I looked over that file of Bootsie Devoss's and there is one thing that sort of caught my attention," she says. "And that is that a couple of years ago Bootsie talked me into giving her a prescription for Fen-Phen. She . . . had a sudden unexplained weight gain. Almost immediately it became apparent that drug was a bad idea, and she never refilled the prescription. But the official line is that if anyone took it, even for a short time, the recommendation is that they have an echocardiogram to rule out heart-valve abnormalities."

An echocardiogram is kind of like an ultrasound of the heart muscle.

"I recommended to Bootsie that she have one, but I don't know that she ever did," Dr. Duty says. "I doubt it would be a problem. But you asked if there was anything in my record that might pertain directly to her surgery, and this does."

"Thanks," I say.

"You're welcome." She hangs up, and I sit there staring at the phone.

Of course I go directly to Harley's office to let him know that the hospital is looking less and less liable. Forget the phenol, forget the missing EMR. Bootsie should have had an echocardiogram done before any type of surgery and she didn't.

"Shit!" Harley says. A curious reaction.

"No, this is good, we're off the hook. The hospital."

Harley looks unconvinced. "Dennis," he says. "Wouldn't he have known this? Wouldn't he have *made* her get the test done?"

"Is that how marriage works?"

Harley's ears turn red.

"How much do you know about Bebe's medical problems?" I ask.

He raises his eyebrows. "But I'm not her doctor."

"And Dennis isn't Bootsie's doctor." He's right, this does sort of look bad for Dennis. Not that bad, though.

"I suppose you have to put this in your report."

"I need to give the information to my experts. Don't worry. They're just looking at hospital stuff, not whether Dennis was a bad husband."

He narrows his eyes.

"Relax," I tell him. "Your good buddy is not going to be in any worse trouble because of this."

This reminds me that Harley was going to check with Bebe about whether she saw Bootsie shooting up. I'll bet a million dollars he didn't.

Instead of putting the information from Dr. Duty in my report, I call my experts and tell them and add that I would like their reports back as soon as humanly possible. Then I call Bebe Sloane.

She sounds stressed. In the background I hear the sounds of small children. Which is odd, as Harley's children are somewhat older: high school girl, junior high boy, something like that.

"I'm baby-sitting," Bebe says. "It's driving me nuts. The woman next door keeps saying she's going on a job interview, can I look after the kids? And I say, Oh, sure. And then she doesn't come home for hours and hours. This is the last time, I swear it."

"Yeah," I say. "You've got to be adamant about these things."

She grunts into the phone. "I can have Harley call you as soon as he gets in."

She doesn't even wonder why I'm calling Harley during business hours when he ought to be here?

"I didn't want Harley, I wanted you."

"Why on earth—"

"Uh, Bebe? Harley seemed to think that at one time you had seen Bootsie inject herself with something. With a needle. I'm looking for confirmation of that."

"Oh, I'd forgotten about it. Yes, I think she was on insulin, but that would be known to her doctors, wouldn't it? I mean, it wouldn't be a factor?"

"She wasn't diabetic."

"Oh." A long beat while Bebe thinks about this.

"I just wanted to know if you saw her using a needle."

"No. I don't believe I ever did. I did, somehow, think she was diabetic. But she wasn't the sort of person who would shoot up in front of anybody."

"Maybe in the ladies' room?"

"Well, but not in front of anyone. You know."

"Okay." I asked, I got.

"Terrible situation," she says. "Terrible for Dennis, and of course even worse for Bootsie. Just a rotten deal all around. You know, there are people these kinds of things should never happen to, and those two, well, that's the kind of people they are. . . ."

It sounds like she's trying to tell me something, but I'm not sure what.

"Bad things can happen to anybody," I say. "Just bad luck. An accident. Or not even an accident, maybe just Bootsie's overall health. Harley seems to think somebody might try to pin this on Dennis. Do you have any reason to think Dennis might have had something to do with Bootsie's condition?"

"I certainly wouldn't want to think so," Bebe says.

"Bebe," I say gently, "what are we up against here? Do you think Dennis could have had something to do with Bootsie's condition? And if so, why?"

"Well, he's not the most . . . He's a charming man, as I said. But he's the kind of man you would think twice about—he's not trustworthy." She laughs. "I mean, I wouldn't mind being in his hands as a patient. But as a wife, well . . ."

"He had affairs?" A little more confirmation wouldn't hurt.

"Only hundreds of them," Bebe says with exasperation. "Now, Bootsie knew, she always knew. And she didn't seem to mind. At least not later. She did at first. Pretty early in their marriage she took a golf club to Dennis's car one day. Really good-looking men are not good husband material. Oh, don't ever tell Harley I told you that! You're laughing, aren't you."

"Absolutely not." Not out loud.

Funny, I never thought of Dennis as incredibly good-looking. He just seemed nice. And Harley. Does she mean that Harley is, or is not, good husband material?

"Dennis," Bebe says, "is the kind of man who would make a good lover but a bad husband. That's what I think about him."

"That's sort of the impression I've been getting. Bad husband." Funny that she used my exact phrase.

"Not that he was a . . . a bad husband, he was very good to Bootsie. But . . . Oh, my God!" She sounds like she just pulled a burning pie pan out of the oven with her bare hand.

"What?" Like there's anything I can do. Tell her to put her hand in cold water until the paramedics arrive.

"I just realized I read that somewhere. Not about Dennis, of course. It was Truman Capote, or Dominick Dunne, or somebody like that, only he was quoting something somebody, some woman, said about Claus von Bülow. I can't believe I said that."

"I'll forget you said it." Along with the bit about how good-looking men are not the ones to marry. Pity. I would have loved using that on Harley.

I hang up to find Langstrom hovering at my door. Since he didn't have Vanessa summon me, I assume this means I have gained some status. It's probably my red suit.

"When can we get your report on Mrs. Devoss?" he asks. "You indicated earlier that it was almost complete."

I did? My report is, at the moment, a bunch of notes in a notebook. I don't say this to Langstrom.

"I need to get comments back from my experts. Usually they send me letters. I did tell them it was pretty urgent."

Right, I told them that *ten minutes ago*.

"Well, I've contacted the authorities," Langstrom says. "Did you see the papers? They put 'accidental' in quote marks."

Langstrom, you would assume, has been around the block enough times to realize that the dailies never get it right.

"Not even an accident," I say. "Just an unexpected outcome."

"They suggest that since he's a high-ranking authority here, obviously something like this couldn't happen without his collusion."

"Bullshit!" Oops. For a moment I forgot myself. But Langstrom doesn't seem to care.

"Totally," he agrees. "Pure bollocks. But we have to avoid even the appearance of collusion, so I thought it might be prudent to call in the police."

"I don't think that's a good idea," I say. Did he just tell me that he'd already done it? "I wish you had talked to me first. I think that might have been a bad move."

Langstrom's lip curls. "They called me. A Captain LeFevre. He said they would be very interested in examining all the evidence we have in our possession."

I forget myself again and blow air through my bangs. *Not a professional gesture.* And another reason for getting rid of these pesky bangs. "They won't know what to make of it," I say.

"And I wanted to talk to them about other matters. Jette."

Oh. Well, I guess that's okay.

"I was wondering if the hospital should offer some kind of a reward for anyone with information on her whereabouts."

"That's a *good* idea," I say, glad to have something to agree with.

"Does five thousand dollars sound about right?" Langstrom asks. "Should it be higher? Or lower?"

I think about this for a minute. That was the amount of my sign-on bonus, when I joined Petter, Forrester & Rommell. It seemed quite generous at the time. It also approximates my bonus last year, at which time it didn't seem nearly as generous.

"I guess . . ."

"We don't want to appear cheap," he says. "We should have done this the first day."

"I'll call Nolan so he can get it into his press release."

"Please see that he does. And, of course, you and I need to sit down to discuss what's to be done about her workload. Farm a lot of things out to our outside counsel, I suppose."

Jette, in fact, has been diverting a great deal of her workload to outside counsel all along. I expect legal expenditures to drop significantly. Depending, of course, on the length of her absence.

"Anyway, when the police show up, I'd like you to be present," he says.

"Sure. Absolutely."

"With your report," he adds significantly. Then he removes himself from my office without a fare-thee-well.

I grit my teeth and peck out three paragraphs on how my investigation has revealed minor inconsistencies and nothing to induce a coma. I spend a few minutes chewing on my pen and wondering whether to go into these inconsistencies, then decide not to. I plug in the notice that the report is confidential and print it.

Then I write another paragraph explaining the attorney-client privilege. For Langstrom.

Basically, in this situation I am the attorney and the hospital is my client.

I'm spell-checking this memo when Gifford calls and tells me the brothers are here if I'd like to talk to them.

"The brothers?" I ask dumbly.

"You know. *Riot*."

Oh. *Those* brothers. I'm not sure whether Gifford means they are siblings or if he's just being political, but I tell him I will be right there.

16

The NonGang Gang

The two boys turn out to be siblings, ages fifteen and thirteen. Unlike Tristan, they have gotten their growth spurts. They tower over me. The older one is well filled out, the thirteen-year-old is skinny. They look like nice boys, as Gifford said, not particularly like gang members. I wouldn't cross the street to avoid them. They even have normal, nongang names.

"Maybe you could just tell us what you saw and what you heard." I direct this toward Ben, the older one, but Steve answers.

"Man," he says. "Dude come to us and told us he wanted us to off his wife and he'd give us money."

"Hey," Ben says. "Wasn't like that. First of all, he didn't come to *us*."

"Okay," I say. "Can you describe him?"

"Was just one guy," the older kid says. "Kind of a big dude. Kinda looked like . . ."

"Like a fat Elvis Presley," Steve says. "Yeah, the one nobody wanted on the stamp, 'cept this guy wa'nt all that old. Had blond hair, though."

When he first said Elvis, I thought of one of our security guards who plays up his slight resemblance to the King. But John isn't fat. Or blond.

"And a ponytail," Ben says. "Fact is, we don't see his hair, 'cause he wearing a cap, 'cept for that tail."

"That's right, yeah," Steve says. "Only it was bleached, that tail. Coulda been a weave. 'Cause, you know, he had these eyebrows. Dark, like."

"How old?"

" 'Bout, well . . . older than us," Steve says. "I'm not studyin' the dude's age, you know?"

"Thirty at least," Ben says. "And dressed kinda poor."

"Okay. Where did he approach you?"

"Oh, man," Steve says. "We weren't doin' nothin', you know? We were hanging out. Looking in this guy's car. A guy we know."

"That Devon, he's bad news," Ben says. "He kind of attracts these situations."

"Okay. So what did this guy say?"

"Comes over and you know, people, like, don't come over to us. We send out anti vibes or something. People cross the street, you know?"

I smile guiltily.

Ben chuckles. "They do that," he agrees. " 'Cause of Devon, mostly."

"So it's weird," Steve says. "This guy comin' over like this. So we think, you know, he wants to cop, like, thinks we have drugs. Or else he's a narc 'cept he don't have that narc look."

"This was when? Thursday? What time?"

"No, Wednesday, but like, after school, maybe four. He come over and he say, 'Hey, brothers' or somethin'. We, like, oh, man, get away, you know? Like, get outa here. He just come on over like he knows us or somethin'."

"But he's got no authority," Ben puts in. "Like, he's not a teacher, he's not a cop. He's just some dude."

Steve takes over again. "So then he says who's the leader here. What he says, I think, is 'Who's the big man here?' And, like, Devon goes, 'You talkin' to me?' Just like that. And the guy says, 'Yeah, okay, I'm talkin' to you. I got this job.' "

"Cool here, he jumps on it," Ben says with disgust. "Got to be in on everything. Says yeah, we can handle it. He's, like, shoooww meeee the moneeeee, dude!"

"Did not," Steve says.

I've done this wrong. If clinical staff members were involved in an incident, I would not let them tell their stories together like this. Too late for that now. I stop the did not/did too litany. "So what did he ask for? In his words, if you remember."

Steve answers. "Says do we know Montmorency? What's he think, we can't read? Says he wants a diversion, he called it that, on Saturday, at the back parking garage. And starts layin' out the whole thing. Look for this car, this license plate, then when you see it do some gunfire. Like a gang war. We shoot this car so it looks like a stray bullet."

"He didn't say shoot the car," Ben says. "He takes care a that. Who do we look like, we're gonna do a thing like that? But he does want shooting. And Devon is like, 'No good, man, you gotta provide the artillery,' like he's gonna *do* some'n' crazy like that."

The scene they describe reminds me of a bit from the soap *General Hospital,* to which I was addicted briefly in my teens. A woman, Heather, befriends the woman who adopted her baby and plots to give the woman LSD so that she can get her baby back.

I can't believe I remember this shit.

Anyway, in one episode, Heather *walks into a drugstore* and asks to buy some LSD. Totally weird; I mean, I was in college at the time—maybe high school even—and *I* knew you couldn't walk into a drugstore and ask for LSD. *Third-graders* knew that. But there she was, on national television, doing this unimaginably dumb thing.

She didn't get the LSD, of course.

"What was supposed to set this all off?" I ask.

"When we see a 1966 T-Bird, red with a cream top," Steve says. "Which the top might be down and it's a blond woman driving it, good-lookin' he says. Then he stops and says maybe she's not driving."

"License plate BTC," Ben offers helpfully. "Something like that. Sounded like a radio station. BCO."

"An' then he comes up with another car," Steve says. "Like

he's just thought, maybe they'll switch cars. White Mercedes license plate, some letters, like MTV, DDV TV. You know, man, we 'posed to hang out there, all afternoon, just outside a this parking garage without getting chewed off by the man or something and watch for this car or that car and if it's got the right license plate. And then start shootin' and whoopin' it up."

"He just nuts, you ax me," Ben says.

"This does sound kind of nutty," I say. "Did he say what the people in the car were supposed to look like? Or why?"

"Yeah, I'm gettin' a that," Steve says. "Okay, Devon all of a sudden ax who he wants wasted and why. And the guy jumps around, says it's his wife, she's messin' around on him, only that part he didn't do real well. And then he says maybe she's not gonna be driving her car, that's the red one, but it's gonna be the guy's car, the guy she's fooling around with, see, and he says she looks real good, and that's when we know this guy's full of it, 'cause look at him and there ain't no way he's married to a hot blonde in a phat car. He's not dressed for it, you know?"

These kids know their clothes and they know their cars.

"We're, like, you wanna smoke a babe like that? Even Devon is like, mister, let's see some green or you full a shit, man, get outa here, you got the wrong guys. And then the guy, he boned out."

I've been taking notes fast, and I finally make the connection with the license plate. As I wrote it down, BTC or BCO, I thought, Boot camp? But it's obvious: Bootsie.

"License plates BOOTC and . . . DDVMD?" I suggest.

"Yeah, sounds like," Steve agrees.

I turn to Gifford. "This fits in with something else going on." I turn back to the kids. "If you were to see this guy again, would you know him? And could you let somebody know if you see him again?"

" 'Less he be in some kinda disguise," Steve says. "Sure, I'd know him."

"Never saw him before," Ben says. "Not gonna see him again, either. Bet on it."

"Whose plates are those?" Gifford asks after the boys are gone. "And how do you know?"

"I'm betting BOOTC is Bootsie Devoss and DDVMD is Dennis Devoss."

Gifford whistles. "You know everybody's license-plate numbers?"

"It was a guess." The way you guess that 555-2020 on your caller ID is your eye doctor. But I can check it easily enough.

"So this is serious," Gifford says.

"It sounds cockeyed. But I don't think those boys made it up. Who's this guy? And what's his problem?"

"Doesn't ring a bell with me," Gifford says. "Don't know the dude, but I'll keep my eyes open."

"Me, too," I say, although I don't know what I'm looking for. Somebody who, for instance, knew Bootsie would be at the hospital on Saturday for surgery but couldn't put it together that she wouldn't be driving herself home.

I detour to the Smoker's Showcase in the hope that a bit of nicotine in my system will help me process this. How does it fit?

It doesn't; in fact, it screws up my whole theory. What it looks like, of course, is that someone *was* after Bootsie. If the gaps caused by the disappearance of her medical record didn't do her in, maybe somebody would give her phenol by mistake, since it was just sitting there in the OR. And if nobody gave her the phenol, then on her way out of the hospital, a gang war would erupt.

This makes no sense at all. I can't even fit Jette, my new favorite suspect, into it. I give it a try, though. Jette *does* have a brother. I have no idea what he looks like. I assume like Jette, but he could resemble Elvis. But he lives in Deer Trail.

This was such a dumb stunt to pull. That's the part that doesn't fit. Jette's smarter than that.

Although Jette was here when the phenol case unfolded at

the hospital across the street. Jette was here when an employee exiting from the parking garage was wounded in some gang cross fire. And she's not here now.

Harley pounces on me the moment I walk into Admin.

"Great, Vicky. Langstrom's in his office with the cops and he wants us both in there, but nobody knew where you were."

I counter by grabbing Harley and dancing him into his office, where I shut the door. "New wrinkle," I say. "Some of Gifford's kids met a guy who wanted to start a riot, Saturday afternoon, as soon as either Dennis's or Bootsie's car came out of the back parking garage."

Harley does a perfect what-me-worry expression of surprise.

While his mouth's still open, I go on. "What I think is that somebody was trying to *make it look* like Dennis was involved. That is, working on the *extremely improbable* theory that someone purposely left phenol in the OR, to raise suspicion, and someone purposely caused Bootsie's EMR to disappear, to raise suspicion, and that same person *pretended* he was Bootsie's husband and he wanted to make Bootsie go away. You follow?"

Harley shakes his head.

"I got a description of the guy and it's sure not Dennis."

Harley nods.

"I think I should tell this to the police."

He shakes his head. He must be getting woozy. Then he finds his voice. "Not yet."

"Don't you see? If anything, this *exonerates* Dennis, not that there's anything to exonerate him from."

"I need to talk to him."

"There's no time! You said the police are in there right now!"

Harley swallows. "Don't tell them yet." He opens his door, straightens his shoulders, and buttons the top button of his blazer before we parade into Langstrom's office.

Langstrom introduces us to two uniformed policemen,

whose names I instantly forget, and a plainclothes detective. *Very* plain clothes. Tan slacks, black T-shirt, flannel jacket, mud-encrusted boots. Detective, not Captain, LeFevre. We all sit down around Langstrom's nice glass-topped table.

Langstrom rubs his hands together. "Always glad to help out our men in blue," he says. "Although I believe it's somewhat premature to be talking at this point."

The uniformed cops look at each other, and I get the distinct impression that Langstrom lied to me, that he called them, not the reverse. But I'll go along with his fiction.

"So this is about our corporate attorney who's disappeared?" I say brightly.

"She's our other attorney," Langstrom adds, even though he already said that when we were introduced. The cops smile politely.

LeFevre clears his throat. "The doctor's wife," he says. "Mr. Langstrom here said you have information that we might be interested in."

"Not at this point." What else is there to say?

Langstrom frowns.

The cops go on to establish that there is no evidence of intentional malfeasance. I rattle off a long string of the tests we are doing—blood chemistry, gas chromatography, CT scan, electroencephalogram, magnetic resonance imaging—using the biggest words I can think of at the moment. They don't like it that we don't know exactly when whatever it was happened. Of course, we don't like that either.

"Could someone have slipped her a substance during surgery or afterward that would cause this kind of reaction?"

"That's possible, although not likely." I sound like a doctor! "But we've found no evidence of that. And it wasn't a reaction, but more a failure to react."

"Whatever. This happened, or I should say was discovered in the area patients are taken after surgery, right?"

"The recovery room, yes."

"Somebody could have sneaked in and gotten to this lady in the recovery room?" LeFevre asks.

"That's not very likely," I assure him. "The staff keeps a pretty close watch on patients as they're coming out of anesthesia."

"So it's more likely it happened in surgery."

"I haven't found any evidence of that, either."

"Well, which is more likely?" the detective asks. "What I mean to say is, how did this happen?"

"We don't know." A nice safe thing to say, as I tell all my doctors who are being deposed: If you don't know, just go right ahead and say you don't know. I didn't realize quite how hard it was to do. Langstrom sits there and lets me deal with it. Even though it makes me sweat profusely, it's probably better that he keeps out of it.

"Hmmm. This recovery room, is it in the same part of the hospital as your emergency room?"

I feel a little prickle of something. "No, they're separate departments."

"So the recovery room is a lot more secure than, say, the emergency room?"

Damn. He knows about the Tanzanian cabdriver. This means that the whole police force knows about the Tanzanian cabdriver.

"Very secure," I say. I try to appear less tense and wait for him to say something about the cabdriver.

The detective smiles a twisted smile. "It might be helpful to us to have your notes," he says to me.

"That's a good idea." Langstrom sees me shaking my head and adds, "Why not?" I guess he didn't read my memo. So I run through it again, telling him and the police, who probably know it anyway, why my notes are privileged.

"I don't know about that," the detective says.

"I can give you cases," I say. "But look, we have every intention of working with you. We will call you at the first indication that a crime has been committed. That's why I said this meeting was a little premature. We have no such indication." I stare into LeFevre's eyes. If he gets the feeling I'm holding something back, well, he's right. I'm holding back the planned riot, and I'd just as soon tell him about it.

"You've had a lot of bad things happen here lately," LeFevre says conversationally.

"It probably seems like it," I agree. Hell, yes. "But . . ." I stumble. I don't want to say that bad things happen here all the time, nor do I want to say they almost never happen. God damn Langstrom anyway.

Langstrom doesn't say a word. "But . . ." I stutter again. "Um, Ms. Wakefield's disappearance is probably not related to her work for the hospital, so you couldn't really count that. So there's just the one incident, and we are working diligently to determine if our procedures were followed, and from what it looks like, they were. . . ." Damn it, I sound like a liar.

Detective LeFevre stands first, then the uniforms, who *haven't* said a word during this interview. As we're shaking hands, LeFevre asks one last question. "The victim's husband, does he happen to be around?"

"He's probably at his wife's bedside," Langstrom answers.

17

Fastball

After the cops leave Langstrom's office, Harley and I stare at each other for probably a full minute. We're like a pitcher and a batter trying to see into each other's head—at least that's what I'm trying to see into. Am I going to defy him and pitch my fastball, and if I do, is Langstrom going to hit it out of the park? Do I tell Langstrom about the rent-a-riot deal? Will he call the cops right back? Odds are, he will.

Harley could be wondering if I'll mention it. I wonder if he *wants* me to mention it so that he doesn't have to, or if he wants me not to, because Dr. Law and Order Langstrom will report it. Of course, it *should* be reported.

Harley said don't tell the cops. He didn't say don't tell Langstrom.

"This hospital," I say, shaking my head. "We need a full-time cop coordinator. You know, somebody who just deals with all our cases that involve the cops, so we're all on the same page."

"What a good idea, Vicky," Harley says smoothly.

Fuck! I should keep my mouth shut. I was only trying to break the tension. I think he means to write this into my job description.

Then I have an even more horrible thought: It's probably *already* in my job description.

Then I decide that he's merely pointing out to Langstrom that I should have handled this and Langstrom should have stayed out of it. At this point, the head games get to be too much for me. In revenge for what I think Harley was thinking, I open my big mouth once again and tell Langstrom what I learned from Gifford and the two boys.

He sighs and runs his fingers around his collar. Harley's mouth sets in a thin line.

"You know, I don't *like* having police in our hospital," Langstrom says. "Not unless it's absolutely necessary. But once they're here, they should be apprised of all the facts."

"I'll notify them." I duck under Harley's glare and head for the refuge of my office.

I cool off first by making nasty phone calls. One to an attorney who filed his client's complaint three days after her statute ran out; this is why I check. Of course the lawyer, who probably took this on contingency, argues with me. A call to yell at our outside counsel, the one who messed up those relatively simple interrogatories a couple of days ago.

Finally I call the police dispatch number, identify myself, and say we had a riot planned for Saturday but it didn't happen and do I need to notify anyone? The dispatcher thinks about it for two seconds and says she doesn't think so, then puts me on hold. Tristan comes to my door clasping a few pages to his breast. I motion him in and hang up the phone.

18

String of Zeros

"Guess what," Tristan says. "I got into those files you wanted. I mean, I didn't get into the files, but I got them printed." He hands me a stack of papers.

"Good job," I say, glancing at them.

"I had to write the file name on them with a pen," he says. "So you'd know which one was which. Oh, and I didn't read them."

Sure, I believe him.

"Did you get some lunch?" I ask.

He makes a face. "My mom packed something. Tuna fish. I ate it at about ten. I hope it was okay to eat it in the office."

"No problem." I dig around in my purse. I come up with a five-dollar bill and spend a long moment considering. Is this too much? Enough? Does it look like a bribe? Does it look like I should give him more? If I give him more, will he realize how important this is and blackmail me? And, finally, *is* it important? I won't know until I read it.

"Oh, no," he says, shrinking away from the money. "I just did it for fun."

"Go to the cafeteria and get something else to eat," I say. "Don't worry, it's not like school-cafeteria food." I don't think. I can't recall ever eating anything from a school cafeteria. "Or there's a Burger King down the street. McDonald's, Taco Bell."

"Hey, no." He edges closer to the bill. "Really. It didn't even take me very long. I got lucky." I continue holding out the five. He shoves his hands into his pockets, then pulls one out. "Uh, thanks." The bill disappears into his pocket. He goes back into Jette's office and I sit down to peruse my loot.

As loot goes, it's not much. The file that caught my attention—the one Jette saved at 9:57 on Wednesday night, after the eating disorders dinner and before disappearing—was directed to Dennis.

To: Dennis Devoss, M.D.
From: Jette Wakefield, Esq.

I have always thought that putting "esquire" after your own name is cheesy and have resisted doing it. But I'm seeing it more and more.

Subject: Medical Records Security

Dennis—

God, I love that breezy way she just gets right into it.

I've spoken with Barney Newman in IS, and I've consulted the following journal articles, attached hereto as Exhibits A through D, regarding tampering with/security of medical records.

"Attached hereto." You gotta love it.

Re: My conversation with Barney, he has authorized me at the Administrator level, which will enable me to track any activity, authorized or not, in EMRAM, via a program called SATAN. It will give the user ID, the files/records accessed, and state whether or not a change was made, or even if they were merely viewed. However, two things are notable. The first is that this access situation will give me access to not only the date the record was accessed . . .

Reading this, I realize that Jette would have given it another edit before sending it off. All those accesses.

The other significant factor is that this Administrator status will enable me, or anyone so authorized, to also note unauthorized accesses. The authorized accessee . . .

"Accessee"? Izzat a word?

. . . will show the seven-digit access code along with initials. Unauthorized users will show up as a string of zeros, but their terminal code will identify their identity.

Unauthorized users will show up as zeros. And then they can get their identity identified. Yep, she definitely would have given this another edit.

Okay, it's just a memo. I'll bet she password-protected it so nobody could read her lousy first draft.

A test run indicated that, interestingly enough, even as I write this, there are two users without access codes around in the system. Barney explained that, for instance, if someone is entering keystrokes too rapidly, they could end up in EMRAM by mistake and be pretty much stuck there. In that case, they would call IS for help in getting unstuck, or else they would turn off their computer . . .

The memo ends there. That could be the point when she realized she could identify the location of at least one of the unauthorized users. She didn't say.

And I have to show this to someone. It indicates that Jette intended to come into work on Thursday. Only she didn't.

For another, it hits on an issue that may be material in the investigation of Bootsie Devoss's bad outcome, owing to the disappearance of Bootsie's EMR.

Could Jette have created the mischief in Bootsie's EMR and then come up with this scenario to cover her tracks? I don't think so, or she wouldn't have slapped a password on this file, but I don't know.

Why would she be messing around in Bootsie's EMR? The only thing I can come up with is, *she* was having an affair with Dennis and wanted Bootsie out of the way. This is pretty lame. After all, she has that nice boyfriend up in Laramie. And the medical record information, while unavailable to me, was readily available to Bootsie's doctors, so what would have been the point?

I debate whether to go into Jette's office and dig around for the journal articles. I sure wish she'd mentioned them by name; all I know is that there are four of them. I'll do it later, when Tristan isn't in there.

SATAN.MEM is pretty much the same. It has a general roundup of what the program does and why the program should not be resident in our system for long: because it exposes vulnerabilities. It, too, is incomplete.

TIME.SHT is just what it sounds like, a timesheet, in table form, of attorney time and clients, similar to those kept at law firms everywhere. Except this isn't a law firm. Jette's corporate counsel and she doesn't have to log her time. I scan the list. She didn't provide a narrative of what she was doing, but she does have names, dates, and times. In quarter-hour increments. It goes back two years. I don't recognize any of the times. I wouldn't even think it was this year's timesheet, except that she last saved it on 4/7, Wednesday night. After entering "Lassiter—.25," I presume.

Work on the side? Work that could have gotten her into trouble? Judging by the entries, not a lot of work, but maybe this is something that should be shared with the cops. And I need to ask Hawkeye if maybe she was doing something for him since Lassiter is his last name. I run down the list of other names. Quite a lot of them, but none look familiar. Jones, Quinones, Randolph, Griego, Chynowski, nothing that strikes any kind of chord, except there's one Sloane. Could this be Harley? I'll have to check.

The other password-protected file, TOGO.GAY, is directions to someplace. She doesn't say where. She doesn't give an address. I don't toss it, because it could be pertinent. It looks like some kind of poem. Damn, I wish she'd included the address. Maybe that's where she is!

Think, Vicky. She has the address in her address book, so she doesn't need to write it down. But why put a password on a file like this?

I feel a headache coming on. I start massaging my head, i.e., pulling on my hair. Then I quit. I've just decided this practice is *giving* me headaches.

Somewhere in this office we have a Denver street guide. I don't know why we have it, but we do. I step outside my office and ask Anita if she knows where it is.

"Why do you need it?" she asks.

Why does she need to know why I need it?

"To look up an address," I say, somewhat snottily. "Do you know where it is?"

"What address?"

"I mean the street guide."

Anita whirls her chair around, yanks open a file cabinet behind her, pulls the guide out, and slams it on the ledge of the secretarial corral.

"Thanks," I say, wondering if maybe Anita could benefit from some hormone therapy. I take the guide into my office, where I laboriously look up the area in question. Another dead end—literally. Following Jette's directions, you'd end up in a cul-de-sac.

And it's way the hell in the suburbs. Talk about a string of zeros.

I take the guide back, opened to the page, and ask Anita if she knows anything about this neighborhood.

"I live there," she mutters.

"Here?" I point to the map.

"I live on the other side of the highway."

"But this is residential, right?"

Anita gives me a look.

"Okay," I say, "here it is. I found these directions in Jette's directory and wondered if they meant anything."

Geri pipes up. "In Littleton?"

"Yeah." I read off the directions, which sound much more poetic when spoken aloud.

Geri makes a face. "My friend Gayle," she says. "She was having a Kitchen Magician party and Jette said she might be able to make it, so I gave her directions. She didn't get there, though."

"Oh." So a dead end both figuratively and literally.

"See," Anita says, "you could have saved yourself a lot of time and trouble by just asking us."

Uh, right. I start back to my office, then get another bright idea. Since they seem to know everything, why don't I ask the assistants what, if anything, they've heard about Dennis and any possible affairs.

I stand by Anita's desk and lower my voice. "Okay," I say, "in you guys' expert opinion, is Dennis Devoss kind of a flirt?"

Instant confirmation. "Oh, lord, yes," Anita says. "A few years ago I was in charge of hiring a secretary to work for him and I just had the worst time."

"She sure did," Vanessa drawls. "She wouldn't hire one girl because her blouse was too low-cut. Didn't want to lead the good doctor into temptation."

"That girl looked like a slut," Anita says, as if it happened yesterday.

This fits. Of course she wouldn't want to lead anyone into temptation.

I notice that Vanessa is avoiding eye contact with me. Good grief, is she one of Dennis's conquests? I wouldn't put it past her. He's a powerful man; she likes powerful men.

She's one of the best players of office politics I've ever seen. Along with Jette.

This is not a compliment exactly.

"So there's a trail of broken hearts?" I direct this question to Vanessa.

"You'll have to ask him," she purrs. "I don't know anything about any broken hearts. He's not an ass-grabber, anyway." Vanessa sets her purse on her desk. Anita attacks her keyboard.

"But I'll tell you this," Vanessa says. "If I *were* going to have an affair with a married man, he'd be high on my list. Not to marry, you understand. But an affair."

Like Bebe said. I go back into my office and sit at my desk, eavesdropping as Geri belatedly joins the conversation. "He's a cutie, all right, and he is kind of a flirt."

Vanessa says something in reply, probably something catty.

"Well," Geri says, "a couple of months ago, I heard him tell Jette that his wife was going to be out of town. In fact, he said it twice."

Another inaudible reply from Vanessa.

"Yeah, she was driving her daughter back to college after Christmas break and then spending a couple of weeks with friends in the east. He made a point of it. I wondered."

I wonder, too: Is Geri implying that *Jette* is one of Dennis's conquests? That would fit my theory perfectly. Too perfectly.

I wonder how come my radar didn't pick that up.

"There was just something strange in the way he said it," Geri says.

This time I hear Vanessa's voice, as she's walking out. "He's the kind of guy who throws out a lot of lines. Who knows whether he pulls them all in?"

Catch and release. I bite my lip and lay it out to myself.

Jette has an affair with a high-level physician. I recall the softening of her hairstyle and yet another new diet. The Lent diet, which always followed the New Year's diet. Jette devises a plan to tamper with the medical record of her lover's wife.

This could work. The medical record thing was something she was working on with Dennis, and under top-secret conditions. A cover for them both?

Somehow I can't see Dennis throwing Bootsie over for Jette. I realize this exposes my prejudices.

Anyway, to follow this thought: Jette screws up her attempt, or maybe she thinks she's successful, so she leaves town.

Man, this theory has all kinds of holes in it. The chief one being, Jette disappeared *before* Bootsie's bad outcome.

I should show her memo to Dennis. He has other things on his mind, but maybe he'd remember something new and helpful if he saw the memo. Or maybe he'd have some kind of reaction that would tell me . . . something. Anyway, the memo has his name on it. I grab the printout and head up to the ICU, hoping to find him there.

19

Terminal Code

Brian Marrote comes out of ICU just as I get there and tells me Dennis is holed up in his office with the cops.

"What lousy timing they have," he says. "I just told Dennis things don't look good. I don't think Bootsie's going to come out of this."

"She's taken a turn for the worse?"

"We've just found out more. The CT scan showed a massive brain hemorrhage that's affected significant portions of her brain. I'm afraid we waited too long before doing a quick surgery. I think if we'd gotten in there two, three hours post-op, we could have identified the source of the bleeder and cauterized it, but now it's too late. The brain just doesn't recover from those kinds of insults."

"So she was misdiagnosed?"

Dr. Brain rubs his face. "We didn't do the MRI until very late in the day. It simply took too long to realize there was any problem." He pats me on the shoulder. "Don't worry. Your experts aren't going to find anything amiss. Everything looked absolutely normal when she came out of surgery. If we'd done the MRI right away, we'd have seen it, but there was no indication for an MRI at that time. That's just my opinion. It may have happened hours later. Anyway, she was checked at appropriate intervals. I've gone over the whole record myself. The only question is whether Bootsie should have had the plastic surgery, because the only piece of information we didn't have—that she passed out inappropriately a couple of weeks ago after having her teeth cleaned—she didn't provide. She made the decision not to provide that, probably because she knew that would delay the surgery."

"Somebody knew. I saw a note in the file when I was going over it on Sunday."

"That was my note," Dr. Brain says. "Dennis told me about the fainting incident, also on Sunday, and I wrote it on the chart. I'm sorry. I should have done it more formally and dated it."

I nod. Yes, he should have. Now it could look as though he's covering something up himself. Except why would he do that? There's no reason. If he'd wanted to cover it up, to protect Dennis or for whatever reason, he wouldn't have made the notation at all.

But wait. Dennis had wanted an exploratory surgery done. Dr. Brain hadn't wanted to do it. For a good reason—he hadn't wanted her to go under anesthesia again. Does this exonerate Dennis or the reverse? Neither, I decide, and at this point it probably doesn't matter.

"So what happens now, to Bootsie?"

"We'll see what happens when she's taken off the respirator," Dr. Brain says. "We've been artificially suppressing some of her brain functions for the tests, autonomic responses, and she may be able to respirate on her own. If not, we have an advance directive not to prolong it. No so-called heroic measures."

"And if she breathes?"

"People have remained in a coma for some time. Years. Although technically, once they're breathing on their own, it's a persistent vegetative state, absent total brain death. She would, of course, still require the feeding tube, but her directive is to continue nutrients and hydration."

"Oh."

"Her body will function. Her hair and nails will grow. She will move, and possibly she will even vocalize. Her eyes will be open part of the time, but whether she will see anything or not, we just don't know. We think not, but we're not absolutely sure. And she could remain in this state for years."

"That's pretty bleak. That's what you told Dennis?"

"Right. But there's still the outside chance that she will regain more function than that. She could have, for instance, the intellect of, say, a six-year-old. I can state with some authority, though, that she will never be able to function independently again."

As I walk back to my office, I feel a deep sorrow for Bootsie—and for Dennis. But I don't feel it inside. It's more like it's walking next to me. I won't cry for Bootsie now. I'll cry some other time—hearing a stupid country-western song on the radio or reading in the newspaper about some tragedy that happened to people I never met. This is how I deal with it, and how I've always dealt with it since the first case that hit me, back at Boston City. We had a little patient, six years old. He was burned over sixty percent of his body, but he was doing well, healing. His mother, who had sacrificed her face and her right hand to get him out of their firetrap apartment, sat at his side and talked about trips to Disneyland, baseball games, camping. We all thought he would make it—but he didn't. He succumbed to an infection, and he went quickly.

His mother was physically unable to weep. But even as I comforted her, I wondered why I wasn't crying myself. I went about my duties as if nothing had happened. I couldn't get him out of my mind, yet I functioned efficiently. As if I had a heart of stone or as if I hadn't cared. For days. And then, in the supermarket checkout line I was reading a magazine (*Redbook,* a mother's story about her baby being misdiagnosed as retarded) when the tears started flowing to the extent that I felt duty-bound to buy the magazine.

Other nurses deal with it in other ways. Some of them, in fact, just go right ahead and cry. Of course they do tell you in nursing school that you don't want to get too emotionally involved with your patients, and that works, to a point.

I stop in my office to make a phone call that is quick but comforting, then head into Harley's lair, with the memo to Dennis still clutched in my hand. If I can't show it to Dennis, I'll show it to Harley.

He's on the phone, which is par for the course in our office. I wave at him, go back to my office, and reconsider. What does this memo tell me that I didn't already know? Only that SATAN could be used both to unearth security breaches and to breach security. Oh, and it demonstrates Jette's intent, as of 9:57 on Wednesday evening, to be in her office on Thursday.

What Harley could get from this memo is that I corrupted an innocent youth and broke into the system to get it. He will wonder what else I'll do in pursuit of my ends. Not that they are my ends.

I wonder if I could find out, one way or another, which terminals were being used at the time of the medical records break-in. If Jette could identify it, I'm sure the Information Systems people can. But can they do it one week later?

I call IS and tell Regina I'd like to find out who was on the system last Wednesday night, or at least find out who Jette had tracked down.

"We uninstalled that SATAN program, if that's what she was using," Regina says.

"I think she was in EMRAM." I read the note.

"Sounds like she was looking at EMRAM, via SATAN. I'll check with Barney, but I'm pretty up on the diagnostics. It's a tedious thing, though. Is it important?"

I don't even know. "I think so. Yes. Doesn't our system track all accesses?"

"It does now," she assures me. "But while we had SATAN running, a sophisticated user could have gotten in without a trace, which is why we've uninstalled it."

"Wouldn't it be a pretty big coincidence that during the one period of a few days when the system was vulnerable, some sophisticated user got in and used it and left no trace?"

Regina snorts. "Haven't you read *The Celestine Prophecy*? There's no such thing as a coincidence."

"But Jette could tell whose terminals were on, last Wednesday."

"She knew who it was?"

"I don't know. Maybe she just knew where it was. The terminal. There was a terminal ID."

"Ohhh," Regina says. "But you don't know which terminal."

"That," I say, gritting my teeth, "is what I'm trying to find out. She said something about a string of zeros."

"Well . . ."

There's a long silence, during which I bite my tongue. Finally Regina speaks.

"Maybe two hundred of these computers are hardwired into the system. The rest of them are like your computer, they have a hard drive and you can run them stand-alone or hook into the network. But the hardwired ones do give a terminal ID. So if she saw a terminal ID it must have been hardwired."

"Yes!" I'm beginning to wonder if Regina is as smart as I thought she was. If she said what I think she said, this narrows it down to one of two hundred instead of one of thousands.

"So maybe it's on the backup record," she muses. "As a string of zeros."

"Yes! Yes! That's what I'm after. I hope I'm not a week too late."

"You might be just in time," Regina says. "I'll see what I can do. Throw some fairy dust on it or something."

"Whatever it takes." I hang up, feeling drained. Throw back my head and see Harley out of the corner of my eye. I stand up.

"Vicky, I was on the phone with the cops. They found Jette's car."

I sit down again.

"They tried to call you, but they got your voice mail, so they transferred to me—"

"Just her car? Not Jette?"

"No Jette," Harley says. "This is not great news."

"Where?"

"Somewhere up north," Harley says. "In an isolated area near the Wyoming border. Some balloonists spotted it early this morning and called it in when they came back to earth."

"A ranch near the Wyoming border?"

"Didn't I just say that? The cops are sending a team up there to see what they can find, and they'll keep us posted."

"Was the car wrecked?" My mind is moving fast. Maybe she *was* going to Laramie.

Harley shrugs.

"I'll bet that boyfriend did it," I say. "Flew down, then drove her out somewhere, killed her, then hopped back in his plane—"

"Vicky," Harley says, "slow down. She could have had car trouble and gone for help."

"It wouldn't take her six days to find help. Did the cops call her brother?"

"I don't know. That detective said it was a progress report and asked if we had learned anything further."

"Shit." Is this progress? "They're sure it's her car?"

Harley shakes his head. "It's a car that matches the description of her car, whatever that is. Forest green or something. Which made it hard to see."

I stare at my nails and decide I won't tell Harley what I found in Jette's locked files. Instead I say I'm going out for a bit.

"Don't even think about going up there," Harley warns.

"I hadn't thought of it." It's beastly of me, I'm sure, but my comforting phone call was to my hairdresser. I said I was desperate and if I couldn't get in today, I was going to take my desk scissors to those fucking bangs.

"I'm going over to see Derek." This new idea just blossomed in my brain, but it makes sense. He's at Jette's, in Cherry Creek; my hairdresser is also in Cherry Creek. And it sounds so much better than telling Harley I'm going for a haircut. He doesn't need to know that. He'd say I could do it on the weekend, only I didn't *have* a weekend.

I call Derek from my car. Yes, the cops called him, but they told him he should not attempt to visit the scene. He's not going to let the Denver cops boss him around. He's on his way out the door.

"This makes sense. She was dating a guy from Wyoming," he says. "A rancher. My guess is she was on her way up to visit him and her car skidded off the road or something, and she decided to hike for help."

Why does everybody think Jette would hike for help? And that once she found it, she'd remain incognito all this time?

Jette is methodical, not impulsive. For instance, she would never decide on the spur of the moment to go get a haircut. She probably scheduled her appointments months in advance.

I call Randall Cryer in Laramie again, hoping he will have mellowed somewhat. The phone rings for the duration of my search for a parking spot, at which point I hang up. Then, for the next forty-five minutes, all I have to do is sit while someone fusses over my hair. Just what I needed.

My relaxed mood wears off quick. On my way back to the office I get stuck in traffic. What is it with all these *cars*? Denver never used to have traffic like this. A few bad intersections, but what *is* this shit? It's not even rush hour.

Although, at this rate, it will be rush hour by the time I get back to the office.

I sit, inhaling fumes and being overtaken repeatedly not only by a woman striding along purposefully but by a homeless man pushing a shopping cart not very purposefully (a cat person if ever I saw one).

Since it's not fulfilling its intended use—to let me know if there are flashing lights behind me—I twist the rearview mirror to study my bangs, and they are . . . *too short*.

It's times like this when I see the apocalypse, and it's one giant fucking traffic jam, with irate drivers, noxious fumes, honking horns, and sirens. I'm thirsty. I have a headache. I need to pee. My bangs are too short. This has to be hell. The ancient beast from the pit is, of course, fossil fuels. Phillips 666. I guess that makes Henry Ford the Antichrist.

I don't even have a nice relaxing tape to plug in. I hit the radio, and who's playing? Traffic, what else? The group, not a report.

Then, just as the jam breaks up, my phone rings. It's Melinda.

"What in the hell is going on at your hospital?" she asks. "You're making news, even way up here."

I steer with my knee, the knee of the leg I *don't* use for the clutch, while I turn the radio off, the better to hear her. I need one more appendage here. Or an automatic. "The usual," I say. "It's a shit job, but somebody's got to do it. And not only that, they cut my bangs too short. What did you hear?"

"The police are investigating a link between the disappearance of your nemesis there and the death of the wife of one of your top doctors."

What! I've been absent from my duties for only an hour and twenty minutes. "They called her my nemesis?"

"No, dummy, *I* called her that," Melinda says. "Sorry about your bangs, by the way."

"And Bootsie *died*?"

"That's what I heard, yes."

"Jesus. You'd think somebody would have paged me."

Then I calm down for a minute. What am I thinking? The media never get it right. And it doesn't sound like Melinda's talking about newspapers anyway; she must be listening to talk radio.

Great; she got all this information and all I got was "The Low Spark of High-Heeled Boys."

"Maybe I heard it wrong. It was just a shock to hear about your hospital on the radio. But it probably shouldn't have been *that* much of a shock, given it's your hospital. . . ."

Oooh. Nice one, Melinda.

A drunk stumbles into the street in front of me. I swerve and change lanes, then curse. I'd honk, but my hands are full. But that's okay. Somebody else honks.

"So when are you coming back?" I ask.

"Maybe next week," Melinda says. "I told you this case has tentacles. There must be twenty lawyers working on this, so you can imagine. It's getting worse and worse. We keep breaking things down into smaller and smaller pieces and then the pieces just . . . grow."

I wrestle the car around a corner using my elbow. "You should have a cat," I say. "Then you would have a reason to get back home on weekends."

"I'd get twenty speeding tickets," she says. "The Wyoming fuzz will give you speeding tickets when you're stopped at a light if you have Colorado plates and are driving a Porsche."

"Hey, are you anywhere near Laramie?"

"Vicky, it's a big state. No, I am not anywhere near Laramie. If I was that close, I would come home."

"Can I borrow your house? Glenn has his kids this weekend and we might need a place to go."

"Mi casa es su casa," she says. "Of course."

I turn onto the street that leads to the parking garage and almost broadside a Channel 9 van. "Oh, shit!"

"You just hit somebody?"

"There are camera crews in front of the hospital." This is never a good sign. I thought we weren't going to have a press conference. Was there a shoot-out? Was Melinda's information accurate?

Hell, it could even be something brand-new.

"Oh, man," Melinda says. "Well, you've got your hands full. As usual."

I pull into my parking spot and turn the key, the wrong way, so that the ignition makes a loud *skrunk*. I guess the key turned in the other direction in the rental car.

"Jeez, Vicky, what did you do to your car?"

"I turned it off."

"No wonder your cars catch fire and things," Melinda says.

After I hang up, I sit for a minute, listening to the pops and creaks of my car cooling off—and yes, making sure there isn't any smoke coming from anywhere. Then I shoot upstairs to find out what in the hell is going on.

It's kind of anticlimactic. Nothing is going on. Nolan, Dennis, and Harley stroll into the office, talking calmly. I feel kind of a surge of hope, looking at Dennis. He doesn't look like a man whose wife just died. He doesn't even look like a man whose beloved wife is in an irreversible coma. He's in his typical business attire: sharp white cuffs, gray pin-striped suit, dark tie with blue stripes. He even got rid of the dandruff. Dennis and Harley go into Langstrom's office. Nolan follows me into mine and perches on the edge of my desk.

"What a press conference," he says.

"Press conference?"

"Yeah, Vicky, one of those things where reporters and people like that come and ask questions and we answer them . . ."

"I know that!" Jesus. Did Langstrom watch me leave and then call the press? "I thought we weren't going to have one. Low-key, I thought we said. Nobody told me."

"There's a reason for that, Vicky. They ran out of duct tape."

Ha-fucking-ha. I can keep my mouth shut as well as the next person. What Nolan is probably alluding to is, at one press conference—*years* ago—somebody asked a question and I jumped in with a "Don't answer that!," which looked pretty stupid, but I can assure you, it was preferable to letting them answer the question.

It is true that at every press conference I've attended on behalf of this hospital, somebody has said something he or she shouldn't have, and apparently I writhe when that happens, which encourages the reporters.

"So how did it go? What was the point?"

"It was great, Vicky. I'll bet you haven't even seen the papers this morning."

"*Au contraire,* but so what? They already got the story, why come here?"

"Because Langstrom thought they weren't getting the whole story. So he called them. Then he called me."

Aha. A picture begins to emerge. Langstrom is the sort of person who needs someone by his side at all times saying, "Don't answer that! Don't *do* that!" He's a great one for saying he's done something, like offered to give a high-admitting physician from another hospital some kind of splendid incentive—like a Jaguar—to bring his or her admissions here instead and then asking if there's any kind of legal problem with what he's just done. And then, when I tell him there *is* a legal problem, he gets pissed off at *me*.

Apparently it's the same with Nolan. Instead of going to Nolan and saying we've got a situation, should we hold a press conference, he fucking calls the press!

"Dennis made a great speech about how he was confident everything that can be done is being done and he has faith in the staff and he feels no one is to blame," Nolan says.

"Well . . . good." Something bothers me about this, but I can't articulate what it is. "Was that Langstrom's idea?"

"I think it was Dennis's idea," Nolan says. "At the end, they also asked about Jette."

"How do they know about Jette?"

"They listen to the police band. What they asked was if it was related. Weird question."

"Really weird question," I agree. "They didn't ask if she's been found?"

"You are out of the loop," Nolan says quietly. "They found her."

I process this. Melinda, in Wyoming, must have heard this live. She just confused the victims.

"Oh." I feel numb.

"Anita fell apart, so Harley sent her home," Nolan says.

This makes sense. Anita is so close to falling apart at any given moment, it doesn't take much.

"I would at least have expected Harley to look sad or something."

"Yeah, well." Nolan raises his eyebrows. "We're guys, what can I say? It's not like we expected her to come bouncing back in here apologizing for her unforeseen absence, is it?"

I shake my head. Somehow, all of us knew, when she didn't show up last Thursday, that we'd never see Jette again.

"Foul play?" I ask weakly.

"They didn't give us details," Nolan says. "They were asking the questions, after all. We were the ones with no answers."

20

Eulogy for Jette

I don't know how Vanessa does it, but she's the only one who, when she buzzes me and talks through the speaker, does not sound like some fuzzy-voiced teenager at the Burger King drive-through.

"Dr. Langstrom would like to see you in his office, if you have a minute."

"I'll be right there," I shout in the general direction of the phone.

"And do you know where Nolan is?"

Nolan shakes his head rapidly. What's he gonna do, hide out in my office? "He's in here, too."

Nolan makes his long face even longer, then sticks his tongue out at me. I jerk my head in the direction of Langstrom's office.

Vanessa stands at the door of Admin with her coat on, as if she's only waiting to steer us into Langstrom's office. "The phone's going to the switchboard," she says. "I got fed up with all the calls. I'm going home."

Langstrom is pacing and biting his lip. "We should have some sort of memorial thing for Jette," he says. "Nolan. Did you get the bit about the reward into your press release?"

"Yeah," Nolan says. "But I didn't get the press release out until after the balloonists had notified the cops. And now I've got to do another one."

"Deflecting all inquiries, of course, until we know that Derek's been informed," I say.

"Absolutely," Nolan says.

Langstrom nods and paces some more, then turns to me. "So, will we have to give these balloonists the reward?"

He's got me there. Jette was the tactician; she would know this. Not only that, she would have known all the contingencies before the reward was even offered. As soon as a reward was mentioned, Jette would have been asking whose budget it was coming out of.

"If they know about it, and ask about it I think we should pay them." I'm thinking karma here. "I don't know the exact legal position on something like this, but we have to think about community goodwill. Whose budget would it come out of?"

"A very good question," Langstrom says. "What was it again? A thousand dollars?"

Nolan and I glance at each other.

"Five thou," Nolan says.

"They may not ask," I add.

Langstrom paces some more. "I guess it's the thing to do," he says. "Even though her car was located before the reward was offered."

"You said yourself we should have offered it days ago," I say.

Langstrom glares at me. "Now. Next item," he snaps. "Can we run our flag at half-mast tomorrow?" He looks from me to Nolan, then back to me.

As a lawyer, I guess I should know this. As a former Girl Scout, I definitely should know this. I don't.

"I don't know," I confess, and look at Nolan.

"Me either," he says. "When it's a cop, or a president, or a state employee—"

"Then the city or the state raises the flag to half-mast," Langstrom says. "So if it's a hospital employee who died in the line of duty, then we should be allowed to raise our flag to half-mast."

"No, you raise it all the way, then lower it," I say. At least I remember that. I'm beginning to think we should fly it upside down.

"Where's Harley?" Langstrom growls. "He probably knows who's in charge of raising the damn thing."

"This is our country's national symbol we're talking about here," Nolan says. "That is, with all due respect, sir, it's not a 'damn thing.'"

"Sorry," Langstrom says.

"The grounds crew, I think," I say. "I'll find out about the protocol and let them know."

Langstrom leans back against his desk and folds his hands in front of him, a gesture that looks about as natural as if he suddenly turned a cartwheel. "Forget the protocol. Just tell them to lower it," he says. "If the governor decides for the state and the mayor decides for flags at city buildings, I think I have the authority to say that flags on hospital buildings hang at half-mast, and that's where they'll hang."

They don't hang, they fly. Or maybe they do hang.

I call the grounds crew from Vanessa's desk. I get some dumb schmuck who asks if we're lowering them on account of it's tax day, so I have to point out that we're lowering them because *Langstrom said to*.

Geri listens to me make the call. She seems a little dazed. Anita didn't work for Jette, but she got to break down and go home. Vanessa didn't work for Jette, and she got fed up and left. But Geri, who not only worked for Jette but who had a prior relationship with her, is still here, sitting at her desk. Not crying or anything.

"Geri?" I say, considering the possibility that she may be in shock.

She turns and smiles thinly.

"You should get out of here, too. I think the office is closed."

She nods. "But I'd just have to wait for my bus, anyway. I might as well stay here."

"Okay. If you're okay."

"I'm okay. Really."

I think she's in denial.

"It's interesting, isn't it," she says, "that the police haven't told us anything, but we all think somebody killed Jette. Don't you find that interesting?"

I draw my breath in. "Well. She wasn't old enough to die of old age. It wasn't cold enough for her to die of exposure. She didn't . . . um . . ."

"She certainly didn't overtax herself running a marathon or anything," Geri says.

I realize I've never heard Geri say anything bad about Jette. Not only that but she's come down on me a few times when I *did* say something bad about Jette. She must be in shock.

"No," Geri says. "Everybody's pretty certain somebody did her in. It's the natural thing to think. But why? Because she was a vile, low person, that's why. I mean, I worked for her because she was smart. But she was also vicious."

"She was a hard person to work for sometimes," I agree.

"A lot of people didn't like her," Geri says. "I mean, practically nobody liked her. But on the other hand, if I ever wanted to harass somebody, to intimidate them, to drive them crazy, to throw everything the law had at them, I'd hire Jette."

"I know what you mean."

Geri leans back in her chair. "There are a lot of things you guys didn't know about her," she says. "For instance, you knew she didn't get a lot of work done. But she was doing work on the side. She called it her pro bono work—that's a laugh. She ran a little business through here, although she mostly did it from home. I got to be in charge of sneaking her the office supplies."

I consciously slow my breathing down. "Anything that . . . do you know who her clients were?" Did I keep that copy of her TIME.SHT?

Geri twists her face into a smile. "Everybody's respectable," she says. "That is, everybody who called here. Small collection firms like Equitable Recovery and a couple of other places like that. The guy I talked to at Equitable used to work for the hospital, guy named Alvin Bales. Remember him? He sent stuff over when he needed a lawyer's signature, and Jette signed it— for a cut. I mean, she didn't draft it, she probably didn't even read it. Just signed it. Every once in a while she had to show up in court on a case, but not real often. She'd get people on the phone and scare the bejesus out of them. And, of course, she wasn't supposed to be doing that."

This isn't as bad as I expected. I wanted to hear that she'd been into dummy corporations and money laundering, things that could give someone a real reason to whack her.

"A lot of lawyers do that," I say. "They don't get killed for it. Do you know anyone who hated her enough to kill her?"

"Maybe," Geri says. "You know those instructions you found, and I said they were to my friend's house? Well, they weren't. We had a party who was being real hard to serve. So Jette made me do it by pretending to deliver flowers. I mean, I had a nice bouquet. It's a gated community, so I told the guy at the gate I had these flowers and he called the house. Took it up to her house, rang the bell, read the card, asked if she was that person. Then handed her the summons." Geri shakes her head. "You know what Jette said? She said don't give her the flowers. But I did leave them."

I close my mouth.

"The lady probably threw them in the trash. She was so mad. Remember when Plains Hospital changed its name to Plains Regional Medical Center? And Jette got a restraining order, claiming they were falsely advertising because they were just a piddly little hospital, not a regional medical center, and that delayed their use of the name by eighteen months? Probably cost them around twenty thousand or so in legal fees."

"And they weren't even a competitor," I say. "But I doubt that Plains put out a hit on her."

Geri laughs. "To Jette, everybody was a competitor. And then she filed corporate names on all these things that we *might* be using someday, everything she could think of. Like Executive Wellness, Executive Lifestyles, Corporate Health, Executive Health, Community Health. Just a whole bunch of trade names we probably aren't ever going to use, so no one else can use them."

I had thought of that as a good business move.

"But when *she* got a cease and desist for the in vitro clinic, Little Miracles, from some adoption agency, she wrote a nasty letter back saying we were using the term and if they didn't like it, they could assume the costs of the litigation to stop us."

Sometimes I have to marvel at Jette's proficiency at legal intimidation. Often it seemed to me that the reason we didn't fire her was that then she'd be working against us rather than for us.

Whatever works.

"Anyway, she made enemies," Geri says.

I get the feeling that this is as close to a eulogy as Jette's going to get.

"Is there any way I could get into her files and find out who . . . else . . . she might have been working for?"

Geri shakes her head. "I already looked. She kept most of that stuff at home. Oh, she's got the Rule 369 interrogatories on file, so she can whip them out if she needs to." These are the nasty postjudgment interrogatories that demand information on the location and nature of any assets you might have, so these things can be seized to fulfill the judgment. "But she didn't have names. Not here. Probably at home."

"Maybe I should talk to Alvin Bales." I don't want to. He's a twisted little man with a twisted little mouth, and he's hard to talk to.

"Don't," Geri says. "He'll know where it came from and, frankly, I'm afraid of that guy. Particularly now that I don't have Jette around to protect me anymore. And don't get me wrong. She took good care of me." Geri leans back again and gazes at the ceiling. "Remember when I got the DUI?"

"Yeah."

"It was my second one. I was going to lose my license. I wasn't really drunk—just unlucky. But I'd been through it before, and I knew to just turn over my license and refuse the test. So that way they don't have a criminal charge, nothing they can prove, but you still have the hearing at the DMV and you lose your license. So what Jette did . . . it was beautiful. She called the Aurora cops, asked for the guy who nailed me, and told him she was somebody from DMV—she used the name of a real person there, I think—and that the hearing date had been vacated. Gave him the new date, cool as you please. So he didn't show up for the hearing, and I didn't lose my license. Didn't have to go to drunk school, didn't have to pay a fine."

"Wow," I breathe.

"First she gave me the name to use. But I didn't have the nerve. So she did it. She called. She could have lost her license for something like that, couldn't she?"

"It was good of you not to mention this until she was dead," I agree. "You didn't, did you?"

"Of course not. And, uh, I go miles out of the way to avoid driving through Aurora anymore."

I'll bet.

"Yeah . . ." she says dreamily. "So, Alvin Bales. He's an investigator, not a lawyer. It hardly ever gets to the point where you need a lawyer. Not with a slimebag like Bales on your case. But when it did, there was Jette. With the legal arsenal."

I'm fascinated. I've known for months that Jette was into *something*. I just didn't know what.

"Geri, go home," I say. "The office is closed. Get out of here. Take tomorrow off, if you want."

"Yeah," she says, still seeming vague. "No, I'm coming in. I want to see that flag hanging at half-mast."

21

Comfort Foods

Waiting for the elevator, I consider the new possibilities. I'm going to have to talk to Bales or somebody else is going to have to. Yeah, somebody else. I'll give him to the cops.

He's twisted physically, as I said, with a tic that pulls his head around to one side. He walks with a limp and sometimes uses a cane. Worst of all—at least for me—he has several missing teeth. And he spits when he talks. And he thinks he's hot shit.

I got trapped into talking with him for about twenty minutes one day when he was waiting for Matt Vanlandingham, the VP of marketing, to show up. He babbled nonstop about how wonderful he was and the great things he was doing for Matt—to wit, a whole bunch of stuff that to me sounded barely legal. Shortly after that Matt fired him.

I run into Hawkeye while waiting for the elevators. "Terrible news about Jette," he says, peeling the wrapper off a Snickers bar. Apparently he is no longer worried about his own health. "I'm gonna go home and eat comfort foods."

"Me, too," I say, though I was thinking along the lines of vodka.

I probably don't have any vodka. I'm not the sort of person who goes home and pours myself a stiff one. I'm the sort of person who hits the bar on the way home. And why not? It's on the same block. Very handy. I'd rather let somebody else buy the liquor and mix the drinks, while I sit there, listening to the jukebox and observing the other patrons. I'll leave a nice tip. All I have at home, usually, is wine.

At Christmas all the hospital brass—Langstrom, Harley, Matt Vanlandingham, and even Nolan—were gifted with bottles of this and that. Tullamore Dew, Glenfiddich, Southern Comfort. *Big* bottles. We girls—even Jette—got flowers, candy, food baskets, and certificates to day spas. Not that I'm knocking gift certificates to day spas, but I could get into a bottle of Tullamore Dew. Sexism strikes again.

I park my car and think about the bar. It's on my block. Very convenient. The bad news, first about Bootsie, then about Jette, and even about Catgirl, has shaken me in strange ways.

I don't want to go to a bar by myself. I guess happy hour has ruined me.

I knock on Glenn's door, even though his car wasn't parked in its space in the garage. No answer.

I open my door and am met by—surprise—Tara, aka FrankenCat, who has been waiting for my return so she can ruin my panty hose, since she missed them this morning. She does this by rubbing her stitches against my ankles. I've heard this is not affection; the cat wishes to mark you with its scent. I look at my ankles, to see how badly shredded the stockings are, and see a trail of feathers. She caught a bird?

Oh, no! She caught the pheasant feather in my fedora. Goddamn cat.

I defuse my hostility toward the cat by picking her up and examining her stitches. "You're healing well," I tell her. "You little survivor, you." I put her down and head for my stash. She follows me, meowing.

I pull out another sample packet of IAMS cat food. I think this stuff is essentially cereal with meat juice. I pour it into the chipped pink dish on the floor. Tara sniffs it, stares at it, then resumes meowing.

The hell with her. She can eat this stuff or she can starve. Where's my booze?

I have two bottles of red wine, which I don't feel like drinking. A chilled bottle of champagne, which I *really* don't feel like drinking. About half a bottle of fake Kahlúa, which somebody I know makes using instant coffee and who knows what else. It tastes lousy, both on its own and mixed with other things, but it might have to do. And—aha—a Cuervo tequila bottle with a couple of inches left. I feel my spirits lift somewhat just finding it.

I don't have anything to mix with it. No orange juice, no sweet-and-sour mix. I don't even have a lemon, although I do have some salt. I pour the tequila into a small glass, stare at it for a moment, then drain the glass and pour another.

At this rate, it's not going to last very long. But tequila is not something you sip. Perhaps there's enough here to get me past my resistance to the fake Kahlúa.

Ugh, not the fake Kahlúa! Next thing you know I'll be hitting up the aftershave.

I take the second shot over to the phone and call Melinda's hotel in Riverton. The phone rings three times and then is picked up by the desk. I leave only the brief message that I called and then hang up, feeling bitter.

If I were an alcoholic, I'd probably feel like I just hit bottom. A little tequila, a little fake Kahlúa, and for companionship a damaged cat.

Said cat leaps up onto the counter and sniffs my glass. I

remove her. My nursing training kicks in and I handle her gently, although I'd like to throw her against the wall. I think about all the bad luck that's crossed my path since she did. Bootsie. Jette. Arinda. Even Lindy, the marathoning doctor. I gulp down the second shot. That's almost a woman a day for the last five days. The tequila makes me feel like it's all this cat's fault. I unscrew the bottle and pour enough tequila to coat the bottom of the glass. At this rate I have about two shots left. Why bother with a glass?

Because tequila, when taken straight, must be taken in a single gulp. I add a little more to the glass, then remove myself and the glass from the vicinity of the bottle. I pull a chair over to my French window and stare down at rush-hour traffic.

The cat, apparently not tuned in to my hostility, leaps onto my shoulder from behind me, claws her way down my front, and plants herself in my field of vision. I knock back the tequila and stare at the glass and think about getting some more. Then I have another idea.

In the depths of my closet there is an old purse, and in this old purse there is—maybe—the last vestige of my real stash, a pinch or two of sensimilla.

The stash used to be much bigger. It used to contain a wider variety. For instance, I always used to have a small quantity of coke. Not that I used a lot of it. It made me feel good to have it around, in case I needed it.

Coke—just a little of it—made me smarter, braver, more coordinated, and better looking. Several months of drug therapy failed to convince me that I could successfully live my life without it. I finally disposed of the last of the coke last fall, when I dated (briefly) a cop and resigned myself to a lesser life. But I kept the pot, because what the hell, it's just pot, and not very much of it. And here it is, more than I remembered. A tablespoon or two in a baby-food jar. Along with some ZigZags so old that the gummed strip has lost most of its stickiness.

I sit on the bed, uncap the jar, rub the product between my

fingers, and then roll it (clumsily) into a joint. It's not the tightest joint I ever rolled, what with the difficulty of getting the edge sealed, but it will do. I light it, inhale, close my eyes, and hold the smoke in. Ahh.

Marijuana does not make me smarter, braver, more coordinated, or better looking. It just makes me not worry about it so much—except the times when it makes me worry about it even more. With a head start of tequila, I'm sure this won't be one of those times.

I stroll back to my window, coughing at the harshness of the weed, and have another hit. Tara follows me like a hallucination.

There's a knock on my door, followed by the sound of a key. Polite Glenn; he knocks, then enters, sniffs, and shuts the door quickly.

"Vicky?"

I've been drug-free the whole time he's known me. Drug-free—I hate that term.

"Do I smell what I think I smell?"

I giggle. (Good; it's working.) "Hi," I say. "I've had a hell of a day. You look cute."

Cute is probably the wrong word. He's wearing a light blue shirt, a dark gray suit with chalk stripe, and a tie with various bright colors swirling through it. Not a real conservative tie. I fixate on it. "Cute tie."

"Cute?" He frowns, looking even cuter.

I exhale with a series of small coughs. "Oh, dear. Caught by a federal agent," I mutter.

"Knock off the federal agent bit, please," he says, looking even more serious. "I don't want to be reminded. I'm having a pretty bad week."

"Oh, have people been dropping dead where you work, too?"

"I don't work in a hospital." He shrugs out of his jacket and stands there a minute with it in his hand. Then he reaches up and loosens his tie. Then he drapes the jacket over a chair. As he turns, I note that his shirt has come almost untucked in the back, which I find quite fetching.

"Tell me about it." I say this as a meaningless phrase, a form of punctuation. He takes it literally.

"I'm in this office, right? These people are not being investigated. We were looking into another company they did a joint venture with, and they had some records we needed to see, so I went over to their offices to have a look."

He removes the tie. His hair, which is blond, very fine, and thinning, is combed straight back when he leaves in the morning. It has loosened and is falling over his forehead. Charming.

"We kept telling them, you are not under investigation. But—I don't know—maybe they have something to hide." He reaches out, takes the sorry excuse of a joint, and takes a hit. "Boy, it's been a long time."

"I'm shocked. What would the IRS say to one of its agents taking illicit drugs?"

He exhales smoke and hands the joint back. "*I'm* not going to tell them. Anyway, I'm not an agent, I'm an accountant. So they put me in this tiny little office. I think it's the janitor's closet. With a table about the size of those desks you have in grade school. Like so." He approximates with his hands. Yep. Small.

"Heaped with papers, but all the wrong papers. It's like they are daring me to investigate *them*, not their old joint-venture partner. And there's not enough room even to set my laptop down."

It still sounds better than people dropping dead or going into comas every time you turn around.

"And nobody talks to me. Usually, when I go into an office like this, people are not exactly friendly, but they aren't hostile. This place, it's like I'm the invisible man. But I sit there all day, trying to get what I need." He takes the joint again, looks at it, then hands it back.

"Usually, in fact, people are nice to you. Usually they have a room set up with a phone. People have installed a separate phone line just for the IRS auditor. These folks seem to be hiding something."

"So investigate them," I say.

"I may recommend that we do just that." He runs his hand through his hair. It falls back, even more engagingly, over his right eyebrow. "So what's happening at your hospital that's so much worse than usual?"

"They found Jette," I say. "Dead, that is."

"Ah, baby." He reaches for me, takes my hand.

"The cops haven't told us any of the circumstances. They never do."

"Because you're all suspects." He massages my shoulder. "I have an idea."

And I just know it's going to be a great idea. The hand on my shoulder is having much the same effect on me as one of his kisses . . . but then he surprises me.

"A great night for a ride," he says. "But you'll want to dress warm. A sweater. Leather—I know you have a leather jacket. Not the coat, that would be too long . . ."

He's finally going to get me onto his motorcycle. And I have no resistance left.

22

Joint Venture

It's mild outside, but I follow his advice and dress warm: the snagged tights, which were still lying on my bed from this morning, topped by my red leather pants; a black turtleneck, topped by my leather bomber jacket.

"I've known you to dress faster," Glenn drawls from my bedroom door.

"You—wow," I say, looking at him and marveling at the change. He still looks cute but in a much different way. Talk about changing your persona. Amazing what jeans and a many-zippered black jacket can do that a chalk stripe can't. The crowning touch is a black knit watch cap.

"You've got an outfit for every occasion," he says. "I'd advise some shoes, though. And gloves."

Right. I put on my Keds high-tops and answer his black knit cap with a cashmere beret. I don't ordinarily wear it because it makes my head sweat, wrecking my hair.

He hands me a helmet. "An extra brain bucket," he says. "I don't think it will help, but it's like a seat belt or belief in a higher power. Can't hurt."

Unlike a seat belt, a motorcycle helmet is not mandatory. But it's mandated by Glenn. "Since it's my machine, you *will* wear it."

"Will it fit over my hat?"

"It's adjustable."

The helmet makes me feel like a space cadet. As I strap it on in the garage, I have a fit of paranoia. "I'm a little drunk."

"Luckily you aren't driving," he says. "Or did you need to throw up?"

"I don't throw up."

"All right then. Hang on. We're off."

We swoop out of the parking garage and then head down Grant. It's like a different city from the one you see in a car. Less remote and more personal.

It's been ages since I rode a motorcycle anywhere. Glenn's has a lift in the back, so I can sort of see over his shoulders. But we still can't talk or listen to music.

As we zoom out on Eighth Avenue and negotiate the turn that takes us to Sixth Avenue, I fall into the thrum and vibration of the motorcycle. Once we're on the highway and going fast, I appreciate the gloves. But the helmet removes one of the things I used to love about riding motorcycles, the wind in my hair.

Still, as we speed toward the mountains and I look at the glittering city behind us, I realize that this is what I need. Something entirely different.

We take Sixth Avenue to I-70, then turn on I-70 and go up Lookout Mountain road, heading to Buffalo Bill's grave. The night air is chilly up here, but a blast of icy air must have been what I needed. And an opportunity to turn off my conscious mind, blow out the cobwebs. We roar up the mountain, past the park that houses the Buffalo Bill museum, and head down the other side, negotiating hairpin turns at just the right speed and getting occasional glimpses of city lights in the distance.

I needed the distance.

We pass a couple of darkened parked cars. Couples necking or drinking beer—or both. Some things are much better suited to cars; we stop only for a moment. During this pause, we don't talk. Lights twinkle from the windows of downtown buildings. I visualize cleaning crews going through them, vacuuming and emptying trash. On Seventeenth Street, accountants are working late because it's tax time and associate attorneys are working late because they have to maintain their billable hours. East of downtown, in the hospital district, patients are being settled in for the night. Interns are grabbing a bit of sleep. Vitals are being checked, drugs are being tallied, dishes are being washed. I lean against Glenn's back and hug him. All during the ride I've been holding on to him a little tighter than I need to.

As we head down to Sixth Avenue again and back to Denver, I realize what I need to do.

I need to find out who Jette discovered breaking into EMRAM. That must have been the last person in the hospital Jette saw. Maybe the last person she ever saw. If he or she hasn't come forward by now, there's a good reason for it.

I'll have to call IS, talk to Regina, and tell her it's more important than I had previously thought to track down that terminal. And if IS can't do it, there must be some other way to get it done. But how?

There are ways to find out who was working that night. I know this because I've had occasion to collect copies of time cards. This time, though, my usual straightforward procedure of marching up to people and asking them things won't work.

On the way back, we get in sync with the wind. We glide into the city. I tell myself that everything is going to be easy.

We push our way exuberantly into my apartment, where:

That cat is nuzzling and drooling on the absolute last of my marijuana, which she has knocked out of the jar and spilled on my bed; and

The phone is ringing.

Completely sober, I pick up the phone. I can feel surliness in my body language and hear it in my voice.

I don't say hello. I snarl a "Yes?" into the receiver.

Two things happen simultaneously. Glenn lets out a gleeful yelp. "Hey, what was that you were smoking? Catnip?"

And Harley says into my ear, "Vicky? I'm on my car phone. I just heard that the cops arrested Dennis."

23

Law and Order

Harley, it turns out, got his information from a ten-second news update on the radio on his way home from his son's soccer match. He has no further information. He's now home and his TV's tuned to 9News, which promised an exclusive.

"Nobody called you or anything?" I ask.

"No. Nobody called you either?"

"I don't know. I was out. I just walked in the door." But even as I say this, I'm checking my caller ID. Nobody called but my poor neglected friends, who I never have time to talk to anymore. If not for them, I would seriously consider ripping this so-called convenience out of my life.

"Do you think maybe you should go over to the hospital?" Harley asks.

I snort into the phone. "Whatever for? Dennis is in jail, not the hospital. Anyway I've had too much to drink." I feel sober, but there's always the blood-alcohol thing.

"Just to check things out," Harley mutters. "I guess it was a bad idea. It seems like somebody should *do* something."

"I'll call you if I hear anything." Not that I'm going to hear anything. I'm not even going to try.

"Something going on?" Glenn asks as I hang up. "By the way, whatever that stuff was I think you can kiss it good-bye."

"I don't even think I'll kiss it." Tara is sprawled on the bed, looking extremely relaxed. Her food bowl is empty.

"Do you have to leave? I could drive you," Glenn offers.

"I'm not leaving. But I think I'll watch the news."

We watch the talking heads until they show a clip of Dennis, flanked by two uniformed police officers, walking away from his house. Or somebody's house. Anyway, not the hospital.

"This is it, right?" Glenn says.

"Yeah. The guy whose wife is in a coma."

"Did he do it? Like that famous case from years ago? Sam Sheppard?"

"I don't think so." Sam Sheppard? Isn't he married to or maybe divorced from Jessica Lange?

"Police today arrested Dr. Dennis Devoss, the head of Montmorency Medical Center, on suspicion of attempted murder. Dr. Devoss's wife, Barbie Devoss, remains in a coma following surgery at her husband's hospital...."

"Her name is *Bootsie*," I say, both to the screen and, as an aside, to Glenn.

On-screen, Dennis looks into the camera for one startled

moment. He doesn't try to hide behind a clipboard or anything. He just looks away.

I take small comfort in the fact that they got Bootsie's name wrong. That means that, just possibly, everything's wrong.

Then they cut to a reporter standing outside of Montmorency, at the Medallion. "LIVE," the screen proclaims, as if there's some benefit to standing outside the hospital's bad piece of sculpture at 10:15 P.M.

"The arrest follows the news that Montmorency Medical Center's head of legal services, Jette Wakefield, missing for several days, was found dead earlier today in a secluded area. . . ."

"Oh, my God. They're making it sound like Dennis had something to do with Jette," I say. "Those bastards."

"Sue them," Glenn suggests.

It's a quick clip and then on to other news. A quickie follow-up interview with the husband of Lindy Fogg, the dead thirty-seven-year-old marathon runner, who adds the information that she was a onetime Olympic contender. Not as a runner. As a skier.

Not a good week for local doctors.

I flip to another station, but for all I can tell the TV station was right about one thing: It was a 9News exclusive.

My phone rings immediately. I was expecting it. It's Nolan.

Another big difference between Jette and me is that I have gone out of my way to make myself available to practically everyone. I draw no boundaries between work and my private life. Jette did. No one would call Jette at home except in the direst of emergencies. The only time I ever tried it was last week.

"Those fuckers," Nolan says. "They are supposed to fucking call me before they air something like this!"

"You're kidding. . . ." He sounds like somebody in a Quentin Tarantino movie, unusual for Nolan.

"I mean, those assholes didn't even give me the complimentary heads-up," he says. "Wait a minute. Did you see the news?"

"I saw it, I saw it."

"I'm going to call them up and raise hell," Nolan says. "Plus, I think the dickheads got it wrong. I don't think they arrested Dennis. I think they just took him in for questioning."

"Same thing. I didn't see if he was handcuffed—"

"He was not handcuffed," Nolan says. "I taped it, of course. I wonder who tipped them off."

"They get the police band. Remember?"

He echoes Glenn's thought. "Can we take some kind of legal action against them? Libel? Slander?"

Jette would have had some good legal trick, I'm sure.

"Hey, Eeyore, there's nothing we can do tonight," I say. "We can do that if it turns out he wasn't arrested. But not tonight. So just calm down and get some sleep."

"Sleep? I want to nail their fucking carcasses to . . . to . . ."

"The Medallion?"

"Yeah."

"Just relax, Nolan. We'll deal with it tomorrow." Tomorrow promises to make today look like a holiday. "What's that thing you always say? There's no such thing as bad publicity?"

"Hah," he says, and hangs up. I click the television off and then turn the phone ringer off.

Glenn and I climb into bed as routinely as an old married couple. He doesn't even ask, as he usually does, if he should go back across the hall to his own place. I don't know if this means anything.

"I don't think your cat likes me," he says.

"It's not *my cat*." Maybe I could give it to Maurice, the homeless guy. He could always use another cat. "What, hasn't it shredded any of your clothes? Hasn't it drooled on the last remnants of your marijuana?"

"No, she just disappears whenever I'm around."

"So stick around," I say. There's a long pause while we cuddle.

"You mean that?" he asks after a moment.

"Yeah," I say. "And not because of the cat." A few more moments of silent cuddling.

"We're practically living together," he says.

"Ah, not really." We aren't sharing a closet.

"I'm hardly ever in my place. I think maybe we should look for a place together."

"What's wrong with this?" It's ideal. Same address but we each have our separate units. Glenn doesn't like that it's a low-rent joint in a bad neighborhood, where gunshots ring out in the night.

"Like I said, I'm hardly ever at my place. You know."

"I've never lived with anyone." It *is* strange, I know, to be almost thirty-seven and never have shacked up with somebody or been married. Still, lots of people *never* get married.

"Why haven't you?"

It's a valid question. "I guess—well, I'm impatient. I think maybe I'm more of a sprinter in the relationship field. But you—you have a history of long, stable relationships," I say.

"Just one. I told you we got married too young. I don't know that it was all that stable, but it was long, yes."

"See, you hung in there. I admire that. You went the distance."

"Not exactly," he says.

"Come on. Fifteen years? That's practically a marathon."

"Sprinters," he says, "can adapt themselves to become distance runners much more easily than the reverse."

"Really?"

"It's true. In fact, it's what happens to a lot of runners as they mature." As they *age*, he means. "There's a lot to be said for hanging in for the long haul."

"There's a lot to be said for sprinting, too. For instance, if you're trying to outrun somebody, it's better if you're a sprinter." You would think we were really talking about running here.

"Hmmm." He rolls over onto his back. "I'm not sure that's true. I've heard that distance runners eventually outrun sprinters. Well, of course they do. When the sprinter runs out of steam."

"But by then . . . well, take this example. You're a distance runner and somebody who's a sprinter is after you. Sure, maybe you can outrun him eventually, but meanwhile he's *caught* you."

"But if you're a sprinter," he says, "you can't run forever. The distance runner will outlast you. Anyway, I think we've lost the metaphor."

No, we haven't.

24

Get Out of Jail Free

I forgot to turn off the ringer of the cordless phone by the bed. As a result, my sleep is interrupted by Langstrom, of all people. And it's not interrupted in the middle of the night although it seems like it. No, it's 5:30 in the morning, and of course I *should* be up at that hour, so I do my damnedest to pretend I am.

Langstrom tells me he gave Dennis my cell-phone number, because Dennis is allowed to call his lawyer anytime. From jail. I guess this means he *was* arrested last night.

Rats. We can't sue the news station for slander.

"I'm not Dennis's lawyer."

"Why not? You're the only lawyer we've got," Langstrom says.

"I don't know criminal law that well." My mind reaches back to grasp the last bit of criminal law I studied, about two hours before I took the bar exam.

"Dennis is not a criminal," Langstrom says. "I feel very deeply guilty that he's being treated this way. I suppose I shouldn't have called in the police."

"Probably not."

"But it was your report that convinced them."

Sleepy as I am, I hear two things in Langstrom's statements. First, he'd lied when he told me the cops had contacted him. As I suspected. Second, despite my protests, he showed them my write-up. Probably even gave them a copy.

"But they didn't *see* my report." This is a test.

Langstrom flunks. He coughs, a guilty cough if ever I heard one.

"They did, somehow, get their hands on your report. Well, it was inevitable that they would."

"Well." It's awfully early to have to deal with things. But if not now, when? "I'll be happy to talk to Dennis. I'll do anything I can to assist him in obtaining a referral to qualified counsel." Sheesh. I don't even have to be in Langstrom's office to start talking this way. I don't even have to be *awake*.

"We'll talk about it when you get in," Langstrom says.

I drag myself into the shower. FrankenCat is still sleeping off her marijuana binge. I scrub and shampoo and wonder how it is that Dennis has ended up in jail. Rich people do not end up in jail even when they commit heinous crimes. And I still don't believe Dennis has committed a heinous crime.

I think of a man I know named Raymond. A lawyer and real estate developer, Raymond also owns a hotel, several bars, and a couple of strip joints. He's really old, but has been known to show up at society galas with multiple dates—like five of them, whose combined ages don't even add up to his.

Raymond has two things going for him. He's very, very rich. And he's likable. Eighty million dollars and, probably, eighty zillion friends. One of his ex-wives turned up dead during a highly publicized squabble over family business interests, somehow passing her voting shares along to Raymond in the process. Two of the ex-wife's children (Raymond's stepkids) felt quite strongly that Raymond had arranged their mother's death. There was some evidence besides his stepkids' suspicions. Eventually there was a trial. He was acquitted.

Now I don't know that Raymond killed his ex. However, he benefited, not just from the shares, but from an old insurance policy. During all this he wasn't even disbarred. And he didn't spend one *minute* in jail.

As far as I know, Dennis would not benefit from Bootsie's death. There's no evidence against him. Anyway, she's not dead. Yet he's in jail.

And I can't be his lawyer. Still, I can't help wondering what they've got on him. They must have unearthed something—and it's sure nothing I have. But it's something I need.

I step into a tailored Jones New York pantsuit and debate whether to wear my fuchsia Escada jacket or stick with the good old Eddie Bauer coat.

Since it's windy as all get-out, I bypass Escada and go for the leather.

By the time I'm ready to go, FrankenCat has roused herself from her pot-induced stupor and is bouncing off the walls. I pour some food into the dish and notice that the few crumbs left in the dish from the night before have attracted a stream of ants. Goddamnit. Ants! I have got to get rid of this cat.

But the first thing I have to do today is talk my way out of being Dennis's lawyer. I start in Harley's office, where, before Harley even says a word, I go through it point by point. I am not a criminal lawyer. *No one* takes me seriously as a lawyer. Exhibit A, I submitted a report with CONFIDENTIAL ATTORNEY-CLIENT WORK PRODUCT written all over it. Fat lot of good that did; the cops have it. Furthermore, I represent the hospital, not the individuals in the hospital. For me to represent Dennis would be foolhardy. It might also be a conflict of interest.

"The courtroom lost a great advocate in you, Vicky," Harley says. "Hey, I'm with you. You don't have to convince me. But I think you should have at least accompanied Dennis to jail."

When he sees my expression, his serious one vanishes. He laughs. "Hey, caught you at a loss for words. That's rare."

I keep my composure. "I assume you mean I should have accompanied him to turn himself in," I say. "That I should have gotten in between him and the cops and we should have carried the whole thing out in a dignified manner."

"Well, yeah. That's what I meant. That would have been a much better media moment for us."

We both stop to consider the footage: our esteemed colleague and high official of the hospital, flanked by uniformed police as if he were a big escape risk. His hands were not cuffed; he habitually walks with his hands behind him, as if deep in thought. But it *looked* like they were cuffed, and appearances are everything. I have to admit, it made a very effective media moment. Hell, I'd have run it if it were my station.

"Okay, well, go down to the jail and get him out. You can do that much without being his official lawyer, can't you?"

Sure, Harley. But I'd like to wait until he calls me.

I return a call from Jette's brother. He sounds exactly the same as he sounded yesterday. He was on his way up I-25 when the cops stopped him. They broke the news in the gentlest way possible, but they haven't yet told him the cause of death. His sister—his other sister—is here now, too. She can't get anything out of the cops either. Can I find anything out?

That's an interesting question. I'll do what I can.

I consult my Rolodex, consult a map (learning, in the process, that Jette's car was found on the route to Laramie), and then call various numbers in Larimer County. I finally learn that Jette's body was taken to Poudre Valley Hospital for autopsy. After a little more Rolodexing, I call an old nursing friend of mine who works there; she says she'll find out what she can.

I look out the window, where the flag is flying, not hanging, at half-mast in a stiff breeze. What now?

I've got the IS number half dialed when Harley appears at my door and jerks his thumb in the direction of Langstrom's office.

I precede him in where, for Langstrom's benefit, I once

again enumerate the reasons why I can't represent Dennis. I hit it hard that I represent the hospital and that it could be a conflict of interest.

"Bollocks," Langstrom says. "That's only if he did it, and I am one hundred percent sure he did not."

"Still, it's a conflict," I say.

"It's in the hospital's interest to have him *well* represented. To tarnish the image of one of our head doctors is to tarnish the image of the hospital."

"I can't represent him *well*," I counter. I don't add that the image of the hospital is pretty well tarnished already.

"As his attorney, you will have access to whatever they've got on him," Langstrom says.

Yeah, I'd thought of that myself.

"Okay," I say. I can masquerade as his lawyer until we can find a better arrangement. "Down the road he's going to need someone who knows the territory, but I'll do what I can now."

Groucho said it best: These are my principles. If you don't like them, I have others.

Then I go into Harley's office. He asks, right off, who I would recommend as a criminal lawyer.

"Brett deVries," I say. I realize that this name probably jumped into my consciousness because of its similarity with the name of the accused: Devoss, deVries. "He's kind of cocky but he's really good."

"A cocky dude'll do," Harley says. I look for something to throw at him.

Brett was one class ahead of me in law school and went straight from there to the DA's office. (The one and only coke-snorting DA I've ever known, although I'm sure there have been others.) After four years he switched to criminal law, joining a small firm with a good reputation for representing people with bad reputations, and he's been golden ever since.

When I ran the legal aid clinic, he did more pro bono work than any other lawyer who has a practice. He won every case I referred to him.

I stop by the supply cabinet to grab another notebook.

"You're pushing it," Anita says.

I count them off on my fingers. "Assault by hussy Wendy Wyeth on cabdriver. Assault by said hussy on Environmental Services worker. One for liability pertaining to potential claim by family of hussy. One for disappearance of Jette. One for bad outcome of Bootsie Devoss. One for defense of Dennis Devoss. And a spare in case anything else happens."

"Can you tell me why you can't just use one up, then start a new one?"

"I might need to find something pertaining to one case in a hurry. I'd have to index it."

"God forbid," Anita says. "Lawyers!"

I make several calls—one to Brett deVries, one to another friend of mine from law school who has a very eclectic practice that includes criminal law, and one to Ken Sharpe, my favorite outside counsel, telling him what I'm up to here. When I come out, the assistants are again discussing legal pads in the files.

"Sometimes there are about a half-dozen in Jette's files. Each with the first two or three pages written on," Anita goes on. "It drives me crazy! Why can't she just fill one up?"

"Who knows?" Geri says.

They ignore the fact that Jette won't be filling any of them up now. I guess this is how they are going to deal with it—talk around it. I choose that moment to leave.

My own preference is spiral notebooks, which take up even more space in the files.

At the city jail, a woman with four-inch fingernails fumbles with the paperwork and X-rays my purse and my briefcase, then goes over me with a metal detector. They make me leave my scissors, a fork, and my cell phone. Fortunately, they don't ask me why I have dinnerware in my briefcase. I came to a fork in the road and picked it up?

I spend about half an hour in a dingy, depressing waiting room. The only other people waiting are a couple of women with babies crawling all over them. After a while I am summoned to another room, where several women are visiting with their incarcerated boyfriends, husbands, brothers, fathers, sons through glass with telephones, and am told I have ten minutes.

"Wait, wait, wait," I say, "I'm Dr. Dennis Devoss's attorney. I need to speak to him in confidence."

The jailer, a baby-faced guy with a lot of keys, purses his lips. "Oh, well, we got that wrong," he says. "Follow me then."

Nobody takes me seriously as a lawyer. *Nobody*. I glance back at the dismal visiting room just in time to see Dennis led in. He's got cuffs on now, in front, and he's wearing a turquoise jumpsuit that looks a lot like scrubs. He looks depressed, especially as I walk out. Baby Face says something on his two-way radio, and the jailer on the other side of the Plexiglas backs Dennis out of the room.

Moments later Dennis and I meet face-to-face in a small room with a table, a marked improvement. Although the handcuffs have been removed, Dennis still looks depressed.

Even in a jail jumpsuit Dennis is a good-looking guy, but a different kind of good-looking. When I saw him yesterday he had had on one of his sharply creased suits. His hair was a little longer than it should have been, which looked cute. He looked like a gentleman, but one who enjoyed life.

Now he looks like an easygoing rogue. It must be the jumpsuit: not his color. Not *anybody's* color. It's short-sleeved, revealing arms with a lot of black hair. His top button is unbuttoned to show tanned skin with a lot of curly black chest hair. He looks like a happy criminal, caught by accident, except that his eyes, while they still have the crinkly laugh lines, are not nearly as merry.

"When can I get out of here?" is his first question, not surprisingly. "This place sucks."

"Right," I say. I pull out the notes from my sources, to tell him what's going to happen, but he's way ahead of me.

"First you have to be charged," he says. "They have to do that within twenty-four hours, and they take you before a judge to do it. You can get bail anytime after you're charged, so that will probably be first thing in the morning."

"You got another lawyer?" No wonder they thought I was a visitor.

"Nope," he says. "My fellow cons. They are all working on getting me out of here. And they know how it's done."

"Well . . . good." I pull out my notebook, on which I have posed several pertinent, hastily assembled questions. As he answers them, I start to feel like a real lawyer. Just what I wanted.

I have a sudden guilt attack: I wanted Jette's job, and now I'm doing it; I wanted to do more lawyerly things, and now I'm doing them. I hadn't considered the cost. I shove the guilt to one side. I don't have time for it at the moment.

"I don't know what evidence they have to hold you," I say. "It's bound to be pretty thin."

"Since I didn't do it," he agrees. "And it's a funny thing; they haven't charged me. At least I don't remember that they did."

My pen pauses, then writes, *Not charged?*

"They didn't say you were under arrest?" This was not one of my questions. "They didn't fingerprint you?"

He shakes his head. "Another thing. I was going to tell you, only I didn't have a chance. Langstrom showed me your report—with the medical record attached—and Vicky, that record is wrong. There's a sheet in there where somebody listed all these drugs Bootsie was supposedly taking. That just wasn't true. I mean, illicit drugs, bad things. Heroin, for God's sake."

"I saw that. That wasn't Bootsie's? I mean, not true?" I had figured Bootsie for a flower child. And a lot of doctors' wives, twenty or thirty years ago, did, in fact, get into bad drugs.

"She did take Fen-Phen. I think she had about four of them," Dennis says. "She had just gotten that prescription when the news started to come out on the stuff. I gave her a couple of journal articles. But the rest? Hey, total bullshit. She may have smoked marijuana a few times, but trust me, she didn't use heroin. And even if she had, she wouldn't have listed it on a sheet like that!" He's beginning to sound hysterical. "She'd have been more likely to tell the truth about her age."

"Okay," I say. "So how did that get into her record?"

"I don't know!"

"It was handwritten—"

"Not her handwriting. Jesus."

"Dennis, that had nothing to do with your being arrested," I say.

"My daughter's coming home from school," he says. "I caught her just before she left for spring break, and I'm supposed to pick her up at the airport this afternoon. She can deal with the personal stuff until I get out."

"Bail," I say, breaking into the personal stuff. I explain how it works: you pay the bondsman ten percent of the total and the bondsman puts up the full amount. Dennis knows all that, thanks to his fellow cons. In fact, he knows more than I do.

If he puts up his house, he can go up to three-quarters of a million dollars! "Only you have to have some kind of form, proving that your taxes are paid up," he says. "That's the sticking point for a lot of people, the taxes. You have to go to the assessor's office and get a certificate."

I didn't know that. I have quite a learning curve here. Once I've covered everything, I'm hesitant to leave.

"Hmmm." I take a deep breath. "Seems to me, if you were never arrested, you're free to leave. It's worth a try."

He smiles and shrugs.

"Let's go," I suggest. I stand up. Dennis stands up. I open the door.

The guard says, "Wait, you were supposed to knock when you were coming out."

"My client has not been charged," I say. "He has not been arrested. He'd like to go home."

"Wouldn't they all," the guard says, but he doesn't say it with much conviction. "He's being held as a material witness."

"We'll need his personal effects. Where would we go to get them?"

"Just a minute now," the guard says. "You can't walk out just like that."

I know we can't. There are all sorts of locked doors.

"Why not?"

"You've got a dangerous criminal there."

This is the prearraignment holding facility. Technically, everybody in this building is innocent.

"You just said he was a witness. So which is it: dangerous criminal or witness?" I ask.

The guard looks as though he'd like to lock *me* up. So does Dennis.

"It's okay," Dennis says. "I mean, we can go back in that room until this is straightened out."

"Yes, sir," the guard says. "Go back in the interview room. I'll see what I can do to get you out of here."

We go back into the drab little room. This time I hear the door lock behind us.

I sit down and cup my chin in my hands. Dennis, on the other side of the table, does the same.

"You should never have gone with them," I say.

"They didn't make that clear."

"They wouldn't." I sigh. "Maybe they'll send somebody in to question you, with your lawyer present." This idea gives me shivers. It won't be like sitting in on a deposition. I have no idea what I should do or say.

"I can't believe anyone would think I'd try to kill Bootsie," he says. "Or anyone—but particularly Bootsie."

"Is there anybody who might want to complicate your life?" I ask. "Maybe somebody whose surgery didn't turn out so hot?"

"No one has ever come after me," he insists. "In court, that is. I've been lucky. And of course I'm damn good."

"So nobody that you know of would try to get to you through Bootsie?"

"Anybody who knew me would know that's the way to do it," he says quietly.

We're interrupted by a sharp rap on the door. But it's not the interrogators, just the guard, to say he can't let Dennis out. Well, we tried.

He looks down at the table. "Somewhere along the line,

somebody got to her," he says. "I didn't think that at first. Not even when I came in here. But now, thinking about that record? Something's going on."

"Could somebody have been jealous?"

"This is kind of extreme for jealousy."

"Yeah," I agree.

We are interrupted again by the guard. "Just to let you folks know," he says. "We can hold him without charging him for up to seventy-two hours."

Dennis groans and puts his head in his hands again.

"You're kidding," I say.

"No, I just checked. It's uncommon, but we can do it. When the situation warrants."

"And what about this situation warrants it?" I demand. The guard shakes his head and exits, locking the door again.

Dennis raises his head. "They told me—the other guys—that nobody spends more than one night here."

I sigh. Then I ask Dennis a few easy questions, like has he ever been arrested before. Like anyone, he's been stopped for speeding, but he got the tickets dismissed. Rushing to a patient's side, et cetera.

At least one *lawyer* tried to use this defense, saying he got his ticket while he was rushing to court. It took the Colorado Supreme Court to reverse the county court's decision that speeding to court was justified.*

"Uh, Dennis? I hate to mention this, but one of the reasons they've probably got you here is that the police always think it's the spouse when something happens." I sigh, then take a deep breath. I look deep into his eyes. "So they look at things like who benefits if, for instance, she dies. Life insurance and like that."

"She's not dead," Dennis says, but his eyes grow lighter.

"No, she's stable. God, I'm sorry."

"Insurance. No. There's a good bit on me," he says. "She may have some from her job, I have no idea. In fact, I think she does, with our daughters as beneficiaries."

---

*People v. Dover, 790 P.2d 834 (Colo. 1990)

"Her office? Where did she work?" This ought to be on the medical record, but I don't recall seeing it.

"She . . . doesn't work there anymore, but she still owns the place," he says. He clears his throat. "Equitable Recovery. Um, it's a collection agency."

"Gee, I didn't know that." I thought Bootsie was one of those ladies who lunch.

"She doesn't tell a lot of people," he says. "She started it, well, when I first got into practice. With thousands of dollars of student loans to repay, she started calling up my patients who were slow pays. She was running my office. Only when people got really late, really, really late, she would say that she was from Equitable Recovery Systems. Which sounded more threatening, I guess. She even incorporated. She knew a lot about accounting and stuff; she was very bright. God. I'm talking about her in the past tense." He runs his hands through his hair.

I write on my pad. Equitable Recovery. Meanwhile, Dennis recovers.

Then I underline it twice. EQUITABLE RECOVERY.

"And she was good at it, damn good. She started doing it for some of my colleagues, then hired some staff, and then she pretty much turned it over to the staff after that."

"To . . ." I search for the name. "To Alvin Bales?"

Dennis makes a face. "He's . . . you know, he wasn't always like that. He got mugged and a couple of thugs worked him over pretty well."

I should feel sympathetic. Instead I wonder if he got his butt stomped because he was already a jerk.

"Bootsie wasn't ashamed of what she did," Dennis says, looking very earnest. "It started as a sideline, then it was her main thing for a while, and then when she got into other things, it just became a sideline again."

"Whatever." The picture of Bootsie gets more interesting. "So do you know how long, approximately, he's been working for her?"

"Not too long. But he couldn't have . . ." Dennis stops, scratches his head. "You know Bales used to work for Montmorency. And he was fired and banned from the hospital a few months ago. I don't think he could have gotten to Bootsie's medical record."

I remember when Bales was banned. At the time I didn't realize we could *do* that.

"He wasn't, uh, one of your patients . . ."

"God, no," Dennis says. "If he'd been my patient he wouldn't be limping."

The guard knocks, then sticks his head in. I throw him a nasty glare, but being a jailhouse guard he's impervious. "Nobody's around to question the doc just now," he says. "But you and your client are free to, uh, take as long as you want."

When he shuts the door, I tell Dennis that Jette, too, had a link to Bales.

"Good grief," he says. "And now they're both—"

"Yeah," I say.

"And he's such an unsavory character," Dennis says.

That's putting it mildly. "Where's Bootsie's office?"

"Pretty close to the hospital," Dennis says. "She doesn't go there anymore. Oh, but you want to talk to Alvin Bales."

I wouldn't say I *want* to, but it seems like a good idea.

Dennis gives me the address and I nearly go into shock. Next door to my apartment. It's a three-story office building that has been in decline—and that's putting it mildly.

I've never seen Bootsie around my neighborhood. She'd stand out. Bales, on the other hand, would fit right in, but I've never seen him around there, either.

Before I knock on the door to let the guard know we're done, I ask one last question.

"Sorry to sound intrusive. But this has been suggested, and the police will find out, so I need to know. Were you having an affair?" I practically cringe as I ask this, but Dennis isn't fazed. In fact, I get a glimmer of a grin.

"Is that an issue?"

"It might be."

"At such time as it becomes an issue, I'll let you know," he says. And the grin turns into a smile.

Almost like he's flirting with me.

25

Equitable Recovery

I get back to the office with a *long* list of people I need to call. Brett deVries again. Anybody I know who might have experience in getting someone out of jail who hasn't been arrested. Somebody who knows what would justify this seventy-two-hour hold without arrest.

It's possible to keep someone in the hospital for that same amount of time on a psych hold, if the person is considered to be a danger to himself or others. But we have to have some justification for it, and I'm sure the police do, too.

The list goes on. The IS people, to check on their progress at finding out who was logged on last Wednesday night at around 9:30. Dennis's accountant, who knows where the papers are to prove Dennis has the money to post bail—now that I know you don't just march down there with the deed to the house. Anybody who knows anything about Alvin Bales. I know just enough to know I don't want to talk to him myself.

But first I have to get by Harley, a maneuver that's gotten harder lately.

"How'd it go at the jail?"

"I didn't get Dennis out, if that's what you mean." Of course that's what he means. "But I learned some stuff," I add.

Harley follows me down the hall to my office. "What stuff?"

"A possible suspect. Remember Alvin Bales?"

"Jesus," Harley says. "That creep. What about him? Hey, you're just acting as a lawyer here, right? Not an investigator?"

I blow air through my bangs, which doesn't work nearly as well now that they're too short. "Right, but there's stuff I need to know. What did Alvin Bales do to get eighty-sixed?"

"Come on, Vicky. You know what happened with him."

"I don't know exactly."

Here's what I know: He used to work for Admin in some semi-official capacity that didn't involve his having office space. He worked with Matt Vanlandingham in Marketing as an industrial spy, although I think he had a different title. If another outfit was planning a new clinic in the southeast sector, he'd know, and maybe we could get our new southeast clinic up and running first. If some other hospital was in secret negotiations for an HMO's business, Bales would find out the details, and we could accelerate our own negotiations accordingly. Or drop them, as the case might be.

Nobody's sure how Bales acquired his information, but the general consensus is that he, like Jette, was kept on the payroll solely so he wouldn't be working against us.

Harley motions me into his office and in his roundabout way tells me Bales *was* working against us.

"He worked for us, and he had business cards saying so. At some point, he got into contract negotiations, supposedly on our behalf, with some doctors in a rehab clinic we were thinking about acquiring. AccuTech. So he's running contracts back and forth and keeping Matt from talking directly to the docs, and of course it's all hush-hush, top secret. He comes in with some contracts with the docs' demands on them, and when he pulls them out in Matt's office, out falls a business card that says he's working for AccuTech. So Matt fired him."

"Yeah." Nobody had told me this part.

"And then, in consideration of confidentiality, we banned him from the hospital. Even as a patient. That's all I know.

You might want to talk to Matt. If you talk to Alvin, for Christ's sake, don't invite him to your office."

"Right, Harley." I'm hoping to avoid talking to Bales. He wouldn't answer my questions, anyway. He's slicker than snot, and about as appealing.

"We think he might have stolen some office equipment," Harley says. "That's what we're holding over his head, to keep him out of the place. Like computers and stuff. What do you want with him, anyway?"

"Bootsie owns a collection agency." Harley's face tells me he already knew this. "Bales worked for her. He also threw some of the collection agency's work to Jette. So there's a connection with two victims, right?"

Harley's voice rises into its upper registers. "Jette?"

"Why would Bootsie hire such a person?"

Harley clears his throat. "Bootsie probably didn't. She's pretty much stepped away from that business. For years. I guess she does still own it."

"So who runs it?"

Harley shrugs. "Bales, for all I know. I mean, I don't know."

"I wish you'd told me everything about this right from the start," I say. "Does Mitch send any business to this agency?" Mitch is the head of Patient Finance.

"He sends deadbeats to lots of places," Harley says. "Probably. You'd have to ask him. Why?"

This is our chief operating officer speaking. Scary.

"Because we ban Bales from the hospital, then give his company our business? That doesn't make sense."

"I'm sure Jette cleared it . . ." Harley starts, then recognition falls over his features. "What was Jette doing?"

"Just a little side job. Some collections. Same agency. Maybe some others."

"Oh." Harley processes this. "We have a disclosure form. She didn't put this on it."

"No kidding. I need to talk to Bales." I'm hoping Harley will discourage me.

"I think we should just give his name to the police. This has nothing to do with your Sleeping Beauty investigation. In fact I thought that was pretty much over."

"Yeah. But Jette," I say. "That was the connection. Bales knew both Bootsie and Jette. I find that interesting."

Harley perks up. "You think it might take some of the heat off Dennis?"

"I don't even know why the heat's on Dennis in the first place," I grumble. "I need to go make some phone calls."

"Vicky, let's hold off on this Bales thing," Harley says. "I mean, don't tell the police yet."

"Hell's bells, Harley, why not? Look, am I investigating this or not? When do we bring the police in on this? When he's murdered someone else?"

Harley frowns.

"What's the downside of my contacting the police? You said yourself I should turn things over to them. You just suggested I give them Bales's name."

Harley shakes his head. "Your call, I guess," he says.

I'm glad we got all that straightened out.

I decide not to tell Harley that I'm trying to find out who might have been logged on the night Jette disappeared. That way, he can't tell me to let the police handle it.

What next? Oh, right, call Regina. But I don't get the chance; my phone rings.

"You're Vicky? I just had to tell you, you're wrong, absolutely wrong, about Dennis. He couldn't have tried to do any harm to anyone, let alone Bootsie! That's bullshit, pardon my French. It's crap."

Whew! "I don't think he did," I say, somewhat cautiously. "Who is this?"

Saralynn Somebody, from Radiology. "You're not the one who had him arrested?"

"I'm the one trying to get him out," I say. "Who told you to call me?"

"Oh, nobody," she says earnestly.

I would believe her, except that as soon as I hang up I get a call from Gwen Cable. She wants to let me know that she's praying for Dennis. And am I going to see him soon? Because she'd like to give him one of her prayer cards.

Gwen, a unit secretary, hands these out to people who need them: hot pink, laminated, the size of a business card. On one side is her prayer, with her copyright notice. (Yes. She copyrighted her prayer.) The other side bears the Serenity Prayer and selected Bible verses, with attribution. She gave me one when I broke my finger, to help me heal. In fact, she gave me two, but they might have stuck together.

"Who is telling people to call me?" I ask. "You're the second call in ten minutes. It's spooky."

"Nobody *told* me to call you. It was a voluntary thing. The word is you got him arrested, but I didn't believe that."

"Uh . . . well, thanks. Hey, do you want a cat? A nice black cat, only a little damaged." I should have been asking *everybody*.

Gwen laughs. "No, thank you, sweetie, I have birds."

Then my cell phone rings. Since it rings somewhat less frequently than my desk phone, I give it a higher priority.

"Helloooo," I sing out, pulling it out of my purse. "This is—"

"I know who this is," Nolan snaps. "They fired me. Langstrom fired my ass."

I barely have time to say, "Oh, shit," when simultaneously my desk phone rings and Harley sticks his head into my office.

"Goddamnit," I say, trying to hide the cell phone with my hair. "Harley, let me get this." I pick up the desk phone and hold it to my unoccupied ear. "This is Vicky."

"Vicky," coos Lisa, my old secretary, "boy, do I need to talk to you. Did you hear? Langstrom just fired Nolan!"

"Wow," I say. "How come?" Then I flip the receiver up, away from my mouth. I think I saw this in a movie once. I talk into the cell phone, "Hey, I just heard you'd been fired." I wave at Harley, who's doubtless come to tell me Nolan's been fired.

"He said something to the press that Langstrom didn't

like," Lisa says. She sounds almost gleeful. I thought she liked Nolan.

"Langstrom doesn't like you saying *anything* to the press. He likes to say it," I say, for the benefit of both Lisa and Nolan. They both talk at once. Harley motions at me.

"And also I heard you're the one who had the police arrest Dennis Devoss," Lisa says.

"That's not quite the whole story," Nolan says.

"Just a second," I say to both of them. I look at Harley. He shakes his head at me, jerks his thumb toward his office, then makes a chopping motion to indicate urgency. I nod.

"I'd love to hear the whole story," I say, again to both of them. "But I've got to go to Harley's office right now."

I hang up on them and stroll into Harley's office. He shuts the door.

"Langstrom fired Nolan," he says. "A direct result of the TV coverage of Dennis's arrest—and there was also a very bad story in *The Denver Post*. Did you read it?"

I shake my head.

"He feels Nolan went too far in what he told them."

My own theory is, he fired Nolan because Nolan corrected his flag etiquette. "Christ. Nolan only said we were investigating this with the same care we always took—"

"I thought you didn't see it." Harley stares at me.

"I didn't *read* it, but I saw it." Suddenly it seems like a strain, speaking to only one person. "That wasn't Dennis's arrest," I say.

"No. That was the media, *staging* Dennis's arrest. Langstrom went ballistic. He thinks, in order to do that, they must have had collusion from someone inside. He blames Nolan."

Collusion. Langstrom's word of the week.

"Nolan wouldn't do that," I say. "In fact, he called me right after I watched the news. He was pretty mad they hadn't given him a heads-up."

"I know, I know. But you see where this puts us? We have a problem."

"Harley, I hope you aren't expecting me to also do Nolan's job. Seeing as I'm already doing mine *and* Jette's."

"We need some kind of barrier between us and the press."

"Helloooo. It ain't gonna be me, Harley. I would be a bad person to do that." As he must realize.

"In the current situation it could be a problem."

"Not my problem. Langstrom's problem, maybe, or Matt's." Matt is Nolan's boss, although it's been a very loose relationship. Marketing is where Matt spends his time. As in *not in the office*.

"Matt's not around."

"Shit, Harley, round him up. Do I have to do all the thinking for *everybody*?"

Harley grins and nods.

"This was a dumb time to do this," I say. "Now, of course, boss, I'll do whatever you want. But if I have to handle the press, I'm going to be spreading myself pretty thin. And I can't suck up to them the way Nolan can."

Harley's pretty far gone. He resists the opportunity to add to his ongoing sexual harassment case.

"Naw," he says, "you're right. You'd be a bad person for that position, even temporarily."

Thanks, Harley.

Nolan is not in his office, although he has managed to procure, quite rapidly, a number of boxes. I head outside, where the spring sun is beaming down and everything looks cheerful until the wind hits you. At least it's a warm wind. I don't see Nolan or smell his cigar. I light up anyway.

Nolan sneaks up behind me. "Thought you'd never get here," he says.

Nolan doesn't look at all depressed about getting fired. But then his long, mournful face looks morose in any case, which is why I call him Eeyore.

"You have a good network," I say. "At the same time you were telling me you got fired, two other people were telling me that you got fired. Where were you when you got fired anyway, on *Oprah*?"

"Damn close," he says. "I'm walking down the hall toward the cafeteria. Somebody yells, 'Hey, Horowitz.' I turn around and it's Langstrom. He yells I'm fired and tells me to get off hospital property. Kee-rist. I thought he was gonna shoot me or something."

"What on earth did he fire you for?"

"For getting Devoss arrested," Nolan says.

"Oh, hell. I thought that was my fault," I say. "He's probably reconsidered by now."

"Tough. He told me I was fired and to get out. And I am packed. And I am getting out."

"Nolan, he's a jerk, but he's not that big a jerk. They need you." I sit there, feeling sorry for Nolan. Goddess knows I've gotten in trouble with Langstrom, and will again, but he's never yelled at me.

Correction: He's never fired me.

"There were witnesses, Vicky," Nolan says after a minute. "Only about fifty of them."

"Still, he could apologize or something. Don't worry, I'll bet you have your job back in half an hour. I'll talk to him."

"You do that, Vicky." He grins again. "That ought to nail it down. Obviously, Langstrom hasn't read my contract, but I'm sure you have."

"I haven't." Uh-oh.

"He didn't check with Human Resources, either." Nolan's grin turns into an outright smile, showing teeth.

Years of severance pay.

"Shit. You're going to be on my incident list." I consider the possibility of being in an adverse position to Nolan. "Damn."

"I'm calling it retirement," Nolan says. "Which, given my advanced age, is how the 401(k) will consider it."

"Well . . . fuck." I feel kind of sad about this. Not that I want to get mushy or anything. "Harley is feeling pretty much up shit creek."

"All right," Nolan says—just as I notice that he's smoking a cigarette rather than his usual cigar. No wonder I didn't see him. "Just for Harley there's a gal in the Graphics Department.

Name's Ruth. She's pretty young, but I think she could do what I do. Plus she'll be one hell of a lot cheaper."

Which could be important, because unless I've guessed badly wrong, we'll still be paying Nolan. What the hell; it's not my money.

I take a puff of my cigarette and am electrified by a sudden thought: Dennis could have falsified Bootsie's record himself. And used Jette and her concern over the sanctity of the EMR to cover it up. Then he could have done away with Jette. Why didn't I think of that?

"Jesus Christ," I say.

"What?" Nolan asks.

"I just thought of something."

"I figured that. I mean, what? What did you just think of?"

"None of your business. You don't work here anymore, bucko. What if you took this story to the competition?"

Nolan screws up his face in a semblance of deep sorrow. "What if I have information to trade?"

"Now you're talking. Assuming, of course, that it's good information."

"Jeez. Hard as nails. I'll call ya."

What the hell, we're alone in the Showcase. "Bootsie's EMR didn't just disappear. It was falsified. According to Dennis."

"He's covering his ass," Nolan says.

"Could be. But this is something we can prove. Handwriting analysis."

"I know somebody who does that," Nolan says. "I'll get you her name."

"Thanks." I mash my half-smoked cigarette into an S and tell Nolan to have a nice retirement.

After trotting somewhat breathlessly upstairs, I run smack into Harley. It's like he's lurking behind the door, waiting for me.

"I went to talk to Nolan," I tell him.

"You talk him into coming back?"

"Hell, no. I didn't fire him; Langstrom did. So it seems to

me that it's up to Langstrom to talk him into coming back, and I don't think he has a prayer." (I know where he could get one, though. Gwen.)

"I'm not getting into that one," Harley says. "You're right. Vanlandingham can deal with it, if he so chooses. Or, hell, *Langstrom* can deal with it. With the press."

This makes us both grin. Grimly. Then Harley goes into his office and I get on with my ear-to-the-ground bit.

I call Regina to ask how she's doing on tracking down the terminal with the string of zeros.

"It would have been easier with SATAN," she says. "You should see that program. It's like a road map."

"Could the computer have been off-site?" I ask, thinking of Bales. "A computer that, maybe, somebody had stolen?"

"No, if Jette could tell the location, it would have to have been on hospital grounds."

"Why?"

"If she could tell where it was, it's one of the hardwired terminals. If somebody took one of those—and people have—it would no longer be hardwired."

There goes the Bales theory. But at least there's hope for locating the terminal. I hang up, get my phone book, and look up the number of Equitable Recovery. While I'm looking, I take two more calls from women who insist that Dennis couldn't have caused Bootsie any harm. Hey, don't tell me, tell the police. No shortage of character witnesses. One of the women is the nurse staffing supervisor and the other is a patient representative. I write down their names.

The patient rep feels that Dennis has been railroaded, much the way Bill Clinton was. Come again?

"Trumped-up charges," she says. "Dennis is a nice guy. No way he'd hurt his wife. Or anyone."

"That seems to be the general consensus."

"These sexy guys, people are always trying to nail them for something," she says. "Just for the crime of being appealing."

Yeah, right. I shake my head, then call Equitable Recovery. If I get voice mail, I'm going to scream. Loud.

I don't. Instead I get a soft-voiced person who almost whispers, "Equitable Recovery. How may I help you?"

"Could I speak to Alvin Bales?"

There's a long pause.

"Okay," the breathless voice says. "Mr. Bales is not available. Would you like his voice mail or could someone else help you?"

"I need to talk to him in connection with a hospital investigation. I'd rather not get into it on the phone."

"Of course," she whispers. "You can leave a number."

I consider leaving a fake name. But Bales is probably smart enough to spot the hospital exchange, particularly since he once worked here.

I don't spell it. Let her write down "Lucky."

Then I realize I need to get the original page of the chart where Bootsie—or somebody—listed all those drugs taken. I only saw it as a computer printout.

Man, I am so out of it! I call Regina back. She assures me that the record, having been scanned into EMRAM, is now back in Medical Records. I thank her for the info and sit back.

That's a procedure? Just put the medical record any old place? My phone rings.

It's Belinda Drinkwine, our physician recruitment coordinator, telling me I'm a hopeless psychotic for having Dennis arrested and asking if there's anything she can do to help get his good name cleared.

"I'm getting pretty tired of being blamed for this," I grumble.

"I've worked with the guy for years. He's an up-front, on-the-level guy, and he was proud of Bootsie. Maybe he was framed," she suggests.

"I've considered that possibility," I say. "Who would frame him?" Silence on the other end.

"An enemy?" Belinda guesses.

"Certainly not a friend. Listen, if you have any information, please call me back." And I write down her name and extension. Am I going to need a whole new notebook for the Friends of Dennis? It looks that way.

I head over to Medical Records. On the way, I try to work out why either Dennis or Alvin Bales would try to damage Bootsie Devoss.

What Harley seems not to have been telling me was that Dennis had a lot of affairs. Still, being a doctor, Dennis would know that causing Bootsie's EMR to disappear wouldn't have much of an effect on anything. Being a doctor, he would have other ways to get rid of her. Like the tried-and-true method of divorce.

Bales, on the other hand, might think sneaking false information into a medical record *would* have an effect. But why would Bales want to? From what I know of him, blackmail comes to mind. That, and revenge. Maybe he blackmailed Bootsie into giving him a job and she fired him anyway? But he wasn't fired. The receptionist at Equitable Recovery said he was not available, not that he no longer worked there.

If Bootsie's recovery had gone well, I wouldn't even know about this medical records problem. Or would I?

Jette still would have disappeared. Or would she? It seems to me that she caught someone breaking into EMRAM, and circumstantial evidence indicates that the record being violated was Bootsie's. So these two incidents are linked, whether I like it or not.

Back to Bales. One of the things he boasted about was that he could get to *anybody*. He could have gotten into Bootsie's record to prove how good he was.

But why Bootsie? The person who owned the place where he worked? Presumably she already knew how good he thought he was.

Maybe she realized what a creep he was and was going to fire him. Maybe she knew something about him that he didn't want known. Maybe one of his associates set up the bit with the riot, to throw a scare into Bootsie. I wouldn't put it past him.

I need to switch my thinking. This is not a Sleeping Beauty

issue. The EMR doesn't relate to her outcome. I'm working a medical records issue that may somehow lead me to the person who abducted Jette. So I guess it's fitting that I have to bully the guy in Medical Records to let me take the page from Bootsie's chart, even though I have assured him of a complete chain of custody. A copy won't do.

Jesus! I remind myself that he's just doing his job. People aren't supposed to be able to waltz in here and take pages from the records. Or add them.

And also Langstrom instituted his own espionage policy, encouraging or even rewarding employees who rat out other employees. For all the medical records clerk knows, this is a test.

Studying the page back in my office, my conviction that a graphologist can prove anything from this weakens. There's not a lot of handwriting on it. Mostly, it's check marks. Check your afflictions: drug addiction? cirrhosis of the liver? And how about your family's health problems? But there are some write-ins—like the mention of heroin.

This is the best evidence of tampering so far. *Nobody* would voluntarily write in that he or she had used heroin.

As I study it, I take a call from Bootsie's old sorority sister Mary Frances, known as Mouse. Who knew that these sorority sisters, Bootsie and Mouse, would go through life with those teenage monikers? Mouse speaks in a bright southern accent, very Liz Taylor in *Cat on a Hot Tin Roof*, and talks my ear off without saying anything. I learn, quite quickly, that she married a guy who's big in oil, and he moved to Denver as a big promotion, and she was just so happy to get back together with Bootsie, because she and Bootsie had been so close, all those years ago. After I switch ears, she says she's coming over to the hospital to see Bootsie about four, after her tennis match, if I'd like to meet her there.

I don't know what Mouse might be able to tell me, but I arrange to meet her at Bootsie's room around four.

"People in a coma can hear you, you know," she says. "And I'm also gonna bring some of her favorite scent. She used to like Shalimar. Dennis always gave her Joy, because somebody told him it was the costliest perfume in the world. I think a little dab of either one of those on her pillow might cast things in an *entirely* different light."

The next time the phone rings I answer, "Vicky Lucci's office," in case it's someone I don't want to talk to and I can pretend to be my own secretary.

It's Regina, a call I wanted. "The fairy dust worked. I think I've got it," she says, and launches into an explanation in a foreign language.

I try to follow, I really do, but I get lost in her explanation. After a minute I tell her to cut to the chase.

"I think we've identified the terminal."

Jesus, why didn't she just say so?

"It's in Medical Informatics. The last officially logged in user was Corky Phillips, a doctor, but that doesn't mean he was the one using it, because of the string of zeros. If it was an authorized user, it was Dr. Phillips. If it was an unauthorized user, there's no way to tell."

"I thought a string of zeros always indicated an unauthorized user."

"It could still be Dr. Phillips. He might have logged in wrong."

"All right. Hey, Regina, thanks."

I call the hospital switchboard and get Corky Phillips's extension. No answer. I call the switchboard again and have him paged.

I know one thing: If I have to meet this guy, it's going to be in broad daylight in a crowded room.

He could have a perfectly plausible reason for being in EMRAM. Doing informatics research. He could have logged in wrong. He probably did. This is probably a dead end.

On the plus side, he calls right back. I explain who I am and, unable to think of a suitable subterfuge, ask him straight out whether he was on his computer last Wednesday night between nine and ten.

"Last Wednesday night? I was in Chicago at a conference," he says. "Why?"

"I'm looking for the last person who saw Jette Wakefield in the hospital." I'm still stuck with the truth.

He says he knew who Jette was. He was sorry to hear about her, but he never met her. Didn't run into her last Wednesday night or anytime. Then, to make absolutely sure he was where he says he was, he starts reading off things from his calendar.

Corky Phillips's schedule illustrates what happens to doctors who are in the bottom half of their medical school class and who want to practice in desirable locations like Denver. He spends fifty percent of his time seeing charity patients in the family medicine clinic, fifty percent of his time in the Alternative Healing Department, and the remaining fifty percent in Medical Informatics.

"I like Informatics the best," he says, "but the pay's just a small stipend, so I don't spend too much time in the office."

Did I want to know this? "So who else uses your terminal?"

"I have no idea," he says, rather stiffly. "I don't have real office space, I have a cubicle. I share it with a person I've never met. When I go there, which is usually early in the morning, there's nobody there, but I assume somebody else uses that terminal at other times during the day."

"When did you say you went to Chicago?"

He sighs. "I left on Wednesday morning, eleven-forty-five. You want to see my ticket?"

"Hang on to it if you've got it. Do you know Alvin Bales?"

"Never heard of him. Sorry."

Damn! I want to bang on something. Maybe smash a window or two. I'm sweating through my silk blouse.

The only thing to do is to go down there and look at how this cubicle is laid out.

I seal the page from Bootsie's record in an envelope and take it to the fire safe, which supposedly is always locked. Anita (naturally) keeps the key. Anybody who gets to this will have to go through her, so it's pretty secure. This is a woman, after all, who records it when you take a notebook or a pen out of the supply cabinet.

Of course, Anita wants to know what's in the envelope. "Evidence," I say.

"And you have a call on two," Anita says, looking sour. "I didn't ask who it was."

I glance at my watch. "Is it Brett deVries?" She shakes her head. "Is it a woman?" She nods. "Send it to voice mail. I've got a meeting. If Brett calls, call me on my cell phone."

26

Handwriting on the Wall

Medical Informatics, room 0436, is in the basement. This is the office space for people with no clout, a part of the hospital that looks more like a cellar than a basement. Creepy, with hissing pipes along the ceiling, puddles on the floor, and lots of BIOHAZARD! stickers on various doors.

But the doors also bear the same good-quality plastic brass nameplates we have up in Admin. The three tacked on the door of room 0436 read: EXECUTIVE WELLNESS, EPIDEMIOLOGY, and MEDICAL INFORMATICS. In that order.

For a terminal in an out-of-the-way location, it's unbeatable. It's not a place I'd want to go to in the middle of the night without Security, either.

Behind the pebbled glass of the door there's a desk, very cramped. Behind the desk is Kathryn Micklin.

There are two components to Epidemiology. There is the

esteemed Gordon Lutz, M.D., Ph.D., who coordinates the data on communicable diseases with the state health department. And there is Kathryn, R.N., B.S. in biology, M.S. in biostatistics, his professional research assistant. Kathryn has a sweet pink face, prematurely white hair, and great legs, which are now propped on her desk.

"Hi, Vicky," she says, tucking her legs demurely under her desk. "And what brings you to our humble abode? I was expecting the interior decorator at any moment."

"Sorry to disappoint you." I like Kathryn, although I feel sorry for her. She's one of those smart, educated women who get paid a pittance to do a fairly complicated job. Which means she gets to sit at a cramped little desk and look like a receptionist. But if her work gives her satisfaction, who am I to pity her?

"I came to check out your computers," I say. "Well, not yours. Corky Phillips's."

"In there." She nods her head toward the first little office, which has a nameplate saying LOWELL GRAVES. An unfortunate name, Graves, for the head of Executive Wellness. She's the one who came in to measure our fat and lecture us about cholesterol.

Even though his name's not on the door, Kathryn assures me that's Corky Phillips's part-time space. Her boss is behind door number one—when he's here—and a large computer is behind door number two.

I stick my head in door number three. A compulsively neat office, although it doesn't look that way at first, being so cramped. A bare desk, with the terminal on it, glowing evilly in the darkness. A stapler, a tape dispenser, and a three-hole punch pushed up against the wall. A bunch of phone numbers written *right on the wall* in pencil.

The computer keyboard's on a shelf under the desk. Cardboard cartons full of material promoting the Executive Wellness Program line the interior.

"Lowell's hardly ever there," Kathryn says helpfully. "For that matter, neither is Corky, although he's here more than Lowell."

"She uses that computer?"

"Hardly ever, I don't think," Kathryn says.

"She writes down phone numbers directly on the wall?"

Kathryn laughs. "I've seen her write phone numbers on her *wrist*. She's a sick person. But no, she doesn't use the computer much. I think she's moving her office. When she does come in, she's on the phone all the time, setting up appointments and just talking to people."

All she has to do is mention phones and mine rings. It's Anita. "I have Brett deVries on the other line for you," she says. "Should I have him hold?"

"Have him call back on my cell phone."

"You're over budget on that cell phone every month."

"Okay, transfer the call down here to"—I lean into the office and get the number—"extension 0436."

"Right," Anita says.

I point my finger at the phone "Ring," I say dramatically. Seconds later it does. Oooh, the power.

The door won't close because the desk is an inch or so too large. Kathryn must overhear every word Lowell says.

Brett tells me to take it easy tomorrow, it's just a bail hearing. Not to try the case. Not to get upset if the prosecutor offers some false or misleading information, as they often do. Get the charges, get the bail, get the papers signed, and get Dennis out of there. "It's a no-brainer," he assures me. "I'll be around, and if I'm free when your case comes up, I'll do the honors. But I've got two cases going, so the odds aren't good."

I thank him and hang up. Probably I would have talked longer if I'd been in my office.

Back to Kathryn. "Other than Lowell and Corky, who else uses the computer?"

"Nobody," Kathryn says. "I have my own system—and the mainframe."

"Wow."

"Good grant writing," Kathryn says. "Vicky, what are you *doing* down here?"

I lick my lips. Is Kathryn the villain here? Would Kathryn

have an affair with Dennis Devoss, try to hack into Bootsie's medical record, and get caught by Jette using someone else's seldom-used terminal? I don't think so, but you never know.

"Looking for Lowell, I guess." I think of the elaborate printouts we all got, with our body fat analysis and our life expectancy charts. From a color printer, in fact. "She never uses the computer? Not the mainframe?"

"The mainframe's ours. The one in her office . . . I couldn't swear she never turns it on, but she doesn't just sit there and pound it. However, she *is* on the phone constantly." Kathryn grins, rather meanly.

Just as I thought. She can hear every word.

I level with her. The quick story, that I'm looking for a person Jette might have had a confrontation with and that the trail led me to this computer, used by Lowell.

"I don't think Lowell ever works that late," Kathryn says. "But what do I know? I get out of here by four, usually earlier." We both look at our watches. Four is when I'm meeting Mouse. "And a lot of times I'm out in the field and don't come in here at all."

I try to think of a noble way to ask her if she overheard any interesting conversations and decide there is only the old-fashioned low-down way. "Did you ever hear Lowell say anything about Bootsie Devoss? Or Jette?"

"I heard things you wouldn't believe, but not about them." She raises her eyebrows at me and I nod to tell her to go on. "All right, check this out. She's living with this woman. Only the woman is two-timing her. With men. Lots of them, apparently."

Now this sounds promising. Could one of them be Dennis? Could all of them be Dennis?

"She and this gal live way up in the mountains and sometimes Lowell doesn't want to make the drive. Didn't. The other woman would take somebody else home on those occasions. My understanding is, Lowell now has her own place and this whole thing is over. Which is a relief."

"Was the guy by any chance Dennis Devoss?"

I watch Kathryn think about this. "I believe it was guys,

plural," she says. "She didn't mention names. She just called this gal up and ragged on her. And threatened her, now that I think about it."

"If you think about it some more and you remember anything significant, let me know, would you?"

Kathryn nods. "Oh, and about those wallpaper samples . . ."

I decide I have time for a smoke on the way back to my office. No sooner have I lit up than I think of several other things I should have asked, like, What was the name of the girlfriend? What was Lowell threatening her with? That would have been interesting even if it had nothing to do with Bootsie or Jette.

I kind of miss Nolan and his stinky stogies at the Showcase. But back in my office I find he's left a message with the phone number of the person he knows who does handwriting analysis.

I'll need a sample of Bootsie's handwriting, not to mention a sample from anyone we suspect of faking this drug history. Dennis, for instance. Alvin Bales. Lowell.

I scrabble through my notes and find the pink sticky Dennis wrote his password on.

Okay, it's not much, a couple of words. But it looks very doctorlike, which is to say almost illegible. Even though he was using a felt-tip pen, he bore down very hard, as if he was making several copies. It's pretty much of a scrawl, and kind of a spiky one at that. The handwriting on the medical record history page looked more rounded and feminine.

It doesn't look like the same handwriting. But these things can be faked. Dennis certainly knew Bootsie's handwriting. You learn these things about people you're close to. When I was in high school, I could fake my mother's signature perfectly.

Then I remember that I didn't get this password from Dennis. I got it from Hawkeye. So much for that.

But I had Dennis write down *something*. I remember seeing it. I sit at my desk with my eyes closed until I remember what it was. Then I dig it out of the folder. The authorization to release medical records, signed by Dennis as Bootsie's attorney-in-fact.

Bootsie will be harder. I can't think of any way to lay my hands on a sample of her handwriting. I sit down and lean my head back. Who might have something she'd written and would that person feel comfortable handing it over?

Harley's wife. Those two were good friends. I have hardly any samples of the handwriting of my good friends, but it won't hurt to ask her. I call her up.

Good thing she's such a homebody. She answers right away.

"Hey, Bebe, I saw Dennis Devoss today—"

"Oh, that poor man. How is he?"

"Not great," I say. "But in better shape than his wife."

"I've got to get down there and see poor Bootsie," she says. "Not that it will do the least good, of course, but you do these things. And maybe, well—gosh, I hate to go there, but what are the visiting hours at the jail?"

"Don't go there, I'm getting him out. Soon."

"They can't have much of a case, can they?" Bebe says. "Oh, what a terrible situation. If there's anything I can do to help . . ."

"Well, yes. I know you and Bootsie were really good friends, and I, um, wondered if you had a sample of Bootsie's handwriting around anywhere."

"Hmmm," she says. "I don't think so. She sends Christmas cards, of course, but I don't keep them. You do know that Dennis tried to talk her out of this surgery, right?"

"I've heard." And it's not material.

"Men are always against these things. You know I wanted breast enhancement, and Harley just went nuts."

Every time I talk to her she tells me something about Harley I do *not* want to hear. Except, in a kind of morbidly fascinated way, I do.

"Hey!" Bebe says. "Here's something. I found it. Her recipe for Key lime pie. In her own handwriting. Would this help?"

"Yes! Could you send it in with Harley tomorrow?"

"I sure can."

"Maybe put it in an envelope?"

"Sure."

That will probably be a first for the handwriting expert: a medical record, a release, and a recipe.

Then I listen to my last message. Charlene starts by saying she's calling about Dennis, big surprise. She's a nurse. Good; I was beginning to worry that the nursing staff seemed underrepresented among the Friends of Dennis. Charlene promises support if he goes to trial. She thinks she can get a bunch of nurses to come out with signs and things, saying he's absolutely not a wife-murderer, if I don't think that would be too Charles Manson.

Too . . . what? I've gotta call this lady back.

"I'm so glad you called," she coos. "The nursing staff is thinking about taking up a collection for his defense. You know how rare that is? You know how many doctors we'd do that for?"

Not many, but who cares. "What on earth did you mean by 'too Charles Manson'?"

"Oh. Well, after I said that, I thought about how those girls hung around on street corners, and carved stuff into their foreheads and things during his trial, and it didn't seem like such a good idea."

"No, I don't think it's a good idea. I'm hoping it won't get to trial."

"I didn't mean *Dennis* was like Charles Manson," Charlene says. "Only he does have this sort of aura. I figure Manson must have had something like that. You know, charisma. But basically, he's just such a nice guy. Dennis, I mean."

"Right. I'm hearing that a lot." We certainly have some flaky people working at this hospital. "Well, thanks anyway."

"Of course I never met Charles Manson," Charlene says.

Probably a damn good thing. "I'm glad to hear it, and thanks for calling—"

"Anyway, I've got an envelope going around. Just let us know where to send the money."

"Right, Charlene." I try to think of a worthy cause. Brett deVries. He'd probably take it.

This is wonderful. My star client has been compared to Claus von Bülow, Charles Manson, and Bill Clinton. Hey, I'm trying to *clear* him, guys.

I do not add Charlene's name and phone number to my ever-growing list.

Then I go wait for Mouse, as arranged, outside Bootsie's room.

It's the first look I've had at Bootsie. She's still connected to a respirator, along with various other feeding tubes and IV lines.

If I knew her well, I'd probably slap her silly and say, "Come on, come on, wake up, you've got things to do, places to go."

Mouse exercises a good deal more restraint. She's telling Bootsie about her tennis match, for which she used self-hypnosis to tell herself she was Martina Navratilova. It worked well enough that she got off an overhead backhand slam for a winner, but the shock of that threw her out of her trance. Oh, well.

She finishes her story and bounces brightly over to me.

"Call me Mouse," she insists.

She's little, dressed ultra-Southwestern: prairie skirt, turquoise squash-blossom necklace. Mouse may have had a face-lift or two herself, but she still looks a good twenty years older than Bootsie. Which is to say, she looks Bootsie's age, which is nearly my mother's age—a surprise.

She gives me a hug. She smells very good. "Now, where can we go for a little chat?"

We go to the chapel, a nice private place. I could think of better places; I tend to prefer bars over chapels as a general rule. However, it seems appropriate, being deserted.

The first thing I ask is Bootsie's real name.

"Before she changed it? Benison," Mouse says promptly. "An old family name—or something that was supposed to sound like one, anyway."

"Benison?"

"I think it was her mother's maiden name. To make it worse, her last name was Carroll. Of course, now girls with perfectly proper names are renaming themselves things like Hunter and Tyler. But Bootsie didn't want to sound like a boy, and I think she was always called Bootsie in her family."

It sounds like she was named after a cat. And then she went on to have a roommate named Mouse . . . interesting.

"Course, Benison means good luck. But everybody heard it as 'Benson' and thought she was a boy. In fact, you know, she got a notice from the draft board to report for a physical. This was back in college, when folks were burning their draft cards."

"Well, it's different." Before I know it, I'm telling her about my sister-in-law, Hepsibah, who changed her name to Happy—with damn good reason, in my opinion—but who then not only married a guy named Lucci but perpetuated bad names on her daughters, naming them Madison, Wallis, and Stratton and calling them Misty, Windy, and Stormy.

Mouse drags me back to the point.

"Now, what can I tell you that will help get poor Denny out of jail?"

Denny? "I don't know. I've gathered that he has . . . affairs, but I don't know if that could be a motive."

"You come right out with it, don't you, honey? Yeah, Denny played around, but you know what? Bootsie could have stopped that if she'd wanted to. If he didn't play around, she'd have lost interest."

"You're kidding."

"Not hardly. Back when we were roommates, she was only attracted to guys who already had girlfriends. She took Denny away from this drab little thing called Muriel, but she'd have dropped him if he'd stopped looking at other girls."

This is an interesting concept, and it goes against all my notions of Southern womanhood.

"There were two things about her," Mouse says. "One was that she could see things in guys that other girls didn't. Like there would be some cute but no-account guy who'd be going out with somebody else. First Bootsie would steal him away and then she'd reform him! And let me tell you, when Bootsie straightened out a guy, he stayed that way. I don't know how she did it."

"A good trick," I say.

"Denny studied too much. He and this girl Muriel? They did things like drove around and reported people who were driving bad on Denny's ham radio. Not a CB, people didn't have those back then. It was one of those things that made him kind of a doofus. A nerd—only we used a different word back then. A nebbish." She shakes her head. "No, that's not exactly the word either."

It's hard to imagine Dennis as a nerd, but not impossible.

"Bootsie took him away from Muriel. Next thing you know, she had him dancing, found out he could play the piano. I thought of him as her senior project. It was a big surprise when they got married. But you know back then we girls got sent to college for one reason, and that was to get our M.R.S. degree. I guess she got tired of reforming them and then turning 'em over to some other gal."

Interesting, but it's not going to get him out of jail.

"Do you think Dennis, or Bootsie, had any enemies? I mean of the sort who would try something either to get Dennis in trouble or . . ."

Mouse shakes her head. "Everybody has enemies, but you know what? I can't think of any for those two. Those aren't the kind of people they know. I don't know about Denny, but Bootsie, who'd do a thing like that?"

"To get her out of the way?"

"She was never in the way, hon. Not like that."

"You said she could have kept him faithful." I don't need to know this; I'm just curious.

"You got a guy you want to keep faithful, there's two things you can do. First, you cook some of your menstrual blood into something he eats."

"Ah . . . gluh . . ."

"Yep, you heard me. That's step one. That keeps him in

love with you. Doesn't have to be a whole lot of it. Then—and this is harder—take a mirror he's looked into, break it up, put it in a pot, and water it once a week. As long as you want to keep him."

"That's harder?"

Mouse laughs. "Takes more commitment," she says.

"Oh," I say, somewhat weakly.

"And you know what? I've got something to help you get that man out of jail." Mouse digs around in her purse, an enormous fringed bag, and comes up with what looks like a spongy piece of bark. Beige and curled.

"Ginger?" I reach out. Gingerly.

"High John the Conqueror," Mouse says. She rips it into two pieces and hands me the smaller piece. "Brought it in for Bootsie. Now what you oughta do is make up some Friendly Judge Oil, but I don't remember all the ingredients off the top of my head, and I don't think you have time. So just put it in your pocket or tuck it into your bra. Don't eat it!"

"I wouldn't dream of eating it."

"Just remember it's there. It gives you the power."

Great. With this little funky root and Gwen's prayer card, I'm all set.

I go back to my office to check my voice mail. One message from Alvin Bales, returning my call.

I called to give him one shot at answering my questions before giving his name to the cops. Does this count as his one shot? A voice-mail message? Probably not. I dial the collection agency number and get voice mail. Then I doodle on my desk blotter and think about calling the cops right now.

Instead I gather up my collection of notebooks, pack them in my briefcase, and head home.

27

The Power

The first thing I notice is that my place has been trashed. My phone and a pile of papers have been knocked off my desk. A round basket that resides on top of the refrigerator and contains odds and ends (quarters, pennies, nail clippers, coupons) has been hurled across the room.

Before I go into full-scale panic I spot the culprit: Franken-Cat. She's curled up, asleep, in the now otherwise empty space on top of the refrigerator. She gets up, stretches, and leaps to the counter, much more heavily than you'd expect for a cat her size. From there she grunts, twitches her tail, and launches herself at me.

This is almost the same way she flung herself into my arms from under the car that first night. I instinctively drop my briefcase to grab her. I don't know why I didn't just let her hit the floor. Cats can fall great distances without getting hurt. They land on their feet. But no.

She purrs in my arms. I never believed cats got attached to people. They like you because you feed them and that's it. But I consider the possibility that Tara misses Arinda or whatever her name was. Phyllis. Perhaps Arinda fed her better-quality cat food, although I notice that the food dish is empty.

"Why'd you knock my stuff off the desk, you little shit?" I put her down and pick up my phone. Could I still get messages even though my phone was off the hook? Apparently so; I have one. It's Glenn, telling me he's going straight from work to some Children's Chorale thing to hear his oldest boy and he'll be in late.

Good. I needed some time to myself. To putter.

I pick up the stuff Tara knocked over, then sit down to apply a coat of nail polish. I've just capped the bottle when Tara leaps into my lap, adding an interesting texture to my polish. She jumps off my lap when the phone rings.

It's Harley. Quite civilly, he asks me what on earth I want with Bootsie Devoss's recipe for Key lime pie. Equally cool, I tell him it's for a sample of Bootsie's handwriting, is that a problem?

Then I remember I wasn't going to tell him about Bootsie's forged drug sheet. Shit. Now I have to. So I do.

"And you've informed the police about this?"

"Not yet. Look, they don't care. Hey, I was going to tell you. I just forgot."

"Did you tell the cops about that guy Bales?"

"No—"

"I didn't think you would. Vicky, you're going to get into trouble!"

"I'm going to tell them, okay?" I don't add that I called Bales.

Harley grumbles into the phone, then says he'll bring in the recipe tomorrow.

I use tweezers to pick cat hairs out of my polish and apply another coat. Then I pull out my notes on how to get somebody out of jail and study them. I tell myself, over and over, that I'm not waiting up for Glenn. And, in fact, when the polish is dry, I go to bed. Without Glenn's warm body, I find it difficult to get to sleep.

And also, without Glenn around, Tara feels free to spend a lot of time knocking noisily around my room. Sometime in the middle of the night, it starts to rain.

28

Friendly Judge Oil

I wake up to the sound of slush hitting my windows. Not only airborne but horizontal, too. The worst: a wet spring snow, coupled with gale-force winds. It's a day to dress warm, but I can't. The only thing to wear today is a court suit. And I have a doozy.

This is a very conservative outfit that used up about ten percent of my sign-on bonus when I joined the law firm of Petter, Forrester & Rommell. I knew I needed something conservative even though I didn't plan to spend a lot of time in court; PF&R was that kind of firm.

The fabric and the cut are pretty straightforward. It's very vertical; a warm gray worsted, with a touch of sienna and a touch of blue interwoven. The jacket, which was altered to fit, is boxy, with a stand-up collar and no lapels. The skirt is straight, with the pattern lined up at all the seams. So as not to shock the sales staff at Brooks Brothers, I permitted them to hem the skirt so that it hits, very conservatively, just above my knees.

The peach silk blouse I bought to wear with it has suffered a bit over the years—hot and sour soup, coffee, and the like—so I put on another silk blouse, a very grayed blue, which pretty well echoes my mood this morning. As I dress, I realize that the peach blouse, although defunct, outlasted the Brooks Brothers store, which has since been turned into a restaurant called the Cheesecake Factory.

BAD LUCK 221

Since I wouldn't dream of taking my taupe Bruno Maglis out in weather like this, I sacrifice my other pair of taupe shoes because they were cheap and because they're killers. Every time I wear these shoes, I have to go out on my lunch hour and buy another pair of shoes.

I park as close to the jail as I can. Only about three blocks. I then proceed, with my umbrella held on the horizontal and my visibility considerably diminished, to the courthouse.

At ten till eight in the City and County Building, there are two kinds of people. There are the purposeful, suited people with briefcases and legal pads, who know where they are going, who they want to see, and where to find them. They walk briskly and confer with confidence.

Then there are the sullen, puffy-eyed people waiting in the halls, people who look like they've been up all night waiting for justice.

Then there's me. I do my best to look like one of the former.

I don't bail people out of jail every day, okay? In fact, I've never done it before. Many lawyers I know have never done it before. Melinda, for instance. Never has, probably never will.

By the time I find the courtroom, I am almost ready to stand in the halls and howl, "Hey, does anybody know how to get somebody out of jail?" Where's my get-out-of-jail-free card?

The magistrate is zipping right through, currently on number three. I find a seat and lean back. A hell of a lot of good the damn suit has done me so far.

But it's instructive to watch. A pattern emerges. The case is announced. The prisoner stands up. Some young guy or gal from the DA's office stands up, too, and says they don't want to grant bail, and then some other lawyer, usually from the public defender's office, says the person should be released on his (or her) own recognizance. A few facts are thrown around. The charge, the details of the case against the prisoner, the mitigating circumstances.

I'm planning my arguments. Your Honor, this man's wife is desperately ill and he needs to be at her side. Hmm. But they think he caused her desperate illness. Strike that one. Anyway, deVries said not to argue the case.

Suddenly there is the purr of a cell phone and it's coming from my bag. I sidle out of the row of seats as unobtrusively as possible—much less obtrusive, for example, than the woman with the restless baby. Nonetheless I get a major glare from the bench. He stops the proceedings to stare me down as I slip out the door.

Sheesh! Too bad I can't answer and put people on hold without saying anything. Now there's a marketing idea. Hit this button and it tells the caller to please hold. The cellular customer you have reached is in the soup at the moment, but just hang in there. An idea whose time has come.

"Hello?"

"Vicky? Nole here."

Nolan. How very annoying. I was hoping it was deVries, saying he was on his way and to hold everything.

"Hi, Nolan. You got me out of court."

Nolan snorts. "Since when have you gone to court?"

I ignore this. "So how's retirement?"

"Cool. Did you know I have a wife and kids? My daughter's in college. I didn't realize, since she's still living at home."

"That's wonderful, Nolan. Have you got something to tell me or did you just call to chat?"

I would feel sorry for him, but then he does have that great clause in his contract. So, instead, I'm jealous.

"I'm sorry. No, I had a couple of questions and I couldn't get you at your office. Didn't mean to drag you out of court."

"That's okay. I'm out now. Might as well ask them."

"Well. Human Resources sent over a settlement agreement I'm supposed to sign, and my wife thinks I shouldn't. But it looks to me like I have to sign it, to get the lump sum payment."

"Yeah, you know, I still don't know what's in your contract. But, Nolan? I represent the hospital's interests here. If you have doubts, you'd better hire a lawyer."

There's a bit of silence. "I know you represent the hospital's interests," he says mournfully. "But, hey, this is just a couple of sheets of paper. And we're buddies."

For God's sake. "Where's your suspicious nature? You must have been in media relations too long. Here's the deal, basically: If you get the money, you can't sue us for wrongful dismissal. I've seen dozens that are similar. Is that pretty much the gist of it?"

He rattles paper in my ear. "Yeah, that's the gist of it. There's something more, referencing the noncompete clause in my contract. 'Incorporated herein by reference,' that kind of thing."

"Yeah, yeah. Don't worry about that. That just means you don't go to work for a competing hospital within so many miles within so many years, whatever it says in your contract. Hey, I'll be happy to look at it for you. Just keep in mind that I'm the hospital's attorney." Too bad, because this, unlike getting somebody out of jail, is something I know about.

"Right," he says. "Call me when you get out of court."

I open the courtroom door and the magistrate stops the proceedings again.

"Excuse me," he pontificates. "There seems to be some confusion about whether this is or isn't a solemn court of law."

Jesus! People were going in and out of this courtroom like fucking worker ants the whole time I was on the phone. I mean, it's not like a symphony concert.

Before I can reply, he goes on. "If you'd taken the trouble to be here when court opened, you would no doubt have heard my admonition against disruptions of the telephone sort as well as certain other disruptions."

Well, excuse me. I got out as fast as I could once it started ringing.

"The phone will be turned off or it will be left outside, do I make myself clear?"

He reminds me of the prof I had for Evidence.

"Right," I say, making a big show of turning it off.

Worse luck, my seat is gone. So I stand, for three or four more cases. At least I get to see that the procedure does, in fact, look very similar. I'm heartened by the fact that most of the people charged look like criminals, most of them have records, and yet the top bail is five thousand dollars. Usually less. *Bang!* Next case!

If a career criminal has to put up only five thou, I can probably handle this.

When Dennis's case is called, there's a glitch. Dennis wasn't brought over. Hell, what do we need *him* for? While we're waiting for him to be led in in chains, in his ill-fitting jumpsuit, the magistrate goes on to the next sad case.

Dennis, who did not look reliable yesterday, looks even worse today. He looks as bad as the career criminals. Something is wrong here. Men with money, position, and power are not supposed to be jailed. Something's fucked in the system.

"You've been tried in the media," I whisper to him.

He nods.

"*You're* counsel of record?" the magistrate asks me as Dennis is led in. "I don't see an entry of appearance here."

"It was faxed yesterday," I say. "I have a copy." I dig around in my bag. DeVries told me I didn't need one just to handle the bond stuff. Bad advice? Should we hire this guy? Damn.

I fish the paper out, and the magistrate doesn't even look at it.

"What's the charge?" he asks, turning his beady little eyes to the DA. "I don't see a charge here." I am relieved that he's turned his sarcasm on the DA, a skinny, well-dressed woman who looks extremely competent.

"Your Honor, the charge will be attempted murder." She waves some papers under the magistrate's nose.

The magistrate looks through his glasses at the papers, then over his glasses at Dennis. Dennis, for reasons I can't fathom, smiles a goofy jailbird smile. His hair is curly and wild and seems much longer than it did yesterday. He's one of those men who has to shave twice a day, meaning he's missed at least two shaves. And, of course, the jumpsuit doesn't add a great deal to his overall aura of trustworthiness.

Then the magistrate looks back at the DA. "So how come

there's no charge on here?" The prosecutor looks in a file folder, as if she expects to find more than the one sheet.

"Highly irregular," the magistrate mutters. "But let us proceed."

We go through the routine. Held without bail! Heinous crime! Off on personal recognizance! Community ties! And somehow the bench comes to the conclusion that Dennis is such a dangerous criminal that he should be held without bail until his arraignment.

Yes, that's right. The magistrate agrees with the DA. Bail denied.

"Wait a minute, listen, this is a travesty of justice," I say. After all, haven't I just seen a whole bunch of real criminals get bonded out? Hasn't the maximum bond I've seen here today been five thousand? *No one* has failed to get bail.

"It's the court's decision," the magistrate says, looking through me. *Bang!* He calls the next case.

The DA, sitting at her little table, does not look smug. I guess it's just routine for her.

Before Dennis is led away, he does a very expressive hand gesture that says, quite clearly, "Hey, what the *fuck*?" I don't know what the fuck. Unless the magistrate took a personal dislike to me, because my phone went off in his goddamned sacred courtroom.

I go outside to the smoking section. Hah! At least at Montmorency you get a place to sit down and a tiny bit of shelter. There's an overhang. Here, on the south side of the building, the most that can be said is that at least it's out of the wind. And out of the wind is out of the snow. Mostly. I turn the phone on. I got a call. An unfamiliar number—maybe deVries's cell phone?

Yes! Finally something goes right. A small thing, but still. And he answers!

"They denied bail," I say.

"Unbelievable. Did they say why?"

"Flight risk, severity of the crime, who knows?"

"Jesus. Well, hang around and talk to the DA, that's what I

usually do, see what they've got on him. Maybe it's more than you thought."

"It can't be." I don't want to talk to the DA. I want to slap her. Then steal her clothes.

I also want to kick my shoes off and scream. I don't.

"Talk to the judge then," he says. "That's fucking ridiculous. All I can figure is, they're misinformed about the medical condition and they're waiting for her to croak. Because the only people who don't get bail are murderers. Not attempted murderers."

"The magistrate hates me." A good lawyer knows the law, a great lawyer knows the judge. There's truth in this. And in this area I don't even know the law!

"I'm hanging out in courtroom 6," he says.

"Apparently, cell phones are permitted there," I say frostily.

"Actually, no. I'm in the hall. Hey, I'll get down and see the DA as soon as I can. Hang in there."

Right. I light another cigarette just as a uniformed cop waves at me. I'll be damned. Sweet Charley Moss, who once wanted me to cook him a steak. How odd, I was just thinking about him and here he is. Another coincidence.

He strolls over. He lights up and tells me he's getting married in June. Presumably to some fine woman who can cook. I congratulate him. Then he bitches a little about being here on a traffic case that's going to a jury, for God's sake. People who get traffic tickets should just pay their fines.

"Yeah. That's what I always do."

"Don't see you down here very often," he says.

"Never at all," I say. "My car caught fire."

He snorts up some coffee. "Well, that would help."

Very funny. I'm wondering if I could get disbarred for failure to get bail for my client.

I tell Charley what I came down for and where I failed.

"Caruso's been on a tear this week," he says. Caruso is the chief of police. "Course, I'm way, way far from the halls of power, but these things filter down." He grins at me. "The word is, two patrolmen went and interviewed your man and

Caruso called them into his office and reamed them for not arresting him."

"Jesus. Why do they have it in for Dennis?"

Charley shakes his head. "Something came down last weekend," he says. "Like I said, I'm too far out of the loop to know. We have the usual tough-on-crime bit, make arrests, all that. And generally, we don't hold someone like this unless there's good reason—say, because we think they'll destroy evidence if they're out on bail, and we want to get the evidence first. But Caruso's being such a schmuck this week, even his snotty son-in-law is steering clear of him."

"Great," I say. "So he's pissed off and taking it out on my client. I jerked the magistrate's chain and he's taking it out on my client. What next?"

Charley asks what I did to the magistrate. I tell him. Apparently, the magistrate's famous for throwing people out when their electronic devices make noise. Courtroom decorum.

"You're lucky he didn't find you in contempt," Charley says.

That's me: lucky, lucky, lucky.

"How can I find out what's going on?" I ask. "I mean, specifically, what they've got against Dennis? Because they sure don't have much in the way of evidence, unless he's been lying to me."

Charley rolls his filter between his fingers and flicks it into the street. "Evidence is the least of your problems. I'm up for a promotion, so I don't want to rattle anybody's cage, otherwise I'd ask Wyeth myself. Not that he'd tell me, but I could ask."

"Who's Wyeth?" The name sounds familiar.

"That's the snotty son-in-law," Charley says. "He's one of the shrinks, pretty ineffective if you ask me, because anything he hears goes straight into Caruso's ear."

Oho. This is making a little more sense. Not a lot more, but some. "Police shrink George Wyeth? Wendy? This guy's married to someone named Wendy?" I try to be cool, but hot damn. I can figure this out. If Wyeth is Caruso's son-in-law, then Wendy Wyeth, erstwhile nutcase and loose woman, is Caruso's daughter.

No wonder he's in a bad mood.

"Yeah," Charley says. "Wendy Caruso. She was Miss South Dakota a few years back, remember that? Cute girl, redhead. Lived here all her life, but she went to college there and . . ."

"I don't keep up with that stuff."

Charley grins.

As long as I'm talking to one of our men in blue, I ask him if he can tell me anything about how Jette was found.

"Sort of," he says. "It was Larimer County, for one thing, so the Larimer County sheriff's in charge of the investigation and they took her body to Poudre for the autopsy. But some of our guys were in on it, too, since the tip came into our office, and they say she didn't appear to be roughed up or anything. She was quite a ways from her car—I'm not sure how far. That's all I know."

"Hey, thanks, Charley," I say, and before he can get away, I stand on tiptoe and give him a kiss. A nice chaste one, on the cheek.

I walk over to the jail to see Dennis. He probably doesn't want to see me, but he doesn't have a choice, they lead him in, what can he say? That he never wants to see his lawyer again? I tell him, first thing, that deVries is going to talk to the DA or the judge, whichever one he can snag first. Then I quickly outline what I think the problem is, viz., he, Dennis Devoss, is Mr. Montmorency. Due to negligence on the part of Montmorency personnel, Caruso's daughter was allowed to escape and disgrace herself, not to mention assaulting two innocents. Further, said situation was handled in such a way that it's quite possible it could have gotten around the police department, although Charley didn't mention it.

"You think that's the problem?"

"It's my best guess," I say. "Boy, I'm really sorry."

"I'm sure you handled the situation as well as anyone could have."

All those people who've been saying Dennis is a nice guy? They're right.

* * *

BAD LUCK

The first person I run into at the hospital is Bootsie's friend Mouse, who comes out of the gift shop with a big bunch of flowers, as I'm heading to my office.

"Hiya," she says.

"Oh, hi."

"You look low. This weather's enough to send a person into hibernation," she says.

"It's not the weather." God, I can feel my lower lip sticking out. "I just went down to get Dennis out of jail, only they denied bail."

"That's *awful*," she gasps. "Lord, sounds like you needed that Friendly Judge Oil after all. You carried the High John, didn't you?"

"You bet." Actually, I think it's sitting on my desk. I forgot all about it.

"Darlin', you think this is just some weird Southern witchery, but this stuff can put you in the right mood, straighten out your thoughts," Mouse says. "But you got to believe. It won't do *all* the work. It just helps you focus, tap into the energy."

"I didn't mean to disparage it," I say. "I just never heard of this stuff."

I slouch into Admin. Harley steps out of his office and hands me an envelope—a return envelope, one of those the charities send out, suggesting that you put your own stamp on it.

"Your recipe for Key lime pie," he says formally.

I take it. "They denied bail," I say.

"You're kidding!"

I shake my head and walk into my office. Then I remember what I have to do with the envelope. I take it back and hand it to Anita, asking her to put it in the large envelope with the other piece of evidence.

"A recipe for Key lime pie?"

"Yeah."

I go back to my office, kick my shoes off, then sit and stew until I'm good and mad. Then I put the piece of High John the Conqueror in my pocket. Then I call the office of the police chief. Leave my name and the fact that I'm corporate counsel with Montmorency, emphasis on *Montmorency*. When the receptionist asks what it's in regard to, I emphasize that it's confidential. I finger the root in my pocket while I wait to see if this works.

She comes back on the line, cooing that Caruso is in a meeting. She encourages me to leave my number. He'll call me back when he gets free. *Sure* he will.

The odds are about 500 to 1. Can I change these odds? Maybe.

I call Nolan. "Hey, want a scoop? The chick who went around giving blow jobs to everybody was the *police chief's daughter*."

Nolan laughs. "Anybody could have found that out."

"But nobody did."

"What do you want me to do about it?"

"Ah, I shouldn't have told you that," I say, lying through my teeth. "I mean, if you still worked here, this would be confidential, but since you're on your own, you might call up the police chief and ask him to verify this ugly rumor."

"Gotcha," Nolan says. "You know, this kind of thing could backfire. I *could* go to the media."

"Yeah, I know. You need work. How about *Westword*?"

Westword is a local weekly that is either gutsy or sleazy, depending on your perspective. It mostly fits in with my own social conscience, but it's run whole articles on popular though unsubstantiated rumors, the dirtier the better, as well as in-depths on controversial subjects. And movie reviews, tons of ads, and a huge personals section. In other words, vastly entertaining—unless you have something to hide, like Caruso. Mentioning it ought to scare the shit out of him.

"What a mind," Nolan says.

"Think of it as greasing the wheels of justice."

While I wait for Caruso to call me back, I try calling Lowell Graves. Not even a personalized voice-mail message at her extension. I consult the hospital directory, which lists another extension for her. She's not there, either. I try Epidemiology, to find out if Kathryn knows any names and what Lowell threatened her girlfriend with. I get voice mail.

I could go have a smoke to calm my nerves. It would be a long walk in bargain shoes, whose fit was not improved by sloshing through puddles, and I might miss Caruso's return call. I decide to let my shoes dry out a little more, and call the Larimer County coroner's office to see if anything further is known about Jette's demise.

"Hi, I'm Vicky Lucci and I work with insurance at Montmorency Medical Center," I say, which is not a lie. "One of our employees, Jette Wakefield, was found dead and was taken to Poudre. I need to know the cause of death as soon as possible—that is, whether it was natural causes or otherwise. For the insurance, you know; it was double indemnity in case of accidental—"

"Right, I understand," the clerk says. "We're pretty informal up here. If you could just give me your phone number and your name again."

I oblige and ask how long it will be before a death certificate is issued.

"I don't think she's been autopsied yet," the clerk says. "Might be a few days before we get the certificate signed. I guess you need a certified copy, right?"

"Ultimately, but could you fax a copy as soon as it's available?"

"We could probably do that." So I give her my fax number.

Then I call my so-called friend, the nurse who works at Poudre who was going to check on this for me and didn't. She's not working today. I go back out front and ask Anita for my evidence envelopes.

Anita cranes her neck to watch me compare handwriting. They don't look the same. The chief difference is that on the recipe the *i* dots are horizontal slashes, almost hooks. On the medical record sheet they are just dots.

Dennis's signature doesn't even seem to *have* an *i* dot.

I leaf through my notes for the number of Nolan's handwriting expert and call her up.

"I'm calling about handwriting analysis," I say. "I've got some samples, I don't have all of them yet, but I wondered if you could tell me about *i* dots."

"What about them?" she asks.

"If somebody does slashes instead of dots, would they always do it?"

Before she answers, she takes down other relevant information, like who to bill for this consultation. I give her Jette's budget. Then she tells me what she needs to do an analysis: originals, at least a page if possible, preferably on unlined paper.

"For one, all I have is a signature."

"Signatures won't work unless you're comparing them to another signature. That is, to see if a signature is authentic."

Bummer! This doesn't help.

"It's very difficult to single out one characteristic and deduce anything from that. Under certain circumstances, *i* dots as slashes indicate high stress levels. If a person was tense when they wrote something and then wrote something another time when they weren't tense, it could be very different."

You would think doing your medical history would be more stressful than writing a recipe. So it must be a different person's handwriting.

You never get the phone call you want when you're sitting in your office waiting for it. I shove my feet back into my shoes and stroll out of my office, gnashing my teeth. So far, I've chewed the tops off three perfectly good pens. It is time to limp downstairs. My plan is, go over to the parking garage to have a smoke, then, since I'll be close, down to Kathryn's office to ask more questions. And maybe see if Lowell left a handwritten sheet in her desk.

"I'm expecting this very important phone call," I say to Anita. "If it comes, could somebody call my cell phone and get me up here?"

Anita frowns at me and looks pointedly at Geri.

"Give me your cell-phone number," Geri says.

I am almost exactly halfway to my destination when my phone rings. "Yes, hello?"

"It's Anita," she says. "You forgot to tell us who the important call was from."

"A guy named Caruso, did he call?"

"No. Alvin Bales." I can hear her disapproval through the phone. "What on earth is he calling you about?"

I roll my eyes. What if he'd been the important call? Anita probably hung up on him.

"Oh, wait, your line's ringing again." She puts me on hold. I wait, on the off chance it's Caruso. It can't be. It's too soon.

It is.

"I'll be right up." In fact, I'm already bolting up the stairs.

I slam breathlessly into my office, pick up the phone, and hear a woman's voice. Well. It doesn't surprise me that Caruso is the kind of person who has his secretary place his calls. "He'll be right with you," she chirps.

Good. I need to catch my breath. I kick off my shoes again.

Anita hovers around my office door. "That's the call, right?"

I nod. And just as well I didn't keep Caruso waiting.

"You should switch to gum," she says. Thinking, no doubt, that I was out having a nicotine fix. Too bad I didn't get that far.

Sorry, I am not a good gum chewer. First off, I don't like it. When I have it, though, I smack. I try to blow bubbles. I chew the hell out of it for about three minutes, then I swallow it. The caps of pens, now those give you something to chew on. I grab one.

"Caruso."

"Victoria Lucci." The "Victoria" sounds funny in my mouth and to my ears.

God, I wish I could smoke in my office. I wonder if I'd get fired? I could open a window . . .

I plow ahead.

"One of our doctors is in your jail. You know, the jail for those who are innocent until proven guilty. He's quite a well-known doctor, with good, strong ties to the community, so it seemed very peculiar to me that he couldn't get bail."

"Uh-huh," Caruso says. "I don't set bail."

"I know that. Anyway, he hasn't been charged. He's just being harassed. I was wondering if this had anything to do with any kind of bad associations anyone there might have with our hospital. Because—"

"Someone from the media called," he says. "You've got a leak there. I know the incident you're talking about."

"We do have leaks," I admit sorrowfully. "We do our best, but sometimes these things happen."

"Lady, you're running a fucking nuthouse over there."

"We have a psych ward, that's true. . . ." I think back to the conversation with the police and Langstrom. Those cops—they knew all about the Wendy Wyeth incident. Probably every cop on the force knows all about it, and Caruso knows they know. His daughter the hussy. Why didn't Charley tell me? Then I realize Charley had. He'd drawn me a road map.

"What do you want?" Caruso asks.

It's such an abrupt switch, I'm not ready. "Just what anybody would want. Charges filed in a timely manner. Bail set at a fair amount, a fair and speedy trial. Not that it surprises me that charges haven't been filed." I marvel that we've never once named any names whatsoever. Including *Westword*.

He sighs.

"It really isn't fair, for one individual to bear the brunt of responsibility for the actions of a whole hospital," I say. "Even in the best-run organizations things can sometimes get out of hand." Hah.

At least I didn't say the best-run *families*.

"And I know you must have *some* influence over there at the courthouse," I add. "Probably a great deal."

"What about the media?"

"I promise you, they'll get nothing official from us. Nothing. Patient confidentiality is—"

"Right," he says, and hangs up on me.

So do we have a deal? I'll just have to wait and see.

I phone Nolan.

"Hey, Caruso called me back."

"You spoke to him? I'm impressed. They told me he was in meetings all day. So . . . did you work it out?"

"Yep. You wanna fax over your papers and let me take a look?"

"Sure," Nolan says. "Ah, shit. That would have been a *great* story."

"Too bad your journalistic ethics wouldn't permit you to write it."

"Uh, yeah. That is a pity."

I put my shoes on again and my phone rings.

It's Brett deVries, who gets right to the point. "I have some good information," he says. "I talked to the DA, who said the word was to hang on to Dennis Devoss, but she didn't know why. I didn't get a chance to talk to the magistrate because he went home sick, but that's good. If you go back, you'll pull somebody else. I talked to a couple of cops, who said some red-hot evidence was supposed to be coming through on Dennis, which would be jeopardized if he got out, but it never materialized. You can go back down there and try again, or I can do it."

I wonder if this fast action is all from my phone call to Caruso. "Just go down there and . . . show up? Say we want another try at bail?"

"Yep."

I ponder this for a good three seconds. "Okay, I'll go. Just anytime?"

"As soon as you can get here, basically. I have to get out to Arapahoe County."

"Half an hour." This is good. I can smoke in my car on the way down there.

"I'll look for you," Brett promises.

29

Sprung

I park the car in the same spot I had this morning, then wade through the slush, once again with my umbrella aimed against the onslaught. I connect with Brett outside courtroom 9. He looks over my notes on why Dennis should be released and nods approvingly.

"I don't know why that didn't work earlier," he says.

I reach into my purse and turn my cell phone off.

A different courtroom, a different person presiding—a judge, not a magistrate. Oh, and, of course, this time I have the High John in my pocket.

"Your Honor," I say, "this man has been held since Tuesday evening without bail and without charges. Might I suggest that you either charge him or release him? We have here a respected member of the community with no prior criminal charges. We have heard no evidence that this man is guilty of any sort of crime, which leads us to believe that the prosecution has no such evidence."

The assistant DA looks like she wants to say something, but she doesn't.

The judge sighs, then apologizes to Dennis. He doesn't grant bail. He tells Dennis he is free to go until such time as charges are filed.

Dennis, in his jumpsuit, brightens considerably. He looks almost respectable. I feel like F. Lee Bailey!

After going back to the jail to get his clothes, Dennis accepts a ride to the hospital.

"I didn't think they were going to let me out," he says. "No paperwork."

"Yikes." I hadn't thought of that. No get-out-of-jail-free card. "Didn't you just . . . tell them?"

"Finally, yes. That's what the cons said to do. Tell the guard it was all a mistake and I was free. It worked, too."

Gee, it didn't work yesterday. Something must have changed.

"Do you know a doctor named Corky Phillips?" I ask, trying to get the most out of the short ride.

"Not well at all, but I know who he is. Over in Family Medicine, right?"

"And Alternative Healing. And Medical Informatics."

Dennis snaps his fingers. "Right. Okay, yes, I know him. Little short guy, about your size. So what?"

"I think the person Jette went after, last Wednesday night, was using the terminal in his office. The Medical Informatics office."

"Hmmm," Dennis says.

"This is not proving helpful," I say. "I'm trying to locate the person Jette went after. Corky says he went to Chicago for a seminar that day, so he wasn't around. I'm trying to figure out who else could have used his terminal."

"I don't know." Dennis yawns. "If he says he was in Chicago, then it couldn't have been him, could it? So very likely someone else was using his terminal. It happens."

"You know where Medical Informatics is?"

Dennis finishes his yawn. "It's kind of out of the way. But that would just make it a better place, if you were going to do something naughty."

Naughty? "Dennis, I think that whoever Jette confronted was the last person to see her alive. I mean, I think whoever it was . . . killed her."

"Not Corky Phillips. He's about half her size."

"Plus being in Chicago. The other person down there is our

Executive Wellness person, Lowell Graves. Do you know her?"

"You think it might have been Lowell?"

Why won't he just answer the question? "She and Corky share the office, the computer, all that. Would she have any reason to break into the computer system?"

"Not that I can think of." Dennis sounds grumpy. And guilty.

"The other possibility is that you lured Jette down there and did away with her, in which case I'm going to be very sorry I got you out of jail."

Dennis laughs. A good, hearty laugh. A guiltless laugh.

"I'm sorry," he sputters between snorts. "I shouldn't laugh about this. I mean, this is *not funny*. My wife is in a coma. One of my valued associates has been killed. I've just gotten out of jail." A deep belly laugh swallows him up. Ho ho ho ho ho. It lasts so long, I start grinning, then it keeps going and I stop.

"But I didn't kill Jette. I don't know what happened to Jette. I'm very, very sorry about Jette. That's ridiculous."

He wipes his eyes. I think his bout of laughter is the kind that's very close to hysteria.

Vicky, you clunk. It *is* hysteria.

"Lowell," he says. "If someone wanted to set me up for attempted murder, Lowell would be a lot more likely a person than Phillips." His chest heaves with residual chortles.

"Why?"

"She doesn't like me. I don't know why. Heh-heh."

"How do you know?" I pull into the parking garage.

"Hoo." He pulls a clean white handkerchief out of a pocket and wipes his eyes. "Boy, all my clothes smell like that jail. Let's see. How do I know? She called up Langstrom to complain about me, for one thing. Tried to get me removed from my position of trust and responsibility."

Langstrom knew this? And he didn't tell me? Hell, why blame Langstrom? Dennis didn't tell me, either, not even when I asked if he had any enemies.

I make my voice as even as I can. "Why would she do that?"

Dennis shakes his head. We both get out of the car and slam our doors. I slam mine harder, but not a lot harder. The glass in my window falls down inside the door frame. "Goddamn fucking car," I swear. For some reason, this sends Dennis off into another fit of hysteria. He pulls out of it long enough to answer my question.

"Got me. I mean, I have no clue. Langstrom treated it pretty much as a joke. I guess he told her if she wanted to file harassment charges with Human Resources, that was up to her, but of course she couldn't do that, since there was no harassment. I've only seen the woman a few times, and I've never interacted with her personally. Anyway, she never filed anything. But, for some reason, she just doesn't like me."

Lowell Graves has just shot to the top of my suspect list. I knew I wanted to talk to her, but now I *need* to talk to her. And I need to have a little chat with Langstrom, too.

30

Executive Workout

I track Lowell down by dialing the number from my wellness form, which invites you to call if you have questions about your evaluation. I get a cheerful person who wants to tell me how I can live forever.

"No, no," I say, "I'm trying to reach Lowell Graves."

"Let me look at her schedule. Just hang on now."

While on hold I dictate a brief memo detailing what I've

done in the evidence department: collected one page of a medical record and one dessert recipe. And what I need to do: get better samples of handwriting from Dennis, Lowell, and Alvin Bales.

"Okay," the voice says. "She's got consultations all morning, but on Thursdays she generally works out at lunch."

It's on the late side of lunch now. "Where's her gym?"

"It's . . . you know where Montmorency Medical Center is?"

"Oh, do I ever. I work here."

"Then you know where the gym is. That's where we are— or where she is. You can probably catch her in the weight room."

"Great!" What I mean is, awful. I don't want to go near the weight room. If I piss Lowell off, she could drop a barbell on me.

On the plus side, during the lunch hour it's pretty crowded. I've heard. So maybe it's as good a place as any to confront Lowell and ask her why she abducted and murdered Jette. Not to mention why she hates Dennis Devoss.

I met Lowell when she presented the Executive Wellness Program to our office, so I'm sure I'll know her again.

That whole workup was a dry run for the program—try it out on hospital management and see how it flies. We liked it. We didn't exactly vote on it, but we did evaluate it.

Executives love this stuff, even though, in my experience, they already take pretty good care of themselves. Run six miles at lunch, lift weights after work. This helps offset all that golf.

Lowell looks like just the person to take the Executive Wellness Program into corporate offices throughout the city: a two-year R.N. degree, followed by a B.A. in physical education, a master's degree in nutrition, and marketing expertise from volunteer work with a sports clinic in Aspen. (She probably got to ski for free.)

She gives an instructive talk, I have to say, with visual aids that include replicas of the kind of blood that clogs arteries (a thick greasy substance in a sealed Baggie, yuck) and five pounds of fat (pale yellow rubber, double yuck). This is on the follow-up visit, when you already know your cholesterol level and percentage of body fat, which makes it even worse.

But in other ways it seems to me she's a bad representative. For one thing—and everybody talks about this—her clothing, her body type, her haircut, and even her name make it a little unclear which sex she belongs to.

Hey, that's okay, I understand that. No harm in being a little butch. But she came across as superior and condescending. For all I know this may be the ideal way to deal with high-level executives. The executives in our office certainly ate it up.

My problem is how to approach her. I need to forget that she took me into a file room and used a caliper to measure my fat. (Actually, she didn't. A rounder, gentler nurse did that, while Lowell supervised and then said, rather critically, that twenty-four percent body fat was not at all bad for a woman my age but that I might think about holding it down a bit with, say, some exercise. When I pointed out that I was not overweight, she said coolly that I wouldn't be, since fat weighs much less than muscle. Grrr.)

I walk across the grounds, wearing my coat. It's still raining slush. Brave and foolish people are out here stretching for their midday run, wearing T-shirts and shorts. Idiots.

Once inside, I feel a tad overdressed, but not too much. Lowell is at some weight machine, working it. Ropes and pulleys and flat weights, which is good because it's nothing she can drop on me.

There's no place to sit, so I stand in front of her, coat dripping. She's got both hands full—with things that look like stirrups—so I don't shake hands. I get right to the point.

"I don't know if you remember me, I'm Vicky Lucci, the risk manager—"

She nods and grunts.

"I was wondering where you got your wellness evaluations printed."

Okay, so I don't get *right* to the point. See, it's easier to start out with a nonthreatening question. However, it doesn't work on Lowell.

"Why would you wonder that? It's on the business plan."

Fuck. Isn't it just like me to do something the hard way when I could have done it the easy way? Not that it matters, since that isn't what I want to know, but it's something I can look up when I get back to the office.

"You do them from your computer in your office?"

She grunts again, strains. Muscles stand out in her arms, muscles in places where I don't even have places.

"No. They go through data entry." She stands and moves to the next station, or whatever they call it. I follow her, noting that she whips her towel out to mop up *before* she sits down, not when she abandons the station. Then she pulls a pin out of a stack of weights behind the equipment and inserts it in a much lower place.

The guy who's next in line performs the same mop-up activity and then, shooting her a glare, moves the pin on that machine in the opposite direction.

"So people in data entry can see all that stuff?" My voice rises slightly in alarm—and what am I doing? *I don't care.* "Uh, never mind. What do you use the computer in your office for?"

"My Christmas list," she says. "Is that a problem?"

The oblique approach is not working very well on this lady.

"Why did you call Langstrom about Dennis Devoss?"

"Oh, Christ, I should have known." She drops her legs and the weights make a loud and threatening *clunk*. "That isn't something I want to talk about, okay?"

"No, not okay. Somebody used the computer in your office to break into confidential medical records."

"Shit. Look, you know, I really don't want to talk about this. Not here. And I have a one-thirty appointment."

She's not getting me into any place secluded, that's for sure.

She gets up suddenly, leaving her towel, and stalks into the women's dressing room. I follow her, feeling a little insecure.

"It was probably Gaynor," she says, wadding her socks into

little balls and stuffing them in a mesh bag. "Gaynor would do anything to get me into trouble, including making it look like I screwed around with somebody's EMR. I don't do *anything* on that computer. *Ever*. That bitch!"

Would this be the ex-girlfriend? "Gaynor?"

"Gaynor Griego. She's a part-time physical therapist and a full-time shit," Lowell says. She stuffs her tank top and shorts in the bag, pulls the drawstring, and then stands in front of the mirror. Naked.

"How would she get into your office?"

"The door doesn't close." She peruses herself frontally, then sideways.

"How about the front door?"

"Everybody and his brother has a key to it." She ends her admiration of her naked self and steps into the shower without pulling the curtain closed. That's okay. I'm far away and protected by a leather coat. Which is already wet.

"Why would she do that?" I raise my voice to talk over the shower.

" 'Cause she's a cunt," Lowell yells back. " 'Cause she's a troublemaker. She's a psychopath."

Okay, okay, sheesh! I pace around outside the shower, wondering who Gaynor is and what she's got to do with anything.

"She's bipolar," Lowell shouts above the shower. "A real nutcase. She's okay when she takes lithium, but she gets it into her head that the lithium's turning her into a robot and she starts self-medicating with herbal shit. Then she really goes off the deep end."

"Why would Gaynor have used your computer?"

"To get *me* in the shit," Lowell says. "I'm telling you, she's vicious."

Lowell steps out of the shower, wipes herself with the towel, then wraps it around her hair. "You interrupted my workout and I forgot to stretch," she mutters, and starts doing just that.

"Gaynor is vicious?" Back to my trusty technique of repeating the last thing said to me.

Lowell towels her hair vigorously, almost to the point of complete dryness. "She's got a bad case of believing her own propaganda. Which is that she is the queen of the world and she can make things happen."

She pulls a comb from her bag—still without putting any clothes on—and styles her hair, precisely forming a side part, then sculpting the front hair up and back. There's a name for this kind of hairstyle, but I can't think of it. Very boyish.

"Things like what?"

"Like . . . her stepmother's death," Lowell says. I get the feeling she was going to say something different.

"Like Bootsie Devoss's medical record?" I ask.

Finally Lowell starts to put on some clothes. She dresses in angry, violent motions. I think I know who's the psychopath. Socks first, but at least she's getting dressed. That's good; I don't know whether I was supposed to admire her, lust after her, or envy her surely-below-twenty-percent body fat. At least, if anyone ever asks, I can attest that she is, in fact, female.

"I don't have anything against Bootsie," Lowell says. "But Gaynor wanted her to die. I don't know why I shouldn't tell you that. Although how she could have accomplished that from my computer, or *anybody's* computer, is way beyond my comprehension. If that's what you were getting at."

"Yes, well . . ." I study my fingernails.

Lowell zips up her tailored, pleated pants.

"It would be so typical of her to fuck that up, if she did do it," Lowell says. "She claims she's a witch."

Another witch. They're everywhere. Not quite as prevalent as SUVs.

"She's one of the most inept witches ever—not that I believe in that shit. You know what she did? She was having trouble with her boss. So—get this—she took a piece of paper and a bottle of water, some kind of springwater, to work, right? Wrote her boss's name on the paper. Waited for her boss's shadow to fall on the piece of paper, then *stuck* the shadow to the paper with a piece of tape. Right, a piece of fucking Scotch tape." Lowell shakes her head and starts lacing her wingtips. "Okay, then, having stuck her boss's shadow to the paper, she takes the paper, puts it in the bottle of springwater, and puts it in the freezer. At work, natch. At the end of the day she brings it home and sticks it in the freezer, where it's supposed to freeze out all the negative influences of the person in question, yada yada yada. You know what? About a week later she got fired. So much for freezing the negative influences, right?"

This sounds like the kind of thing Mouse would recommend.

"Ah, but if you work for evil purposes, it comes back to you three times over," I say, like I know what the fuck I'm talking about.

"In that case Gaynor is due for some pretty heavy shit coming down on her real soon." Lowell shrugs into her jacket. I note that, unlike every jacket I've ever owned, it has an inside breast pocket. Now this I envy.

"But why would she want Bootsie out of the way?" I don't believe for a minute that Gaynor wanted Bootsie out of the way; I think Lowell did. And with the added bonus of getting Dennis in trouble for it.

Lowell pauses, shoots her cuffs. She's perfect. She's got a clinical background. She knows how things work at the hospital. And I can prove she had a grudge—or something—against Dennis.

"Bootsie was her boss, the one whose bad influences she tried to freeze," Lowell says. "And then, according to Gaynor, Bootsie went and did all this other shit to her, like screwed up her mortgage. I believed all that at the time, but now I've got to wonder, why on earth would Bootsie even bother with a slutty piece of garbage like Gaynor?"

Lowell picks up the bag and strides out of the locker room. I follow her, feeling like I've gotten no answers at all.

"The answer is, Bootsie wouldn't," Lowell says. "She would have forgotten Gaynor, like totally, five seconds after she handed her that pink slip. The rest of it is all in Gaynor's fucked-up head."

I follow her, walking fast, back to the hospital, at which point she heads toward employee parking.

"She's so screwed up she believes this stuff! She believes, for instance, that she can make herself invisible. So there's your explanation: she made herself invisible, came into my office, and used my computer to get rid of Bootsie."

"That's nuts."

"Gaynor's a nutcase," she says. "Excuse me. I think I mentioned that I've got an appointment at one-thirty. I'm late."

"You knew Bootsie?" It's lame, but it's the best I can do; Lowell's not cooperating.

"Never met her," she says.

"Why did you almost file a harassment complaint against Dennis Devoss?"

Not even this stops Lowell's momentum.

"I didn't," she says. "I reconsidered. Now if you'll excuse me . . ." She unlocks a white Mazda Miata, climbs in, and slams the door.

I think of great parting lines, like "The cops may have something to say about that." But where am I really? What have I learned?

That Lowell has a great deal of anger toward a part-time physical therapist named Gaynor.

A couple of things from Lowell's rant stick in my mind. One, she didn't mention Jette, only Bootsie. Two, she questioned how Gaynor could attempt to kill Bootsie from a computer terminal, which is a damned good question. And three, she didn't deny that she *considered* filing a harassment suit against Dennis.

Lowell's carrying a lot of attitude. She remains high on my suspect list, to the point that I think maybe I'll call the cops as soon as I get back to my office. Give them Lowell Graves and Alvin Bales.

But first I go back down to the basement. Kathryn is sitting at the desk that looks like a reception desk, erasing something from a gigantic spreadsheet.

"Vicky! You brought the wallpaper samples?"

"What?" Then I remember that we're doing a fiction that I'm the decorator. The hell with that. "Oh, sorry. Listen, you said Lowell's on the phone a lot. Did you ever hear her mention Gaynor Griego? Was she the other woman? Can you tell me what she threatened her with?"

Kathryn leans back in her chair and smiles. "Are you asking me to repeat . . . gossip?"

"I'll try to catch it the first time."

"Old joke, Vicky. Let's see. No, I cannot confirm that Gaynor was the name of the woman Lowell was living with. It does sound familiar, but I couldn't swear to it." She leans back. "Am I going to have to swear to any of this?"

"Probably not. Please go on. The threats particularly."

"Okay. Now, I don't know that Dr. Devoss was the person, of those men, but at one point Lowell was saying things like, 'I'm going straight to the CEO and I'm going to get him for harassment.' But she seemed to be using this as a threat more against whoever she was talking to. For whatever that's worth."

"She told Gaynor this?"

"I don't know who she was talking to. Then she said something about some kind of gift, or something, that Lowell could take away. Let's see. Something like 'I know what he gave you, and it's going back.' I don't know why that sounded like a threat, but it did."

After talking to Lowell, *I* can see why it sounded like a threat. Kathryn pulls a nail file out of her desk drawer and sands a snag off the desk. "But then she also threatened to expose the fact that the person she was talking to had a record and lied about it on her application."

"A criminal record?"

"I don't think she said criminal record, now that I think about it. Just something that the other person had failed to disclose. For some reason it almost seems like maybe she mentioned a stint in the loony bin. Which would fit if this person works here." Kathryn replaces the file in her desk.

"I think this person does work here," I say. "You sure heard a lot."

"Lowell acted like I wasn't even here."

The invisible woman.

"She's pretty open," I say.

"Entirely too open," Kathryn agrees. "Some things should just remain dirty little secrets. I was about ready to go to the CEO myself. Thinking maybe it was Lowell who'd been in the loony bin."

Why are nutty people so attracted to hospitals? Never mind—I'm sure I don't want to know the answer. Kathryn goes back to erasing.

"Do you know this Gaynor Griego?"

"Like I said, I've heard the name. I can't put a face to it. I don't recall where I've heard it."

"Did you ever see Lowell's girlfriend? Did she come down here?"

"Not while I was here. I don't even know what she looks like, but basically nobody comes down here. Not even Lowell much anymore. And about that I'm happy."

"Lowell's a reptile," I agree, thinking about how cold she seemed, doing her presentation in our office. "Well, thanks."

"Oh, anytime," Kathryn says airily.

I go into Lowell's office. I open the top drawer: paper clips, pens, sticky notes. Nothing with handwriting on it. Except the wall, of course. I wonder if that would work. But getting it to the graphologist would be a bit of a problem.

I thank Kathryn again on the way out. "Someday you'll have to let me know what this is all about," she says.

"You're a statistician. You'll figure it out."

31

Protocol

I stop at the hospital cafeteria and buy myself a hamburger that's been sitting on the steam table for hours and a Mountain Dew. Sitting in a quiet, out-of-the-way booth, I eat voraciously. I'm on my last bite when Hawkeye stops by. Which is good, because he will take food right off your plate if there's any left.

"Hawkeye, do you know a person named Gaynor Griego?"

He nods. "She's been around awhile. Flipped out while in medical school, which a lot of people do. Didn't finish, but got a degree in physical therapy, and now she's working in our rehab clinic. Or some damn place. Dressed as a nun last Halloween."

"Ohhh." Now I know *exactly* who he's talking about. Not everybody dresses in costume for Halloween around here, but enough people do that it doesn't look strange. Still, the nun stood out.

"Did you ever finalize your report on Sleeping Beauty?" Hawkeye asks. "I never saw it."

"I'll finalize it when my experts get back to me, but right now it looks like the trouble was endocarditis, previously undetected. I see the responsibility as about twenty-five percent doctors, because they don't seem to have been very diligent at tracking down the record or of checking the patient's presurgical condition. Thirty-five percent staff, mainly for not guarding the record. And forty percent patient."

"Good girl!" Hawkeye gets up and strikes me on the shoulder, nearly dislodging my last mouthful. "That adds up to one hundred percent! That's the way we like 'em."

It also means no one was more than fifty percent responsible, which is good for some reason. I forget why.

I go back to my office, where I slurp down two big glasses of water while looking up Gaynor's number. I call her and get . . . a voice-mail message with an English accent.

Gaynor Griego speaks with an English accent. Interesting. I wonder if it's a put-on. I don't remember ever hearing her say anything, although I have a very clear memory of her waddling around in her nun outfit. Wimple, gold cross, rosary, and all.

God, I'm tired of this case. "This is Vicky, the vice president of risk management," I say, throwing my title around. "I'm calling looking for information on unauthorized use of a computer terminal in the basement area, a week ago Wednesday. If you have any information on that incident, I would appreciate it if you'd call me back."

There. If this person is guilty, she will not call back.

Right. Vicky, you stupid doody-head, if she's innocent, she won't call back either, because she will have no information. You phrased that inquiry quite badly. Try again. Later. Better.

I call Equitable Recovery again and instead of connecting with the soft-voiced receptionist, I get a guy. "Alvin Bales," I say crisply.

"Speaking. Who's calling, please?"

"Ah, Vicky Lucci at Montmorency—"

"Right," he says. "I remember you. Not wasting any time assuming your old boss's duties, are you?"

"I guess not—"

"I suppose you want the same action she got. Excellent choice, by the way. You sign your name to a little piece of paper and you get twenty percent of any judgment amount; it's a sweet deal. Makes me wish I'd gone to law school."

"That's not why I'm calling . . ." And I'll bet Jette got more than twenty percent, too.

"I haven't been anywhere near your hospital," he says.

"Not for months. Everything Jette did went via courier. Sometimes the hospital courier, sometimes not, but that was Jette's call. So—why are you calling?"

"Your name keeps coming up," I say. "On my suspect list, that is. You knew Bootsie Devoss and you knew Jette, and something bad has happened to both of them."

"Bad things happen to everyone," he says. "How am I supposed to have accomplished this, or can't you tell me? I'm sure I have alibis for all relevant periods."

I'm glad he said that; it stops me from saying what the relevant periods are. In fact, I can't tell this guy about any aspect of the investigation. I was right the first time. Let the police handle Bales.

"I'm basically just calling to, uh—" Why the fuck am I calling? "I'm going to have to give your name to the cops because of the connection."

"Oh, the poor cops. They can't round up their own suspects?"

"I just wanted to let you know. Or find out if you knew anything."

"A courtesy call. Well, thank you. You know, if you'd let me into that hospital for two hours, I'd know *everything*. Think the cops would like that? All wrapped up and delivered to their door?"

How could I have forgotten this guy's monumental ego? It nags at me for a minute. What if he's right?

"Sorry, I don't have the authority."

"That's not surprising. Neither did Jette. You'd have to clear it through Harley Sloane, and it would take him two blessed years to make up his mind."

He obviously knows Harley. Since anything I ask might reveal something about the situation here, I am at a loss for words. Bales isn't, though.

"Thanks so much for the heads-up, that the cops might be calling on me," he says. "I appreciate it. I'll be ready for them."

Goddamnit. I hang up, very pissed off at myself. I *knew* I didn't want to talk to the guy.

Then I go to see Langstrom, observing all the protocol—which is to say I stop at Vanessa's desk and ask if Langstrom has a minute. Yes, he does.

"Ben," I say (using his first name, like Harley does), "I have a little problem with this Dr. Devoss thing."

Ooops. Wrong. Langstrom has said that he is the sort who likes solutions, not problems. Well, tough shit.

"My *problem* is that apparently Dr. Devoss had some kind of *problem* with a female employee who called you up, seeking—"

"She wanted his resignation," Langstrom says. "Those kinds of people should not be encouraged."

"Let me finish. My information is that you talked to her and told her if she had a *problem*, she should file a grievance."

"Isn't that our procedure? What's the *problem*?"

"Two problems," I say. I feel remarkably calm, considering that I'm chewing out my boss's boss and I can't utter a sentence without throwing in the word *problem* two or three times, and it's beginning to lose its meaning. "One, I was investigating an action that could be construed as an action against Dr. Devoss, and I needed this kind of information. It's not inconceivable that an employee with an issue might take some kind of covert action against the object of her rage."

Here I am again, going into Langstrom-speak.

"The other problem, uh, *issue* is, when a female employee has this kind of problem, we need to take it seriously. I'm not saying you need to go around firing doctors just because some woman says there's a . . . an issue, but people with complaints like this need to be treated with dignity." I stare at him for a minute.

"All right," he says. "I'll take the next one seriously."

He says it in such a way that my whole position just became preposterous.

"Thanks," I say.

I always feel like I should back out of Langstrom's office bowing. This time, for what strange reason I cannot say, I do it.

Langstrom doesn't look even mildly surprised.

BAD LUCK 253

I come out and face the assistants—who are pretending they didn't see it. "Who'll be the next one fired?" I ask. "Anybody want to start a pool?" Then I go back into my office and shut the door.

Sometimes I just need to write myself a script. While waiting for Langstrom to come in and fire me, I open my notebook and scribble out a much less wimpy and inconclusive message for Gaynor.

"Disregard my earlier message. I need to talk to you, it's very important, please call me back." Then I pick up the phone and dial her number again.

Surprise! I don't get her voice mail. I get her. Her English accent is less pronounced in person, but it's still there. She says she knows who I am and she'll be happy to talk to me if I think it will help. She can meet me right after her next patient, in about forty-five minutes. We agree to meet in the atrium between the hospital and the medical office building, where physical therapy is located.

I sit down and scribble up some notes on my conversation with Lowell, thinking of things I need to ask Gaynor on my way to the truth. My theory—that Lowell committed the assault on Bootsie's record—kind of falls apart without a motive.

Gaynor doesn't seem like Dennis's type, in her nun outfit or in her regular attire. But what do I know about Dennis's type? He seems to have been flirting with every woman in the hospital.

I still have a few minutes to kill before meeting her, so I run over to the neurological unit, where Bootsie's been moved, to see if Dennis is there. He is—and wearing a fresh outfit. He doesn't seem particularly glad to see me. Which is to say, he smiles tiredly and says, "So we meet again."

"I have a couple more questions in connection with Lowell," I say. "Apparently she was mad at you because of someone named Gaynor Griego, so I need to ask. Do you know Gaynor, and would Gaynor have anything against Bootsie?"

Dennis studies me. "I know Gaynor. She's a physical

therapist. I don't know what she has to do with Lowell, though. I can't fathom how my knowing Gaynor had anything to do with Lowell. Why it would make her mad."

Lowell seems like a pretty easy person to piss off, but I don't mention that.

"Does Gaynor have anything to do with Bootsie?"

"Well, she knows her. Gaynor spent some time working for the foundation back when Bootsie headed it."

So we're back to the Disease of the Year bunch. This is interesting, with what I now know about Bootsie. The foundation devotes most of its efforts to coming up with funds to provide treatment for indigent patients. It sometimes gets in a bit of trouble, though, as its funds go directly to Montmorency—not to the indigent. It occurs to me that, as the owner of a collection agency that mainly pursues folks who haven't paid Montmorency's doctors, Bootsie might have a conflict of interest, being the director of the foundation. But that's irrelevant, since she's no longer the director.

"Why would a physical therapist be working at the foundation?"

Dennis shrugs. "Got me. I think it was just a way for her to pick up some extra money. They worked together for a while. Bootsie liked having someone with an English accent answering the phones. Thought it gave the operation some class."

"Yeah, how does someone named Gaynor Griego end up with a British accent?"

"I don't know. Maybe it's her married name?"

If he's involved with this Gaynor person, he's being awfully coy about it.

I don't ask if he was involved with Gaynor. I'll soften her up with the question about her accent, then ask her.

"Is she any good as a physical therapist?"

"She is, yes. She's maybe a little sensitive for the job. Too gentle. Not that you want a sadist, but sometimes you have to push people past their limits. You have to hurt them, to put it bluntly. So if I have a patient who's an athlete, who needs that push, I schedule somebody else. But if it's a little old lady who's had hip surgery, or a kid, then Gaynor's the best."

"Okay." I check my watch, then head to the atrium to meet her.

She's easy to spot. Of course, I saw her when I went for physical therapy for my broken finger. Yes, physical therapy. What can I say, it was a bad break.

Even out of the habit, she looks more like a nun than a lesbian witch. She has the kind of benign countenance I associate with people who are pleased with the way their life has gone. She looks like somebody's grandmother. Well, not just anybody's grandmother. A hippie grandmother, the kind of person who, instead of trading LSD for a BMW, went to live off the land. Like maybe how Janis Joplin would have looked, had she stuck around.

She doesn't look like a Griego, that's for sure.

"I've got half an hour until my next scheduled patient," she says. She looks around the area. "Let's get out of here."

"Okay, where?"

She flips a long braid over her shoulder and starts walking, heading outside. As she brushes by me I get a strong odor of old-hippie perfume. Frangipani. I follow her, even though I'm not wearing my coat.

She's not wearing a coat either, but she has on a lot of layers. Over a turtleneck (or maybe it's a dickey) she has on a flowered flannel dress and a heather-gray sweater buttoned halfway up. Over that she's wearing a beige lab coat with her ID dangling from its pocket.

And around her neck a moon-goddess pendant, exactly like the one Arinda had worn, or very nearly. Therefore, just like the one I used to have. I guess it wasn't as unique as I thought.

Gaynor seems to be aiming to get off hospital property by the most direct method, cutting through a little fake park by the parking garage. I say "fake" because although it's set up to look like a park—there's even a birdbath—it's too narrow for anyone to play in, and it's one of the places where the grounds staff piles snow during the winter. However, despite the slushy conditions earlier, most of the snow piles have melted. And it's out of the wind.

I quickly discover piles of another sort. Apparently, it's a rest area for dogs. You can guess how this information comes to me. I stop and try to scrape it onto the grass. My killer bargain shoes have about had it; they've been through numerous slushy puddles today and now dog shit.

"Merde," Gaynor says cheerfully. She pulls a cigarette from her purse and lights it.

"Right." Good for her, she can say *shit* in French. I've never seen her at the Showcase. I thought I knew most of the smokers.

This cigarette smells like she does. Like frangipani. Or no, it's clove.

"Merde. It's an expression of good fortune," Gaynor says. "No, really. It's considered to be a harbinger of good luck."

I drag my shoe through a pile of slush, then through wet grass. It probably means, in subtext if not literal translation, *better luck next time*.

"You don't look like a Griego," I venture. "Or sound like one."

She smiles, exposing a gap between her two upper front teeth. "You're not the first one it's confused. Me da," she says, going *real* heavy on the accent, "nice country boy from La Junta, sent to England during the war, married Mum, and had me. He came back over when she died, so I got the experience of finishing up in American high schools. It was lovely, being thought an illegal alien on two different fronts."

She answered that extremely personal question willingly enough, so I go on to the harder ones.

"You know I'm trying to shed some light on the situation with Bootsie Devoss," I say.

"Right. Told me that on the phone, you did. Your message."

I did? I thought I only mentioned the computer incident. I pause and study my shoe. Damn it, it's going to stink up my office. I wish I had a paper towel.

Gaynor looks through her pockets and pulls out a brown paper towel. She hands it over.

"If I were going to arrest a person, Dennis is who I'd pick," she says. "Although it looks to me like just one of those things. Unfortunate and all, but these things happen, don't they?"

"You'd pick Dennis?"

"If I had to arrest someone? Yes. He's clever, that man. He's effing brilliant, don't you know. I mean, assuming it didn't just happen. It could be an elaborate scheme to get his wife out of the way, which no one would ever suspect, but with one mistake. She's not out of the way, is she now? No, in a sense she's more in the way than ever."

"And it's not like no one suspected, either," I say. "But you're the first person I've talked to who feels that way."

"I saw through him. I see through everyone. Bit of a curse, that."

She *did* hand me a paper towel, but anyone could have seen I needed one.

Gaynor goes on. "Mind, he *is* a sweetheart. But I saw in the depths of his soul that he wished his wife was out of his life. A very deep wish, and not a new one."

"I've heard he depended on her utterly."

Gaynor shoots me a look. "Utter dependence is hardly an excuse to keep someone around. More the opposite, I would say. Most people dislike being dependent, particularly utterly so, and resent the person depended upon."

I inspect my taupe shoe.

"It's too bad, because Dennis is a nice guy. He's suffering from a karmic disruption, though. Much bigger than merely the disability of his wife. I don't think he should have become a doctor. I think he should have been maybe a car mechanic."

What an idea—Dennis Devoss as a mechanic.

"What makes you think he did it?"

Gaynor laughs. "Maybe he wished it, but I don't think he *did* it."

"You said—"

"I said he's who I'd arrest, if I had to arrest someone. Me, I think what happened to Bootsie was just one of those things. But I don't think he's all that torn up about it."

An interesting take. I don't either, but that could be his clinical distance.

"If somebody did something to affect that outcome, look at it, he's perfect. He had the know-how. He could have gotten to the medical record easy enough. Could probably have gotten into the OR. And wouldn't he know what bad drug interactions his own wife has? And I think you have to have a DEA license to have access to phenol. If that's what caused her problem."

"That seems to be what the cops are thinking." Okay, so don't count Gaynor as a character witness. And you don't need a DEA license to have access to phenol.

"You're a lawyer, so you'd know this stuff," Gaynor says. "Say he did know something about her that her doctors didn't know. Something that would affect the surgical outcome. If he didn't tell, would that be attempted murder?"

A good question. "I'm not a criminal lawyer, but I think the person has to die through your action," I say. "And intent, of course."

"But in this case the person didn't die, so he's clear. Legally. Right?"

"He seems to be. Anyway, he's out of jail." Better not get into this any further. "Lowell said—"

"Lowell!" Gaynor almost spits. "Doubtless Lowell told you that I did it, all of it, out of spite because he wouldn't leave his wife."

"Leave his wife? No, she didn't say that. Was there something between you two? I mean, you and Dennis?"

"Not like that. He'd call sometimes and we'd have a bit of a chat, usually about a patient but sometimes about other things. Deep subjects, you know, like what movies we'd seen."

"Lowell was thinking of filing a harassment charge," I say. "I just wondered if there was any merit to that."

"If you mean that he harassed Lowell, all I have to say is, *in her dreams*." Gaynor laughs. "I'm sorry. He has an eye for the ladies, I'll say that. Is Lowell one of the ladies? You tell me."

"You and Lowell were roommates," I say. "Have I got that right? And now you're not."

"We were not roommates, we were lovers," Gaynor says. "I am not in the closet about my sexuality. I'll be quite honest, I've reached that stage in my life where if someone appeals to me, male or female, I will go for it. Life is short, and if I'd wanted a ball and chain, I'd have gotten married, wouldn't I, like anyone else."

Is she asking *me*?

"And I didn't. Now, Lowell wanted a rent-free place to stay and some fun and games. Good times, as they say in the personals. Quiet romantic evenings in front of the fire. But she also wanted to turn me into a bull-dyke. She wanted me to cut my hair, splash on some Aqua Vulva, and never look at another woman *or* another man. That's not where I am in my life right now." Gaynor throws her braid over her shoulder.

"So she was jealous of your relationship with Dennis?"

"She was jealous of my relationship with *anyone*. Any kind of relationship," Gaynor says. "I'm a natural healer. Did Lowell mention I was a witch?"

"She mentioned that, yeah."

"Another thing I'm not in the closet about. Or the broom closet, as we call it." She laughs a low, throaty chuckle. "Lowell was jealous about that, too. She is *not* a healer, not naturally or any other way."

That I can believe.

"You are, I think," she says. "And Dennis is, which was why he would have made a good auto mechanic."

What a strange connection.

"Lowell said you'd do it to get her in trouble. And you had it in for Bootsie Devoss."

"I cussed Bootsie out every month when I wrote out my mortgage check, because she conspired to ruin my credit rating," Gaynor says.

Ah. Now *this* sounds unbalanced.

"She ruined your credit, so you put a curse on her."

"No, no," Gaynor said. "See what I mean? I said I cussed her out, not that I put a curse on her. That's one of those misconceptions about witches, that they go around trying to turn people into frogs. No, although if Bootsie got a little tingle every month when I wrote out that check, well, I couldn't help that, now could I? It costs me one hundred and ten dollars a month more because of her conspiracy, and I can't help but think about it. But if negative thoughts could put people into comas, wouldn't we be seeing an epidemic?"

Maybe not an epidemic, but I can think of several people who might be in somewhat worse shape. Lowell, for instance.

"Witchcraft isn't about flying around on broomsticks and putting evil spells on people. It's about ways to influence ourselves so that we get what we want."

That's sort of what Arinda had said, and even Mouse. "That pendant, the moon goddess," I say. "Is that some kind of a witch thing?"

She looks down, giving herself a triple chin. "No, this is just something I picked up because I happen to like it. The witch thing would be a pentacle."

"Oh. Because I used to have one just like that. Or almost. Only I lost it." I sound downright whiny when I say this; I hate sounding like that. "I thought mine was one of a kind."

Gaynor gives me a steady blue-eyed look. "You bargained for it, didn't you?"

I open my mouth. I got it at the Capitol Hill People's Fair, years ago, one of the first years I was in Denver, when it was still held at East High School. It was the second day of the fair, it looked like rain, and I talked the vendor into giving it to me for half-price.

My mouth is still open when Gaynor says, "I thought so. No wonder you lost it then. You never haggle for magical objects. It's bad luck."

Would Arinda have known Gaynor? That would be an odd connection. Of course, it's odd to run into two such pendants in a week after all these years. Then, thinking of Arinda, I remember the cat.

"Hey, do you need a cat? A nice black cat, very affectionate? Already spayed." Only a little damaged.

Gaynor laughs. "Sure. A witch needs a black cat, right?"

"I'm not kidding. I've got this cat I have to get rid of."

"I'm not kidding, either. I could use a cat. I live in the mountains and I have this mouse problem. It wasn't a problem for a while. A couple of mice I can handle. But they're taking over."

"All right!" I say. "Hey, I can go get it right now."

"Now hold on," Gaynor says, laughing, "I've got another patient, then another patient after that. And I don't know how comfortable a cat would be in Rehab. There's a dog there."

"A very well-trained dog." Connie's Seeing Eye shepherd.

"The cat wouldn't know that, would she?"

"I've got a carrier," I say, as if that solves the whole problem. Then I drag myself back to my questioning. "Were you ever . . . did you ever go to Lowell's office?"

Gaynor thinks about this, then shakes her head. "I knew where she worked, but no, I don't think I ever went there. Discretion and all that. What else did she say about me?"

"That you have Bootsie's name in a bottle of springwater in your freezer," I say.

Gaynor snorts. "I might've expected that," she says. "One problem. I have a cabin in the mountains. Indoor plumbing, but no electricity. In other words, I don't even *have* a freezer."

Gaynor shakes her head as we stroll back toward the atrium. "Now about this cat. I have my last patient at four-thirty. A thirty-minute session."

"I'll have her back here by, say, five? Maybe a few minutes after?" Gaynor nods. Yes!

Back in my office, I lean my head on my hand and close my eyes for two seconds. Harley chooses those two seconds to stick his head in my office. "Hey! No sleeping on company time."

"I was just resting my eyes." It's true!

"You've put in a hard week. You can go home if you want." While I'm wondering if this means Langstrom told Harley to fire me, he goes on. "Heard you kicked butt in court today. Good job. Dennis was impressed."

I suppress a snicker. Sure he was.

I should take Harley's advice and go home, but instead I go through my in-box. It's been filling up with incident reports (minor), interoffice mail (I check the return addresses and then dump all but the most intriguing back into interoffice mail; they'll come back to me in another couple of days), and interoffice mail addressed to Jette. A lease somebody wants reviewed. An announcement that the Project Review Committee meeting has been rescheduled from this morning to next Friday morning. A couple of biennial reports from the secretary of state.

I put sticky notes on the biennial reports, write "Please handle" on them, and drop them on Geri's desk. Then I dictate my notes of my interviews with Lowell and Gaynor.

The only time Gaynor lost her cool was when I mentioned Lowell. Whereas Lowell was spitting and hissing about Gaynor the whole time. But Gaynor had to think about whether she'd been to Lowell's office. Surely she'd remember. And I also noted that she knew about the phenol. I left that out of my report, but in fairness I had asked several nurses whether it would be routinely added to the tray, so it could be common gossip.

I can't see either Gaynor or Lowell dragging Jette into the wilderness. Lowell might have the muscle, but Gaynor seems soft.

I'm drifting off again—in thoughts, not in sleep—when the phone startles me. It's the clerk in the Larimer County coroner's office who has called to tell me the autopsy on Jette has been done.

"Still don't have a copy of the death certificate," she says, "but I have the autopsy report. I don't suppose it'll help you much if you needed to know whether the death was accidental."

"It won't?"

"Just doesn't say. Death by drowning; could have been an accident, could have been suicide. But if you ask me it wasn't suicide."

Drowning. That's a surprise.

"Why not suicide?"

"She was found in a crick. She'd been conscious, she could have just lifted her head."

It's so refreshing to hear somebody pronounce *creek* that way. That's what my grandparents would have called it, unless it had a name. If it had a name, it would be a *creek*. Spelled the same but pronounced with a long *e*.

"There's your double indemnity," the clerk says. "And also, it won't say this in the report either, but that crick was dry when she landed there. Not many suicides would have figured on the runoff, unless she was from around here."

The clerk runs through the autopsy report briefly. Blood alcohol level of .001 percent, very low. But a high level of a sedative. A slight head injury, blunt object to the temple, but not the cause of death. Time of death, based on digestion of stomach contents, body temperature, and ambient temperature, approximately 10 A.M. Thursday. "But you know," the clerk adds, "the body had been in cold water, so that's not very precise. If you needed to be precise."

I think back. At 10 A.M. Thursday, a week ago, Jette hadn't even been missed yet. I was still looking around for a ride to the CHARM meeting.

"The head injury," I say. "Did it happen before or after ingestion of the sedative?"

"Well, now, I can't tell you that. Not from the report. But if somebody had a load of sedative on board, why would anybody need to hit them?"

Good point.

I thank her. I wonder what this means. Particularly the bit about the ditch being dry. Whoever killed Jette hadn't intended to kill her? But that didn't make sense. Knock her out, throw her in a ditch—no, my guess is, whoever dumped her there knew there'd be water in it soon. It's spring, after all.

I dig the detective's card out of my notes and tell his voice mail that I have unearthed some people with connections to Bootsie and to Jette, then leave Bales's name and Lowell's. Graves and Bales. Sounds like a law firm. I leave Gaynor's name, too. But what the hell. It sounds like Lowell's office was virtually abandoned after four o'clock. Anyone could have gone in there.

Then I realize that I left names but nothing about the office or how I got to it. I call back, sure that the cops will say I should have told them as soon as I knew. Fuck that. They get it when they get it. I haven't known all that long and I've been busy.

Instead of voice mail I get the man himself. LeFevre, the casually dressed detective who was in our offices the other day. He's not the lead investigator on Jette's case, but he knows a lot about it. *Now*. After he establishes who I am, he thanks me for the names and goes a little deeper into the connections. But I'd like to know a few things, too.

He grunts. Cops do *not* like sharing their information. "And what do you think you need to know?"

"Mainly, I need to know if anyone else is in danger of being abducted."

"What makes you think Miss Wakefield was abducted?"

"Oh, please. I knew her; she wasn't the type who would go off on a hike in the wilderness. I even think I know why she was abducted."

"Then you should have told us that, when we were in your office. We gave you every opportunity."

"I didn't know then."

I tell him Jette may have caught somebody falsifying the EMR. If he wants the technical stuff, he'll have to talk to someone in IS.

"That's it?" he asks. It doesn't sound like much, when you put it like that.

"I don't know if they lured her to her car or took her there under duress, or if they went to her car and waited for her," I say. "But—"

"But you're pretty convinced these two things were related. You don't think it's possible, say, that someone entirely unrelated to this computer terminal waited in her car. Or that maybe she interrupted somebody breaking into her car—or even her house. You don't know if she went home first, or maybe out for a beer, or maybe she even picked up a hitchhiker."

He doesn't mention the sedative and the head injury. I don't either. "I can state with absolute assurance that she didn't pick up a hitchhiker." I guess he doesn't want to hear about the computer.

"What else do you think you know?" LeFevre says. "It's best to tell us everything."

"I want to help," I say. "Maybe if I knew more, I would think of more. I'm assuming you've got her car and are going over it for evidence. I'm assuming there was somebody else in the car and there's no sign that she had car trouble."

"You're wrong," he says. "One of the tires was flat."

I think for a minute. Would Jette have changed the flat, or would she have struck off through the wilderness for help? Neither. She had a cell phone, like everyone else in this great country. She would have called AAA.

"What made the tire flat?" I ask.

There's a long silence. Then he suggests that I might like to come down and speak to somebody in person.

"No, I wouldn't. The phone is an excellent medium of communication."

"So what else do you know?" he persists.

I'm sure the cops don't want to hear about Lowell and Gaynor and their domestic travails. I tell him anyway.

I was right. He stops me midway and asks, "What else?"

"This terminal, it's out of the way. Practically anybody could have used it. But there might be . . . fingerprints."

"Unless it's fingerprints of known criminals, it won't help," he says.

"Everybody gets fingerprinted when they come to work here." Even risk managers. "And we do a criminal check." We do a criminal check when an applicant says he or she has a record. If the applicant says no to that question, we don't check. Ass-backwards, yes? Sometimes it seems like that's how we do everything.

"We'll check it out," he says. "I don't suppose you could isolate that terminal, so nobody else leaves their fingerprints on it, could you?"

"Probably. Now, can you tell me, please, if anybody else here at Montmorency needs to be worried about abduction?"

"You should take all precautions. You in particular," he says. He considers a moment, then adds, "Here's what we've got. You hit it; there was a second person in that vehicle. Couple of footprints. Size-twelve waffle-stompers, so we're thinking tall but not too heavy, maybe one-eighty, two hundred. You know anybody like that?"

Dennis? I'm bad at guessing people's weights, but I'll bet he weighs more than that. It sure doesn't sound like Lowell and not much like Gaynor. Gaynor I'd guess between to be 130 and 150. Depending on how many sweaters and shawls she was wearing, of course.

"So if you find yourself looking at a guy, slightly above average height, but with the height in the torso, not the legs, you might want to be extra-careful. We think he might have been driving, with Miss Wakefield unconscious in the passenger seat."

"Wow. How do you know all that?"

"We measure the distance between footprints, for one thing. Also considered the position of the car seat, which was not that far back."

I digest this for a moment. "Jette was tall."

"We know that. We also figure it took a fairly big fellow to get her out and down the hill. But not someone big enough to throw her over his shoulder."

This seems to rule out not only Gaynor and Lowell but also Corky Phillips and Alvin Bales—who is, after all, virtually a cripple. And I guess it rules me out, too, or LeFevre wouldn't be telling me this.

I tell him I probably can't isolate the whole computer, but I can get the keyboard and the mouse. "Couldn't hurt," he says. "Put it in some kind of loose wrapping and try not to get your own fingerprints on it."

Who does he think he's dealing with here? I knew that!

I go to the supply cabinet and get an extra-large Jiffy padded envelope.

"Why do you need that?" Anita snaps.

"More evidence," I snap back. "Are you going to be here for the next fifteen minutes?" I ask that because she has her purse on her desk, as do Vanessa and Geri.

"I leave at five."

"Then give me the key to the fire safe, or leave it somewhere I can find it, because I'm going to need to put something in it."

Anita scowls. "Vicky, haven't you ever heard of Miller Time? And I'm not leaving my key out."

"Fine, then give it to me."

Anita slowly opens her drawer, then shuts it. "All right!" she says crossly. "I'll wait. Hurry up, though."

I make the trip as quickly as I can. First to a file cabinet just outside IS, which is full of keyboards, mouses (or are they mice?), and mouse pads. I grab one of each, then skip down the stairs to the basement.

The door to Informatics/Epidemiology/Executive Wellness is locked. Growling and muttering, I go in search of someone who can unlock it. I find a guy—just the type I'm supposed to avoid, which is to say tall—wearing gray overalls and banging on a pipe with a wrench of some kind. "I need to get into an office," I say. "I need to change this keyboard, and I'm in a hurry." My hope, of course, is that he concludes I'm with IS and have a perfect right to go around exchanging keyboards.

"Which office?" He pulls a ring of keys from his belt with one of those sliding tape things.

"Zero four three six. Epidemiology."

"Oh, that one." The keys fly back up the metal strip to his belt. "You do need a key, but any key will work on that lock."

"Come again?"

"You got a key on you? Use it," he says. "We've rekeyed it so often, any key will work."

I go back down the hall and try my house key. It works. Lowell said everybody and his brother had the key to this door, and, by Goddess, she was right. This is the easiest office to break into in the history of the world.

I pull on latex gloves. The old keyboard, mouse, and mouse pad go into my large envelope. As I leave, I make certain the superfluous lock is locked.

I make it back to Admin, slightly breathless, at ten after. Hey! Langstrom's gone! I managed to get through the day without getting fired, despite having tried pretty hard. I hand the envelope over to Anita, who glares as she puts it in the growing evidence file and slams the safe shut. "In your absence," she says frostily, "Geri wanted to know who's supposed to be the registered agent on those corporations. Jette used to be."

"I'll leave her a note."

My next move is simple. Go home, pack up the cat and her assorted food samples, and get her back to the hospital atrium, say, before 5:30. Piece of cake. Except, it turns out, that's not my next move. Harley appears at my door—I thought he'd gone home—and tells me Jette's brother and sister are on their way over. "There are things they have to fill out to get Jette's last check," he says. "I guess I can handle it."

Something in the droopy way he says this makes me want to let him handle it, but I don't. Instead I call Gaynor to tell her I'll be a few minutes late with the cat, like I'm not already.

"Gaynor? Hey, I'm on my way. I'll be there by five-forty-five. Tops. All I have to do is run home and get her."

"I have to leave here by five-thirty," Gaynor says. "I need to

BAD LUCK

get home before dark, because one of my headlights is out. I'm an hour away from my place, and the sun goes behind my mountain at about four-thirty. No streetlights."

Now, this is depressing. Again everything's happening at once. I can't tell Harley I won't speak to Jette's next of kin because I have to unload a cat.

"Tomorrow then?" I try to conceal my eagerness to get this cat out of my life.

"I'm not coming in tomorrow. No clients," Gaynor says. "The guy who took over Dennis's patients during his troubles is using a different therapist, and I'm not driving down the mountain for two half-hour appointments."

Could I leave now and come right back? I don't want the bereaved siblings to have to wait. Not too long, anyway. Not that long.

"Maybe I could drive the cat up this weekend."

"I don't mind," Gaynor says. "It's a long drive, though. Call before you come, to make sure I'll be around." I write her number down. Then she gives me directions, which takes such a long time that I probably *could* have driven home and back. Take Colorado 72 west, go a mile past Indian Peak Road, turn left at Divide View Trail, the first Divide View. If I come to the second one, then I've gone too far.

"How will I know if it's the first one or the second one?"

"You just have to pay attention. If it's the second one, then you won't find my house."

Sheesh. Take Divide View the First two point two miles, at which point there will be a bunch of mailboxes. Just after I pass those mailboxes, veer left and take that street to a fork in the road, then take a right, which goes up sharply, then go past two houses that have For Sale signs and the next left is her driveway. I scribble like mad, trying to get this right. During the course of this conversation, Harley appears in my doorway and jerks his thumb toward the reception area.

"And your driveway leads straight to your house?"

"It doesn't lead anywhere else, but it's not exactly straight. When you get to the broad space with a cliff above it, which is the only place big enough to turn around, you turn right, the only way you can turn. It doesn't look it, but my place is just a few yards from there."

"Do you have an address?"

"Yeah, but it's meaningless. There's not even a number on my house."

How very helpful.

Jette's siblings are, like Jette, blond giants. Derek must be six and a half feet tall, and her sister, Viveca, is not much shorter. Maybe six-four. Her flaxen hair is long, pulled back in a ponytail, with neat bangs, cut very straight, not feathered. Very schoolgirlish. She looks like what she is, a Minnesota farm girl, except—

Except for the web of intricate tattoos on her arms, all the way down to her wrists. These are expertly done, unlike the one just above her white anklet. That one is an unmistakable jailhouse tattoo. Prick yourself with a pin, go over it with a ballpoint, and voilà, you have a permanent cross on your skin. A little memento of your time in the slammer.

They are both very polite, shaking my hand as Harley introduces us. Viveca is red-eyed. We mouth a few senseless phrases about the tragedy. Then Harley splits.

"I don't understand it," Derek says. "Drowning? I'll never understand it. I thought it was just an accident."

"The city," Viveca says. She picks up a framed picture on Jette's desk, her only framed picture. A little blond girl and a dog. Where, in Jette's family, could you find a *little* blond girl?

Derek looks around Jette's office, which seems much smaller with these two in it. "What should we take?"

"Her . . . diploma," I say, none too helpfully. Goddamnit, I'm crying. I don't even care about Jette, but her brother and sister look like such nice people. If you like tattooed giants. I decide not to call attention to my tears by apologizing.

Of course you don't want your boss to get knocked off. Well, maybe you do. I read a survey somewhere that four out of ten Americans, given the chance, would do away with their bosses.

And since she's been gone I've been using her secretary—and her budget—shamelessly. But why tears for Jette and, say, no tears for Bootsie? Or Catgirl?

"Her diploma, yes," Derek says. "Okay, and her pen, and—"

"I can't do this," Viveca says. "It's too soon. I can't deal with it."

"But I suppose somebody else wants this office," Derek says, giving me a meaningful look.

"Not for a while." I pull myself together. I don't want this office, and I'm not even sure that I want this job anymore. "Listen, would it be better if I went through her things and boxed them up, then sent them to you? Later?"

"Yes," Viveca says, and stalks out.

"I appreciate it," Derek tells me. "It's a hard thing to come to terms with. That your sister has been murdered and you don't even know why. I mean me. I'm the one who doesn't know why. Not you. Of course you don't know either...."

"The police are working on it." And so, in my own ineffectual way, am I.

"I'll be staying at her place for a while, to wrap things up," Derek says. "I don't suppose you know of anybody who'd take her cat."

This makes me laugh, snort, and then sends me in the opposite direction, blubbering like a baby. "I'm sorry," I gasp. "Bad things are happening to people I like, and it's hard to deal with."

"Eh, I'll take the cat to my ranch," Derek says. "It's a city cat, so it'll have some adapting to do. One of the more spoiled cats I've known in my life."

I'd offer him Tara, but it doesn't seem appropriate. Besides, I already found a home for that cat, and I'll get her to Gaynor if I have to hand-deliver her.

32

Leo Rising

I go home to an empty apartment, which I find kind of refreshing. Of course it isn't really empty. Tara is here somewhere. Somebody has very thoughtfully placed a six-pack of Heineken in my refrigerator. This, and the absence of Tara, makes me suspect that Glenn has been here, but he's not here now.

I find the cat in my closet, sleeping on top of a pink angora sweater that is now a pink and black angora sweater. I pick up the black cashmere cowlneck right next to it and put it on. Along with some black leggings. Comfort clothes. Then I grab a beer, pop the cap, and start polishing my shoes.

Every time I buy shoes I resolve to polish them after each wearing, to protect my investment. For some reason, this becomes a very low priority. So every few weeks I have to make like a shoeshine girl.

When I get to my Diego Della Valle boots I find out that they have *toothprints* on them. Little tiny toothprints. It doesn't take a master detective to figure out whose teeth.

Damn it, I knew puppies liked to chew up shoes, but I hadn't realized cats did. "You're history, cat," I announce, wishing it were true. Tara doesn't even look interested.

I polish the boots as best I can. When I take them back to the closet, I notice a wet-looking stain on my bedspread. I grind my teeth. At least Tara, up to this point, has been using her litter box perfectly.

Worse luck, it's water. A murderous rage envelops me. "You goddamned little beast!" I scream at her. "You inconsequential stitched-up motherfucking fur ball, you wrecked my waterbed!"

I have to get out of here. I've had a really bad day. I pull on an old pair of socks and my cowboy boots and pace around my bedroom. Then I peel back the linen to see how bad the damage is. I have a repair kit, somewhere, but in ten years I've never needed it.

I dig through various drawers. Before I find it, my phone rings. I grab it, hoping it's somebody who wants to meet me for a drink somewhere. "Yes!" I yell.

It's Kate, who's used to my rude answering techniques. "Hey, lady, good news. You're in the right profession after all."

It takes me a few seconds to remember our last conversation. It seems like weeks ago. I was bitching about my job. "No, I'm not."

"Oh, yes. I got my friend Nina to do your chart. She did a fabulous job."

"My chart?" I immediately think medical records.

"Astrological chart, girlfriend. She's the one who does the charts of all the big execs at Azimuth Oil, among other things."

Whenever Azimuth, the oil company that helped make Kate's daddy rich, hires a new executive, the company gets the new hire's chart done to see if said exec will be compatible with the rest of the management staff. Team building. Whatever floats your boat. At Montmorency they use the somewhat more conventional Myers-Briggs profile. I, for instance, am an ESTP.

"Listen to this," Kate says. "You're a triple Leo, which is rare. Maybe even a quadruple Leo. I guess that would be depending on latitude, longitude, et cetera, which of course I couldn't tell her."

I don't know myself. I was born on an army base near Bad Kreuznach, Germany, ten days before my father's post ended. My mother has not spared any details of what a monumental pain I was on the trip home, but she didn't mention latitude or longitude.

"Okay, here goes. 'Your birth sign, as well as your rising sign, your moon, and Mercury, are in Leo, which makes this a particularly influential sign in many aspects of your life. Leo is a seeker of heat and light, and therefore a seeker of truth, and therefore a seeker of justice. Because of the element of heat, you do not shy away from conflict or controversy, but you understand that the path to truth is never easy.'"

"That sounds like my profession all right," I mutter.

"Anyway, this is great, there's stuff about your love life, your pets, your cars, your apartment. It's kinda weird how Nina doesn't even know you, yet she got so many of these things right."

"My *pets*?"

"Come on, you triple Leo, you know it has to be a cat."

No no no no no! "She have it in there that my car caught fire?"

Kate giggles. "Well, a seeker of heat and light, I guess that would qualify on both counts."

I can hardly wait to read about my love life.

The path to truth is never easy. How very profound. I suppose next I will start believing this stuff.

I ask Kate if she'd like to drive up into the mountains with me and she says not tonight. Then I call Gaynor, hoping she's had enough time by now to get home. I am not keeping the goddamned cat all weekend. And also I don't know where I'm going to sleep.

She doesn't answer. I leave a message asking her to call me as soon as she gets in. I pace around my apartment. Tara is nowhere to be seen. I suppose I will have to be nice to this freaky cat so I can catch her in order to get rid of her. I *have* been nice. Haven't thrown her against the wall once despite a lot of provocation.

My pets. A cat? Holy Jesus Christ. No way. I point my finger at the phone and command it to ring—it worked once. But it doesn't work this time.

I find the waterbed patch kit, with instructions, in the very top drawer of the kitchen, the one I have to stand on a chair to reach. But at least I find it. While I'm up there, Tara decides to reappear and let me know that this is the moment when she's desperate for food.

I use the opportunity to put her in the cat carrier. This cat is going. She's history. If Gaynor doesn't call back, I'll take her to the Dumb Friends League.

I read the instructions on the patch kit. "Drain the waterbed . . ." Fuck! I look at the cat carrier. *Nine minutes*. I stalk into the bedroom, find a bucket, fail to find the hose. After all, what would I be doing with a hose? *Six minutes*.

I go back to the kitchen and pull out a notebook to write a message to Glenn. And there's the note I forgot to leave Geri earlier, about how to deal with the biennial reports.

I still don't want to miss Gaynor's call, so I use my cell phone to leave a message. Geri should replace Jette's name as registered agent with mine. Not only that, we should go through *all* our corporate books and make the replacement everywhere. We should check to see if Jette made a list of corporations she's RA for. Jette was forward thinking and detail oriented, so maybe she did. In any case we should start such a list for me, in the case of my own unanticipated demise. I hang up and check my watch. *Two minutes* . . . The phone rings.

"Sorry to bother you, but can I bring that cat up tonight?" Gaynor says sure, no problem, it's about an hour's drive and am I okay with the directions? I think so.

I leave a note for Glenn telling him where I'm going and why. Oh, boy, tonight I can stay at his place, on his mattress on the floor. Roughing it. I pull on my black leather coat. It takes me two trips to load the cat and all her paraphernalia into the car. Then we head for the hills.

33

Speak of the Devil

Coal Creek Canyon has missed out on a lot of the development that's been going on in a lot of other mountain communities—although I don't suppose the people here miss it, exactly. I notice a sign for the grange. Things haven't changed much since my last trip up this canyon, which was at least ten years ago.

At that time I thought this was pretty much the typical old-style mountain community, full of typical mountain people: hillbillies. I don't know why. The people I knew who lived up here were old hippies, which should mean that Gaynor fits in perfectly.

There seems to be a rule that at least five vehicles must occupy each yard, with at least one of them up on blocks. Oh, and you have to have two or three nasty-looking dogs.

Anyway, in the fading twilight, this is what I see:

A wooden fence, a barn, a tractor, and a couple of pickups under a mercury vapor light. Patches of snow, or in some cases whole drifts, on the north side of the highway (I think). I get only glimpses as I creep along the road, which gets smaller, ruttier, and steeper as I follow Gaynor's directions. She mentioned it was steep. I downshift into second and then into first. The area is heavily wooded. I tell myself that if I went off the road, I wouldn't go far; these trees would catch me. *Sure* they would.

It gets worse. When I come to the fork, the hill I go up is so steep that for a minute I'm afraid I'll have to roll back down and get a running start, but I make it. Barely. One For Sale sign. Who's going to see it up here? Then another. And finally her driveway.

I can't believe she calls this a driveway. It's a steep, rocky, deer trail. I hesitate at the clear space—she said this was the only place you could turn around, but she also said her house wasn't much farther up, and a straight shot at that.

This is four-wheel-drive territory, for sure. Yet I make it, with my car struggling to breathe (or at least that's what it sounds like—panting and gasping).

It's a fairly new cabin, not what I expected, in a hexagon shape. It seems built into the hill, with a deck jutting off one side.

I pull in behind a scrofulous-looking VW, cut my lights, and am immediately in total darkness. Okay, not total. There is a very dim porch light. About fifteen watts.

I thought she said she didn't have electricity.

So maybe it's a candle. Without the headlights, I'm in blackness so thick I can taste it.

I hear a dog barking somewhere in the distance, but other than that just a lot of quiet. When I stayed with friends in this area long ago, it was so quiet that I couldn't get to sleep. I don't lock my car, but you'd better believe I set my parking brake—something I never do. I turn on the overhead light to collect the cat carrier. Without benefit of streetlights or the glow that bounces off the clouds in the city, it's like being in a black pit. I grope my way past the Volkswagen and stumble over what must be a porch.

If there's a knocker or a bell of any kind, I can't see it. But I guess I made enough noise. Just as I bump into the door it opens, letting out a wave of frangipani-scented air and revealing Gaynor.

"Hey," she says softly. "You made it."

"Your cat." I hold up the cat carrier. Gaynor takes it and then tells me it's a house rule to remove footwear.

"Oh, I won't come in," I say.

"Of course you will. You can leave the boots on if it's important. You don't want to just hand the kitty over like an inanimate object, do you?"

I don't care, but I step into the entry, slip my boots off, and add them to several other pairs, in varying sizes, scattered under and around a bench in the entry.

"Neat socks," Gaynor notes as she opens the carrier.

They are wild socks. A little thin on the bottom but presentable enough otherwise, a black-and-white-check pattern sprinkled with fluorescent grapes.

Tara pops her head out of the cat carrier and looks around with interest. "She still looks bad," I say. An understatement: She still looks like FrankenCat. "But she's okay. And spayed and everything." Now that I'm getting rid of her, her ears look rather dear, particularly the tattered one.

"That will give her status," Gaynor says, touching the cat's ear. "She'll look like the veteran of many fights."

Tara leaps out of the carrier and walks around slowly, smelling things, then rubbing against them.

Gaynor's place is cozy: a room with a potbellied stove blasting away, a leather chair, a small round table (cable spool) with two chairs, and lit by a hurricane lamp. The table contains a bunch of other stuff, too: an ashtray, a pile of paper, a green paperback called *Wiring Simplified*. Tara will be sure to knock all this stuff to the floor, but I don't mention that.

"You said you had indoor plumbing," I say. "Can I avail myself?"

"Sure. That way."

I can see into the kitchen, separated from the main room by—what else?—strands of beads and also illuminated by lamplight. But bright compared with the permeating dark outside. A window over a small sink looking out into the mountain blackness, herbs under a Gro-Lite. Ah, growing your own. What a nice witchlike thing to do.

A Gro-Lite? Maybe she has a generator. Couldn't be solar, not if she's in shadow most of the day, as she says.

The bathroom is darker, lit by a tall black candle. Other

than that, and the fact that there are no square corners, it looks like any bathroom—sink, tub, towels. Black soap. This would freak me out except that I've seen it before. I'd never have suspected Gaynor of being the Laszlo type, but if that's what keeps her skin looking so great, I may be a convert.

"Hey, did you ever know a girl called Arinda? Her real name was Phyllis something," I say.

"No," she says shortly. "Would you like a cup of tea? Or some wine?"

I'd like hot chocolate with a splash of peppermint schnapps, but what the hell. "Sure. Tea."

"Have a seat," Gaynor says.

I choose the leather chair. In addition to the hurricane lantern, Gaynor has a candle burning in here. I stare into the flame, watching it squat, then stretch, whipping out a ribbon of black smoke.

I sit at an angle to a pair of sliding patio doors. A bamboo curtain is pulled to one side—not that a bamboo curtain would provide much in the way of insulation. But the pot-bellied stove throws out so much heat that I shrug out of my coat.

"I wanted to talk to you a little more about this Bootsie thing," Gaynor says. "I just wondered if I would be questioned because of my attitude, because of what Lowell said. In some kind of official investigation."

"The official investigation is over." The unofficial one isn't about Bootsie; it's about Jette.

"Oh, okay," Gaynor says. "Good."

Tara noses her way back into the room and leaps into my lap, causing a slight tea spill. I should drink this tea and get out of here.

"Nice place," I venture. "Even with no electricity. Cozy."

Gaynor apparently picks up on my irony here. "You might have noticed, I do have electricity coming to the house. The house itself isn't wired, though."

Ah. So that *wasn't* a candle burning over the porch.

"Keep meaning to do that, don't I," she says. "Wire it. Thought I'd get me bruv to help out. He's handy that way."

"What brothers are for," I agree, taking a big gulp of tea and burning my mouth somewhat. What *is* this stuff? It tastes like hot cough syrup. "Cat, you're in the wrong lap."

Tara purrs and kneads.

"That's one thing that a hundred and ten a month would have helped out with," Gaynor says. "Among many others. Almost lost the place."

I sip the tea, rather delicately, wondering how much she could have paid for a place like this, small, with no electricity, up an impossible road.

"Bootsie ruined my reputation, she did," Gaynor says darkly. "But that wasn't enough for her. Oh, no."

"What happened?" I feel I have to ask.

"I was working for the foundation. This was a couple of years ago, when Bootsie was head of it. I was, like, the peon, the one who answered phones, ran papers around, made the tea. Well I had my patients, didn't I, only I wasn't full-time then as a PT. So I worked around that. Cheesed her off, not that *she* worked full-time. So then the petty cash comes up short, and as it was stashed in the file cabinets behind my desk, I was blamed."

"Petty cash?"

"Four hundred dollars, or so they said. Mind, I don't know. I didn't take it. But the circumstances were such that it looked like I could have taken it. And in the end the agreement was that I wouldn't be charged for it, but I would resign. Sacked, right, but that was fine with me. I was getting more clients then, and it wasn't the best job. Miss Bootsie didn't think I dressed well enough to be her part-time peon, but fine. Okay, I resigned; no hint that I resigned under a cloud or anything like that. But then, when I went for financing on this place, come to find out that Miss Bootsie had gone to court and entered a judgment against me in the amount of four hundred dollars, plus collection costs, which was bullshit. *What* collection costs? I have the resignation; it made no mention of repaying this money that I *supposedly* stole. And who the bloody hell has *four hundred dollars* lying around in petty cash? And I'd had no notice. None of those letters that said this is an attempt to collect a debt—I know what they look like."

For some reason I flash on Geri, using floral delivery to camouflage a summons. I'll bet it's really hard to serve somebody with no address. If Gaynor was living here then.

"Not only that but Miss Bootsie was friendly enough when I ran into her. Not a word about where's my money. She could have said something. So I had to write my own letter, send it to the credit agency, saying I knew nothing whatsoever about this so-called debt and hadn't received any notice and didn't owe it, and meanwhile I was scrabbling about for the financing. I'd been living here for years and didn't want to leave, start all over. And I was getting the place for a good price, less than my rent, if I could have gotten the financing. So I did what I had to do, went up a few points, talked to lawyers, the works."

Gaynor delivers all this without bile. She's simply recounting a tale. A bit of sarcastic emphasis on some of the words is the only hint that she's upset about it; she even smiles at times.

"So the next time I ran into Bootsie I asked her why the bloody hell she did this to me, and she said it must have been a mistake. You know, somebody wrote off the loss as a bad loan to an employee and it accidentally went to collection. The only problem being, it was Bootsie's own collection agency." Gaynor laughs. "Expect me to believe she doesn't know that stuff? Doesn't sign things? Come on. I can't figure it. Even if she thinks I really stole the money—and I guess she does. Or did."

Who knows? Do I want to go back and investigate the dismissal of a part-time employee from the hospital's charitable foundation? I always thought of the foundation as a bunch of nice ladies with nothing better to do but have a catered lunch in our boardroom every once in a while, certainly not as a bunch of vindictive old bats who would become crazed over the loss of four hundred dollars from petty cash. And that *does* seems like a lot of petty cash.

But I'll have to check this out. Maybe Jette, doing her so-called pro bono work, signed the papers. Maybe Gaynor has a motive after all.

Now Gaynor turns bitter. "I mean, why pick on me? Bootsie had it all, didn't she—good looks, money, nice home, nice car, nice kids, nice husband. *She had it all,* and she'd had it all from the beginning. I had nothing to start with, built myself up, lost it, had to start over. There were people in that office she could've pinned it on with less harm. Why kick a bloke who's already down?"

Gaynor shakes herself back into cheerfulness. "Well, now, enough negative energy on Bootsie. If that didn't put her over the edge, nothing will, right?"

Gaynor looks the same as she did before: a gentle, aging flower child. But her house no longer seems hospitable to me. I glug down some more of the tea. It's cooler now, which has not improved its taste.

"Celestial Seasonings cranberry, in case you wondered," Gaynor says. "I should have asked if you wanted honey or sugar in it, but it's pretty sweet on its own."

That it is.

"Why would you think I knew this Arinda person?" she asks, sitting down opposite me.

"Oh . . . like all risk managers in Denver know each other, all witches in Denver know each other. This was Arinda's cat."

Arinda's cat jumps off my lap onto an upright piano and walks along the keyboard, playing a spooky tune. Then she leaps to the top of the piano and looks around.

Gaynor launches into the tale of how she got the piano into the cabin. Seems the piano movers got it up the hill okay but abandoned it on the porch. She and her brother had to get it inside, just the two of them.

"My half brother," she says. "He's kind of . . . well, I watch over him, seeing as he was so young when his mother died. A right trollop she was, and he's suffered because of it. She drank, that is, and he's a little on the dim side, maybe the drinking, and maybe just the fact she died when he was so young. Nine, he was."

I don't want to hear about it. I'm thinking about the trip down the mountain.

Get a grip. As she said, it's a straight shot backing down the driveway, assuming you could *see*, and of course there are all those nice trees to keep you from falling *all* the way down. A comforting thought.

"It's little things," she says. "It's not that he's dumb or anything. He just can't seem to plan very far ahead. He doesn't see consequences. Poor impulse control."

I nod. I suffer from that myself. Coming up here in the dark, for instance.

"But he's a good strong boy and he wants to be helpful," she says as though the kid is still nine years old. "Ah, Dickie. You know, he was the most beautiful child. Wouldn't think it to look at him today, but he was so blond. And so handsome. Not that he's not still cute and all."

I drain the tea, which leaves me feeling as though I've eaten something meant for a horse. A definite alfalfa aftertaste and bitter, too. I expected better from Celestial Seasonings. I stand, feeling tilted. Gaynor stands. She picks up the candle.

I don't know what the altitude is here, but sometimes I get a little light-headed in the mountains. My ears pop and my equilibrium disappears. I'm not sure I'm standing up straight. The fact that Gaynor's place has no square corners doesn't help.

"I'll walk you out," she says. But before I can get into my coat, the door opens and a guy walks in.

Gaynor seems delighted. "Speak of the devil," she says. "Here's Dickie now, me bruv. Dickie, hey, you blocked her car, you'll have to back down. Vicky's just leaving."

"Quiet car," I say to the guy on the porch.

"Keeps it purring like a kitten," Gaynor agrees. "Dickie, this is Vicky. Speaking of kitties, she brought me one—"

"You!" Dickie says. He steps a little farther into the light.

Before he was just a large, dark shape. The light turns him into someone I know from somewhere.

I make the connection with the next thing he says, even though he says it to Gaynor. "She knows. She's known from the beginning. Arinda brought her here."

34

Sit a Spell

I feel a chill creep down my back, the kind of chill that no amount of hot tea, and not even the potbellied stove, can dispel. Gaynor's brother is Arinda's boyfriend. I couldn't pick him out of a lineup—or identify him from police photos—but I'm sure now.

And he's right. Arinda did bring me here in a roundabout way. This gives me another chill, one that goes down to my fingertips.

I start easing my arms into my coat, pretending I didn't hear him. What is it that he knows I know? That the police are looking for him in connection with Arinda's death?

He's not bad-looking, although not the kind of guy who appeals to me. I favor a more intelligent look. He does not have a mustache, but I know why I remembered his eyebrows. They are dark precise arches over his eyes.

My mind immediately processes that Gaynor lied to me when she said she didn't know Arinda. She must have. Not just because Arinda's a witch; because Arinda was living with her brother. She lied about the electricity. And what else? Something is nagging at me.

Dickie has gone pale. "We can't get away from her," he says.

We?

"She came to the house the night after that thing with the little black kids—"

"*Will* you shut up!" Gaynor barks.

So Dickie was the brilliant dude who tried to buy a riot. How did he know the make and model of the Devosses' cars?

Dickie shuts up. My immediate reaction is to check for weapons—both the kind that could be used against me and the kind I could use against them, if they try to keep me here. How could I leave? Dickie's truck is pulled up behind my car.

I could duck out the door and roll down the hill. In fact, that sounds good. I reach my foot around, hoping to snag one of my boots.

"You can't go," Gaynor says. "We have to figure this out."

I try to divert them from the fact that Dickie's wanted for his girlfriend's murder and I know it.

"Look, I don't care. He's the guy who tried to get some kids to start a riot around the hospital? Doesn't matter, because it didn't happen. None of the stuff you tried to pull on Bootsie had any effect, either." Except the last thing, which had its effect on Jette.

"Maybe, maybe not," Gaynor says in her new, hard voice. "But it's my brother I've got to think about, isn't it?"

I make a fast move toward the door. The hell with footwear. I have to get out of here.

"Grab her!" Gaynor says. Dickie obliges. He smells quite strongly like Bob's Bump Shop, that same greasy mechanic smell. I can't move; I try to catch his chin with my head and miss. My feet are off the ground, kicking ineffectively. My arms are uselessly pinned beneath his. I'm immobilized, although I'm not uncomfortable.

"She knows all about those kids," Dickie says, not even panting. "I don't know how she knew. I didn't tell anybody."

Dickie is not the most analytical soul I've run into lately. He's focused on the riot, which was nothing, and not the murder of his girlfriend. But that's okay. Maybe I can use that.

"He hasn't done anything," I say. "The riot never happened."

"I never told him to do that," Gaynor says. "He thought that one up on his own."

The awful thought hits me that perhaps Dickie murdered Arinda because she brought me, the hospital lawyer, into his home, at a time when he was feeling guilty. He hadn't been interested in me at all until Arinda said I was a lawyer.

I turn to Gaynor. "None of your spells worked. You had nothing to do with Bootsie's condition. There's no reason to keep me here."

"Workings, sure," Gaynor says. "I know that. You don't have to do anything, you know. You simply invoke our old friend Murphy's Law. And help it along, however."

"The phenol, the record, the computer—"

"Whatever," Gaynor says. She makes a face. "The computer."

"But you have nothing to worry about. You didn't kill Bootsie."

"You are a dimwit," Gaynor says. "Bootsie's not dead."

Oh . . . right. True. As good as, though.

"Back inside," Gaynor says to Dickie, who moves me back as if I were a store mannequin. It's no use fighting him. If I had my boots on, I could try to stomp on his instep. Not a very practical idea, since my feet are several inches above his insteps. I note that the no-footwear-in-the-house prohibition has not been extended to Dickie. He's wearing mud-encrusted boots, size twelve at least. Size-twelve waffle-stompers. Yeah, and he's big enough to have carted Jette around without too much trouble.

"You can let her go," Gaynor says. "Just don't let her get away." He releases me, and I sink back into the leather chair as if Dickie's grip has somehow removed my muscles. Dickie stands a few feet away with his head lowered. Gaynor throws her hair to one side, rubs her neck, and then lights a cigarette.

Even though it's clove, it smells wonderful. It gives me an idea. A very small one, one that probably won't work.

"Do you mind if I smoke?" A lit cigarette might not stop Dickie, but it could slow him down.

Gaynor thinks about this for a minute. "Why not?"

I lean down to my purse and then I have another idea. My cell phone. I hit the button that will automatically dial the last number called. Who was the last person I called? Geri. Too bad it wasn't 911, but you can't have everything. Whatever Gaynor says has a good chance of being immortalized on Geri's voice mail. If, for instance, I'm not around to tell people. Although I intend to be.

I pull the cigarette out and light it and try to steady my nerves. The important thing is not to panic.

"I've got it," Gaynor says. "Dickie, you have to be cool about this." He raises his head and looks at Gaynor.

These people probably mean to kill me as surely as they killed Jette. Blunt object to the temple, narcotic overdose, then dumped unconscious in the nearest mountain stream. As surely as they—or at least Dickie—killed Arinda. I never knew how, but anyway, she's dead. And here I'm thinking the important thing is not to panic. But at least somebody will have a clue.

A clue! I need to leave one. "Gaynor, you and Dickie don't have to do this," I say, so the names Gaynor and Dickie will register on Geri's voice mail.

Gaynor ignores me. Will she hit me, or will Dickie just pick me up and choke the life out of me? I feel sort of numb, but not, oddly enough, panicky.

"Keep an eye on her," Gaynor says. "I'll be right back." She goes into the kitchen and Dickie just stands there.

This is the worst moment so far. I figure she's going after a knife. I can barely get my voice to work, but on the off chance the voice mail will stop recording if there's a silence, I keep talking. "I think maybe you and your sister need to talk things over in private." I attempt to survey the situation without seeming desperate. Potential weapons: the hurricane lamp, the candle, the fireplace poker. Potential escape route: the patio door, if I could jump over the arm of the chair and open the door before Dickie got to me. Dickie is big but not terribly vigilant. Of course, then I'd be on Gaynor's deck. But that seems preferable to being in Gaynor's cabin.

If I can disable Dickie, I'll have only Gaynor to deal with. "I'm sure you didn't mean what happened to Arinda." As I say it, I'm convinced it's true. He doesn't know his own strength. He has poor impulse control.

"I didn't," Dickie says. "I miss her." He looks at me suspiciously, almost as if he's afraid of me. He thinks Arinda brought me here (so do I). Could I use that? Too bad I don't have any magical powers. I don't even have the High John the Conqueror in my pocket.

I wonder where the cat has gotten to. The goddamned little cat who started all this.

I raise my voice slightly. "And I guess you and Gaynor also killed Jette, but you probably didn't mean that either."

Dickie shakes his head—not very helpful for recording purposes—and Gaynor comes back in, moving fast, with my teacup in her hand. But no knife.

"He had nothing to do with Jette. Nothing," she says.

I don't know why I should believe a word she says.

She sets the cup down beside me, then stands back and crosses her arms. Right; so who left the prints from the size-twelve waffle-stompers near Jette's car?

"It's sure hard to believe you dragged Jette out of the hospital by yourself," I say.

"Not that it matters, but it was pretty darned easy."

"But why? So she caught you messing around with Lowell's computer." I'm sure I've got that right, and Gaynor doesn't deny it. "That's nothing compared to murder."

"I didn't murder Jette," Gaynor says.

"Somebody did." I stare at the tea. "Was she the lawyer who signed those papers Bootsie filed against you?"

Gaynor shakes her head. "We can do this easy, or we can do it hard," she says grimly. "Now drink your tea. Same stuff you had before."

I make a face. I didn't like it before and now I'm about one hundred percent sure it's drugged. "No, thank you. Did you have Dickie stationed in the parking garage to grab Jette? After trying to talk the neighborhood kids into starting a riot?"

Gaynor sits down and looks at me. "Drink your tea. You will feel better. You will feel very good. On the whole, I prefer a gentle way of doing things."

I guess she means if I drink the drugged tea, then I will just pass out and she won't have to knock me upside of the head with the poker. It *does* sound better.

"I don't feel like contributing to my own demise." That's putting it bluntly. In fact, I don't feel like *participating* in my own demise.

"You're nuts," Dickie says. He seems to be addressing Gaynor, not me. "You'll get us into more trouble. Who's Jette?"

"Jette was also a lawyer," I tell him. "Tall, blond. Does that ring a bell?" He shakes his head.

"I tell you, he had nothing to do with that. Just so you won't be wondering, I didn't kill Jette. I simply removed her from the premises."

"I'm not going to be so easy. People know that I came here. They'll be expecting me to come back. When I don't show up . . ."

"They won't be expecting you to have a wreck on your way home," Gaynor says. "But just so you know, I don't espouse violence. Jette crept up on me when I was working at the computer, and I panicked and hit her on the head with a three-hole punch. I admit it. I should have been tougher mentally. I shouldn't have panicked."

"For God's sake, that wouldn't have killed her." Talk about panic. This is not one of those cases where the truth shall set you free.

"Of course not," Gaynor says. "But it would have been hard to explain."

She couldn't explain knocking Jette out with a hole punch, so she killed her?

Perhaps the thing to do is to foster the belief that I am sipping

Gaynor's drugged tea and it's having an effect. I take a small sip, sit back, and close my eyes.

"So I gave her a syringe of Mepergan while I got my faculties back, to figure out what to do," Gaynor says, sounding quite pleased with herself. "You know, I never much liked her."

Nobody did. But that's no reason to kill her.

"I took her down to the parking garage and poured her into her car. Drove her out to the woods and left her," Gaynor says. "I planted in her mind the belief that she had been abducted and raped. She would have believed it, when she came to, only I guess she never did."

Poor Gaynor, innocent all the way. I'll bet she did kill her stepmother.

It's funny, though, she still seems warm and friendly to me. Like I just can't believe she's going to kill me. Or maybe she's not. Maybe she's just going to leave me facedown in some ditch with some wild idea planted in my brain like I was abducted by aliens.

"How did you get an unconscious person through the hospital without anyone seeing you?" I ask. "Oh—no, Lowell told me that. You can become invisible."

Gaynor smiles, a friendly, open smile. "It's true. It's not invisible, more like just blending in. I put her on a gurney, see, and I grabbed some scrubs out of a closet, and I just walked her through the halls with a sheet over her and a mask over her face. Connected to an IV."

Well, of course. These twosomes are constantly strolling through the hospital.

"So when did you bring Dickie in? Or did he work there?" I'm thinking he might be ... trainable. An Environmental Services person.

"Dickie had nothing to do with any of that. He didn't even know about it."

"Yeah, well, what about the size-twelve boots?"

"I wore them," Gaynor says. "Also extra weight, ankle weights and that, to throw them off about my size."

"I guess Dickie was going to handle the rape part."

"He didn't know anything about it," she insists.

"Was all that really necessary?" I no longer trouble to make my words sound crisp. My voice sounds dysarthric, like that of a stroke victim.

"You said a person needed an action and an intent in order to be found guilty of murder, right?" Gaynor asks.

Boy, I barely remember that conversation. "Something like that," I mutter. This tea tastes the same as the first cup—very syrupy—but it seems to pack quite a wallop, or else I am insanely suggestible. I am going to have to walk quite a line here, to keep my faculties while pretending I'm losing them.

"I think I should just go," Dickie says.

"Not yet," Gaynor snaps. "I'll need you in a minute." She looks back at me. I shut my eyes, doing my best to appear out of it.

"Right back," she says, and I hear the clatter of the beaded curtains. More tea? Doesn't matter; this may be my only chance. I come to life, jump over the arm of the chair, and make for the patio door.

It helps, somewhat, that the room is cluttered and that Dickie is large. I flip the lock on the patio door, but the door doesn't open. Too late I see why: in addition to the lock, there's a broomstick inserted in the tracks to keep the door from opening. Before I can toe it out, Dickie grabs me in his immobilizing grip. And Gaynor's back in the room. Smiling.

I give it one more desperate try. "If you guys haven't done anything, then what's the big deal? Just let me go home."

"It doesn't matter anymore," Gaynor says. "It doesn't even matter that you've got your recording device going in that purse, because that device is going to disappear." She moves in close to where Dickie is holding me and I feel a jab in my arm. "But I did not kill Jette, and Dickie did not help." I can't even look down to see what caused the jab. A needle, I assume. Gaynor goes on talking. "I put her in her car, then I drove her to a place I know about. I stopped home for a change of clothing, because she was asleep; she didn't care. I dropped her off, left her car, left the boots, and hitchhiked back in time for my first patient." Gee. She could have just taken her broom.

Gaynor steps back, holding a syringe. Just as I figured.

"So you're telling me you didn't do anything. So you're in the clear." I feel like I'm swaying, which is not possible since Dickie's holding me quite firmly.

Being a nurse, I'm much more concerned about where that syringe has been than about what was in it.

"Fortunately, I can go without sleep for days, when I need to," Gaynor says.

I feel a sudden fury. "What was the point?"

"Just helping Murphy's Law along."

As my rage dissolves, I suddenly feel as if I have gone for days without sleep. Mental toughness, I tell myself. My life may depend on keeping some part of me awake. Correction: I'm convinced my life depends on it.

I close my eyes, chanting over and over to myself: Stay awake, stay alert. Stay angry. Simultaneously, I try to let myself go limp.

I don't know if Gaynor is convinced that I've lost consciousness, but Dickie is. He carries me into the entry again and then drops me, more or less, onto the floor.

"You'll need to get your truck down the hill," Gaynor says. "Let me make sure she's out first."

Two things keep me awake: fear of what she's going to do to me to make sure I'm out, which, of course, I'm not, and the realization of what she means to do. She's going to put me in the car, unconscious (well, hopefully not), and then point me down that hill.

To test for consciousness, she stabs the back of my hand with a pin, the same kind of noxious stimulation used on Bootsie to test her reflexes. Whatever she shot me with must have been some heavy-duty painkiller, because the pinpricks feel like, well, like pinpricks, but they don't hurt, and I don't flinch.

Then she presses her fingertips lightly on my wrist. Pent-up anger is making my heart race and there's nothing I can do about it. After a few seconds she removes her fingers. I guess I passed.

"Okay," she says. "Get the truck out of the way, then get back here. Hurry. I don't know how long she'll be out."

Is this my chance? I don't think so. I'd have to get to my feet, get past Gaynor, and get out the door. No . . . I think I will make my move when she puts me in the car. Or am I just procrastinating because I'm too limp to move? *Am* I too limp to move? There's no way to test it without blowing my unconscious act.

This is a great drug in a way. I feel liquid and warm and floaty. It would be so easy to just go with it and pass out.

Next thing I know, Dickie is hoisting me up. That was fast. My sense of time is distorted. I remain limp. There's a certain way your limbs dangle when you're unconscious. Dickie probably wouldn't know if I did it wrong, but Gaynor might. It's all I can do not to kick him in the balls, but if I did that, even Dickie would know I was not unconscious.

He throws me over his shoulder as if I weigh nothing. I engage in mental calculations: Maybe he *wasn't* involved in getting rid of Jette. He'd have had no trouble carrying her. The air is sharp and cold. Would an unconscious person get goosebumps?

"The overlook?" Dickie says.

"That's on a highway," Gaynor points out to him. "No, I think just before the turnoff. That will look better. Don't you worry about it, I'll find a place."

The overlook. Jesus. Now I really have goosebumps.

I hear the sound of Gaynor digging through my purse for my car keys. Wrong, Gaynor, they're in my coat pocket.

"Shoot," Gaynor says, "a cell phone. I thought it was a tape recorder. I wonder who she was trying to call?"

I guess that's the end of the message. Gaynor must not have one of these gadgets or she'd know that it will automatically redial the last number called. Not that I give a shit. The message is on Geri's voice mail, and it will stay there until Geri retrieves it, even if I'm not there. There is *nothing* Gaynor can do to erase it.

She locates the keys in the pocket of my coat. "We'd better get her coat on," she says. She and Dickie wrestle me around, trying to put my arms in my coat. I don't make it any easier. *Limp* is the word here. It's probably more like trying to force a strand of cooked spaghetti through a straw than like trying to put a cat into a cat carrier. "Okay, so we'll hang it over the seat."

I would like to help her out here. Tell her that I would never go outside with my coat off—people will know that—and that I always, always wear my seat belt. Being a risk manager and all.

Whoever finds my body will think that's most peculiar . . . wait a minute. Whoever finds my *body*?

In a stroke of brilliance, I allow myself to drool rather than swallowing my saliva. Eeyuw.

"Something in the seat," Dickie says. "You want her in the passenger side, right?"

"For now," Gaynor says. "Darn it. She brought the cat box. We'll have to get that out. She would have left it." She pulls out the box and the bag of kitty litter and Dickie stuffs me into the seat.

"And her boots. We better get those on, she wouldn't be driving around barefoot. Get her in there. *Hurry.* I'll take this stuff inside and get her boots."

Dickie may have poor impulse control but he doesn't move fast. He arranges me so I'm sitting in the seat, but—being unconscious—I'm slumped over. My chest rests on my thighs, my arms dangle, and my feet are still hanging out the door. It's a great imitation of unconsciousness if I do say so myself. I should get an Oscar.

Dickie leans down to put my feet in, and I fall out of the car with minimum pain. He grunts, squats, and hoists me up again. I hear Gaynor's front door creak, and while he's still squatting, I knee him in the crotch as hard as I can. It didn't seem that hard to me, but he howls and bends at the waist, giving me a chance to whack him in the jaw with my elbow. His hands grab at me as I roll out of the way. It would have been a bonus if I could have knocked him down, but no such luck.

It's very hard to go from being completely limp to up and running within a split second. Especially while drugged. I don't manage it. Instead I sort of scrabble around the car, crablike, to the edge of the road—the steep edge.

Still, by the time Dickie lets out a growl and turns to come after me, I've got a decent lead. With all the grace and speed of a three-toed sloth, I flip over the berm and roll. Like a kid rolling down a hill, except it's rocky, and I don't get very far before I hit a tree. With my head.

35

Freeze Tag

It's just like the cartoons—little birdies flying around my head in a circle, going tweet-tweet-tweet. Oddly enough, it wakes me up.

"She's gone! I've lost her!" Dickie yells. I take the opportunity to slide a few more feet and run into another tree.

What an idiot. How could he have lost me when I went rolling down the hill with all these bells and jangles, not to mention the chirping birds?

Well . . . for one thing, it's *really* dark.

"You idiot!" I hear Gaynor yell. It sounds like it's coming from a long way off. I move drunkenly from tree to tree, sort of hand-over-hand, swinging around and doing everything possible to be even farther from Gaynor's voice. "Here, I'm throwing you a flashlight. Find her!"

A beam of light flashes through the darkness. I slither around to the other side of the tree. It's not a very thick tree, but anything helps. I move slowly to the next tree and the next. They are all skinny trees. My legs are like wet sponges. But I'm no longer in danger of falling asleep.

Dickie shines the flashlight right over my head, then aims it a few yards to the right. I continue to grope my way from tree to tree. I couldn't run through this; I would be constantly dodging trees (or, rather, hitting them, since it's so dark). But then I could slither my way through these trees much faster than Dickie could.

However, I don't. I hear Dickie slide. I pull my cowlneck over my face, for warmth and camouflage. For the same reasons, I pull the ends of my sleeves over my hands. I move cautiously, so as not to give myself away with sound. Not long ago I dreamed I was running through the woods in my socks in the snow and a phone was ringing. Instead, I am creeping through the woods, no phone is ringing, there's no snow, but my socks *do* have holes in them.

I try to be invisible and silent. I clamp my teeth together so that they won't give me away by chattering. In the mountain stillness it seems these two could track me through the pounding of my heart.

I slide a little, going downhill fast. Almost immediately a flashlight beam shines weakly through the trees. But the dense trees screen the beam, reflecting the light backward.

In the distance a dog barks. I try to time my moves with his sound: *bark bark bark bark bark. Bark. Bark. Bark bark bark bark bark.*

It would be very helpful if I knew where I was going. *Away.* A good bet would be toward the nearest house—only I'm on the far side, away from the houses, sliding down an unknown dark mountain very slowly.

I'm cold, I have a headache, and I need to pee. I stop, breathe through my mouth, and try to pick up the sounds of pursuit. I can hear somebody, far to one side, and going away from me. I assume it's Dickie. But he, too, seems to have adopted silence as his mode of travel. Or have I gone deaf? No, because there's that dog barking. I wait, hear nothing, and keep waiting. My eyes have adapted somewhat. I see more now, not that there's a lot to see. Trees. No lights. My breathing slows. I try to compensate for my high-altitude disorientation. Then I hear a very slight sound close by. At the same time I smell Dickie. He must have a shop rag in his pocket.

In response sweat pours from my armpits, something I can't control. Great; now Dickie can smell *me*. Or no. If I can smell him, I guess that means I'm downwind of him. It would be nice to keep it that way. At any rate I freeze. Touch the nearest tree just slightly to steady myself. I feel myself swaying and I can't seem to stop.

Then I hear him breathing. He's moving quietly for a big guy, but he's still making noise. Other than the pounding of my heart, I'm not.

Very slowly, I try to hide in my sweater. I crouch down. It's no use running. He's got the whole forest here, and he's coming straight for me.

Some distance away a flashlight pricks the darkness and circles like a beacon. Far away I hear a train blowing a C minor chord. The sound floats and echoes all around the mountains; it seems to reverberate off each tree. The dog barks again. Then, from somewhere up above, I hear a car start. My car. I hear crunches, then headlights sweep the tops of the trees high above me.

What is she doing? Trying to catch me in my own headlights? The lights disappear. Then more crunches, slowly fading away.

Maybe Gaynor figures I'll head for the road and has gone down to block me.

For a seeker of heat and light, I'm striking out. I crouch and grope, looking for a big rock. My thought is that I will throw it; Dickie will hear the sound, some distance away, and think I'm where the sound is. Okay, it's a dumb idea, but he's not the brightest bulb in the chandelier, and I'm desperate. I am suppressing a cough, a sneeze, and probably a scream. The strain is wearing.

My fingers grope a nice rock, the size of a baseball glove. Unfortunately, it's embedded in dirt.

One nice thing about whatever it was Gaynor stuck me with; it's completely worn off.

I wonder why Dickie quit using the flashlight, but then it comes to me; he's getting his eyes accustomed to the dark. The flashlight, although big, doesn't cast a wide beam. And when it reflects off the trees it's probably less than helpful.

He must have sensed something, because he's not moving farther into the forest. He's getting closer to me all the time. I make all kinds of deals: If I get out of this, I will quit smoking. If I get out of this, I will do more pro bono work. If I get out of this, I will become a better person. Learn to cook. Contribute to charity.

I consider my options. I don't have many. Climb a tree—who do I think I'm kidding? The rock idea was good, but there isn't a suitable rock. I seem to be left with one option: Sit where I am and let him find me—or not.

I don't like that option. There has to be something else.

I consider various heroic possibilities—like I could jump up, grab a branch, and swing into his gut with my feet, knocking him off the mountain. I must have seen that one in a movie somewhere. Trouble is, the branches are too high and they are scrawny. Screw that idea.

The idea I like is that I move . . . back up the hill. There were some good rocks up there; I know this because I stepped and/or stubbed my toe on quite a few of them. Too bad I didn't have the wits to pick one up.

If I'm uphill from him, that gives me an advantage I don't usually have: height. And things to hide behind: cars, Gaynor's deck, trash cans. I move uphill, away from the tree. Not exactly retracing my steps. I try to find the least steep way up, the direct opposite of the way I came down.

The disadvantage is that once I move away, I don't know where Dickie is. Another disadvantage manifests itself; it starts to snow. Just lightly, but that means I'll leave footprints.

For a long moment I feel Dickie's presence. Then I hear him

scuff, farther away than before. The forest seems to exhale gently, and I inhale and exhale along with it and move on.

Eons later, I'm at the steepest part of the hill—the part I rolled down. *I'm lucky:* the snow has not yet made it slippery. Just wet. I inch my way up and find it hard to believe I made it. All I have to do is climb over it and I'm back in Gaynor's clearing. I do this on all fours, trying not to make noise. I think . . . I *hope* . . . Dickie is still down below, getting farther away, but I don't know anymore.

As I lift my head above the edge of the road, I see movement. I duck, but not quickly enough. Something is coming for me. Then I realize what it is.

It's my cat.

If she blows my cover now, I'm going to kill her. I'm going to pick her up by her tail, swing her around my head in a circle, and let her fly. She deserves it. She got me into this. She might even make a nice weapon.

I pull myself up lizard-style onto the so-called driveway and let out my breath in relief. It looks like the tableau of a disappearing woman: two boots, one standing up, the other lying a few feet away, the coat a few feet from that, the purse, contents spilled out, a few feet from that.

My car, however, is definitely gone.

As soon as I stand up, Tara rubs against my ankles, purring loudly. I tell myself it couldn't be *that* loud, but she sounds like a goddamn helicopter. A lawn mower at the very least.

I pull my boots on first. They're cold, of course, and the one that was upright has some snow in it. Doesn't matter; my feet are wet anyway. My socks are in tatters, but I feel better. If noisier. Then the coat, which appears to have been run over by my car. I stuff things back into my purse. Gaynor even left the cell phone. What a dumb cluck. Wait, not so dumb. The battery's gone.

Well, shit.

But there's a phone in Gaynor's house. I know this because I called her. I move, still cautiously, to the door.

Locked.

I can't get in via the deck, because of the broomstick in the patio door, but there has to be another window.

There's not—at least not one I can reach. Another patio door, leading, I guess, to the bedroom and guarded by another broomstick. The small, high kitchen window. Under the deck, there's a woodpile and a freezer, but no window. And, damn it, no ladder.

Holy shit, a freezer. I can't resist. I open it.

I never fed this cat anything out of a refrigerator, but somebody did because as soon as I open it Tara meows. *Shut up, you stupid cat.*

If there ever was a light, it's burned out. No problem. I dig my lighter out of my purse and inspect the contents.

Sure enough, a bottle of Calistoga water, frozen solid, with a piece of paper inside. I can't read the blurred writing on it but I'm about one hundred percent sure it says "Bootsie."

I flick out the lighter. I need to hurry before Dickie gets the idea I'm up here.

With Tara sticking as close as my shadow, I creep around the house, looking for a window I can open—or break. What do I care? I even pick up some kind of weird, rusty weight, oblong, with heavy twine through a hole at one end. I have no idea what it is, but it would make a handy window breaker. Of course, that would make noise. I'd like to avoid noise.

What I'd really like is to burn Gaynor's house down. See what that does to her mortgage rate. I must be suffering from hypothermia, because I consider how to do it, not that it would be hard. Light all the candles, find the lamp fuel, spill a little, knock the lamp over, and get the hell out. I'm a seeker of heat and light, what can I say? If I can't find it, I can create it.

I'm on the hill on the far side, still looking for an accessible window, when I hear a hiss. I glance, startled, at Tara, who has suddenly become a double-Tara, with her tail puffed out, back arched, and all her hair standing up. She's hissing at a white face in the darkness: Dickie. About five feet away, crouching.

I react by throwing the thing in my hand straight at his face.

Luckily I didn't have too long to think about it or I would have missed. He goes down with a grunt. The earth seems to shake when he hits.

At first I think he's faking it, to get me closer so that he can grab me. I get only close enough to retrieve my weapon and his flashlight (which is about the same heft as the thing I threw). Finally I can move fast. I goddamn well better. Leaving Dickie lying there, I climb up the deck (no great feat) and use the weight, or whatever it is, to break the glass in the patio door. It shatters and falls in a very satisfying way. I head for the kitchen, where I find a phone and dial 911.

I wonder who you get when you dial 911 up here? "I need help," I say to the voice on the other end. "But I'm not sure where I am. Up Liberty Drive . . ."

"Don't worry. We know where you are. What's the problem?"

I make it simple. The long, strange story can come later. "A guy was after me and I knocked him out and his sister stole my car. I may have killed him." (I don't think so, but it's possible. I find I'm okay with that possibility for the moment. At any rate, maybe this will hurry them along.) "If he comes to, I'll have to hit him again."

"Can you leave the area?"

"His sister took my car. She might be waiting for me." She might even come back!

"We'll get there as quick as we can."

Even inside Gaynor's warm place I'm shivering. Of course, there's a reason for that. There's no longer a patio door to keep the cold out.

Unless she comes up the hill without headlights, I'll be able to see her from the turnaround. I go outside, taking the fireplace poker, and stand guard over Dickie until the cops arrive.

Lucky for him, he doesn't come to.

36

Heat and Light

It's twenty minutes before the muddy pickup with the stick-on magnetic flashing light arrives, and during those minutes Dickie doesn't move. This is, frankly, a long time for someone to be out.

"I was beginning to think I'd killed him," I blurt out when the guy gets out of the pickup. One guy—middle-aged, grizzled, tired.

"You didn't check?"

"Hell, no. I didn't want to get that close to him."

"Paramedics right behind me," he growls, and then, without checking for signs of life, he pulls Dickie's limp arms behind him and snaps handcuffs on.

This activity prompts Dickie to moan and make a choking noise, just as the paramedics show up to take over. I admit to feeling a certain amount of relief that I didn't kill Dickie, which surprises me. Mixed with the relief is a soupçon of regret, which doesn't.

A plastic name badge pinned to the lawman's khaki shirt identifies him as M. R. Tedesco. He motions me out of the glare of his headlights and asks what happened. I've had twenty minutes to think about my long, strange story, so I don't tell it. It's enough to say that Denver wants this guy for a domestic, that he tried to kill me, and that his sister drove off with my car.

Tedesco's raised eyebrow looks like a woolly black and gray caterpillar making for his hairline.

"I broke Gaynor's window," I admit. "To get in, so I could use the phone."

"Everybody's guilty," Tedesco says.

"This cat started it all," I say. "Can you arrest this cat?" He thinks I'm kidding. "Evidence, this cat is evidence." I guess I am kidding. The damn cat saved my life.

The paramedics get Dickie into good enough shape to hang out at the local lockup, wherever that is, until Denver can come for him. While I stand there shivering, Tedesco gets on his cell phone and calls people until he finds someone who can drive me back to Denver. I'm not sure of this person's official standing—in fact, I'm not even sure of Tedesco's official standing—but Tedesco can't drive me if I take the cat, on account of his Rottweiler, a cutie he calls Marybeth, accompanied him here.

I consider leaving the cat here in the mountains, but that would be irresponsible.

The ride he locates turns out to be a lanky young guy, also driving a pickup. We get down the mountain a lot more quickly than it took me to get up there. Along the way I decide to change the cat's name to Pandora.

I walk in my door, drop the cat, and I remember why I needed to get rid of her. She starts complaining that she's hungry. When Gaynor's place became an official crime scene, Tedesco wouldn't let me back in, so I left everything up on the mountain: food, litter box, carrier. Tough shit, cat. *I* don't have a bed.

Or a car.

Defying Tedesco's order to stay put so that the Denver officers could contact me at home, I knock on Glenn's door.

"Good lord, what happened to you?"

"I rolled down a mountain. Hey, I need cat food, another litter box, more cat sand, and to drop by the hospital, and I don't have a car again. I'll tell you about it on the way."

He grabs his keys, but we don't get far. Obviously I need to freshen up a bit—I've got leaves in my hair, for chrissake.

And then, just as we step out the door, two Denver detectives come up the hall. I assault them with questions.

"So did you find Gaynor? Did you locate my car? That woman is crazy, I'm telling you, she could be anywhere—"

Without being too obvious about it they tell me to shut up and ask to hear what I've got on tape. I dial up Geri's extension and then, with my fingers crossed, dial what I think is probably her access code, the last four digits. Voilà! It works. I hand the phone over to the detective. He listens—it seems to take forever—then asks me how to repeat the message. I save the message, then call it up again. The other guy listens, forever again. They nod at each other, then repeat it yet again. They keep calling it a tape.

It starts to bother me that it's not something I can just pull out of an answering machine and hand over. What *is* voice mail, anyway? It must be on tape somewhere. My ignorance is astonishingly vast, when I think about it, which I prefer not to. Finally, they hand the phone back to me so that I can hear my handiwork.

I still hate the sound of my voice, especially when I start sounding drugged. Fortunately, both Gaynor and Dickie come through real well. Particularly the part where Gaynor talks about wearing the size-twelve hiking boots, which fits in perfectly with the cops' evidence. If only LeFevre were here, but he'll hear it eventually.

I interrupt my self-congratulations to leave Geri a message not to erase any of her messages. I flag it as urgent, which will put it in front of nonurgent new messages and all saved messages.

One of the detectives clears his throat. "The threat to you didn't come across real well, though," he says.

"It would have been real clear if I had crashed my car, wouldn't it?"

"I'm not sure it will work as a confession," he says.

I don't know why they need a confession. She stole my car.

"If you find her with my car, you won't need one," I point out. "Meanwhile, who knows what she's up to? She could be around here. In my parking garage. At the hospital. Anywhere."

"She'll surface," he says. "How long do you have to wait to collect on a stolen car with your insurance company?"

Hell, I don't know. To date it's only malfunctioned. As if that's the only thing I have to worry about.

He clears his throat again. "There are no guarantees, of course," he offers, "but it seems more likely that she fled, hoping to stay out of trouble, than come here to get into more trouble. Based upon what you've told us, she went to a lot of trouble to cover up this crime."

"She's sneaky," I say. "She holds grudges."

"Be careful," he says. "But I wouldn't worry about it too much."

Oddly enough, I don't. Glenn takes me to the hospital to have a blood sample drawn, so I can find out what Gaynor injected into me. (It turns out to have been tetrahydrocannabinol, the active ingredient in marijuana. She spiked my tea—and me—with *tea*.) Then on to the store to get Pandora's box, et cetera. Then back home, where I curl up on Glenn's mattress on the floor.

I sleep like a baby. But I wake up with one hell of a hangover, a fuzzy yet metallic taste in my mouth, and extremely sore muscles. Since I don't get hangovers, I blame the bed and mourn the loss of my waterbed, but of course I'm trying to ignore my various scrapes and bruises and a pinwheel on one side of my vision.

"Those people at the hospital didn't notice?" Glenn says unbelievingly. "Are they incompetent or what?"

Don't get me started. "I could hardly expect them to notice a pinwheel in *my* field of vision, and I didn't mention it," I say drily.

I dose myself with several varieties of over-the-counter painkillers and skip off to work. Early, but not as early as Geri. Before I can open my mouth to tell her not to erase any messages, she tells me that she's already listened to them. "Don't worry, I didn't erase anything. I heard all that. How'd you do that?"

"Redial button," I say modestly. Then I go into my office, where, big surprise, I have a few messages on my own phone.

Detective Montoya, sounding somewhat breathy: "Hey, thanks for all your assistance, give me a call and let me know when you can come down and give a statement." Hey, yourself, lady, I think, didn't I already give you a statement? But I don't erase it.

Detective LeFevre, sounding grumpy: "Just wanted to ease your mind about your car. We found it. It's totaled. Call me back if you have any questions."

And thanks so much for easing my mind. You bet your life I have questions. I dial and actually get the guy. "So tell me about my car," I say.

"Wrecked," he says succinctly. "Like I said."

"How about the driver?"

He hesitates, then apparently figures it's okay to tell me. "Seems she got caught in a snowstorm. It happens. Lost control. Went off the road." My car wasn't bad in snow, although probably not as stable as an old Bug. "Looks like she was heading toward the same area where she dumped your boss."

"And she's in custody?"

"In the Poudre Valley Hospital," he says. "Unconscious but stable."

I snort. Same hospital Jette ended up in. "And locked to a bed, I hope."

He ignores that comment. "Car's unquestionably totaled. We'll get you a report on that. I don't know if you need pictures, but it's been towed somewhere."

"Has it been towed somewhere where it will cost me money?"

"You lawyers." He sighs. "Always thinking the worst. No, just some junkyard, okay?" He gives me a phone number.

"Really smashed up?" I ask hopefully.

"Irreversibly damaged. Sorry about that. I mean that we didn't get her before she wrecked your car."

"No problem." Great news; my car is well and truly fucked

and the insurance company will have to pay me. I can get a new car!

"I guess they told you we can't use that stuff you taped. Not in court, that is. Maybe we can play it for her, and if she doesn't know the score, we can use it as leverage. I don't know what we're going to charge her with."

"Murder? Kidnapping? Attempted murder?"

"That's a possibility. If we get some proof."

"Grand theft auto?"

"Yeah, we can lay that one on her. No jail time if it's a first offense."

Can you believe this? "Theft of medical records?" I suggest.

"Oh, yeah."

"Hey," I say, "in case you didn't know, that's a Class 6 felony under Colorado law.*" LeFevre harrumphs.

"Look at the crime scene for a sample of her handwriting," I say. "If it matches the alterations in Bootsie's medical record, we're in business."

"Thanks for your help. We'd have never thought of that," he says sarcastically.

"Bite me," I think, apparently out loud.

"What was that?"

"Thanks." I hang up and call my buddy at Poudre, who is happy to give me the details on Gaynor's condition. She's in better shape than Jette, granted. Better shape than the car. Better shape than Bootsie. Probably in better shape than I'd have ended up in. But not in what you'd consider great shape.

"In the crash, the rearview mirror effectively scalped her," Judy says. The last act of my car; I'm proud of it. "She'll probably come through without permanent brain damage, but she'll have one hell of a scar. She looks awful. Her scalp's sewn on a couple of inches above the eyebrows. Big, ugly, black stitches." Shades of FrankenCat.

"Brow-lift, anyone?" I say.

Judy snorts. "She could use one."

---

*C.R.S. § 18-4-412(3)

Then I hit the Showcase. Dennis Devoss is sitting there, in what's turning into a beautiful spring day, studying a medical text. He lays it aside as I walk up to him. Plum & Posner, *Treatment and Diagnosis of Stupor and Coma*.

"I guess you've heard all the new developments," I say.

He nods. "It's hard to believe. Jette . . . and Bootsie." He shakes his head. "What a miserable bitch that Gaynor turned out to be. She didn't seem like that at all."

"She didn't," I agree. As Lowell told me, she was a bad witch, but a *very good* liar. "I didn't know you smoked."

"Don't. Stopped, years ago," he says. "Smoked a pipe for a while, until I couldn't smoke in my office anymore."

This illustrates our age difference. I've *never* had an office I could smoke in.

"I just wanted to be outside," he says. "Can the cops nail Gaynor for Bootsie?"

"They'd have to prove the harm." Dennis of all people should realize I have only slightly more criminal expertise than I did a week ago, which is still barely any at all. "I think they can get her for Jette, though." I'm being optimistic here. "There's evidence of how she did it on the tape. They can get her brother for killing his girlfriend, and they can probably get both of them for some kind of conspiracy. Put them away for a long time."

Dennis picks up his book. He doesn't care about Dickie or his girlfriend, just Gaynor. A pity she didn't end up in an irreversible coma. That would be perfect retribution.

Even though I didn't say it, Dennis picks up on the thought. "I think Bootsie will come out of it," he says. Here we are, two optimists shining sunlight on each other. "It's only been a week, after all. She's opened her eyes a couple of times. Of course, this isn't my specialty."

I think he's deluding himself. "I hope she will."

But if she doesn't, he has the means to provide good care for her. And he has all his very good friends to help him get through his grief.

I get very little work done, although I do spend a great deal of time on the phone with my insurance company, figuring out what kind of car I will get next. Some nice, practical little two-seater is what I have in mind. You'd think such a car, particularly with a fabric top, would be a *lot* cheaper than a sedan.

But not terribly practical. Glenn was counting on that sedan. When he comes to get me at the end of the day, we have to work out on our fingers how we're going to pick up his kids and get them to Melinda's house. Two kids in his Alfa with me—the two smallest ones—and the larger one on the back of Glenn's motorcycle.

Gulp. I will be *alone in a car with two of his children*.

"Don't worry," he says. "They won't get out of hand. I told them you single-handedly apprehended two dangerous criminals. In fact, they can't wait to meet you."

Lucky me.

If you enjoyed *BAD LUCK*, don't miss Suzanne Proulx's debut novel *BAD BLOOD*...

BAD BLOOD

By Suzanne Proulx

Victoria Lucci's job as a risk manager for a Denver hospital is about to take an unlucky turn: Patients are winding up dead, and it looks like someone in the hospital is responsible. Four people have been given tainted blood. Vicki has suspects, leads, evidence, even the cops on her side. The trouble is, she can't help taking matters into her own hands...

**Published by Fawcett Books.
Available in your local bookstore.**

More hospital menace awaits in the Adele Monsarrat, R.N., series by Echo Heron:

PULSE

✢

PANIC

✢

PARADOX

✢

Published by Fawcett Books.
Available in your local bookstore.

Don't miss these breathtaking medical thrillers by Peter Clement:

LETHAL PRACTICE

DEATH ROUNDS

Spellbinding suspense from a real-life ER doctor

Published by Fawcett Books.
Available in your local bookstore.

Murder on the Internet

Ballantine mysteries are on the Web!

Read about your favorite Ballantine authors and upcoming books in our electronic newsletter MURDER ON THE INTERNET, at
www.randomhouse.com/BB/MOTI

Including:
- What's new in the stores
- Previews of upcoming books for the next four months
- In-depth interviews with mystery authors and publishing insiders
- Calendars of signings and readings for Ballantine mystery authors
- Profiles of mystery authors
- Mystery quizzes and contest

To subscribe to MURDER ON THE INTERNET, please send an e-mail to
join-mystery@list.randomhouse.com
with "subscribe" as the body of the message. (Don't use the quotes.) You will receive the next issue as soon as it's available.

Find out more about whodunit! For sample chapters from current and upcoming Ballantine mysteries, visit us at
www.randomhouse.com/BB/mystery